ACCLAIM FOR ONE OF THE LEGENDARY GRAND MASTERS OF SPECULATIVE FICTION— INTERNATIONAL BESTSELLER ARTHUR C. CLARKE

O   O   O

"Arthur Clarke is probably the most critically admired of all currently active writers of science fiction . . . awesomely informed about physics and astronomy, and blessed with one of the most astounding imaginations I ever encountered in print."
—*New York Times*

"Our most important visionary writer."
—*Playboy*

"Intellectually provocative."
—*Newsday*

"Sets the standard for science fiction that is both high-tech and high-class."
—*Entertainment Weekly*

"Remarkable."
—*Los Angeles Times Book Review*

ARTHUR C. CLARKE

THE GHOST FROM THE GRAND BANKS

and

THE DEEP RANGE

A Time Warner Company

The Ghost from the Grand Banks, copyright © 1990 by Arthur C. Clarke
Introduction copyright © 2001 by Arthur C. Clarke

The Deep Range, copyright © 1957, 1985 by Arthur C. Clarke
Introduction copyright © 1987, 2001 by Arthur C. Clarke

Aspect® name and logo are registered trademarks of Warner Books, Inc.

Warner Books, Inc., 1271 Avenue of the Americas, New York, NY 10020

Visit our Web site at www.twbookmark.com.

For information on Time Warner Trade Publishing's online program, visit www.ipublish.com.

 A Time Warner Company

Printed in the United States of America

First Printing: September 2001

10 9 8 7 6 5 4 3 2 1

Library of Congress Cataloging-in-Publication Data

Clarke, Arthur Charles
    The ghost from the Grand Banks; and, The deep range / Arthur C. Clarke.
       p. cm.
    ISBN 0-446-67795-7
       1. Titanic (Steamship)—Fiction.   2. Underwater explosion—Fiction.   3. Shipwrecks—Fiction.   4. Science fiction, English.   5. Sea stories, English.   I. Clarke, Arthur Charles, 1917-   Deep range. II. Title.

PR6005.L36 G484 2001
823'.914—dc21   2001017738

Book design by Bernadette Evangelist
Cover design by Jon Valk / Don Puckey
Cover illustration by Don Dixon

ARTHUR C. CLARKE

THE GHOST FROM THE GRAND BANKS

and

THE DEEP RANGE

ASPECT®

WARNER BOOKS

A Time Warner Company

The Ghost from the Grand Banks, copyright © 1990 by Arthur C. Clarke
Introduction copyright © 2001 by Arthur C. Clarke

The Deep Range, copyright © 1957, 1985 by Arthur C. Clarke
Introduction copyright © 1987, 2001 by Arthur C. Clarke

Aspect® name and logo are registered trademarks of Warner Books, Inc.

Warner Books, Inc., 1271 Avenue of the Americas, New York, NY 10020

Visit our Web site at www.twbookmark.com.

For information on Time Warner Trade Publishing's online program, visit www.ipublish.com.

 A Time Warner Company

Printed in the United States of America

First Printing: September 2001

10 9 8 7 6 5 4 3 2 1

Library of Congress Cataloging-in-Publication Data

Clarke, Arthur Charles
    The ghost from the Grand Banks; and, The deep range / Arthur C. Clarke.
        p.   cm.
    ISBN 0-446-67795-7
        1. Titanic (Steamship)—Fiction. 2. Underwater explosion—Fiction. 3.
    Shipwrecks—Fiction. 4. Science fiction, English. 5. Sea stories, English. I. Clarke,
    Arthur Charles, 1917-   Deep range. II. Title.

PR6005.L36 G484 2001
823'.914—dc21   2001017738

Book design by Bernadette Evangelist
Cover design by Jon Valk / Don Puckey
Cover illustration by Don Dixon

THE GHOST FROM THE GRAND BANKS

For my old friend Bill MacQuitty—
who, as a boy, witnessed the launch of R.M.S. Titanic,
and, forty-five years later,
sank her for the second time.

Contents

Introduction

Much has happened in the more than a decade since I wrote this book. There has been a dive to the wreck almost every year—one with paying passengers! And of course James Cameron's magnificent movie has been seen all around the world. (Alas, the television series Michael Deakin and I wrote on my lunar version of a similar disaster, *A Fall of Moondust*, was turned down at the last moment.)

As everyone knows, the world survived the "Century Syndrome" (Chapter 4). Now we have plenty of time to prepare for Y3K.

Finally, I am indebted to Charlie Pellegrino for his latest book, *Ghosts of the Titanic* (William Morrow, 2000). This exhaustive coverage of the last hours of the ship, and the stories of its survivors, is packed with heartrending and often astonishing incidents. As Jim Cameron remarks on the jacket, Pellegrino brings the *Titanic* back to life.

Colombo, Sri Lanka

PRELUDE

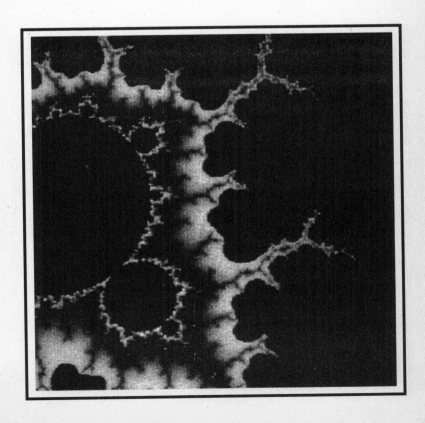

SUMMER OF '74

There must be better ways, Jason Bradley kept telling himself, of celebrating one's twenty-first birthday than attending a mass funeral; but at least he had no emotional involvement. He wondered if Operation JENNIFER's director, or his CIA sidekicks, even knew the names of the sixty-three Russian sailors they were now consigning to the deep.

The whole ceremony seemed utterly unreal, and the presence of the camera crew added yet another dimension of fantasy. Jason felt that he was an extra in a Hollywood movie, and that someone would shout "Action!" as the shrouded corpses slid into the sea. After all, it was quite possible—even likely—that Howard Hughes himself had been in the plane that had circled overhead a few hours before. If it was not the Old Man, it must have been some other top brass of the Summa Corporation; no one else knew what was happening in this lonely stretch of the Pacific, a thousand kilometers northwest of Hawaii.

For that matter, not even *Glomar Explorer*'s operations team—carefully insulated from the rest of the ship's crew—knew anything about the mission until they were already at sea. That they were attempting an unprecedented salvage job was obvious, and the smart money favored a lost reconnaissance satellite. No one dreamed that they were going to lift an entire Russian submarine from water two thousand fathoms deep—with its nuclear warheads, its codebooks, and its cryptographic equipment. And, of course, its crew. . . .

Until this morning—yes, it had been quite a birthday!— Jason had never seen Death. Perhaps it was morbid curiosity that had prompted him to volunteer, when the medics had asked for help to bring the bodies up from the morgue. (The planners in Langley had thought of everything; they had provided refrigeration for exactly one hundred cadavers.) He had been astonished—and relieved—to find how well preserved most of the corpses were, after six years on the bed of the Pacific. The sailors who had been trapped in sealed compartments, where no predators could reach them, looked as if they were sleeping. Jason felt that, if he had known the Russian for "Wake up!" he would have had an irresistible urge to shout it.

There was certainly someone aboard who knew Russian, and spoke it beautifully, for the entire funeral service had been in that language; only now, at the very end, was English used as *Explorer*'s chaplain came on line with the closing words for burial at sea.

There was a long silence after the last "Amen," followed by a brief command to the Honor Guard. And then, as one by one the lost sailors slid gently over the side, came the music that would haunt Jason Bradley for the rest of his life.

It was sad, yet not like any funeral music that he had ever heard; in its slow, relentless beat was all the power and mystery of the sea. Jason was not a very imaginative young man, but he felt that he was listening to the sound of waves marching forever against some rocky shore. It would be many years before he learned how well this music had been chosen.

The bodies were heavily weighted, so that they entered the water feet first, with only the briefest of splashes. Then they vanished instantly; they would reach their final resting place intact, before the circling sharks could mutilate them.

Jason wondered if the rumor was true, and that in due course the film of this ceremony would be sent to Moscow. It would have been a civilized gesture—but a somewhat ambiguous one. And he doubted that Security would approve, however skillfully the editing was done.

As the list of the sailors returned to the sea, the haunting music ebbed into silence. The sense of doom that had hung over *Explorer* for so many days seemed to disperse, like a fog-bank blown away by the wind. There was a long moment of complete silence; then the single word "Dismiss" came from the PA system—not in the usual brusque manner, but so quietly that it was some time before the files of men standing at attention broke up and began to drift away.

And now, thought Jason, I can have a proper birthday party. He never dreamed that one day he would walk this deck again—in another sea, and another century.

THE COLORS OF INFINITY

Donald Craig hated these visits, but he knew that they would continue as long as they both lived; if not through love (had it ever *really* been there?), at least through compassion and a shared grief.

Because it is so hard to see the obvious, it had been months before he realized the true cause of his discomfort. The Torrington Clinic was more like a luxury hotel than a world-famous center for the treatment of psychological disorders. Nobody died here; trolleys never rolled from wards to operating theaters; there were no white-robed doctors making Pavlovian responses to their beepers; and even the attendants never wore uniforms. But it was still, essentially, a *hospital*; and a hospital was where the fifteen-year-old Donald had watched his father gasping for breath, as he slowly died from the first of the two great plagues that had ravaged the twentieth century.

"How is she this morning, Dolores?" he asked the nurse after he had checked in at Reception.

"Quite cheerful, Mr. Craig. She asked me to take her shopping—she wants to buy a new hat."

"Shopping! That's the first time she's even asked to go out!"

Donald should have been pleased, yet he felt a twinge of resentment. Edith would never speak to him; indeed, she seemed unaware of his presence, looking through him as if he did not even exist.

"What did Dr. Jafferjee say? Is it okay for her to leave the clinic?"

"I'm afraid not. But it's a good sign: she's starting to show interest in the world around her again."

A new *hat*? Thought Craig. That was a typically feminine reaction—but it was not at all typical of Edith. She had always dressed . . . well, sensibly rather than fashionably, and had been quite content to order her clothes in the usual fashion, by teleshopping. Somehow, he could not imagine her in some exclusive Mayfair shop, surrounded by hatboxes, tissue paper, and fawning assistants. But if she felt that way, so be it; anything to help her escape from the mathematical labyrinth which was, quite literally, infinite in extent.

And where was she now, in her endless explorations? As usual, she was sitting crouched in a swivel chair, while an image built up on the meter-wide screen that dominated one wall of her room. Craig could see that it was in hi-res mode— all two thousand lines—so even the supercomputer was going flat out to paint a pixel every few seconds. To a casual observer, it would have seemed that the image was frozen in a partly completed state; only close inspection would have shown that the end of the bottom line was creeping slowly across the screen.

"She started this run," whispered Nurse Dolores, "early yesterday morning. Of course, she hasn't been sitting here *all* the time. She's sleeping well now, even without sedation."

The image flickered briefly, as one scan line was completed and a new one started creeping from left to right across the

screen. More than ninety percent of the picture was now displayed; the lower portion still being generated would show little more of interest.

Despite the dozens—no, hundreds—of times that Donald
Craig had watched these images being created, they had never
lost their fascination. Part of it came from the knowledge that
he was looking at something that no human eye had ever seen
before—or ever would see again, if its coordinates were not
saved in the computer. Any random search for a lost image
would be far more futile than seeking one particular grain of
sand in all the deserts of the world.

And where was Edith now, in her endless exploring? He
glanced at the small display screen below the main monitor,
and checked the magnitude of the enormous numbers that
marched across it, digit after implacable digit. They were
grouped in fives to make it easier for human eyes to grasp,
though there was no way that the human mind could do so.

. . . Six, seven, eight clusters—forty digits all told. That
meant—

He did a quick mental calculation—a neglected skill in this
day and age, of which he was inordinately proud. The result
impressed, but did not surprise him. On this scale, the original
basic image would be much bigger than the Galaxy. And the
computer could continue expanding it until it was larger than
the Cosmos, though at *that* magnification, computing even a
single image might take years.

Donald could well understand why Georg Cantor, the dis-
coverer (or was it inventor?) of the numbers beyond infinity,
had spent his last years in a mental home. Edith had taken the
first steps on that same endless road, aided by machinery beyond the dreams of any nineteenth-century mathematician.
The computer generating these images was performing trillions
of operations a second; in a few hours, it would manipulate
more numbers than the entire human race had ever handled,

since the first Cro-Magnon started counting pebbles on the floor of his cave.

Though the unfolding patterns never exactly repeated themselves, they fell into a small number of easily recognized categories. There were multipointed stars of six-, eight-fold, and even higher degrees of symmetry; spirals that sometimes resembled the trunks of elephants, and at other times the tentacles of octopods; black amoebae linked by networks of contorted tendrils; faceted, compound insect eyes. . . . Because there was absolutely no sense of scale, some of the figures being created on the screen could have been equally well interpreted as bizarre galaxies—or the microfauna in a drop of ditchwater.

And ever and again, as the computer increased the degree of magnification and dived deeper into the geometric depths it was exploring, the original strange shape—looking like a fuzzy figure eight lying on its side—that contained all this controlled chaos would reappear. Then the endless cycle would begin again, though with variations so subtle that they eluded the eye.

Surely, thought Donald, Edith must realize, in some part of her mind, that she is trapped in an endless loop. What had happened to the wonderful brain that had conceived and designed the '99 Phage which, in the early hours of 1 January 2000, had briefly made her one of the most famous women in the world?

"Edith," he said softly, "this is Donald. Is there anything I can do?"

Nurse Dolores was looking at him with an unfathomable expression. She had never been actually unfriendly, but her greetings always lacked warmth. Sometimes he wondered if she blamed him for Edith's condition.

That was a question he had asked himself every day, in the months since the tragedy.

A Better Mousetrap

Roy Emerson considered himself, accurately enough, to be reasonably good-natured, but there was one thing that could make him *really* angry. It had happened on what he swore would be his last TV appearance, when the interviewer on a Late, Late Show had asked, with malice aforethought: "Surely, the principle of the Wave Wiper is very straightforward. Why didn't someone invent it earlier?" The host's tone of voice made his real meaning perfectly clear: "Of course *I* could have thought of it myself, if I hadn't more important things to do."

Emerson resisted the temptation of replying: "If you had the chance, I'm sure you'd ask Einstein, or Edison, or Newton, the same sort of question." Instead, he answered mildly enough: "Well, *someone* had to be the first. I guess I was the lucky one."

"What gave you the idea? Did you suddenly jump out of the bathtub shouting 'Eureka'?"

Had it not been for the host's cynical attitude, the question would have been fairly innocuous. Of course, Emerson had heard it a hundred times before. He switched to automatic mode and mentally pressed the PLAY button.

"What gave me the idea—though I didn't realize it at the time—was a ride in a high-speed Coast Guard patrol boat off Key West, back in '03 . . ."

Though it had led him to fame and fortune, even now Emerson preferred not to recall certain aspects of that trip. It had seemed a good idea at the time—a short pleasure cruise through Hemingway's old stomping grounds, at the invitation of a cousin in the Coast Guard. How amazed Ernest would have been at the target of their antismuggling activities— blocks of crystal, about the size of a matchbox, that had made their way from Hong Kong via Cuba. But these TIMs—Terabyte Interactive Microlibraries—had put so many U.S. publishers out of business that Congress had dusted off legislation that dated back to the heydays of Prohibition.

Yes, it had sounded very attractive—while he was still on terra firma. What Emerson had forgotten (or his cousin had neglected to tell him) was that smugglers preferred to operate in the worst weather they could find, short of a Gulf hurricane.

"It was a rough trip, and about the only thing I remembered afterwards was the gadget on the bridge that allowed the helmsman to see ahead, despite the torrents of rain and spray that were being dumped on us.

"It was simply a disc of glass, spinning at high speed. No water could stay on it for more than a fraction of a second, so it was always perfectly transparent. I thought at the time it was far better than a car's windshield wiper; and then I forgot all about it."

"For how long?"

"I'm ashamed to say. Oh, maybe a couple of years. Then one day I was driving through a heavy rainstorm in the New Jersey countryside, and my wipers jammed; I had to pull off the road until the storm had passed. I was stuck for maybe half an hour; and at the end of that time, the whole thing was clear in my mind."

"*That's* all it took?"

"Plus every cent I could lay my hands on, and two years of fifteen-hour days and seven-day weeks in my garage." (Emerson might have added "And my marriage," but he suspected that his host already knew that. He was famed for his careful research.)

"Spinning the windshield—or even part of it—obviously wasn't practical. *Vibrations* had to be the answer; but what kind?

"First I tried to drive the whole windshield like a loud-speaker cone. That certainly kept the rain off, but then there was the noise problem. So I went ultrasonic; it took kilowatts of power—and all the dogs in the neighborhood went crazy. Worse still, few windshields lasted more than a couple of hours before they turned into powdered glass.

"So I tried *sub*sonics. They worked better—but gave you a bad headache after a few minutes of driving. Even if you couldn't hear them, you could feel them.

"I was stuck for months, and almost gave up the whole idea, when I realized my mistake. I was trying to vibrate the whole massive sheet of multiplex safety glass—sometimes as much as ten kilograms of it. All I needed to keep dancing was a thin layer on the outside; even if it was only a few microns thick, it would keep the rainwater off.

"So I read all I could about surface waves, transducers, impedance matching—"

"Whoa! Can we have that in words of one syllable?"

"Frankly, no. All I can say is that I found a way of confining low-energy vibrations to a very thin surface layer, leaving the main bulk of the windshield unaffected. If you want details, I refer you to the basic patents."

"Happy to take your word for it, Mr. Emerson. Now, our next guest—"

Possibly because the interview had taken place in London, where the works of the New England transcendentalist were not everyday reading, Emerson's host had failed to make the connection with his famous namesake (no relation, as far as he knew). No American interviewer, of course, missed the opportunity of complimenting Roy on inventing the apocryphal Better Mousetrap. The automobile industry had indeed beaten a path to his door; within a few years, almost all the world's millions of metronoming blades had been replaced by the Sonic Wave Windshield Wiper. Even more important, thousands of accidents had been averted, with the improvement of visibility in bad-weather driving.

It was while testing the latest model of his invention that Roy Emerson made his next breakthrough—and, once again, he was very lucky that no one else had thought of it first.

His '04 Mercedes Hydro was cruising in benign silence down Park Avenue, living up to its celebrated slogan "You can drink your exhaust!" Midtown seemed to have been hit by a monsoon: conditions were perfect for testing the Mark V Wave Wiper. Emerson was sitting beside his chauffeur—he no longer drove himself, of course—quietly dictating notes as he adjusted the electronics.

The car seemed to be sliding between the rain-washed walls of a glass canyon. Emerson had driven this way a hundred times before, but only now did the blindingly obvious hit him with paralyzing force.

Then he recovered his breath, and said to the carcom: "Get me Joe Wickram."

His lawyer, sunning himself on a yacht off the Great Barrier Reef, was a little surprised by the call.

"This is going to cost you, Roy. I was just about to gaff a marlin."

Emerson was in no mood for such trivialities.

"Tell me, Joe—does the patent cover *all* applications—not just car windshields?"

Joe was hurt at the implied criticism.

"Of course. That's why I put in the clause about adaptive circuits, so it could automatically adjust to any shape and size. Thinking of a new line in sunglasses?"

"Why not? But I've got something slightly bigger in mind. Remember that the Wave Wiper doesn't merely keep off water—it shakes off *any* dirt that's already there. Do you remember when you last saw a car with a really dirty windshield?"

"Not now you mention it."

"Thanks. That's all I wanted to know. Good luck with the fishing."

Roy Emerson leaned back in his seat and did some mental calculation. He wondered if all the windshields of all the cars in the city of New York could match the area of glass in the single building he was now driving past.

He was about to destroy an entire profession; armies of window cleaners would soon be looking for other jobs.

Until now, Roy Emerson had been merely a millionaire. Soon he would be rich.

And bored. . . .

THE CENTURY SYNDROME

When the clocks struck midnight on Friday, 31 December 1999, there could have been few educated people who did not realize that the twenty-first century would not begin for another year. For weeks, all the media had been explaining that because the Western calendar started with Year 1, not Year 0, the twentieth century still had twelve months to go.

It made no difference; the psychological effect of those three zeros was too powerful, the fin de siècle ambience too overwhelming. *This* was the weekend that counted; 1 January 2001 would be an anticlimax, except to a few movie buffs.

There was also a very practical reason why 1 January 2000 was the date that really mattered, and it was a reason that would never have occurred to anyone a mere forty years earlier. Since the 1960s, more and more of the world's accounting had been taken over by computers, and the process was now essentially complete. Millions of optical and electronic memories held in their stores trillions of transactions—virtually all the business of the planet.

And, of course, most of these entries bore a date. As the last decade of the century opened, something like a shock wave passed through the financial world. It was suddenly, and belatedly, realized that most of those dates lacked a vital component.

The *human* bank clerks and accountants who did what was still called "bookkeeping" had very seldom bothered to write in the "19" before the two digits they had entered. These were taken for granted; it was a matter of common sense. And common sense, unfortunately, was what computers so conspicuously lacked. Come the first dawn of '00, myriads of electronic morons would say to themselves "00 is smaller than 99. Therefore today is earlier than yesterday—by exactly 99 years. Recalculate all mortgages, overdrafts, interest-bearing accounts on this basis. . . ." The results would be international chaos on a scale never witnessed before; it would eclipse all earlier achievements of artificial stupidity—even Black Monday, 5 June 1995, when a faulty chip in Zurich had set the bank rate at 150 percent instead of 15 percent.

There were not enough programmers in the world to check all the billions of financial statements that existed, and to add the magic "19" prefix wherever necessary. The only solution was to design special software that could perform the task, by being injected—like a benign virus—into all the programs involved.

During the closing years of the century, most of the world's star-class programmers were engaged in the race to develop a "Vaccine '99"; it had become a kind of Holy Grail. Several faulty versions were issued as early as 1997—and wiped out any purchasers who hastened to test them before making adequate backups. The lawyers did very well out of the ensuing suits and countersuits.

Edith Craig belonged to the small pantheon of famous

women programmers that began with Byron's tragic daughter Ada, Lady Lovelace, continued through Rear Admiral Grace Hopper, and culminated with Dr. Susan Calvin. With the help of only a dozen assistants and one SuperCray, she had designed the quarter million lines of code of the DOUBLEZERO program that would prepare any well-organized financial system to face the twenty-first century. It could even deal with *badly* organized ones, inserting the computer equivalent of red flags at danger points where human intervention might still be necessary.

It was just as well that 1 January 2000 was a Saturday; most of the world had a full weekend to recover from its hangover— and to prepare for the moment of truth on Monday morning.

The following week saw a record number of bankruptcies among firms whose accounts receivable had been turned into instant garbage. Those who had been wise enough to invest in DOUBLEZERO survived, and Edith Craig was rich, famous . . . and happy.

Only the wealth and the fame would last.

EMPIRE OF GLASS

Roy Emerson had never expected to be rich, so he was not adequately prepared for the ordeal. At first he had naively imagined that he could hire experts to look after his rapidly accumulating wealth, leaving him to do exactly what he pleased with his time. He had soon discovered that this was only partly true: money could provide freedom, but it also brought responsibility. There were countless decisions that he alone could make, and a depressing number of hours had to be spent with lawyers and accountants.

Halfway to his first billion, he found himself chairman of the board. The company had only five directors—his mother, his older brother, his younger sister, Joe Wickram, and himself.

"Why not Diana?" he had asked Joe.

Emerson's attorney looked at him over the spectacles which, he fondly believed, gave him an air of distinction in this age of ten-minute corrective eye surgery.

"Parents and siblings are forever," he said. "Wives come and go—*you* should know that. Not, of course, that I'm suggesting . . ."

Joe was right; Diana had indeed gone, like Gladys before her. It had been a fairly amicable, though expensive, departure,

and when the last documents had been signed, Emerson disappeared into his workshop for several months. When he
emerged (without any new inventions, because he had been
too engrossed in discovering how to operate his wonderful new
equipment to actually *use* it) Joe was waiting for him with a
new surprise.

"It won't take much of your time," he said, "and it's a great
honor: Parkinson's are one of the most distinguished firms in
England, established over two hundred years ago. And it's the
first time they've *ever* taken a director from outside the family—let alone a foreigner."

"Ha! I suppose they need more capital."

"Of course. But it's to your mutual interest—and they really respect you. You know what you've done to the glass business, worldwide."

"Will I have to wear a top hat and—what do they call
them—spats?"

"Only if you want to be presented at court, which *they*
could easily arrange."

To his considerable surprise, Roy Emerson had found the
experience not only enjoyable, but stimulating. Until he joined
the board of Parkinson's and attended its bimonthly meetings
in the City of London, he thought he knew something about
glass. He very quickly discovered his mistake.

Even ordinary plate glass, which he had taken for granted
all his life—and which contributed to most of his fortune—
had a history which astonished him. Emerson had never asked
himself how it was made, assuming that it was squeezed out of
the molten raw material between giant rollers.

So indeed it had been, until the middle of the twentieth
century—and the resulting rough sheets had required hours of
expensive polishing. Then a crazy Englishman had said: Why
not let gravity and surface tension do all the work? Let the glass
float on a river of molten metal: that will automatically give a
perfectly smooth surface. . . .

After a few years, and a few million pounds, his colleagues suddenly stopped laughing. Overnight, "float glass" made all other methods of manufacturing obsolete.

Emerson was much impressed by this piece of technological history, recognizing its parallel with his own breakthrough. And he was honest enough to admit that it had required far more courage and commitment than his own modest invention. It exemplified the difference between genius and talent.

He was also fascinated by the ancient art of the glassblower, who had *not* been wholly replaced by technology and probably never would be. He even paid a visit to Venice, now cowering nervously behind its Dutch-built dikes, and goggled at the intricate marvels in the Glass Museum. Not only was it impossible to imagine how some of them had been manufactured, it was incredible that they had even been *moved* intact from their place of origin. There seemed no limit to the things that could be done with glass, and new uses were still being discovered after two thousand years.

On one particularly dull board meeting Emerson had been frankly daydreaming, admiring the nearby dome of St. Paul's from one of the few vantage points that had survived commercial greed and architectural vandalism. Two more items on the agenda and they'd be at Any Other Business; then they could all go to the excellent lunch that was waiting in the Penthouse Suite.

The words "four hundred atmospheres pressure" made him look up. Sir Roger Parkinson was reading from a letter which he was holding as if it were some species of hitherto unknown insect. Emerson quickly riffled through the thick folder of his agenda and found his own copy.

It was on impressive stationery, but the usual polynomial legal name meant nothing to him; he noted approvingly, however, that the address was in Lincoln's Inn Fields. At the bottom of the sheet, like a modest cough, were the words "Est. 1803," in letters barely visible to the naked eye.

"They don't give the name of their client," said young (thirty-five if he was a day) George Parkinson. "Interesting."

"Whoever he is," interjected William Parkinson-Smith— the family's secretly admired black sheep, much beloved by the gossip channels for his frequent domestic upheavals—"he doesn't seem to know what he wants. Why should he ask for quotes on such a range of sizes? From a millimeter, for heaven's sake, up to a half-meter radius."

"The larger size," said Rupert Parkinson, famous racing yachtsman, "reminds me of those Japanese fishing floats that get washed up all over the Pacific. Make splendid ornaments."

"I can think of only one use for the smallest size," said George portentously. "Fusion power."

"Nonsense, Uncle," interjected Gloria Windsor-Parkinson (100 Meters Silver, 2004 Olympics). "Laser-zapping was given up years ago—and the microspheres for that were *tiny.* Even a millimeter would be far too big—unless you wanted a house-broken H-bomb."

"Besides, look at the quantities required," said Arnold Parkinson (world authority on Pre-Raphaelite art). "Enough to fill the Albert Hall."

"Wasn't that the title of a Beatles song?" asked William. There was a thoughtful silence, then a quick scrabbling at keyboards. Gloria, as usual, got there first.

"Nice try, Uncle Bill. It's from *Sergeant Pepper*—'A Day in the Life.' I had no idea you were fond of classical music."

Sir Roger let the free-association process go its way unchecked. He could bring the board to an instant full stop by lifting an eyebrow, but we was too wise to do so—yet. He knew how often these brainstorming sessions led to vital conclusions—even decisions—that mere logic would never have discovered. And even when they fizzled out, they helped the members of his worldwide family to know each other better.

But it was Roy Emerson (token Yank) who was to amaze the massed Parkinsons with his inspired guess. For the last few minutes, an idea had been forming in the back of his mind. Rupert's reference to the Japanese fishing floats had provided the first vague hint, but it would never have come to anything without one of those extraordinary coincidences that no self-respecting novelist would allow in a work of fiction.

Emerson was sitting almost facing the portrait of Basil Parkinson, 1874–1912. And everyone knew where *he* had died, though the exact circumstances were still the stuff of legend—and at least one libel action.

There were some who said that he had tried to disguise himself as a woman, so that he could get into one of the last boats to leave. Others had seen him in animated conversation with Chief Designer Andrews, completely ignoring the icy water rising around his ankles. This version was considered—at least by the family—to be far more probable. The two brilliant engineers would have enjoyed each other's company, during the last minutes of their lives.

Emerson cleared his throat, a little nervously. He might be making a fool of himself . . .

"Sir Roger," he said. "I've just had a crazy idea. You've all seen the publicity and speculations about the centennial, now that it's only five years to 2012. A few million bubbles of toughened glass would be just right for the job everyone's talking about.

"*I* think our mystery customer is after the *Titanic*."

6

"A Night to Remember"

Although most of the human race had seen his handiwork, Donald Craig would never be as famous as his wife. Yet his programming skills had made him equally rich, and their meeting was inevitable, for they had both used supercomputers to solve a problem unique to the last decade of the twentieth century.

In the mid-90s, the movie and TV studios had suddenly realized that they were facing a crisis that no one had ever anticipated, although it should have been obvious years in advance. Many of the classics of the cinema—the capital assets of the enormous entertainment industry—were becoming worthless, because fewer and fewer people could bear to watch them. Millions of viewers would switch off in disgust at a western, a James Bond thriller, a Neil Simon comedy, a courtroom drama, for a reason which would have been inconceivable only a generation before. *They showed people smoking.*

The AIDS epidemic of the '90s had been partly responsible

for this revolution in human behavior. The twentieth century's Second Plague was appalling enough, but it killed only a few percent of those who died, equally horribly, from the innumerable diseases triggered by tobacco. Donald's father had been among them, and there was poetic justice in the fact that his son had made several fortunes by "sanitizing" classic movies so that they could be presented to the new public.

Though some were so wreathed in smoke that they were beyond redemption, in a surprising number of cases skillful computer processing could remove offending cylinders from actors' hands or mouths, and banish ashtrays from tabletops. The techniques that had seamlessly welded real and imaginary worlds in such landmark movies as *Who Framed Roger Rabbit* had countless other applications—not all of them legal. However, unlike the video blackmailers, Donald Craig could claim to be performing a useful social function.

He had met Edith at a screening of his sanitized *Casablanca*, and she had at once pointed out how it could have been improved. Although the trade joked that he had married Edith for her algorithms, the match had been a success on both the personal and professional levels. For the first few years, at least . . .

". . . This will be a very simple job," said Edith Craig when the last credits rolled off the monitor. "There are only four scenes in the whole movie that present problems. And what a joy to work in good old black and white!"

Donald was still silent. The film had shaken him more than he cared to admit, and his cheeks were still moist with tears. What is it, he asked himself, that moves me so much? The fact that this *really* happened, and that the names of all the hundreds of people he had seen die—even if in a studio reenactment—were still on record? No, it had to be something more than that, because he was not the sort of man who cried easily. . . .

Edith hadn't noticed. She had called up the first logged sequence on the monitor screen, and was looking thoughtfully at the frozen image.

"Starting with Frame 3751," she said. "Here we go—man lighting cigar—man on right screen ditto—end on Frame 4432—whole sequence forty-five seconds—what's the client's policy on cigars?"

"Okay in case of historical necessity; remember the Churchill retrospective? No way we could pretend *he* didn't smoke."

Edith gave that short laugh, rather like a bark, that Donald now found more and more annoying.

"I've never been able to imagine Winston without a cigar— and I must say he seemed to thrive on them. After all, he lived to ninety."

"He was lucky; look at poor Freud—years of agony before he asked his doctor to kill him. And toward the end, the wound stank so much that even his dog wouldn't go near him."

"Then you don't think a group of 1912 millionaires qualifies under 'historical necessity'?"

"Not unless it affects the story line—and it doesn't. So I vote clean it up."

"Very well—Algorithm Six will do it, with a few subroutines."

Edith's fingers danced briefly over the keyboard as she entered the command. She had learned never to challenge her partner's decisions in these matters; he was still too emotionally involved, though it was now almost twenty years since he had watched his father struggling for one more breath.

"Frame 6093," said Edith. "Cardsharp fleecing his wealthy victims. Some on the left have cigars, but I don't think many people would notice."

"Agreed," Donald answered, somewhat reluctantly. "If we

can cut out that cloud of smoke on the right. Try one pass with the haze algorithm."

It was strange, he thought, how one thing could lead to another, and another, and another—and finally to a goal which seemed to have no possible connection with the starting point. The apparently intractable problem of eliminating smoke, and restoring hidden pixels in partially obliterated images, had led Edith into the world of Chaos Theory, of discontinuous functions, and trans-Euclidean meta-geometries.

From that she had swiftly moved into fractals, which had dominated the mathematics of the Twentieth Century's last decade. Donald had begun to worry about the time she now spent exploring weird and wonderful imaginary landscapes, of no practical value—in *his* opinion—to anyone.

"Right," Edith continued. "We'll see how Subroutine 55 handles it. Now Frame 9873—just after they've hit. . . . This man's playing with the pieces of ice on deck—but note those spectators at the left."

"Not worth bothering about. Next."

"Frame 21,397. No way we can save this sequence! Not only *cigarettes*, but those page boys smoking them can't be more than sixteen or seventeen. Luckily, the scene isn't important."

"Well, that's easy; we'll just cut it out. Anything else?"

"No—except for the sound track at Frame 52,763—in the lifeboat. Irate lady exclaims: 'That man over there—he's smoking a cigarette! I think it's disgraceful, at a time like this!' We don't actually *see* him, though."

Donald laughed.

"Nice touch—especially in the circumstances. Leave it in."

"Agreed. But you realize what this means? The whole job will only take a couple of days—we've already made the analog-digital transfer."

"Yes—we mustn't make it seem too easy! When does the client want it?"

"For once, not last week. After all, it's still only 2007. Five years to go before the centennial."

"That's what puzzles me," said Donald thoughtfully. "Why so early?"

"Haven't you been watching the news, Donald? No one's come out into the open yet, but people are making long-range plans—and trying to raise money. And they've got to do a lot of *that*—before they can bring up the *Titanic*."

"I've never taken those reports seriously. After all, she's badly smashed up—and in two pieces."

"They say that will make it easier. And you can solve any engineering problem—if you throw enough cash at it."

Donald was silent. He had scarcely heard Edith's words, for one of the scenes he had just watched had suddenly replayed itself in his memory. It was as if he was watching it again on the screen; and now he knew why he had wept in the darkness.

"Goodbye, my dear son," the aristocratic young Englishman had said, as the sleeping boy who would never see his father again was passed into the lifeboat.

And yet, before he had died in the icy Atlantic waters, that man had known and loved a son—and Donald Craig envied him. Even before they had started to drift apart, Edith had been implacable. She had given him a daughter; but Ada Craig would never have a brother.

THIRD LEADER

From the London *Times* (Hardcopy and NewsSat) 2007 April 15:

A Night to Forget?

Some artifacts have the power to drive men mad. Perhaps the most famous examples are Stonehenge, the Pyramids, and the hideous statues of Easter Island. Crackpot theories—even quasi-religious cults—have flourished around all three.

Now we have another example of this curious obsession with some relic of the past. In five years' time, it will be exactly a century since the most famous of all maritime disasters, the sinking of the luxury liner *Titanic* on her maiden voyage in 1912. The tragedy inspired dozens of books and at least five films—as well as Thomas Hardy's embarrassingly feeble poem, "The Convergence of the Twain."

For seventy-three years the great ship lay on the bed of the Atlantic, a monument to the 1,500 souls who were lost with her; she seemed forever beyond human ken. But in

1985, thanks to revolutionary advances in submarine technology, she was discovered, and hundreds of her pitiful relics brought back to the light of day. Even at the time, many considered this a kind of desecration.

Now, according to rumour, much more ambitious plans are afoot; various consortia—as yet unidentified—have been formed to raise the ship, despite her badly damaged condition.

Frankly, such a project seems completely absurd, and we trust that none of our readers will be induced to invest in it. Even if all the engineering problems can be overcome, just what would the salvors *do* with forty or fifty thousand tons of scrap iron? Marine archaeologists have known for years that metal objects—except, of course, gold—disintegrate rapidly when brought into contact with air after long submergence.

Protecting the *Titanic* might be even more expensive than salvaging her. It is not as if—like the *Vasa* or the *Mary Rose*—she is a "time capsule" giving us a glimpse of a lost era. The twentieth century is adequately—sometimes all *too* adequately—documented. We can learn nothing that we do not already know from the debris four kilometres down off the Grand Banks of Newfoundland.

There is no need to revisit her to be reminded of the most important lesson the *Titanic* can teach—the dangers of over-confidence, of technological hubris. Chernobyl, *Challenger, Lagrange* 3 and Experimental Fusor One have shown us where *that* can lead.

Of course we should not forget the *Titanic*. But we should let her rest in peace.

PRIVATE VENTURE

Roy Emerson was bored, as usual—though this was a fact that he hated to admit, even to himself. There were times when he would wander through his superbly equipped workshop, with its gleaming machine tools and tangles of electronic gear, quite unable to decide which of his expensive toys he wished to play with next. Sometimes he would start on a project suggested by one of the countless network "magazines," and join a group of similarly inclined hobbyists scattered all over the world. He seldom knew their names—only their often facetious call signs—and he was careful not to give his. Since he had been listed as one of the hundred richest men in the United States, he had learned the value of anonymity.

After a few weeks, however, the latest project would lose its novelty, and he would pull the plug on his unseen playmates, changing his ident code so that they could no longer contact him. For a few days, he would drink too much, and waste time exploring the personal notice boards whose contents would have appalled the first pioneers of electronic communication.

Occasionally—after the long-suffering Joe Wickram had checked it out—he would answer some advertisement for "personal services" that intrigued him. The results were seldom very satisfying, and did nothing to improve his self-respect. The news that Diana had just remarried hardly surprised him, but left him depressed for several days, even though he tried to embarrass her by a vulgarly expensive wedding present.

All play and no work was making Emerson a very dull Roy. Then, overnight, a call from Rupert Parkinson, aboard his racing trimaran in the South Pacific, abruptly changed his life.

"What's your phone cipher?" was Rupert's unexpected opening remark.

"Why . . . normally I don't bother. But I can switch to NSA 2 if it's really important. Only problem, it tends to chop speech on long-distance circuits. So don't talk too fast, and don't overdo that Oxford accent."

"Cambridge, please—*and* Harvard. Here we go."

There was a five-second pause, filled with strange beepings and twitterings. Then Rupert Parkinson, still recognizable though subtly distorted, was back on the line.

"Can you hear me? Fine. Now, you remember that last board meeting, and the item about the glass microspheres?"

"Of course," Emerson answered, a little nervously; he wondered again if he had made a fool of himself. "You were going to look into it. Was my guess correct?"

"Bang on, old man—to coin an expression. Our lawyers had some expensive lunches with *their* lawyers, and we did a few sums together. They never told us who the client was, but we found out easily enough. A British video network—doesn't matter which—thought it would make a splendid series—in real time, culminating with the actual raising. But they lost interest when they found what it would cost, and the deal's off."

"Pity. What *would* it cost?"

"Just to manufacture enough spheres to lift fifty kilotons, at least twenty million dollars. But that would be merely the beginning. You've got to get them down there, properly distributed. You can't just squirt them into the hull; even if they'd stay put, they'd soon tear the ship apart. And I'm only talking about the forward section, of course—the smashed-up stern's another problem.

"Then you've got to get it unstuck from the seabed—it's half buried in mud. That will mean a lot of work by submersibles, and there aren't many that can operate four klicks down. I don't think you could do the job for less than a hundred million. It might even be several times as much."

"So the deal's off. Then why are you calling me?"

"Never thought you'd ask. I've been doing a little private venturing of my own; after all, we Parkinsons have a vested interest. Great-Granddad's down there—or at least his baggage, in suite three, starboard."

"A hundred megabucks worth?"

"Quite possibly—but that's unimportant; some things are beyond price. Have you ever heard of Andrea Bellini?"

"Sounds like a baseball player."

"He was the greatest craftsman in glass that Venice ever produced. To this day, we don't know how he made some of his— Anyway, back in the eighteen-seventies we managed to buy the cream of the Glass Museum's collection; in its way it was as big a prize as the Elgin Marbles. For years, the Smithsonian had been begging us to arrange a loan, but we always refused—too risky to send such a priceless cargo across the Atlantic. Until, of course, someone built an unsinkable ship. *Then* we had no excuse."

"Fascinating—and now you've mentioned him, I remember seeing some of Bellini's work the last time I was in Venice. But wouldn't it all be smashed to pieces?"

"Almost certainly not: it was expertly packed, as you can imagine. And anyway, masses of the ship's crockery survived even though it was completely unprotected. Remember that White Star dining set they auctioned at Sotheby's a couple of years ago?"

"Okay—I'll grant you that. But it seems a little extravagant to raise the whole ship, just for a few crates."

"Of course it is. But it's one major reason why we Parkinsons should get involved."

"And the others?"

"You've been on the board long enough to know that a little publicity doesn't do any harm. The whole world would know *whose* product did the lifting."

Still not good enough, Emerson said to himself. Parkinson's was doing very nicely—and by no means all of the publicity would be favorable. To many people, the wreck was almost sacred; they branded those who tampered with it as graverobbers.

But he knew that men often concealed—even failed to recognize—their true motives. Since he had joined the board, he had grown to know and like Rupert, though he would hardly call him a close friend; it was not easy for an outsider to get close to the Parkinsons.

Rupert had his own account to settle with the sea. Five years ago, it had taken his beautiful twenty-five-meter yacht *Aurora*, when she had been dismasted by a freak squall off the Scillies, and smashed to pieces on the cruel rocks that had claimed so many victims through the centuries. By pure chance, he had not been aboard; it had been a routine trip—a "bus run"—from Cowes to Bristol for a refit. All the crew had been lost—including the skipper. Rupert Parkinson had never quite recovered; at the same time he had lost both his ship and, as was well known, his lover. The playboy image he now wore in self-defense was only skin deep.

"All very interesting, Rupert. But exactly what do you have in mind? Surely you don't expect *me* to get involved!"

"Yes and no. At the moment, it's a—what do they call it?—*thought experiment.* I'd like to get a feasibility study done, and I'm prepared to finance that myself. Then, if the project makes any sense at all, I'll present it to the board."

"But a *hundred million*! There's no way the company would

risk that much. The shareholders would have us behind bars in no time. Whether in a jail or a lunatic asylum, I'm not sure."

"It might cost more—but I'm not expecting Parkinson's to put up all the capital. Maybe twenty or thirty M. I have some friends who'll be able to match that."

"Still not enough."

"Exactly."

There was a long silence, broken only by faintly querulous bleeps from the real-time decoding system as it searched in vain for something to unscramble.

"Very well," said Emerson at last. "I'll go fifty-fifty with you—on the feasibility report, at any rate. Who's your expert? Will I know him?"

"I think so. Jason Bradley."

"Oh—the giant octopus man."

"That was just a sideshow. But look what it did to *his* public image."

"And his fee, I'm sure. Have you sounded him out? Is he interested?"

"Very—but then, so is every ocean engineering firm in the business. I'm sure some of them will be prepared to put up their own money—or at least work on a no-profit basis, just for the P.R."

"Okay—go ahead. But frankly, I think it's a waste of money; we'll just end up with some very expensive reading matter, when Mr. Bradley delivers his report. Anyway, I don't see what you'll do with fifty thousand tons, or whatever it is, of rusty scrap iron."

"Leave that to me—I've a few more ideas, but I don't want to talk about them yet. If some of them work out, the project would pay for itself—eventually. You might even make a profit."

Emerson doubted if that "you" was a slip of the tongue. Rupert was a very smooth operator, and knew exactly what he was doing. And he certainly knew that his listener could easily underwrite the whole operation—if he wished.

"Just one other thing," Parkinson continued. "Until I give the okay—which won't be until I get Bradley's report—not a word to anyone. *Especially* Sir Roger—he'll think we're crazy."

"You mean to say," Emerson retorted, "that there could be the slightest possible doubt?"

Prophets With Some Honor

To: The Editor, The London *Times*
From: Lord Aldiss of Brightfount, O.M.
      President Emeritus, Science Fiction World Association

Dear Sir,

    Your Third Leader (07 Apr 15) concerning plans to raise the *Titanic* again demonstrates what an impact this disaster—by no means the worst in maritime history—has had upon the imagination of mankind.

    One extraordinary aspect of the tragedy is that it had been described, with uncanny precision, *fourteen years in advance.* According to Walter Lord's classic account of the disaster, *A Night to Remember*, in 1898 a "struggling author named Morgan Robertson concocted a novel about a fabulous Atlantic liner, far larger than any that had ever been built. Robertson loaded it with rich and complacent people, and then wrecked it one cold April night on an iceberg."

The fictional liner had almost exactly the *Titanic*'s size, speed, and displacement. It also carried 3,000 people, and lifeboats for only a fraction of them. . . .

Coincidence, of course. But there is one little detail that chills my blood. Robertson called his ship the *Titan*.

I would also like to draw attention to the fact that two members of the profession I am honoured to represent— that of writers of science fiction—went down with the *Titanic*. One, Jacques Futrelle, is now almost forgotten, and even his nationality is uncertain. But he had attained sufficient success at the age of thirty-seven with *The Diamond Master* and *The Thinking Machine* to travel first class with his wife (who, like 97% of first-class ladies, and only 55% of third-class ones, survived the sinking).

Far more famous was a man who wrote only one book, *A Journey in Other Worlds: A Romance of the Future*, which was published in 1894. This somewhat mystical tour around the Solar System, in the year 2000, described antigravity and other marvels. Arkham House reprinted the book on its centennial.

I described the author as "famous," but that is a gross understatement. His name is the *only* one that appears above the huge headline of the *New York American* for 16 April 1912: "1,500 TO 1,800 DEAD."

He was the multi-millionaire John Jacob Astor, sometimes labelled as "the richest man in the world." He was certainly the richest writer of science fiction who ever lived— a fact which may well mortify admirers of the late L. Ron Hubbard, should any still exist.

> I have the honor to be, Sir,
> Yours sincerely,
> Aldiss of Brightfount, O.M.
> President Emeritus, SFWA

10

"The Isle of the Dead"

Every trade has its acknowledged leaders, whose fame seldom extends beyond the boundaries of their profession. At any given time, few could name the world's top accountant, dentist, sanitary engineer, insurance broker, mortician ... to mention only a handful of unglamorous but essential occupations.

There are some ways of making a living, however, which have such high visibility that their practitioners become household names. First, of course, are the performing arts, in which anyone who becomes a star may be instantly recognizable to a large fraction of the human race. Sports and politics are close behind; and so, a cynic might argue, is crime.

Jason Bradley fit into none of these categories, and had never expected to be famous. The *Glomar Explorer* episode was more than three decades in the past, and even if it had not been shrouded in secrecy, his role had been far too obscure to be noteworthy. Although he had been approached several times by writers hoping to get a new angle on Operation JEN-NIFER, nothing had ever come of their efforts.

It seemed likely that, even at this date, the CIA felt that the single book on the subject was one too many, and had taken steps to discourage other authors. For several years after 1974, Bradley had been visited by anonymous but polite gentlemen who had reminded him of the documents he signed when he was discharged. They always came in pairs, and sometimes they offered him employment of an unspecified nature. Though they assured him that it would be "interesting and well paid," he was then earning very good money on North Sea oil rigs, and was not tempted. It was now more than a decade since the last visitation, but he did not doubt that the Company still had him carefully stockpiled in its vast data banks at Langley—or wherever they were these days.

He was in his office on the forty-sixth floor of the Teague Tower—now dwarfed by Houston's later skyscrapers—when he received the assignment that was to make him famous. The date happened to be April 2nd, and at first Bradley thought that his occasional client Jeff Rawlings had got it a day late. Despite his awesome responsibilities as operations manager on the Hibernia Platform, Jeff was noted for his sense of humor. This time, he wasn't joking; yet it was quite a while before Jason could take his problem seriously.

"Do you expect me to believe," he said, "that your million-ton rig has been shut down . . . by an *octopus*?"

"Not the whole operation, of course—but Manifold 1— our best producer. Forty thou barrels a day. Five flowlines running into it, all going full blast. Until yesterday."

The Hibernia project, it suddenly occurred to Jason, had the same general design as an octopus. Tentacles—or pipelines—ran out along the seabed from the central body to the dozen wells that had been drilled three thousand meters through the oil-rich sandstone. Before they reached the main platform, the flowlines from several individual wells were combined at a production manifold—also on the seabed, nearly a hundred meters down.

Each manifold was an automated industrial complex the size of a large apartment building, containing all the specialized equipment needed to handle the high-pressure mixture of gas, oil, and water erupting from the reservoirs far below. Tens of millions of years ago, nature had created and stored this hidden treasure; it was no simple matter to wrest it from her grasp.

"Tell me exactly what happened."

"This circuit secure?"

"Of course."

"Three days ago we started getting erratic instrument readings. The flow was perfectly normal, so we weren't too worried. But then there was a sudden data cutoff; we lost all monitoring facilities. It was obvious that the main fiber-optic trunk had been broken, and of course the automatics shut everything down."

"No surge problems?"

"No; slug-catcher worked perfectly—for once."

"And then?"

"S.O.P.—we sent down a camera—Eyeball Mark 5. Guess what?"

"The batteries died."

"Nope. The umbilical got snagged in the external scaffolding, before we could even go inside to look around."

"What happened to the driver?"

"Well, the kitchen isn't completely mechanized, and Chef Dubois can always use some unskilled labor."

"So you lost the camera. What happened next?"

"We haven't lost it—we know *exactly* where it is—but all it shows are lots of fish. So we sent down a diver to untangle things—and to see what he could find."

"Why not an ROV?"

There were always several underwater robots—Remotely

Operated Vehicles—on any offshore oilfield. The old days when human divers did all the work were long since past.

There was an embarrassed silence at the other end of the line.

"Afraid you'd ask me that. We've had a couple of accidents—two ROVs are being rebuilt—and the rest can't be spared from an emergency job on the Avalon platform."

"Not your lucky day, is it? So that's why you've called the Bradley Corporation—'No job too deep.' Tell me more."

"Spare me that beat-up slogan. Since the depth's only ninety meters, we sent down a diver, in standard heliox gear. Well—ever heard a man screaming in helium? Not a very nice noise . . .

"When we got him up and he was able to talk again, he said the entire rig was covered by an octopus. He swore it was a hundred meters across. That's ridiculous, of course—but there's no doubt it's a monster."

"However big it is, a small charge of dynamite should encourage it to move."

"Much too risky. *You* know the layout down there—after all, you helped install it!"

"If the camera's still working, doesn't it show the beast?"

"We did get a glimpse of a tentacle—but no way of judging its size. We think it's gone back inside—we're worried that it might rip out more cables."

"You don't suppose it's fallen in love with the plumbing?"

"Very funny. My guess is that it's found a free lunch. You know—the bloody Oasis Effect that Publicity's always boasting about."

Bradley did indeed. Far from being damaging to the environment, virtually all underwater artifacts were irresistibly attractive to marine life, and often became a target for fishing boats and a paradise for anglers. He sometimes wondered how fish had managed to survive, before mankind generously provided them with condominiums by scattering wrecks across the seabeds of the world.

"Perhaps a cattle prod would do the trick—or a heavy dose of subsonics."

"We don't care *how* it's done—as long as there's no damage to the equipment. Anyway, it looked like a job for you—and Jim, of course. Is he ready?"

"He's *always* ready."

"How soon can you get to St. John's? There's a Chevron jet at Dallas—it can pick you up in an hour. What does Jim weigh?"

"One point five tons."

"No problem. When can you be at the airport?"

"Give me three hours. This isn't my normal line of business—I'll have to do some research."

"Usual terms?"

"Yes—hundred K plus expenses."

"And no cure, no pay?"

Bradley smiled. The centuries-old salvage formula had probably never been invoked in a case like this, but it seemed applicable. And it would be an easy job. A hundred meters, indeed! What nonsense . . .

"Of course. Call you back in one hour to confirm. Meanwhile please fax the manifold plans, so I can refresh my memory."

"Right—and I'll see what else I can find out, while I'm waiting for your call."

There was no need to waste time packing; Bradley always had two bags ready—one for the tropics, one for the Arctic. The first was very little used; most of his jobs, it seemed, were in unpleasant parts of the world, and this one would be no exception. The North Atlantic at this time of year would be cold, and probably rough; not that it would matter much, a hundred meters down.

Those who thought of Jason Bradley as a tough, no-

nonsense roughneck would have been surprised at his next action. He pressed a button on his desk console, lay back in his partially reclining chair, and closed his eyes. To all outward appearances, he was asleep.

It had been years before he discovered the identity of the haunting music that had ebbed and flowed across *Glomar Explorer*'s deck, almost half a lifetime ago. Even then, he had known it must have been inspired by the sea; the slow rhythm of the waves was unmistakable. And how appropriate that the composer was Russian—the most underrated of his country's three titans, seldom mentioned in the same breath as Tchaikovsky and Stravinsky . . .

As Sergey Rachmaninoff himself had done long ago, Jason Bradley had stood transfixed before Arnold Boecklin's "Isle of the Dead," and now he was seeing it again in his mind's eye. Sometimes he identified himself with the mysterious, shrouded figure standing in the boat; sometimes he was the oarsman (Charon?); and sometimes he was the sinister cargo, being carried to its last resting place beneath the cypresses.

It was a secret ritual that had somehow evolved over the years, and which he believed had saved his life more than once. For while he was engrossed in the music, his subconscious mind—which apparently had no interest in such trivialities— was very busy indeed, analyzing the job that lay ahead, and foreseeing problems that might arise. At least that was Bradley's more-than-half-seriously-held theory, which he never intended to disprove by too close an examination.

Presently he sat up, switched off the music module, and swung his seat around to one of his half-dozen keyboards. The NeXT Mark 4 which stored most of his files and information was hardly the last word in computers, but Bradley's business had grown up with it and he had resisted all updates, on the sound principle "If it works, don't fix it."

"I thought so," he muttered, as he scanned the encyclopedia entry "Octopus." "Maximum size when fully extended may be as much as ten meters. Weight fifty to one hundred kilograms."

Bradley had never seen an octopus even approaching this size, and like most divers he knew considered them charming and inoffensive creatures. That they could be aggressive, much less dangerous, was an idea he had never taken seriously.

"See also entry on 'Sports, Underwater.' "

He blinked twice at this last reference, instantly accessed it, and read it with a mixture of amusement and surprise. Although he had often tried his hand at sports diving, he had the typical professional's disdain for amateur scubanauts. Too many of them had approached him looking for jobs, blissfully unaware of the fact that most of his work was in water too deep for unprotected humans, often with zero light and even zero visibility.

But he had to admire the intrepid divers of Puget Sound, who wrestled with opponents heavier than themselves and with four times as many arms—and brought them back to the surface without injuring them. (That, it seemed, was one of the rules of the game; if you hurt your octopus before you put it back in the sea, you were disqualified.)

The encyclopedia's brief video sequence was the stuff of nightmares: Bradley wondered how well the Puget Sounders slept. But it gave him one vital piece of information.

How *did* these crazy sportsmen—and sportswomen, there were plenty of them as well—persuade a peaceable mollusk to emerge from its lair and indulge in hand-to-tentacle combat? He could hardly believe that the answer was so simple.

Pausing only to place a couple of unusual orders with his regular supplier, he grabbed his travel kit and headed for the airport.

"Easiest hundred K I ever earned," Jason Bradley told himself.

ADA

A child with two brilliant parents has a double handicap, and the Craigs had made life even more difficult for their daughter by naming her Ada. This well-advertised tribute to the world's first computer theorist perfectly summed up their ambitions for the child's future; it would, they devoutly hoped, be happier than that of Lord Byron's tragic daughter: Ada, Lady Lovelace.

It was a great disappointment, therefore, when Ada showed no particular talent for mathematics. By the age of six, the Craigs' friends had joked, "She should at least have discovered the binomial theorem." As it was, she used her computer without showing any real interest in its operation; it was just another of the household gadgets, like vidphones, remote controllers, voice-operated systems, wall TV, colorfax . . .

Ada even seemed to have difficulty with simple logic, finding AND, NOR, and NAND gates quite baffling. She took an instant dislike to Boolean operators, and had been known to burst into tears at the sight of an IF/THEN statement.

"Give her time," Donald pleaded to the often impatient Edith. "There's nothing wrong with her intelligence. I was at least ten before I understood recursive loops. Maybe she's going to be an artist. Her last report gave her straight A's in painting, clay modeling—"

"And a D in arithmetic. What's worse, she doesn't seem to *care*! That's what I find so disturbing."

Donald did not agree, but he knew that it would only start another fight if he said so. He loved Ada too much to see any faults in her; as long as she was happy, and did reasonably well at school, that was all that mattered to him now. Sometimes he wished that they had not saddled her with that evocative name, but Edith still seemed determined to have a genius-type daughter. That was now the least of their disagreements. Indeed, if it had not been for Ada, they would have separated long ago.

"What are we going to do about the puppy?" he asked, eager to change the subject. "It's only three weeks to her birthday—and we promised."

"Well," said Edith, softening for a moment, "she still hasn't made up her mind. I only hope she doesn't choose something enormous—like a Great Dane. Anyway, it wasn't a promise. We told her it would depend on her next school test."

You told her, Donald thought. Whatever the result, Ada's going to get that puppy. Even if she wants an Irish wolfhound—which, after all, would be the appropriate dog for this huge estate.

Donald was still not sure if it was a good idea, but they could easily afford it, and he had long since given up arguing with Edith once she had made up her mind. She had been born and reared in Ireland, and she was determined that Ada should have the same advantage.

Conroy Castle had been neglected for over half a century, and some portions were now almost in ruins. But what was left was more than ample for a modern family, and the stables were in particularly good shape, having been maintained by a local riding school. After vigorous scrubbing and extensive chemical warfare, they provided excellent accommodation for computers and communications equipment. The local residents thought it was a very poor exchange.

On the whole, however, the locals were friendly enough. After all, Edith was an Irish girl who had made good, even if she had married an Englishman. And they heartily approved of the Craigs' efforts to restore the famous gardens to at least some vestige of their nineteenth-century glory.

One of Donald's first moves, after they had made the west-wing ground floor livable, was to repair the camera obscura whose dome was a late-Victorian afterthought (some said excrescence) on the castle battlements. It had been installed by Lord Francis Conroy, a keen amateur astronomer and telescope maker, during the last decade of his life; when he was paralyzed, but too proud to be pushed around the estate in a wheelchair, he had spent hours surveying his empire from this vantage point—and issuing instructions to his army of gardeners by semaphore.

The century-old optics were still in surprisingly good condition, and threw a brilliant image of the outside world on to the horizontal viewing table. Ada was fascinated by the instrument and the sense of power it gave her as she scanned the castle grounds. It was, she declared, much better than TV—or the boring old movies her parents were always screening.

And up here on the battlements, she could not hear the sound of their angry voices.

A MOLLUSK OF UNUSUAL SIZE

The first bad news came soon after Bradley had settled down to his belated lunch. Chevron Canada fed its VIPs well, and Jason knew that as soon as he hit St. John's he'd have little time for leisurely, regular meals.

"Sorry to bother you, Mr. Bradley," said the steward, "but there's an urgent call from Head Office."

"Can't I take it from here?"

"I'm afraid not—there's video as well. You'll have to go back."

"Damn," said Bradley, taking one quick mouthful of a splendid piece of Texas steak. He reluctantly pushed his plate aside, and walked to the communications booth at the rear of the jet. The video was only one way, so he had no compunction about continuing to chew as Rawlings gave his report.

"We've been doing some research, Jason, about octopus sizes—the people out on the platform weren't very happy when you laughed at their estimate."

"Too bad. I've checked with my encyclopedia. The very *largest* octopus is under ten meters across."

"Then you'd better look at this."

Though the image that flashed on the screen was obviously a very old photograph, it was of excellent quality. It showed a group of men on a beach, surrounding a shapeless mass about the size of an elephant. Several other photos followed in quick succession; they were all equally clear, but of *what* it was impossible to say.

"If I had to put any money on it," said Bradley, "my guess would be a badly decomposed whale. I've seen—and smelled—several. They look just like that; unless you're a marine biologist, you could never identify it. That's how sea serpents get born."

"Nice try, Jason. That's exactly what most of the experts said at the time—which, by the way, was 1896. And the place was Florida—Saint Augustine Beach, to be precise."

"My steak is getting cold, and this isn't exactly helping my appetite."

"I won't take much longer. That little morsel weighed about five tons; luckily, a piece was preserved in the Smithsonian, so that fifty years later scientists were able to reexamine it. There's no doubt that it *was* an octopus; and it must have had a span of almost seventy meters. So our diver's guess of a hundred may not have been all that far out."

Bradley was silent for a few moments, processing this very unexpected—and unwelcome—piece of information.

"I'll believe it when I see it," he said, "though I'm not sure that I want to."

"By the way," said Rawlings, "you haven't mentioned this to anyone?"

"Of course not," snapped Jason, annoyed at the very suggestion.

"Well, the media have got hold of it somehow; the newsfax headlines are already calling it Oscar."

"Good publicity; what are you worried about?"

"We'd hoped you could get rid of the beast without everyone looking over your shoulder. Now we've got to be careful; mustn't hurt dear little Oscar. The World Wildlife people are watching. Not to mention Bluepeace."

"Those crazies!"

"Maybe. But WW has to be taken seriously; remember who they have as president. We don't want to upset the palace."

"I'll do my best to be gentle. Definitely no nukes—not even a small one."

The first bite of his now tepid steak triggered a wry memory. Several times, Bradley recalled, he had eaten octopus—and quite enjoyed it.

He hoped he could avoid the reverse scenario.

PYRAMID POWER

When the sobbing Ada had been sent to her room, Edith and Donald Craig stared at each other in mutual disbelief.

"I don't understand it," said Edith at last. "She's never been disobedient before; in fact, she always got on very well with Miss Ives."

"And this is just the sort of test she's usually very good at—no equations, only multiple choices and pretty pictures. Let me read that note again. . . ."

Edith handed it over, while continuing to study the examination paper that had caused all the trouble.

Dear Mr. Craig,

I am very sorry to say that I have had to suspend Ada for insubordination.

This morning her class was given the attached Standard Visual Perception Test. She did extremely well (95%) with all the problems except Number 15. To my surprise, she was the *only* member of the class to give an incorrect answer to this very simple question.

When this was pointed out to her, she flatly denied that

she was wrong. Even when I showed her the printed answer, she refused to admit her mistake and stubbornly maintained that everyone else was in error! At this point it became necessary, for the sake of class discipline, to send her home.

I am truly sorry, as she is usually such a good girl. Perhaps you will talk to her and make her see reason.

Sincerely,
Elizabeth Ives (Head Mistress)

"It almost looks," said Donald, "as if she was *deliberately* trying to fail."

Edith shook her head. "I don't think so. Even with this mistake, she'd have got a good pass."

Donald stared at the little set of brightly colored geometrical figures that had caused all the trouble.

"There's only one thing to do," he said. "You go and talk to her and calm her down. Give me ten minutes with a scissors and some stiff paper—then I'll settle it once and for all, so there can't be any further argument."

"I'm afraid that will only be tackling the symptoms, not the disease. We want to know *why* she kept insisting she was right. That's almost *pathological*. We may have to send her to a psychiatrist."

The thought had already occurred to Donald, but he had instantly rejected it. In later years, he would often remember the irony of this moment.

While Edith was consoling Ada, he quickly measured out the necessary triangle with pencil and ruler, cut them from the paper, and joined up the edges until he had made three examples of the two simplest possible solid figures—two tetrahedrons, one pyramid, all with equal sides. It seemed a childish exercise, but it was the least he could do for his beloved and troubled daughter.

15 (a) [he read]. Here are two identical tetrahedrons. Each has 4 equilateral triangles for sides, making a total of 8.

If any of the two faces are placed together, how many sides does the new solid have?

It was such a simple thought experiment that any child should be able to do it. Since two of the eight sides were swallowed up in the resulting diamond-shaped solid, the answer was obviously six. At least Ada had got *that* right. . . .

Holding it between thumb and first finger, Donald spun the little cardboard diamond a few times, then dropped it on his desk with a sigh. It split apart at once into the two components.

15 (b). Here are a tetrahedron and a pyramid, each with edges of the same length. The pyramid, however, has a *square* base as well as 4 triangular sides. Altogether, therefore, the two figures have 9 sides.

If any two of the triangular faces are placed in contact, how many sides does the resulting figure have?

"Seven, of course," Donald muttered, since two of the original nine will be lost inside the new solid. . . .

Idly, he tilted the little cardboard shapes until a pair of triangles merged.

Then he blinked.

Then his jaw dropped.

He sat in silence for a moment, checking the evidence of his own eyes. A slow smile spread across his face, and he said quietly into the housecom: "Edith—Ada—I've got something to show you."

The moment Ada entered, red-eyed and still sniffling, he reached out and took her in his arms.

"Ada," he whispered, stroking her hair gently, "I'm very

proud of you." The astonishment on Edith's face delighted him more than it should have.

"I wouldn't have believed it," he said. "The answer was so obvious that the people who set the paper never bothered to check it. Look . . ."

He took the five-sided pyramid and stuck the four-sided tetrahedron on one face.

The new shape had only five sides—not the "obvious" seven. . . .

"Even though I've found the answer," Donald continued— and there was something like awe in his voice as he looked at his now smiling daughter—"I can't *visualize* it mentally. How did you *know* that the other sides lined up like this?"

Ada looked puzzled.

"What else could they do?" she answered.

There was a long silence while Donald and Edith absorbed this reply, and almost simultaneously came to the same conclusion.

Ada might have little comprehension of logic or analysis— but her feeling for space—her geometrical intuition—was altogether extraordinary. At the age of nine, it was certainly far superior to that of her parents. Not to mention those who had set the examination paper. . . .

The tension in the room slowly drained away. Edith began to laugh, and presently all three of them embraced with almost childlike joy.

"Poor Miss Ives!" chortled Donald. "Wait until we tell her that she's got the Ramanujan of geometry in her class!"

It was one of the last happy moments of their married life; they would often cling to its memory in the bitter years to come.

14

CALLING ON OSCAR

Why are these things always called Jim?" said the reporter who had intercepted Bradley at St. John's Airport. He was surprised there was only one, considering the excitement his mission seemed to be generating. One, of course, was often more than enough; but at least there was no Bluepeace demonstration to contend with.

"After the first diver who wore an armored suit, when they salvaged the *Lusitania*'s gold back in the thirties. Of course, they've been enormously improved since then. . . ."

"How?"

"Well, they're self-propelled, and I could live in Jim for fifty hours, two kilometers down—though it wouldn't be much fun. Even with servo-assisted limbs, four hours is maximum efficient working time."

"You wouldn't get *me* into one of those things," said the reporter, as the fifteen hundred kilos of titanium and plastic that had accompanied Bradley from Houston was being carefully hoisted into a Chevron helicopter. "Just *looking* at it gives me claustrophobia. Especially when you remember—"

Bradley knew what was coming, and escaped by waving goodbye and walking toward the chopper. The question had been put to him, in one form or another, by at least a dozen interviewers hoping to get some reaction. They had all been disappointed, and had been forced to concoct such imaginative headlines as THE IRON MAN IN THE TITANIUM SUIT.

"Aren't you afraid of ghosts?" he had been asked—even by other divers. They were the only people he had answered seriously.

"Why should I be?" he had always replied. "Ted Collier was my best friend; God alone knows how many drinks we shared." ("And girls," he might have added.) "Ted would have been delighted; no other way I could have afforded Jim back in those days—got him for a quarter of what he'd cost to build. State of the art, too—never had a mechanical failure. Sheer bad luck Ted was trapped before they could get him out from that collapsed rig. And you know . . . Jim kept him alive three hours longer than the guarantee. Someday I may need those three hours myself."

But not, he hoped, on this job—if his secret ingredient worked. It was much too late to pull out now; he could only trust that his encyclopedia, which seemed to have let him down badly in one important detail, had been accurate in other matters.

As always, Jason was impressed by the sheer size of the Hibernia platform, even though only a fraction of it was visible above sea level. The million-ton concrete island looked like a fortress, its jagged outline giving a field of fire in all directions. And indeed it was designed to ward off an implacable, though nonhuman, enemy—the great bergs that came drifting down from their Arctic nursery. The engineers claimed that the structure could withstand the maximum possible impact. Not everyone believed them.

There was a slight delay as the helicopter approached the landing platform on the roof of the multistoried topside building; it was already occupied by an RAF chopper, which had to be rolled aside before they could touch down. Bradley took one glance at its insignia, and groaned silently. How *did* they know so quickly? he wondered.

The president of World Wildlife was waiting for him as soon as he stepped out onto the windswept platform, and the big rotors came slowly to rest.

"Mr. Bradley? I know your reputation, of course—I'm delighted to meet you."

"Er—thank you, Your Highness."

"This octopus—is it *really* as big as they say?"

"That's what I intend to find out."

"Better you than me. And how do you propose to deal with it?"

"Ah—that's a trade secret."

"Nothing violent, I hope."

"I've already promised not to use nukes . . . sir."

The Prince gave a fleeting smile, then pointed to the somewhat battered fire extinguisher which Bradley was carefully nursing.

"You must be the first diver to carry one of *those* things underwater. Are you going to use it like a hypodermic syringe? Suppose the patient objects?"

Not a bad guess, thought Bradley; give him six out of ten. And I'm not a British citizen; he can't send me to the Tower for refusing to answer questions.

"Something like that, Your Highness. And it won't do any permanent harm."

I hope, he added silently. There were other possibilities; Oscar might be completely indifferent—or he might get annoyed. Bradley was confident that he would be perfectly safe inside Jim's metal armor, but it would be uncomfortable to be rattled around like a pea in a pod.

The Prince still seemed worried, and Bradley felt quite certain that his concern was not for the human protagonist in the coming encounter. His Royal Highness's words quickly confirmed that suspicion.

"Please remember, Mr. Bradley, that this creature is unique—this is the first time anybody has ever seen one alive. And it's probably the largest animal in the world. *Perhaps the largest that's ever existed.* Oh, some dinosaurs certainly weighed more—but they didn't cover as much territory."

Bradley kept thinking of those words as he sank slowly toward the seabed, and the pale North Atlantic sunlight faded to complete blackness. They exhilarated rather than alarmed him; he would not have been in this business if he scared easily. And he felt that he was not alone; two benign ghosts were riding with him into the deep.

One was the first man ever to experience this world—his boyhood hero William Beebe, who had skirted the edge of the abyss in his primitive bathysphere, back in the 1930s. And the other was Ted Collier, who had died in the very space that Bradley was occupying now—quietly, and without fuss, because there was nothing else to do.

"Bottom coming up; visibility about twenty meters—can't see the installation yet."

Topside, everyone would be watching him on sonar and—as soon as he reached it—through the snagged camera.

"Target at thirty meters, bearing two two zero."

"I see it; current must have been stronger than I thought. Hitting the deck now."

For a few seconds everything was hidden in a cloud of silt, and—as he always did at such moments—he recalled Apollo 11's "Kicking up a little dust." The current swiftly cleared the obscuring haze, and he was able to survey the massive engineering complex now looming up in the twin beams from Jim's external lights.

It seemed that a fair-sized chemical factory had been dumped on the seabed, to become a rendezvous for myriads of fish. Bradley could see less than a quarter of the whole installation, as most of it was hidden in distance and darkness. But he knew the layout intimately, for he had spent a good deal of expensive, frustrating, and occasionally dangerous time in almost identical rigs.

A massive framework of steel tubes, thicker than a man, formed an open cage around an assembly of valves, pipes, and pressure vessels, threaded with cables and miscellaneous minor plumbing. It looked as if it had been thrown together without rhyme or reason, but Bradley knew that every item had been carefully planned to deal with the immense forces slumbering far below.

Jim had no legs—underwater, as in space, they were often more of a nuisance than they were worth—and his movements could be controlled with exquisite precision by low-powered jets. It had been more than a year since Bradley had worn his mobile armor, and at first he overcorrected, but old skills quickly reasserted themselves.

He let himself drift gently toward his objective, hovering a few centimeters above the seabed to avoid stirring up silt. This was a situation where good visibility was important, and he was glad that Jim's hemispheric dome gave him an all-around view.

Remembering the fate of the camera—it lay a few meters away in a tangle of pencil-thin cabling—Bradley paused just outside the framework of the manifold, considering the best way of getting inside. His first objective was to find the break in the fiber-optic monitor link; he knew its exact routing, so this should not present any problems.

His second was to evict Oscar; that might not be quite so easy.

"Here we go," he reported to topside. "Coming in through the tradesman's entrance—Access Tunnel B . . . not much room to maneuver, but no problem. . . ."

He scraped once, very gently, against the metal walls of the circular corridor, and as he did so became aware of a steady, low-frequency *thump, thump, thump* . . . coming from somewhere in the labyrinth of tanks and tubes around him. Presumably some piece of equipment was still functioning; it must have been very much noisier around here when everything was running full blast. . . .

The thought triggered a long-forgotten memory. He recalled how, as a small boy, he had silenced the speakers of a local fairground's PA system with well-aimed shots from his father's rifle—and had then lived for weeks in fear of being found out. Maybe Oscar had also been offended by this noisy intruder into his domain, and had taken similar direct action to restore peace and quiet.

But where *was* Oscar?

"I'm puzzled—I'm right inside now, and can see the whole layout. Plenty of hiding places—but none of them big enough to conceal anything larger than a man. Certainly nothing as big as an elephant! Ah—this is what you're looking for!"

"What have you found?"

"Main cable trunk—looks like a plate of spaghetti that's been dropped by a careless waiter. Must have taken some strength to rip it open; you'll have to replace the whole section."

"What could have done it? Hungry shark?"

"Or angry moray eel. But no teeth marks—I'd expect some. And teeth, for that matter. An occi's still the best bet. But whoever did it isn't at home."

Taking his time, Bradley made a careful survey of the installation, and could find no other sign of damage. With any luck, the unit should be operational within a couple of days—unless the secret saboteur struck again. Meanwhile, there was nothing more that he could do; he began to jet his way delicately back the way he had come, steering Jim in and out of the maze of girders and pipes. Once he disturbed a small, pulpy mass that was indeed an octopus—perhaps as much as a meter across.

"Cross *you* off my list of suspects," he muttered to himself.

He was almost through the outer framework of massive

tubes and girders when he realized that the scenery had changed.

Many years ago, he had been a reluctant small boy on a school tour of a famous botanical garden in southern Georgia. He remembered practically nothing of the visit, but there was one item that, for some reason, had impressed him greatly. He had never heard of the banyan, and was amazed to discover that there was a tree that could have not one trunk, but dozens—each a separate pillar serving to support its wide-spread canopy of branches.

In the present case, of course, there were exactly eight, though he did not bother to count them. He was staring into the huge, jet-black eyes, like fathomless pools of ink, that were regarding him dispassionately.

Bradley had often been asked "Have you ever been frightened?" and had always given the same answer: "God, yes—many times. But always when it was over—that's why I'm still around." Though no one would ever believe it, he was not in the least frightened now—only awed, as any man might be by some unexpected wonder. Indeed, his first reaction was: "I owe an apology to that diver." His second was: "Let's see if this works."

The cylinder of the fire extinguisher was already grasped by Jim's left external manipulator, and Bradley servoed it up toward the aiming position. Simultaneously, he moved the right limb so that its mechanical fingers could work the trigger. The whole operation took only seconds; but Oscar reacted first.

He seemed to be mimicking Bradley's actions, aiming a tube of flesh toward him—almost as if imitating his hastily modified fire extinguisher. Is he going to squirt something at *me*? Bradley wondered. . . .

He would never have believed that anything so big could move so quickly. Even inside his armor, Bradley felt the impact of the jet-stream, as Oscar switched to emergency drive; this was no time for walking along the seabed like an eight-legged table. Then everything disappeared in a cloud of ink so dense that Jim's high-intensity lights were completely useless.

On his leisurely way back to the surface, Bradley whispered softly to his dead friend: "Well, Ted, we did it again—but I don't think we can take much credit."

Judging by the manner of his going, he did not believe that Oscar would return. He could see the animal's point of view—even sympathize with it.

There the peaceable mollusk was, quietly going about his business of preventing the North Atlantic from becoming a solid mass of cod. Suddenly, out of nowhere, appeared a monstrous apparition blazing with lights and waving ominous appendages. Oscar had done what any intelligent octopus would do. He had recognized that there was a creature in the sea much more ferocious than himself.

"My congratulations, Mr. Bradley," said H.R.H. as Jason slowly emerged from his armor. This was always a difficult and undignified operation, but it kept him in good shape. If he put on another couple of centimeters, he would never be able to squeeze through the O-ring of the helmet seal.

"Thank you, sir," he replied. "All part of the day's work."

The Prince chuckled.

"I thought we British had a monopoly on understatement. And I don't suppose you're prepared to reveal your secret ingredient?"

Jason smiled and shook his head.

"One day I may need to use it again."

"Whatever it was," said Rawlings with a grin, "it cost us a pretty penny. When we tracked him on sonar—amazing what a feeble echo he gives—Oscar was certainly moving fast toward deep water. But suppose he comes back when he gets hungry again? There's nowhere else in the North Atlantic where the fishing's so good."

"I'll make a deal with you," Jason answered, pointing to his battered cylinder. "If he does, I'll rush you my magic bullet—

and you can send down your own man to deal with him. It won't cost you a cent."

"There's a catch somewhere," said Rawlings. "It can't be that easy."

Jason smiled, but did not answer. Though he was playing strictly by the rules, he felt a slight—very slight—twinge of conscience. The "No cure, no pay" slogan also implied that you got paid when you effected a cure, no questions asked. He had earned his hundred K bucks, and if anyone ever asked him how it was done, he would answer: "Didn't you know? An octopus is easy to hypnotize."

There was only one mild cause for dissatisfaction. He wished he'd had a chance of checking the household hint in the old Jacques Cousteau book that his encyclopedia had providentially quoted. It would be interesting to know if *Octopus giganteus* had the same aversion to concentrated copper sulphate as his midget ten-meter cousin, *Octopus vulgaris.*

15

CONROY CASTLE

The Mandelbrot Set—hereinafter referred to as the M-Set—is one of the most extraordinary discoveries in the entire history of mathematics. That is a rash claim, but we hope to justify it.

The stunning beauty of the images it generates means that its appeal is both emotional and universal. Invariably these images bring gasps of astonishment from those who have never encountered them before; we have seen people almost hypnotized by the computer-produced films that explore its—quite literally—infinite ramifications.

Thus it is hardly surprising that within a decade of Benoit Mandelbrot's 1980 discovery it began to have an impact on the visual arts and crafts, such as the designs of fabrics, carpets, wallpaper, and even jewelry. And, of course, the Hollywood dream factories were soon using it (and its relatives) twenty-four hours a day. . . .

The psychological reasons for this appeal are still a mystery, and may always remain so; perhaps there is some structure, if one can use that term, in the human mind that resonates to the patterns in the M-Set. Carl Jung would have been surprised—and delighted—to know that thirty years after his death, the computer revolution whose beginnings he just lived to see would give new impetus to his theory of archetypes and his belief in the existence of a "collective unconscious." Many patterns in the M-Set are strongly reminiscent of Islamic art; perhaps the best example is the familiar comma-shaped "Paisley" design. But there are other shapes that remind one of organic structures—tentacles, compound insect eyes, armies of seahorses, elephant trunks . . . then, abruptly, they become transformed into the crystals and snowflakes of a world before any life began.

Yet perhaps the most astonishing feature of the M-Set is its basic *simplicity. Unlike almost everything else in modern mathematics, any schoolchild can understand how it is produced. Its generation involves nothing more advanced than addition and multiplication; it does not even require subtraction or division, much less any higher functions. . . .*

In principle—though not in practice!—it could have been discovered as soon as men learned to count. But even if they never grew tired, and never made a mistake, all the human beings who have ever existed would not have sufficed to do the elementary arithmetic required to produce an M-Set of quite modest magnification. . . .

(From "The Psychodynamics of the M-Set," by Edith and Donald Craig, in Essays Presented to Professor Benoit Mandelbrot on his 80th Birthday: *MIT Press, 2004.)*

"Are we paying for the dog, or the pedigree?" Donald Craig had asked in mock indignation when the impressive sheet of parchment had arrived. "She's even got a coat of arms, for heaven's sake!"

It had been love at first sight between Lady Fiona McDonald of Glen Abercrombie—a fluffy half-kilogram of Cairn terrier—and the nine-year-old girl. To the surprise and disappointment of the neighbors, Ada had shown no interest in ponies. "Nasty, smelly things," she told Patrick O'Brian, the head gardener, "with a bite at one end and a kick at the other." The old man had been shocked at so unnatural a reaction from a young lady, especially one who was half Irish at that.

Nor was he altogether happy with some of the new owners' projects for the estate on which his family had worked for five generations. Of course, it was wonderful to have *real* money flowing into Conroy Castle again, after decades of poverty— but converting the stables into computer rooms! It was enough to drive a man to drink, if he wasn't there already.

Patrick had managed to derail some of the Craigs' more eccentric ideas by a policy of constructive sabotage, but they— or rather Miz Edith—had been adamant about the remodeling of the lake. After it had been dredged and some hundreds of tons of water hyacinth removed, she had presented Patrick with an extraordinary map.

"*This* is what I want the lake to look like," she said, in a tone that Patrick had now come to recognize all too well.

"What's it supposed to be?" he asked, with obvious distaste. "Some kind of bug?"

"You could call it that," Donald had answered, in his don't-blame-me-it's-all-Edith's-idea voice. "The Mandelbug. Get Ada to explain it to you someday."

A few months earlier, O'Brian would have resented that remark as patronizing, but now he knew better. Ada was a strange child, but she was some kind of genius. Patrick sensed that both her brilliant parents regarded her as much with awe as with admiration. And he liked Donald considerably more than Edith; for an Englishman, he wasn't too bad.

"The lake's no problem. But moving all those grown cypress trees—I was only a boy when they were planted! It may kill them. I'll have to talk it over with the Forestry Department in Dublin."

"How long will it take?" asked Edith, totally ignoring his objections.

"Do you want it quick, cheap, or good? I can give you any two."

This was now an old joke between Patrick and Donald, and the answer was the one they both expected.

"Fairly quick—and *very* good. The mathematician who discovered this is in his eighties, and we'd like him to see it as soon as possible."

"Nothing *I'd* be proud of discovering."

Donald laughed. "This is only a crude first approximation. Wait until Ada shows you the real thing on the computer; you'll be surprised."

I very much doubt it, thought Patrick.

The shrewd old Irishman was not often wrong. This was one of the rare occasions.

THE KIPLING SUITE

Jason Bradley and Roy Emerson had a good deal in common, thought Rupert Parkinson. They were both members of an endangered, if not dying, species—the self-made American entrepreneur who had created a new industry or become the leader of an old one. He admired, but did not envy them; he was quite content, as he often put it, to have been "born in the business."

His choice of the Kipling Suite at Brown's for this meeting had been quite deliberate, though he had no idea how much, or how little, his guests knew about the writer. In any event, both Emerson and Bradley seemed impressed by the *ambience* of the room, with the historic photographs around the wall, and the very desk on which the great man had once worked.

"I never cared much for T. S. Eliot," began Parkinson, "until I came across his *Choice of Kipling's Verse.* I remember telling my Eng. Lit. tutor that a poet who liked Kipling couldn't be all bad. He wasn't amused."

"I'm afraid," said Bradley, "I've never read much poetry. Only thing of Kipling's I know is 'If—' "

"Pity: he's just the man for you—the poet of the sea, *and* of engineering. You really *must* read 'McAndrew's Hymn'; even though its technology's a hundred years obsolete, no one's ever matched its tribute to machines. And he wrote a poem about the deep sea cables that you'll appreciate. It goes:

"The wrecks dissolve above us; their dust drops down from
    afar—
Down to the dark, to the utter dark, where the blind white
    sea-snakes are.
There is no sound, no echo of sound, in the deserts of the
    deep,
Or the great grey level plains of ooze where the shell-burred
    cables creep."

"I like it," said Bradley. "But he was wrong about 'no echo of sound.' The sea's a very noisy place—if you have the right listening gear."

"Well, he could hardly have known *that*, back in the nineteenth century. He'd have been absolutely fascinated by our project—especially as he wrote a novel about the Grand Banks."

"He did?" both Emerson and Bradley exclaimed simultaneously.

"Not a very good one—nowhere near *Kim*—but what is? *Captains Courageous* is about the Newfoundland fishermen and their hard lives; Hemingway did a much better job, half a century later and twenty degrees further south. . . ."

"I've read *that*," said Emerson proudly. "*The Old Man and the Sea*."

"Top of the class, Roy. I've always thought it a tragedy that Kipling never wrote an epic poem about *Titanic*. Maybe he intended to, but Hardy beat him to it."

"Hardy?"

"Never mind. Please excuse us, Rudyard, while we get down to business. . . ."

Three flat display panels (and how *they* would have fascinated Kipling!) flipped up simultaneously. Glancing at his, Rupert Parkinson began: "We have your report dated thirtieth April. I assume that you've no further inputs since then?"

"Nothing important. My staff has rechecked all the figures. We think we could improve on them—but we prefer to be conservative. I've never known a major underwater operation that didn't have some surprises."

"Even your famous encounter with Oscar?"

"Biggest surprise of all. Went even better than I'd expected."

"What about the status of *Explorer*?"

"No change, Rupe. She's still mothballed in Suisun Bay."

Parkinson flinched slightly at the "Rupe." At least it was better than "Parky"—permitted only to intimate friends.

"It's hard to believe," said Emerson, "that such a valuable— such a *unique*—ship has only been used once."

"She's too big to run economically, for any normal commercial project. Only the CIA could afford her—and it got its wrist slapped by Congress."

"I believe they once tried to hire her to the Russians."

Bradley looked at Parkinson, and grinned. "So you know about that?"

"Of course. We did a lot of research before we came to you."

"I'm lost," said Emerson. "Fill me in, please."

"Well, back in 1989 one of their newest Russian submarines—"

"Only Mike class they ever built."

"—sank in the North Sea, and some bright chappie in the Pentagon said: 'Hey—perhaps we can get some of our money back!' But nothing ever came of it. Or *did* it, Jason?"

"Well, it wasn't the Pentagon's idea; no one there with that much imagination. But I can tell you that I spent a pleasant week in Geneva with the deputy director of the CIA and three admirals—one of ours, two of theirs. That was . . . ah, in the spring of 1990. Just when the Reformation was starting, so everyone lost interest. Igor and Alexei resigned to go into the export-import business; I still get Xmas cards every year from their office in Lenin—I mean Saint Pete. As you said, nothing ever came of the idea; but we all put on about ten kilos and took weeks to get back into shape."

"I know those Geneva restaurants. If you had to get *Explorer* shipshape, how long would it take?"

"If I can pick the men, three to four months. That's the only time estimate I can be sure of. Getting down to the wreck, checking its integrity, building any additional structural supports, getting your billions of glass balloons down to it—frankly, even those *maximum* figures I've put in brackets are only guesstimates. But I'll be able to refine them after the initial survey."

"That seems very reasonable: I appreciate your frankness. At this stage, all we really want to know is whether the project is even *feasible*—in the time frame."

"Timewise—yes. Costwise—who knows? What's your ceiling, anyway?"

Rupert Parkinson pretended to wince at the bluntness of the question.

"We're still doing our sums—aren't we, Roy?"

Some signal passed between them that Bradley could not interpret, but Emerson gave a clue with his reply.

"I'm still prepared to match anything the board puts up, Rupert. If the operation succeeds, I'll get it all back on Plan B."

"And what, may I ask, is Plan B?" said Bradley. "For that matter, what's Plan A? You still haven't told me what you intend to do with the hull, when you've towed it to New York. Do a *Vasa*?"

Parkinson threw up his hands in mock dismay. "He's guessed Plan C," he said with a groan. "Yes, we had thought of putting her on display, after we'd brought her into Manhattan—a hundred years behind schedule. But you know what happens to an iron ship when it's brought to the surface after a few decades underwater—preserving a *wooden* one is bad enough. Pickling *Titanic* in the right chemicals would take decades—and probably cost more than raising her."

"So you'll leave her in shallow water. Which means you'll be taking her to Florida, just as that TV show suggested."

"Look, Jason—we're still exploring *all* options: Disney World is only one of them. We won't even be disappointed if we have to leave her on the bottom—as long as we can salvage what's in Great-Grandfather's suite. It's lucky he refused to let all those chests be carried as cargo; his very last marconigram complained that he had no space for entertaining."

"And you're confident that all that fragile glass will still be intact?"

"Ninety percent of it. The Chinese discovered centuries ago that their wares could travel safely the length of the Silk Road—if they were packed in tea leaves. No one found anything better until polystyrene foam came along; and of course you can sell the tea, and make a nice profit on that as well."

"I doubt it, for this particular consignment."

"Afraid you're right. Pity—it was a personal gift from Sir Thomas Lipton—the very best from his Ceylon estates."

"You're quite sure it would have absorbed the impact?"

"Easily. The ship plowed into soft mud at an angle, doing about thirty knots. Average deceleration two gee—maximum five."

Rupert Parkinson folded down the display panel and clicked shut the miracle of electronic intelligence which was now as casually accepted as the telephone had been a lifetime earlier.

"We'll call you again before the end of the week, Jason," continued Parkinson. "There's a board meeting tomorrow, and I hope it will settle matters. Again, many thanks for your report; *if* we decide to go ahead, can we count on you?"

"In what way?"

"As O.i.C. operations, of course."

There was a long pause; a little too long, Parkinson thought.

"I'm flattered, Rupe. I'd have to think it over—see how I could fit it into my schedule."

"Really, Jason—you wouldn't have any 'schedule' if this goes ahead. It's the biggest job you'll ever be offered." He almost added "Perhaps it's too big," but then thought better of it. Jason Bradley was not the sort of man one cared to annoy, especially if one hoped to do business with him.

"I quite agree," Bradley said, "and I'd like to take it on. Not just for the cash—which I'm sure will be okay—but the challenge. Win or lose. Very nice meeting you both—gotta run."

"Aren't you seeing *anything* of London? I can get you tickets to the new Andrew Lloyd Webber–Stephen King show. There aren't many people who can make that claim."

Bradley laughed. "Love to go—but they've managed to total a slugcatcher in the Orkneys field, and I've promised to be in Aberdeen by this afternoon."

"Very well. We'll keep in touch. . . ."

"What do you think, Roy?" Parkinson asked, when the room was quiet again.

"Tough little guy, isn't he? Do you suppose he's holding out for the highest bidder?"

"That's just what I was wondering. If he is, he'll be out of luck."

"Oh—our legal eagles have done their thing?"

"Almost; there are still some loose ends. Remember when I took you to Lloyd's?"

"I certainly do."

It had indeed been a memorable occasion for an out-of-town visitor; even in this twenty-first century, the "new" Lloyd's building still looked positively futuristic. But what had most impressed Emerson had been the Casualty Book—the register of wrecks. That series of massive volumes recorded all the most dramatic moments in maritime history. Their guide had shown them the page for 15 April 1912, and the copper-plate handwriting encapsulating the news that had just stunned the world.

Heart-stopping though it was to read those words, they had less impact on Roy Emerson than an awesome triviality he noticed when skimming through the earlier volumes.

All the entries, spanning a period of more than two hundred years, seemed to be in the same handwriting. It was an example of tradition and continuity that would be very hard to beat.

"Well, Dad's been a member of Lloyd's for ages, so we have—ah—a certain influence there."

"*That* I can well believe."

"Thank you. Anyway, the board's had some discussions with the International Seabed Authority. There are dozens of conflicting claims, and the lawyers are doing rather well. They're the only ones who can't lose—whatever happens."

Roy Emerson sometimes found Rupert's discursiveness exasperating; he never seemed in a hurry to get to the point. It was hard to believe that he could act quickly in an emergency—yet he was one of the best yachtsmen in the world.

"It would be nice if we could claim exclusive ownership—after all, she was a British ship—"

"—built with American money—"

"A detail we'll overlook. At the moment, she doesn't belong to anyone, and it will have to be settled in the World Court. That could take years."

"We don't have years."

"Precisely. But we think we can get an injunction to stop anyone else trying to raise her—while we go ahead quietly with our own plans."

"Quietly! You must be joking. Know how many interviews I've turned down lately?"

"Probably about as many as I have." Rupert glanced at his watch. "Just in time. Like to see something interesting?"

"Of course." Emerson knew that whatever Parkinson called

"interesting" was likely to be something he would never have another chance of seeing in his life. The *real* crown jewels, perhaps; or 21b Baker Street; or those books in the British Museum Library that were curiously named curious, and weren't listed in the main catalogue. . . .

"It's just across the road—we can walk there in two minutes. The Royal Institution. Faraday's lab—where most of our civilization was born. They were rearranging the exhibit when some clod managed to drop the retort he used when he discovered benzene. The director wants to know if we can match the glass, and repair it so that no one will ever notice."

It was not every day, Emerson told himself, that you had a chance of visiting Michael Faraday's laboratory. They crossed the narrow width of Albemarle Street, easily dodging the slow-moving traffic, and walked a few meters to the classical facade of the Royal Institution.

"Good afternoon, Mr. Parkinson. Sir Ambrose is expecting you."

DEEP FREEZE

I hope you don't mind meeting us at the airport, Mrs. Craig . . . Donald . . . but the traffic into Tokyo is getting worse every day. Also, the fewer people who see us, the better. I'm sure you'll understand."

Dr. Kato Mitsumasa, the young president of Nippon-Turner, was, as usual, immaculately dressed in a Savile Row suit that would remain in style for the next twenty years. Also as usual, he was accompanied by two samurai clones who remained in the background and would not say a word during the entire proceedings. Donald had sometimes wondered if Japanese robotics had made even more advances than was generally realized.

"We have a few minutes before our other guest arrives, so I'd like to go over some details that only concern us. . . .

"First of all, we've secured the world cable and satellite rights for your smokeless version of *A Night to Remember*, for the first six months of '12, with an option of another six months' extension."

"Splendid," said Donald. "I didn't believe even you could manage it, Kato—but I should have known better."

"Thank you; it wasn't easy, as the porcupine said to his girl-friend."

During the years of his Western education—London School of Economics, then Harvard and Annenberg—Kato had developed a sense of humor that often seemed quite out of keeping with his present position. If Donald closed his eyes, he could hardly believe that he was listening to a native-born Japanese, so perfect was Kato's mid-Atlantic accent. But every so often he would produce some outrageous wisecrack that was uniquely his own, owing nothing to either East or West. Even when his jokes appeared to be in bad taste—which was not infrequent—Donald suspected that Kato knew exactly what he was doing. It encouraged people to underestimate him; and that could cause them to make very expensive mistakes.

"Now," said Kato briskly, "I'm happy to say that all our computer runs and tank tests are satisfactory. If I may say so, what we're going to do is unique, and will seize the imagination of the whole world. No one, but *no one* else, can even attempt to raise *Titanic* the way we're going to do!"

"Well, part of her. Why just the stern?"

"Several reasons—some practical, some psychological. It's much the smaller of the two portions—less than fifteen thousand tons. And it was the last to go under, with all the remaining people on deck still clinging to it. We'll intercut with the scenes from *A Night to Remember*. Thought of reshooting them—or colorizing the original—"

"No!" said both Craigs simultaneously.

Kato seemed taken aback. "After what *you've* already done to it? Ah, the inscrutable Occident! Anyway, since it's a night scene it's just as effective in b/w."

"There's another editing problem we've not resolved," said Edith abruptly. "*Titanic's* dance band."

"What about it?"

"Well, in the movie it plays 'Nearer My God to Thee.' "

"So?"

"That's the myth—and it's utter nonsense. The band's job was to keep up the passengers' spirits, and prevent panic. The very *last* thing they'd play would be a doleful hymn. One of the ship's officers would have shot them if they'd tried."

Kato laughed. "I've often felt that way about dance bands. But what did they play?"

"A medley of popular tunes, probably ending with a waltz called 'Song of Autumn.'"

"I see. That's true to life—but we can't have *Titanic* sinking to a waltz tune, for heaven's sake. *Ars longa, vita brevis*, as MGM almost used to say. In this case, art wins, and life takes second place."

Kato glanced at his watch, then at one of the clones, who walked to the door and disappeared down the corridor. In less than a minute, he returned accompanied by a short, power-fully built man with the universal insignia of the global execu-tive—a carryall bag in one hand, an electronic briefcase in the other.

Kato greeted him warmly.

"Very pleased to meet you, Mr. Bradley. Someone once said that punctuality is the thief of time. I've never believed it, and I'm glad you agree. Jason Bradley, meet Edith and Donald Craig."

As Bradley and the Craigs shook hands with the slightly distracted air of people who thought they should know each other, but weren't quite certain, Kato hastened to put the record straight.

"Jason is the world's number one ocean engineer—"

"Of course! That giant octopus—"

"Tame as a kitten, Mrs. Craig. Nothing to it."

"—while Edith and Donald make old movies as good as new—or better. Let me explain why I've brought you together, at such rather short notice."

Bradley smiled. "Not very hard to guess, Mr. Mitsumasa. But I'll be interested in the details."

"Of that I'm sure. All this, of course, is highly confidential."

"Of course."

"First we plan to raise the stern, and shoot a really spectacular TV special as it comes to the surface. Then we'll tow it to Japan, and make it part of a permanent exhibit at Tokyo-on-Sea. There'll be a three-hundred-sixty-degree theater, the audience sitting in lifeboats rocking on water—beautiful starry night—almost freezing—we'll give them topcoats, of course, and they'll see and *hear* the last minutes as the ship goes underwater. Then they can go down into the big tank and view the stern through observation windows at various levels. Though it's only about a third of the whole ship, it's so big that you can't see it all at one time; even with the distilled water we'll use, visibility will be less than a hundred meters. The wreck will just fade away into the distance—so why bring up any more? The viewers will have a perfect illusion of being on the bottom of the Atlantic."

"Well, that seems logical," said Bradley. "And, of course, the stern is the easiest part to raise. It's already badly smashed up—you could lift it in sections weighing only a few hundred tons, and assemble them later."

There was an awkward silence. Then Kato said: "That won't look very glamorous on TV, will it? No. We have more ambitious plans. This is the bit that's top secret. Even though the stern portion is smashed to pieces, we're going to bring it up in a single operation. *Inside an iceberg.* Don't you think that's poetic justice? One iceberg sank her—another will bring her back to the light of day."

If Kato expected his visitor to be surprised, he was disappointed. By this time, Bradley had heard just about every scheme for raising the *Titanic* that the ingenious mind of man and woman could conceive.

"Go on," he said. "You'll need quite a refrigeration plant, won't you?"

Kato gave a triumphant smile. "No—thanks to the latest

breakthrough in solid-state physics. You've heard of the Peltier Effect?"

"Of course. The cooling you get when an electric current is passed through certain materials—I don't know exactly which. But every domestic icebox has depended on it since 2001, when the environmental treaties banned fluorocarbons."

"Exactly. Now, the common or kitchen Peltier system isn't very efficient, but it doesn't have to be as long as it quietly manufactures ice cubes without blasting holes in the poor old ozone layer. However, our physicists have discovered a new class of semiconductors—a spinoff from the *super*conductor revolution—that ups efficiency several times. Which means that every icebox in the world is obsolete, as of last week."

"I'm sure"—Bradley smiled—"that all the Japanese manufacturers are heartbroken."

"The scramble for the patent licenses is on right now. And we haven't overlooked the advertising tie-in—when the biggest ice cube in the world surfaces—carrying the *Titanic* inside it."

"I'm impressed. But what about the power supply?"

"That's another angle we hope to exploit—swords into plowshares, though the metaphor is a little farfetched in this case. We're planning to use a couple of decommissioned nuclear subs—one Russian, one U.S. They can generate all the megawatts we need—and from several hundred meters down, so they can operate through the worst Atlantic storms."

"And your time scale?"

"Six months to install the hardware on the seabed. Then two years of Peltier cooling. Remember—it's almost freezing down there. We only have to drop the temperature a couple of degrees, and our iceberg will start to form."

"And how will you stop it from floating up before you're ready?"

Kato smiled.

"Let's not go into details at this stage—but I can assure you our engineers have thought of that small item. Anyway, this is where you come in—if you want to."

Does he know about the Parkinsons? Bradley wondered. Very probably; and even if he's not certain, he'll have guessed that they've made an offer.

"Excuse me a moment," said Kato apologetically, turning away and opening his briefcase. When he faced his visitors again, barely five seconds later, he had been transformed into a pirate chief. Only the barely visible thread leading to the keyboard in his hand revealed that the eye patch he was wearing was very hi-tech indeed.

"I'm afraid this proves I'm not a genuine Japanese—bad manners, you know . . . my father still uses a laptop, late Ming Dynasty. But monocs are so much more convenient, and give such superb definition."

Bradley and the Craigs could not help smiling at each other. What Kato said was perfectly true; many portable video devices now used compact microscreens that weighed little more than a pair of spectacles and indeed were often incorporated in them. Although the monoc was only a centimeter in front of the eye, a clever system of lenses made the postage-stamp-sized image appear as large as desired.

This was splendid for entertainment purposes—but it was even more useful for businessmen, lawyers, politicians, and anyone who wanted to access confidential information in total privacy. There was no way of spying on another person's electronic monocle—short of tapping the same data stream. Its chief disadvantage was that excessive use led to new types of schizophrenia, quite fascinating to investigators of the "split-brain" phenomenon.

When Kato had finished his litany of megawatt-hours, calorie-tons, and degrees-per-month coefficients, Bradley sat for a moment silently processing the information that had been dumped into his brain. Many of the details were too technical to be absorbed at first contact, but that was unimportant;

he could study them later. He did not doubt that the calculations would be accurate—but there might still be essential points that had been overlooked. He had seen that happen so many times. . . .

His instincts told him, however, that the plan was sound. He had learned to take first impressions seriously—*especially* when they were negative, even if he could not pinpoint the exact cause of his premonition. This time, there were no bad vibes. The project was fantastic—but it could work.

Kato was watching him covertly, obviously trying to gauge his reactions. I can be pretty inscrutable when I want to, thought Bradley. . . . Besides, I have my reputation to consider.

Then Kato, with the ghost of a smile, handed him a small slip of paper, folded in two. Bradley took his time opening it. When he saw the figures, he realized that even if the project was a total disaster, he need give no further thought to his professional career. In the natural course of events, it could not last many more years—and he had not saved this much in his entire lifetime.

"I'm flattered," he said quietly. "You're more than generous. But I still have some other business to settle, before I can give you a definite answer."

Kato looked surprised. "How long?" he asked, rather brusquely.

He thinks I'm still negotiating with someone else, thought Bradley. Which is perfectly true—

"Give me a week. But I can tell you right away—I'm quite sure no one will match your offer."

"I know," said Kato, closing his briefcase. "Any points you want to make—Edith, Donald?"

"No," said Edith, "you seem to have covered everything." Donald said nothing, but merely nodded in agreement. This is a strange partnership, Bradley told himself, and not a very happy one. He had taken an immediate liking to Donald, who seemed a warm, gentle sort of person. But Edith was tough and domineering—almost aggressive; she was obviously the boss.

"And how is that delightful child prodigy who happens to be your daughter?" Kato asked the Craigs as they were about to leave. "Please give her my love."

"We will," Donald replied. "Ada's fine, and enjoyed her trip to Kyoto. It made a change from exploring the Mandelbrot Set."

"And just what," asked Bradley, "is the Mandelbrot Set?"

"Much easier shown than described," answered Donald. "Why don't you visit us? We'd like to take you around our studio—wouldn't we, Edith? Especially if we'll be working together—as I hope we will."

Only Kato noticed Bradley's momentary hesitation. Then Bradley smiled and answered: "I'd enjoy that—I'm going to Scotland next week, and think I could fit it in. How old is your girl?"

"Ada's almost nine. But if you asked her age, she'd probably tell you 8.876545 years."

Bradley laughed. "She *does* sound a prodigy. I'm not sure I could face her."

"And this," said Kato, "is the man who scared away a fifty-ton octopus. I'll *never* understand these Americans."

IN AN IRISH GARDEN

W hen I was a small boy," said Patrick O'Brian wistfully, "I used to love coming up here to watch the magic pictures. They seemed so much brighter—and more interesting— than the *real* world outside. No telly in those days, of course— and the traveling tent cinema only came to the village about once a month."

"Don't you believe a word, Jason," said Donald Craig. "Pat isn't really a hundred years old."

Though Bradley would have guessed seventy-five, O'Brian might well be in his eighties. So he must have been born in the 1930s—perhaps even the '20s. The world of his youth already seemed unimaginably remote; reality outdid storytelling exaggeration, even by Irish standards.

Pat shook his head sadly, as he continued pulling on the cord that rotated the big lens five meters above their heads. On the matte-white table around which they were standing, the lawns and flowerbeds and gravel paths of Conroy Castle performed a stately pirouette. Everything was unnaturally bright and clear, and Bradley could well imagine that to a boy this beautiful old machine must have transformed the familiar outside world into an enchanted fairyland.

" 'Tis a shame, Mr. Bradley, that Master Donald doesn't know the truth when he hears it. I could tell him stories of the old lord—but what's the use?"

"You tell them to Ada, anyway."

"Sure—and *she* believes me, sensible girl."

"So do I—sometimes. Like those about Lord Dunsany."

"Only after you'd checked up on me with Father McMullen."

"Dunsany? The author?" asked Bradley.

"Yes. You've read him?"

"Er—no. But he was a great friend of Dr. Beebe—the first man to go down half a mile. That's how I know the name."

"Well, you should read his stories—especially the ones about the sea. Pat says he often came here, to play chess with Lord Conroy."

"Dunsany was grand master of Ireland," Patrick added. "But he was also a very kind man. So he always let the old lord win—just. How he'd have loved to play against your computer! Especially as he wrote a story about a chess-playing machine."

"He did?"

"Well, not exactly a machine; maybe an imp."

"What's it called? I must look it up."

"*The Three Sailors' Gambit*—ah, there she is! I might have guessed."

The old man's voice had softened appreciably as the little boat came into the field of view. It was drifting in lazy circles at the center of a fair-sized lake, and its sole occupant appeared to be completely engrossed in a book.

Donald Craig raised his wristcom and whispered: "Ada— we have a visitor—we'll be down in a minute." The distant figure waved a languid hand, and continued reading. Then it dwindled swiftly away as Donald zoomed the camera obscura lens.

Now Bradley could see that the lake was approximately heart-shaped, connected to a smaller, circular pond where the point of the heart should have been. That in turn opened into a third and much smaller pond, also circular. It was a curious arrangement, and obviously a recent one; the lawn still bore the scars of earth-moving machines.

"Welcome to Lake Mandelbrot," said Patrick, with noticeable lack of enthusiasm. "And be careful, Mr. Bradley—*don't* encourage her to explain it to you."

"I don't think," said Donald, "that any encouragement will be necessary. But let's go down and find out."

As her father approached with his two companions, Ada started the motor of the tiny boat; it was powered by a small solar panel, and was barely able to match their leisurely walking pace. She did not head directly toward them, as Bradley had expected, but steered the boat along the central axis of the main lake, and through the narrow isthmus connecting it to its smaller satellite. This was quickly crossed, and the boat entered the third and smallest lake of all. Though it was now only a few meters away from them, Bradley could hear no sound from its motor. His engineer's soul approved of such efficiency.

"Ada," said Donald, calling across the rapidly diminishing expanse of water. "This is the visitor I told you about—Mr. Bradley. He's going to help us raise the *Titanic*."

Ada, now preparing to enter the harbor, merely acknowledged his presence with a brief nod. The final lake—really no more than a small pond that would be overcrowded by a dozen ducks—was connected to a boathouse by a long, narrow canal. It was perfectly straight, and Bradley realized that it lay precisely along the central axis of the three conjoined lakes. All this was obviously planned, though for what purpose he could not imagine. From the quizzical smile on Patrick's face, he guessed that the old gardener was enjoying his perplexity.

The canal was bordered on either side by beautiful cypress trees, more than twenty meters high; it was, Bradley thought, like a miniature version of the approach to the Taj Mahal. He had only seen that masterpiece briefly, years ago, but had never forgotten its splendid vista.

"You see, Pat, they're all doing fine—in spite of what you said," Donald told the head gardener.

Patrick pursed his lips and looked critically at the line of trees. He pointed to several which, to Bradley's eyes, appeared indistinguishable from the rest.

"*Those* may have to be replanted," he said. "Don't say I didn't warn you—and the Missus."

They had now reached the boathouse at the end of the tree-lined canal, and waited for Ada to complete her leisurely approach. When she was only a meter away, there was a sudden hysterical yelp and something closely resembling a small floor mop leaped out of the boat and hurled itself at Bradley's feet.

"If you don't move," said Donald, "she may decide you're harmless, and let you live."

While the tiny Cairn terrier was sniffing suspiciously at his shoes, Bradley examined her mistress. He noticed, with approval, the careful way that Ada tied up the boat, even though that was quite unnecessary; she was, he could already tell, an extremely well-organized young lady—quite a contrast to her hysterical little pet, who had switched instantly to fawning affection.

Ada scooped up Lady with one hand, and hugged the puppy to her breast while she regarded Bradley with a look of frank curiosity.

"Are you really going to help us raise the *Titanic*?" she asked.

Bradley shifted uncomfortably and avoided returning that disconcerting stare.

"I hope so," he said evasively. "But there are lots of things we have to talk over first." And this, he added silently, is neither the time nor the place. He would have to wait until they had joined Mrs. Craig, and he was not altogether looking forward to the encounter.

"What were you reading in the boat, Ada?" he asked lightly, trying to change the subject.

"Why do you want to know?" she asked. It was a perfectly polite question, with no hint of impertinence. Bradley was still struggling for a suitable reply when Donald Craig interjected hastily: "I'm afraid my daughter hasn't much time for the social graces. She considers there are more important things in life. Like fractals and non-Euclidean geometry."

Bradley pointed to the puppy. "*That* doesn't look very geometric to me."

To his surprise, Ada rewarded him with a charming smile. "You should see Lady when she's been dried out after a bath, and her hair's pointing in all directions. Then she makes a lovely three-D fractal."

The joke was right over Bradley's head, but he joined in the general laughter. Ada had the saving grace of a sense of humor; he could get to like her—as long as he remembered to treat her as someone twice her age.

Greatly daring, he ventured another question.

"That number 1.999 painted on the boathouse," he said. "I suppose that's a reference to your mother's famous end-of-century program."

Donald Craig chuckled.

"Nice try, Jason; that's what most people guess. Let him have it gently, Ada."

The formidable Ms. Craig deposited her puppy on the grass, and it scuttled away to investigate the base of the nearest cypress. Bradley had the uncomfortable impression that Ada was trying to calibrate his I.Q. before she replied.

"If you look carefully, Mr. Bradley, you'll see there's a minus sign in front of the number, and a dot over the last nine."

"So?"

"So it's really *minus* 1.9999 . . . forever and ever."

"Amen," interjected Patrick.

"Wouldn't it have been easier to write minus two?"

"Exactly what I said," Donald said with a chuckle. "But don't tell that to a *real* mathematician."

"I thought you were a pretty good one."

"God, no—I'm just a hairy-knuckled byte-basher, compared to Edith."

"And this young lady here, I suspect. You know, I'm beginning to feel out of my depth. And in my profession, that's not a good idea."

Ada's laugh helped to lift the curious sense of unease that Bradley had felt for the last few minutes. There was something depressing about this place—something ominous that hovered just beyond the horizon of consciousness. It was no use trying to focus upon it by a deliberate act of will—the fugitive wisp of memory scuttled away as soon as he attempted to pin it down. He would have to wait; it would emerge when it was ready.

"You asked me what book I was reading, Mr. Bradley—"

"—please call me Jason—"

"—so here it is."

"I might have guessed. He was a mathematician too, wasn't he? But I'm ashamed to say I've never read *Alice*. The nearest American equivalent is *The Wizard of Oz*."

"I've read that too, but Dodgson—Carroll—is *much* better. How he would have loved this!"

Ada waved toward the curiously shaped lakes, and the little boathouse with its enigmatic inscription.

"You see, Mr. Brad—Mr. Jason—that's the Utter West. Minus two is infinity for the M-Set—there's absolutely *nothing* beyond that. What we're walking along now is the Spike—and this little pond is the very last of the mini-sets on the negative side. One day we'll plant a border of flowers—won't we, Pat?— that will give some idea of the fantastic detail around the main lobes. And over there in the east—that cusp where the two bigger lakes meet—that's Seahorse Valley, at minus .745. The origin—zero, zero, of course—is in the middle of the biggest lake. The set doesn't extend so far to the east; the cusp at Elephant Crossing—over there, right in front of the castle—is around plus .273."

"I'll take your word for it," Bradley answered, completely overwhelmed. "You know perfectly well I haven't the faintest idea what you're talking about."

That was not perfectly true: it was obvious enough that the Craigs had used their wealth to carve this landscape into the shape of some bizarre mathematical function. It seemed a harmless enough obsession; there were many worse ways of spending money, and it must have provided a great deal of employment for the locals.

"I think that's enough, Ada," said Donald, with much more firmness than he had shown hitherto. "Let's give Mr. Jason some lunch—before we throw him head-over-heels into the M-Set."

They were leaving the tree-lined avenue, at the point where the narrow canal opened out into the smallest of the lakes, when Bradley's brain unlocked its memory. Of course—the still expanse of water, the boat, the cypresses—all the key elements of Boecklin's painting! Incredible that he hadn't realized it before. . . .

Rachmaninoff's haunting music welled up from the depths of his mind—soothing, familiar, reassuring. Now that he had identified the cause of his faint disquiet, the shadow lifted from his spirit.

Even later, he never really believed it had been a premonition.

"RAISE THE TITANIC!"

Slowly, reluctantly, the thousands of tons of metal began to stir, like some marine monster awakening from its sleep. The explosive charges that were attempting to jolt it off the seabed blasted up great clouds of silt, which concealed the wreck in a swirling mist.

The decades-long grip of the mud began to yield; the enormous propellers lifted from the ocean floor. *Titanic* began the ascent to the world she had left, a long lifetime ago.

On the surface, the sea was already boiling from the disturbance far below. Out of the maelstrom of foam, a slender mast emerged—still carrying the crow's nest from which Frederick Fleet had once telephoned the fatal words, "Iceberg right ahead."

And now the prow came knifing up—the ruined superstructure—the whole vast expanse of decking—the giant anchors which had taken a twenty-horse team to move—the three towering funnels, and the stump of the fourth—the great cliff of steel, studded with portholes—and, at last:

TITANIC
LIVERPOOL

The monitor screen went blank; there was a momentary silence in the studio, induced by a mixture of awe, reverence, and sheer admiration for the movie's special effects.

Then Rupert Parkinson, never long at a loss for words, said ruefully: "I'm afraid it won't be quite as dramatic as that. Of course, when that movie was made, they didn't know she was in two pieces. Or that *all* the funnels had gone—though that should have been obvious."

"Is it true," asked Channel Ten's host Marcus Kilford— "Mucus" or "Killjoy" to his enemies, who were legion—"that the model they used in the movie cost more than the original ship?"

"I've heard that story—could be true, allowing for inflation."

"And the joke—"

"—that it would have been cheaper to lower the Atlantic? Believe me, I'm tired of hearing that one!"

"Then I won't mention it, of course," said Kilford, twirling the notorious monocle that was his trademark. It was widely believed that this ostentatious antique served only to hypnotize his guests, and had no optical properties whatsoever. The Physics Department of King's College, London, had even run a computer analysis of the images reflected when it caught the studio lights, and claimed to have established this with ninety-five percent certainty. The matter would only be settled when someone actually captured the thing, but all attempts had so far failed. It appeared to be immovably attached to Marcus, and he had warned would-be hijackers that it was equipped with a miniaturized self-destruct device. If this was activated, he would not be responsible for the consequences. Of course, no one believed him.

"In the film," continued Kilford, "they talked glibly about pumping foam into the hull to lift the wreck. Would that have worked?"

"Depends on how it was done. The pressure is so great— four *hundred* times atmospheric!—that all ordinary foams would collapse instantly. But we obtain essentially the same result with our microspheres—each holds its little bubble of air."

"They're strong enough to resist that enormous pressure?"

"Yes—just try and smash one!"

Parkinson scattered a handful of glass marbles across the studio coffee table. Kilford picked one up, and whistled with unfeigned surprise.

"It weighs hardly anything!"

"State of the art," Parkinson answered proudly. "And they've been tested all the way down to the bottom of the Marianas Trench—three times deeper than the *Titanic*."

Kilford turned to his other guest.

"You could have done with these on the *Mary Rose*, back in 1982—couldn't you, Dr. Thornley?"

The marine archaeologist shook her head. "Not really. That was a totally different problem. *Mary Rose* was in shallow water, and our divers were able to place a cradle under her. Then the biggest floating crane in the world pulled her up."

"It was touch and go, wasn't it?"

"Yes. A lot of people nearly had heart attacks when that metal strap gave way."

"I can believe it. Now, that hull has been sitting in Southampton Dock for a quarter century—and it *still* isn't ready for public display. Will you do a quicker job on *Titanic*, Mr. Parkinson—assuming that you do get her up?"

"Certainly; it's the difference between wood and steel. The sea had four centuries to soak into *Mary Rose*'s timbers—no wonder it's taking decades to get it out. All the wood in *Titanic* has gone—we don't have to bother about it. Our problem is rust; and there's very little at that depth, thanks to the cold and lack of oxygen. Most of the wreck is in one of two states: excellent—or terrible."

"How many of these little ... microspheres ... will you need?"

"About fifty billion."

"Fifty *billion*! And how will you get them down there?"

"Very simply. We're going to *drop* them."

"With a little weight attached to each one—another fifty billion?"

Parkinson smiled, rather smugly.

"Not quite. Our Mr. Emerson has invented a technique so simple that no one believes it will work. We'll have a pipe leading down from the surface to the wreck. The water will be pumped out—and we'll simply pour the microspheres in at the top, and collect them at the bottom. They'll take only a few minutes to make the trip."

"But surely—"

"Oh, we'll have to use special air locks at both ends, but it will be essentially a continuous process. When they arrive, the microspheres will be packaged in bundles, each a cubic meter in volume. That will give a buoyancy of one ton per unit—a comfortable size for the robots to handle."

Marcus Kilford turned to the long-silent archaeologist.

"Dr. Thornley," he asked, "do you think it will work?"

"I suppose so," she said reluctantly, "but I'm not the expert on these matters. Won't that tube have to be very strong, to stand the enormous pressure at the bottom?"

"No problem; we'll use the same material. As my company's slogan says, 'You can do anything with glass'—"

"No more commercials, *please*!"

Kilford turned toward the camera, and intoned solemnly, though with a twinkle in his eye: "May I take this opportunity of denying the malicious rumor that Mr. Parkinson was spotted in a BBC cloak room, handing me a shoe box stuffed with well-used bank notes."

Everyone laughed, though behind the thick glass of the control room the producer whispered to his assistant: "If he uses that joke once again, I'll suspect it's true."

"May I ask a question?" said Dr. Thornley unexpectedly. "What about your . . . shall I say, rivals? Do you think they'll succeed first?"

"Well, let's call them friendly competitors."

"Indeed?" said Kilford skeptically. "Whoever brings their section up to the surface first will get all the publicity."

"*We're* taking the long-term view," said Parkinson. "When our grandchildren come to Florida to dive on the *Titanic*, they won't care whether we raised her up in 2012 or 2020—though of course we hope to make the centennial date." He turned to the archaeologist. "I almost wish we could use Portsmouth, and arrange for a simultaneous opening. It would be nice to have Nelson's *Victory*, Henry Eight's *Mary Rose*, and *Titanic* side by side. Four hundred years of British shipbuilding. Quite a thought."

"I'd be there," said Kilford. "But now I'd like to raise a couple of more serious matters. First of all, there's still much talk of . . . well, 'desecration' seems too strong a word, but what do you say to the people who regard *Titanic* as a tomb, and say she should be left in peace?"

"I respect their views, but it's a little late now. *Hundreds* of dives have been made on her—and on countless other ships that have gone down with great loss of life. People only seem to raise objections to *Titanic*! How many people died in *Mary Rose*, Dr. Thornley? And has anyone protested about your work?"

"About six hundred—almost half as many casualties as *Titanic*—and for a ship a fraction of the size! No—we've never had any serious complaints; in fact the whole country approved of the operation. After all, it was mostly supported by private funds."

"Another point which isn't widely realized," added Parkinson: "Very few people could have actually died *in* the *Titanic*; most of them got off, and were drowned or frozen."

"No chance of bodies?"

"None whatsoever. There are lots of very hungry creatures down there."

"Well, I'm glad we've disposed of that depressing subject. But there's something perhaps more important. . . ." Kilford picked up one of the little glass spheres, and rolled it between thumb and forefinger. "You're putting *billions* of these in the sea. Inevitably, lots of them will be lost. What about the ecological impact?"

"I see you've been reading the Bluepeace literature. Well, there won't be any."

"Not even when they wash to shore—and our beaches are littered with broken glass?"

"I'd like to shoot the copywriter who coined that phrase— or hire him. First of all, it will take *centuries*—maybe millennia—for these spheres to disintegrate. And please remember what they're made of—*silica*! So when they do eventually crumble, do you realize what they'll turn into? That well-known beach pollutant—sand!"

"Good point. But what about the other objection? Suppose fish or marine animals eat them?"

Parkinson picked up one of the microspheres, and twirled it between his fingers just as Kilford had done.

"Glass is totally nonpoisonous—chemically inert. Anything big enough to swallow one of these won't be hurt by it."

And he popped the sphere into his mouth.

Behind the control panel, the producer turned to Roy Emerson.

"That was terrific—but I'm still sorry you wouldn't go on."

"Parky did very well without me. Do you think I'd have gotten in any more words than poor Dr. Thornley?"

"Probably not. And that was a neat trick, swallowing the microsphere—don't think I could manage it. And I'll make a bet that from now on, everyone's going to call them Parky's Pills."

Emerson laughed. "I wouldn't be surprised. And he'll he asked to repeat the act, every time he goes on TV."

He thought it unnecessary to add that, besides his many other talents, Parkinson was quite a good amateur conjurer. Even with freeze-frame, no one would be able to spot what had *really* happened to that pill.

And there was another reason why he preferred not to join the panel—he was an outsider, and this was a family affair.

Though they lay centuries apart, *Mary Rose* and *Titanic* had much in common. Both were spectacular triumphs of British shipbuilding genius—sunk by equally spectacular examples of British incompetence.

INTO THE M-SET

It was hard to believe, Jason Bradley told himself, that people actually *lived* like this, only a few generations ago. Though Conroy Castle was a very modest example of its species, its scale was still impressive to anyone who had spent most of his life in cluttered offices, motel rooms, ships' cabins—not to mention deep-diving minisubs, so cramped that the personal hygiene of your companions was a matter of crucial importance.

The dining room, with its ornately carved ceiling and enormous wall mirrors, could comfortably seat at least fifty people. Donald Craig felt it necessary to explain the little four-place table that looked lost and lonely at its center.

"We've not had time to buy proper furniture. The castle's own stuff was in terrible shape—most of it had to be burned. And we've been too busy to do much entertaining. But one day, when we've finally established ourselves as the local nobility . . ."

Edith did not seem to approve of her husband's flippancy, and once again Bradley had the impression that she was the leader in this enterprise, with Donald a reluctant—or at best passive—accomplice. He could guess the scenario: people with

enough money to squander on expensive toys often discovered
that they would have been happier without them. And Conroy
Castle—with all its surrounding acres and maintenance staff—
must be a very expensive toy indeed.

When the servants (servants!—that was another novelty)
had cleared the remnants of an excellent Chinese dinner flown
in especially from Dublin, Bradley and his hosts retreated to a
set of comfortable armchairs in the adjoining room.

"We won't let you get away," said Donald, "without giving
you our Child's Guide to the M-Set. Edith can spot a Mandel-
virgin at a hundred meters."

Bradley was not sure if he qualified for this description. He
had finally recognized the odd shape of the lake, though he
had forgotten its technical name until reminded of it. In the
last decade of the century, it had been impossible to escape
from manifestations of the Mandelbrot Set—they were appearing all the time on video displays, wallpaper, fabrics, and
virtually every type of design. Bradley recalled that someone
had coined the word "Mandelmania" to describe the more
acute symptoms; he had begun to suspect that it might be applicable to this odd household. But he was quite prepared to
sit with polite interest through whatever lecture or demonstration his hosts had in store for him.

He realized that they too were being polite, in their own
way. They were anxious to have his decision, and he was
equally anxious to give it.

He only hoped that the call he was expecting would come
through before he left the castle. . . .

Bradley had never met the traditional stage mother, but he
had seen her in movies like—what was that old one called?—
ah, *Fame*. Here was the same passionate determination on the
part of a parent for a child to become a star, even if there was
no discernible talent. In this case, he did not doubt that the
faith was fully justified.

"Before Ada begins," said Edith, "I'd like to make a few

points. The M-Set is the most complex entity in the whole of mathematics—yet it doesn't involve anything more advanced than addition and multiplication—not even subtraction or division! That's why many people with a good knowledge of math have difficulty in grasping it. They simply can't believe that something with too much detail to be explored before the end of the Universe can be generated without using logs or trig functions or higher transcendentals. It doesn't seem reasonable that it's all done merely by adding numbers together."

"Doesn't seem reasonable to me, either. If it's so simple, why didn't anyone discover it centuries ago?"

"Very good question! Because so much adding and multiplying is involved, with such huge numbers, that we had to wait for high-speed computers. If you'd given abacuses to Adam and Eve and *all* their descendants right up to now, they couldn't have found some of the pictures Ada can show you by pressing a few keys. Go ahead, dear. . . ."

The holoprojector was cunningly concealed; Bradley could not even guess where it was hiding. Very easy to make this old castle a haunted one, he thought, and scare away any intruders. It would beat a burglar alarm.

The two crossed lines of an ordinary x-y diagram appeared in the air, with the sequence of integers 0, 1, 2, 3, 4 . . . marching off in all four directions.

Ada gave Bradley that disconcertingly direct look, as if she were once again trying to estimate his I.Q. so that her presentation could be appropriately calibrated.

"Any point on this plane," she said, "can be identified by two numbers—its x- and y-coordinates. Okay?"

"Okay," Bradley answered solemnly.

"Well, the M-Set lies in a very small region near the origin—it doesn't extend beyond plus or minus two in either direction, so we can ignore all the larger numbers."

The integers skittered off along the four axes, leaving only the numbers one and two marking distances away from the central zero.

"Now suppose we take any point inside this grid, and join it to the center. Measure the length of this radius—let's call it *r*."

This, thought Bradley, is putting no great strain on my mental resources. When do we get to the tricky part?

"Obviously, in this case *r* can have any value from zero to just under three—about two point eight, to be exact. Okay?"

"Okay."

"Right. Now Exercise One. Take any point's *r* value, and square it. *Keep on squaring it.* What happens?"

"Don't let me spoil your fun, Ada."

"Well, if *r* is exactly one, it stays at that value—no matter how many times you square it. One times one times one times one is always one."

"Okay," said Bradley, just beating Ada to the draw.

"If it's even a *smidgin* more than one, however, and you go on squaring it, sooner or later it will shoot off to infinity. Even if it's 1.0000 . . . 0001, and there are a million zeros to the right of the decimal point. It will just take a bit longer.

"But if the number is *less* than one—say .99999999 . . . with a million nines—you get just the opposite. It may stay close to one for ages, but as you keep on squaring it, suddenly it will collapse and dwindle away down to zero—okay?"

This time Ada got there first, and Bradley merely nodded. As yet, he could not see the point in this elementary arithmetic, but it was obviously leading somewhere.

"Lady—stop bothering Mr. Bradley! So you see, simply squaring numbers—and going on squaring them, over and over—divides them into two distinct sets. . . ."

A circle had appeared on the two crossed axes, centered on the origin and with radius unity.

"Inside that circle are all the numbers that disappear when you keep on squaring them. Outside are all those that shoot off to infinity. You could say that the circle of radius one is a fence—a boundary—a *frontier*—dividing the two sets of numbers. I like to call it the S-set."

"S for squaring?"

"Of cour— Yes. Now, here's the important point. The numbers on either side are totally separated; yet though nothing can pass through it, the boundary hasn't any thickness. It's simply a line—you could go on magnifying it forever and it would stay a line, though it would soon appear to be a straight one because you wouldn't be able to see its curvature."

"This may not seem very exciting," interjected Donald, "but it's absolutely fundamental—you'll soon see why—sorry, Ada."

"Now, to get the M-Set we make one teeny-*weeny* change. We don't just square the numbers. We square and *add* . . . square and *add*. You wouldn't think it would make all that difference—but it opens up a whole new universe. . . .

"Suppose we start with one again. We square it and get one. Then we add them to get two.

"Two squared is four. Add the original one again—answer five.

"Five squared is twenty-five—add one—twenty-six.

"Twenty-six squared is six hundred seventy-six—you see what's happening! The numbers are shooting up at a fantastic rate. A few more times around the loop, and they're too big for any computer to handle. Yet we started with—*one*! So that's the *first* big difference between the M-Set and the S-set, which has its boundary at one.

"But if we started with a much smaller number than one— say zero point one—you'll probably guess what happens."

"It collapses to nothing after a few cycles of squaring and adding."

Ada gave her rare but dazzling smile.

"*Usually.* Sometimes it dithers around a small, fixed value— anyway, it's trapped inside the set. So once again we have a map that divides all the numbers on the plane into two classes. Only this time, the boundary isn't something as elementary as a circle."

"You can say that again," murmured Donald. He collected a frown from Edith, but pressed on. "I've asked quite a few people what shape they thought would be produced; most suggested some kind of oval. No one came near the truth; no one ever could. All *right*, Lady! I won't interrupt Ada again!"

"Here's the first approximation," continued Ada, scooping up her boisterous puppy with one hand while tapping the keyboard with the other. "You've already seen it today."

The now-familiar outline of Lake Mandelbrot had appeared superimposed on the grid of unit squares, but in far more detail than Bradley had seen it in the garden. On the right was the largest, roughly heart-shaped figure, then a smaller circle touching it, a much smaller one touching *that*—and the narrow spike running off to the extreme left and ending at—2 on the x-axis.

Now, however, Bradley could see that the main figures were barnacled—that was the metaphor that came instantly to mind—with a myriad of smaller subsidiary circles, many of which had short jagged lines extending from them. It was a much more complex shape than the pattern of lakes in the garden—strange and intriguing, but certainly not at all beautiful. Edith and Ada, however, were looking at it with a kind of reverential awe, which Donald did not seem to entirely share.

"This is the complete set with no magnification," said Ada, in a voice that was now a little less self-assured—in fact, almost hushed.

"Even on this scale, though, you can see how different it is from the plain, zero-thickness circle bounding the S-set. You could zoom *that* up forever and ever, and it would remain a line—nothing more. But the boundary of the M-Set is *fuzzy*—it contains infinite detail: you can go in anywhere you like, and magnify as much as you please—and you'll always discover something new and unexpected—look!"

The image expanded; they were diving into the cleft between the main cardioid and its tangent circle. It was, Bradley told himself, very much like watching a zip-fastener being pulled open—except that the teeth of the zipper had the most extraordinary shapes.

First they looked like baby elephants, waving tiny trunks. Then the trunks became tentacles. Then the tentacles sprouted eyes. Then, as the image continued to expand, the eyes opened up into black whirlpools of infinite depth. . . .

"The magnification's up in the millions now," Edith whispered. "The picture we started with is already bigger than Europe."

They swept past the whirlpools, skirting mysterious islands guarded by reefs of coral. Flotillas of seahorses sailed by in stately procession. At the screen's exact center, a tiny black dot appeared, expanded, began to show a haunting familiarity—and seconds later revealed itself as an exact replica of the original set.

This, Bradley thought, is where we came in. Or is it? He could not be quite sure; there seemed to be minor differences, but the family resemblance was unmistakable.

"Now," continued Ada, "our original picture is as wide as the orbit of Mars—so this mini-set's really far smaller than an atom. But there's just as much detail all around it. And so on forever."

The zooming stopped; for a moment it seemed that a sample of lacework, full of intricate loops and whorls that teased the eye, hung frozen in space. Then, as if a paintbox had been spilled over it, the monochrome image burst into colors so unexpected, and so dazzlingly beautiful, that Bradley gave a gasp of astonishment.

The zooming restarted, but in the reverse direction, and in a micro-universe now transformed by color. No one said a word until they were back at the original complete M-Set, now an ominous black fringed with a narrow border of golden fire, and shooting off jagged lightnings of blues and purples.

"And where," asked Bradley when he had recovered his breath, "did all those colors come from? We didn't see them on the way in."

Ada laughed. "No—they're not really part of the set—but aren't they gorgeous? I can tell the computer to make them anything I like."

"Even though the actual colors are quite arbitrary," Edith explained, "they're full of meaning. You know the way map makers put shades of blue and green between contour lines, to emphasize differences in level?"

"Of course; we do just the same thing in oceanography. The deeper the blue, the deeper the water."

"Right. In this case, the colors tell us how many times the computer's had to go around the loop before it decides whether a number definitely belongs to the M-Set—or not. In borderline cases, it may have to do the squaring and adding routine thousands of times."

"And often for hundred-digit numbers," said Donald. "*Now* you understand why the set wasn't discovered earlier."

"Mighty good reason."

"Now watch this," said Ada.

The image came to life as waves of color flowed outward. It seemed that the borders of the set itself were continually expanding—yet staying in the same place. Then Bradley realized that nothing was really moving; only the colors were cycling around the spectrum, to produce this completely convincing illusion of movement.

I begin to understand, Bradley thought, how someone could get lost in this thing—even make it a way of life.

"I'm almost certain," he said, "that I've seen this program listed in my computer's software library—with a couple of thousand others. How lucky I've never run it. I can see how addictive it could get."

He noticed that Donald Craig glanced sharply at Edith, and realized that he had made a somewhat tactless remark. However, she still seemed engrossed by the flow of colors, even though she must have seen this particular display countless times.

"Ada," she said dreamily, "give Mr. Jason our favorite quotation from Einstein."

That's asking a lot from a ten-year-old, thought Bradley—even one like this; but the girl never hesitated, and there was no trace of mechanical repetition in her voice. She understood the words, and spoke from the heart:

" 'The most beautiful thing we can experience is the mysterious. It is the source of all true art and science. He to whom this emotion is a stranger, who can no longer pause to wonder and stand wrapt in awe, is as good as dead.' "

I'll go along with that, thought Bradley. He remembered calm nights in the Pacific, with a sky full of stars and a glimmering trail of bioluminescence behind the ship; he recalled his first glimpse of the teeming life-forms—as alien as any from another planet—gathered around the scalding cornucopia of a Galápagos mid-ocean vent, where the continents were slowly tearing apart; and he hoped that before long he would feel awe and wonder again, when the tremendous knife edge of *Titanic*'s prow came looming up out of the abyss.

The dance of colors ceased: the M-Set faded out. Although nothing had ever been *really* there, he could somehow sense that the virtual screen of the holograph projector had switched off.

"So now," said Donald, "you know more about the Mandelbrot Set than you want to." He glanced momentarily at Edith, and once again Bradley felt that twinge of sympathy toward him.

It was not at all the feeling he had expected, when he came

to Conroy Castle; "envy" would have been a better word. Here was a man with great wealth, a beautiful home, and a talented and attractive family—all the ingredients which were supposed to guarantee happiness. Yet something had obviously gone wrong. I wonder, Bradley thought, how long it is since they went to bed together. It could be as simple as that—though *that*, of course, was seldom simple. . . .

Once again he glanced at his watch; they must think he was deliberately avoiding the issue—and they were perfectly right. Hurry up, Mr. Director-General! he pleaded silently.

As if on cue, he felt the familiar tingling in his wrist.

"Excuse me," he said to his hosts. "I've a very important call coming through. It will only take a minute."

"Of course. We'll leave you to it."

How many million times a day this ritual was now carried out! Strict etiquette dictated that everyone else offer to leave the room when a personal call was coming through; politeness demanded that only the recipient leave, with apologies to all. There were countless variations according to circumstances and nationalities. In Japan, so Kato was fond of complaining, the formalities often lasted so long that the caller hung up in disgust.

"Sorry for the interruption," Bradley said as he came back in through the French windows. "That was about our business—I couldn't give you a decision until I'd received it."

"I hope it's a favorable one," said Donald. "We need you."

"And I would like to work with you—but—"

"Parky's made you a better offer," said Edith, with scarcely veiled contempt.

Bradley looked at her calmly, and answered without rancor.

"No, Mrs. Craig. Please keep these figures confidential. The Parkinson group's offer was generous—but it was only half of yours. And the offer which I've just received is much less than one tenth of *that*. Nevertheless, I'm considering it very seriously."

There was a resounding silence, broken at last by an un-characteristic giggle from Ada.

"You must be crazy," said Edith. Donald merely grinned.

"You may be right. But I've reached the stage when I don't need the money, though it's always good to have some around." He paused, and chuckled softly.

"Enough is enough. I don't know if you ever heard the wise-crack that *Titanic's* most famous casualty, J. J. Astor, once made: "A man who has a million dollars is as well off as one who is rich." Well, I've made a few million during my career, and some of it's still in the bank. I don't really need any more; and if I do, I can always go down and tickle another octopus.

"I didn't *plan* this—it was a bolt from the blue—two days ago I'd already decided to accept your offer."

Edith now seemed more perplexed than hostile.

"Can you tell us who's . . . *underbid* Nippon-Turner?"

Bradley shook his head. "Give me a couple of days; there are still a few problems, and I don't want to fall between *three* stools."

"I think I understand," said Donald. "There's only one rea-son to work for peanuts. Every man owes something to his profession."

"That sounds like a quotation."

"It is: Dr. Johnson."

"I like it; I may be using it a lot, in the next few weeks. Meanwhile, before I make a final decision, I want a little time to think matters over. Again, many thanks for your hospital-ity—not to mention your offer. I may yet accept it—but if not, I hope we can still be friends."

As he lifted away from the castle, the downwash of the he-licopter ruffled the waters of Lake Mandelbrot, shattering the reflections of the cypresses. He was contemplating the biggest break in his career; before he made his decision, he needed to relax completely.

And he knew exactly how to do that.

A HOUSE OF GOOD REPUTE

Even the coming of hypersonic transportation had not done much to change the status of New Zealand; to most people it was merely the last stop before the South Pole. The great majority of New Zealanders were quite content to keep it that way.

Evelyn Merrick was one of the exceptions, and had defected at the (in her case, very) ripe age of seventeen to find her destiny elsewhere. After three marriages which had left her emotionally scarred but financially secure, she had discovered her role in life, and was as happy as anyone could reasonably expect to be.

The Villa, as it was known to her wide-ranging clientele, was on a beautiful estate in one of the still unspoiled parts of Kent, conveniently close to Gatwick Airport. Its previous owner had been a celebrated media tycoon, who had placed his bet on the wrong system when high-definition TV swept all before it at the end of the twentieth century. Later attempts to restore his fortune had misfired, and he was now a guest of His Majesty's government for the next five years (assuming time off for good behavior).

Being a man of high moral standards, he was quite indignant about the use which Dame Eva had now made of his property, and had even attempted to dislodge her. However, Eva's lawyers were just as good as his; perhaps better, since she was still at liberty, and had every intention of remaining so.

The Villa was run with meticulous propriety, the girls' passports, tax returns, health and pension contributions, medical records, and so forth being instantly available to any government inspector—of whom, Dame Eva sometimes remarked sourly, there always seemed to be a copious supply. If any ever came in the hope of personal gratification, they were sadly disappointed.

On the whole, it was a rewarding career, full of emotional and intellectual stimulus. She certainly had no ethical problems, having long ago decided that anything enjoyed by adults of voting age was perfectly acceptable, as long as it was not dangerous, unhygienic, or fattening. Her main cause of complaint was that involvement with clients caused a high rate of staff turnover, with resulting heavy expenditure on wedding presents. She had also observed that Villa-inspired marriages appeared to last longer than those with more conventional origins, and intended to publish a statistical survey when she was quite sure of her data; at the moment the correlation coefficient was still below the level of significance.

As might be expected in her profession, Evelyn Merrick was a woman of many secrets, mostly other peoples'; but she also had one of her own which she guarded with special care. Though nothing could have been more respectable, if it came out it might be bad for trade. For the last two years, she had been employing her extensive—perhaps unique—knowledge of paraphilia to complete her doctor's degree in psychology at the University of Auckland.

She had never met Professor Hinton, except over video circuits—and even that very rarely, since both preferred the digital impersonality of computer file exchanges. One day—perhaps a decade after she had retired—her thesis would be published, though not under her own name, and with all the case histories disguised beyond identification. Not even Professor Hinton knew the individuals involved, though he had made some shrewd guesses at a few.

"Subject O.G.," Eva typed. "Age fifty. Successful engineer."

She considered the screen carefully. The initials, of course, had been changed according to her simple code, and the age had been rounded down to the nearest decade. But the last entry was reasonably accurate: his profession reflected a man's personality, and should not be disguised unless it was absolutely necessary to avoid identification. Even then, it had to be done with sensitivity, so that the displacement was not too violent. In the case of a world-famous musician, Eva had altered "pianist" to "violinist," and she had converted an equally celebrated sculptor into a painter. She had even turned a politician into a statesman.

". . . As a small boy, O.G. was teased and occasionally captured by the pupils of a neighboring girl's school, who used him as a (fairly willing) subject for lessons in nursing and male anatomy. They frequently bandaged him from head to foot, and though he now asserts that there was no erotic element involved, this is rather hard to believe. When challenged, he shrugs his shoulders and says, 'I just don't remember.'

"Later, as a young man, O.G. witnessed the aftermath of a major accident which caused many deaths. Though not injured himself, the experience also appears to have affected his sexual fantasies. He enjoys various forms of bondage (see List A) and he had developed a mild case of the Saint Sebastian Complex, most famously demonstrated by Yukio Mishima. Unlike Mishima, however, O.G. is completely heterosexual, scoring only 2.5 +/− 0.1 on the Standard Mapplethorpe Phototest.

"What makes O.G.'s behavior pattern so interesting, and perhaps unusual, is that he is an active and indeed somewhat aggressive personality, as befits the manager of an organization in a demanding and competitive business. It is hard to imagine him playing a *passive* role in any sphere of life, yet he likes my personnel to wrap him up in bandages like an Egyptian mummy, until he is completely helpless. Only in this way, after considerable stimulation, can he achieve a satisfactory orgasm.

"When I suggested that he was acting out a death wish, he laughed but did not attempt to deny it. His work often involves physical danger, which may be the very reason why he was attracted to it in the first place. However, he gave an alternative explanation which, I am sure, contains a good deal of truth.

" 'When you have responsibilities involving millions of dollars and affecting many men's lives, you can't imagine how delightful it is to be *completely* helpless for a while—unable to control what's happening around you. Of course, I *know* it's all play-acting, but I manage to pretend it isn't. I sometimes wonder how I'd enjoy the situation if it was for real.'

" 'You wouldn't,' I told him, and he agreed."

Eva scrolled the entry, checking it for any clues that might reveal O.G.'s identity. The Villa specialized in celebrities, so it was better to be excessively cautious than the reverse.

That caution extended to the celebrities themselves. The Villa's only house rule was "No blood on the carpets," and she recalled, with a grimace of disgust, a third world country's chief-of-staff whose frenzies had injured one of her girls. Eva had accepted his apologies, and his check, with cold disdain, then made a quick call to the Foreign Office. The general would have been most surprised—and mortified—to know exactly why the British ambassador now found so many reasons for postponing his next visit to the United Kingdom.

Eva sometimes wondered what dear Sister Margarita would have thought of her star pupil's present vocation; the last time she had wept was when the notice of her old friend's death had reached her from the Mother Superior. And she remembered, with wistful amusement, the question she had once been tempted to ask her tutor: exactly *why* should a vow of perpetual chastity be considered any nobler—any *holier*—than a vow of perpetual constipation?

It was a perfectly serious query, not in the least intended to scandalize the old nun or shake the sure foundations of her faith. But on the whole, perhaps it was just as well left unasked.

Sister Margarita already knew that little Eva Merrick was not meant for the church; but Eva still sent a generous donation to St. Jude's every Christmas.

BUREAUCRAT

Article 156
Establishment of the Authority
1. There is hereby established the International Seabed Authority, which shall function in accordance with this Part.
2. All States Parties are *ipso facto* members of the Authority.

. . . . .

4. The seat of the Authority shall be in Jamaica.

Article 158
Organs of the Authority
2. There is hereby established the Enterprise, the organ through which the Authority shall carry out the functions referred to in article 170, paragraph 1.

(United Nations Convention on the Law of the Sea, signed at Montego Bay, Jamaica, on 10 December 1982.)

S orry about the emoluments," said Director-General Wilbur Jantz apologetically, "but they're fixed by U.N. regulations."

"I quite understand. As you know, I'm not here for the money."

"And there *are* very considerable fringe benefits. First, you'll have the rank of ambassador . . ."

"Will I have to dress like one? I hope not—I don't even have a tux, let alone the rest of that damned nonsense."

Jantz laughed.

"Don't worry—we'll take care of details like that. And you'll be VIPed everywhere, of course—that can be quite pleasant."

It's a long time, thought Jason Bradley, since I've *not* been VIPed, but it would be rather tactless to say so. Despite all his experience, he was a new boy in this environment; maybe he shouldn't have made that crack about ambassadors. . . .

The D.G. was scanning the readout scrolling on his desk display, giving an occasional PAUSE command so that he could examine some item in detail. Bradley would have returned a substantial slice of his income to his new employers for the privilege of reading that file. I wonder if they know, he thought, about the time that Ted and I "salted" that wreck off Delos with fake amphorae? Not that I've got a guilty conscience: it caused a lot of trouble to people who thoroughly deserved it.

"I think I should tell you," said the D.G., "that we did have one small problem—though I shouldn't worry about it. Some of our more, ah, aggressively independent states-parties may not be too happy about your CIA connection."

"That was more than thirty years ago! And I didn't even know it was a CIA job until long after I'd signed up—as an ordinary seaman, for heaven's sake. . . . I thought I was joining Hughes' Summa Corporation—and so I was."

"Don't let it lose you any sleep; I mention it just in case someone brings it up. It's not likely, because in all other respects your qualifications are superb. Even Ballard admitted that."

"Oh—he did?"

"Well, he said you were the best of a bad bunch."

"That sounds like Bob."

The D.G. continued to examine the readout, then sat for a moment with a thoughtful expression.

"This has nothing to do with your appointment, and please excuse me if I'm speaking out of turn. I'm talking to you as man to man—"

Hello, thought Jason, they know about the Villa! I wonder how they got through Eva's security?

But it was a much bigger surprise than *that*. . . .

"It seems that you lost contact with your son and his mother more than twenty years ago. If you wish, we can put you in touch."

For a moment, Bradley felt a constriction in his chest; it was almost as if something had happened to his air supply. He knew the sensation all too well, and felt the clammy onset of that disabling panic which is a diver's worst enemy.

As he had always managed to do before, he regained control by slow, deep breathing. Director-General Jantz, realizing that he had opened some old wound, waited sympathetically.

"Thank you," Bradley said at last. "I would prefer not to. Are they . . . all right?"

"Yes."

That was all he needed to know. It was impossible to turn back the clock: he could barely remember the man—*boy!*—he had been at twenty-five, when he had finally gone to college. And, for the first and last time, fallen in love.

He would never know whose fault it was, and perhaps now it did not matter. They could have contacted him easily enough, if they had wished. (Did J.J. ever think of him, and recall the times they had played together? Bradley's eyes stung, and he turned his mind away from the memory.)

He sometimes wondered if he would even recognize Julie if they met in the street; as he had destroyed all her photographs (why had he kept that one of J.J.?), he could no longer clearly remember her face. There was no doubt, however, that the experience had left indelible scars on his psyche, but he had learned to live with them—with the help, he wryly admitted, of Dame Eva. The ritual he had institutionalized at the Villa had brought him mental and physical relief, and had allowed him to function efficiently. He was grateful for that.

And now he had a new interest—a new challenge—as deputy director (Atlantic) of the International Seabed Authority. He could just imagine how Ted Collier would have laughed his head off at this metamorphosis. Well, there was much truth in the old saying that poachers made the best gamekeepers.

"I've asked Dr. Zwicker to come and say hello, as you'll be working closely together. Have you ever met him before?"

"No—but of course I've seen him often enough. Last time was only yesterday, on the Science News Channel. He was analyzing the Parkinson scheme—and didn't think much of it."

"Between you and me, he doesn't think much of anything he hasn't invented himself. And he's usually right, which doesn't endear him to his colleagues."

Most people still thought it slightly comic that the world's leading oceanographer had been born in an alpine valley, and there had been endless jokes about the prowess of the Swiss Navy. But there was no getting away from the fact that the bathyscaphe had been invented in Switzerland, and the long shadow of the Piccards still lay across the technology they had founded.

The director-general glanced at his watch, and smiled at Bradley.

"If my conscience would allow it, I could win bets this way." He started a quiet countdown, and had just reached "One" when there was a knock on the door.

"See what I mean?" he said to Bradley. "As they're so fond of saying, 'Time is the art of the Swiss.' " Then he called out: "Come in, Franz."

There was a moment of silent appraisal before scientist and

engineer shook hands; each knew the other's reputation, and each was wondering, "Will we be colleagues—or antagonists?" Then Professor Franz Zwicker said, "Welcome aboard, Mr. Bradley. We have much to talk about."

PREPARATIONS

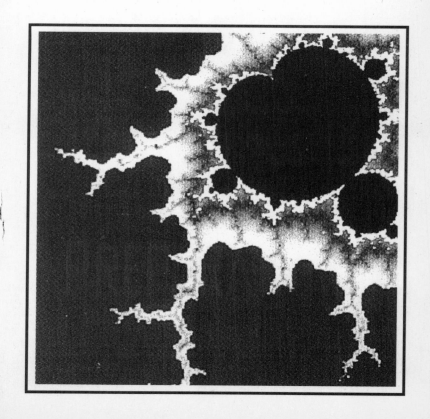

PHONE-IN

There can't be many people," said Marcus Kilford, "who don't know that it's now less than four years to the *Titanic* centennial—or haven't heard about the plans to raise the wreck. Once again, I'm happy to have with me three of the leaders in this project. I'll talk to each of them in turn—then you'll have a chance of calling in with any specific questions you have. At the right time, the number will flash along the bottom of the screen. . . .

"The gentleman on my left is the famous underwater engineer Jason Bradley; his encounter with the giant octopus in the Newfoundland oil rig is now part of ocean folklore. He's currently with the International Seabed Authority, and is responsible for monitoring operations on the wreck.

"Next to him is Rupert Parkinson, who *almost* brought the America's Cup to England last year. (Sorry about that, Rupert.) His firm is involved in raising the forward portion of the wreck—the larger of the two pieces into which the ship is broken.

"On my right is Donald Craig, who's associated with the Nippon-Turner Corporation—now the world's largest media chain. He will tell us about the plans to raise the stern, which was the last part to sink—carrying with it most of those who were lost on that unforgettable night, ninety-six years ago. . . .

"Mr. Bradley—would it be fair to call you a referee, making sure that there's no cheating in the race between these two gentlemen?"

Kilford had to hold up his hand to quell simultaneous protests from his other two guests.

"Please, gentlemen! You'll both have your turn. Let Jason speak first."

Now that I'm disguised as a diplomat, thought Bradley, I'd better try to act the part. I know Kilford's trying to needle us—that's his job—so I'll play it cool.

"I don't regard it as a *race*," he answered carefully. "Both parties have submitted schedules which call for the raising mid-April 2012."

"On the fifteenth itself? *Both* of them?"

This was a sensitive matter, which Bradly had no intention of discussing in public. He had convinced ISA's top brass that nothing like a photo finish must be allowed. Two major salvage operations could not possibly take place *simultaneously*, less than a kilometer apart. The risk of disaster—always a major concern—could be greatly increased. Trying to perform two difficult jobs at once was a very good recipe for achieving neither.

"Look," he said patiently, "this isn't a one-day operation. *Titanic* reached the bottom in a matter of minutes. It's going to take days to lift her back to the surface. Perhaps weeks."

"May I make a point?" said Parkinson, promptly doing so. "We have no intention of bringing our section of the wreck *back to the surface*. It's always going to remain completely underwater, to avoid the risk of immediate corrosion. *We're* not engaged in a TV spectacular." He carefully avoided looking at Craig; the studio camera was less diffident.

I feel sorry for Donald, thought Bradley. Kato should have been here instead: he and Parky would be well matched. We might see some real fireworks, as each tried to be more sardonically polite than the other—in, of course, the most gentlemanly way possible. Bradley wished that he could help Donald, toward whom he had developed a warm, almost paternal feeling, but he had to remember that he was now a friendly neutral.

Donald Craig wriggled uncomfortably in his chair, and gave Parkinson a hurt look. Kilford seemed to be enjoying himself.

"Well, Mr. Craig? Aren't you hoping to film the stern rising out of the water, with your synthetic iceberg looming over it?"

That was exactly what Kato intended, though he had never said so in public. But this was not the sort of secret that could be kept for more than a few milliseconds in the electronic global village.

"Well—er," began Donald lamely. "If we *do* bring our section up above sea level, it won't be there for long—"

"—but long enough for some spectacular footage?"

"—because just as you intend to do, Rupert, we'll tow it underwater until it reaches its final resting place, at Tokyo-on-Sea. And there's no danger of corrosion; most of the ironwork will still be enclosed in ice, and all of it will be at freezing point."

Donald paused for a second; then a slow smile spread over his face.

"And by the way," he continued, obviously gaining confidence, "haven't I heard that *you* are planning a TV spectacular? What's this story about taking scuba divers down to the wreck, as soon as it's within reach? How deep will that be, Mr. Bradley?"

"Depends what they're breathing. Thirty meters with air. A hundred or more with mixtures."

"Then I'm sure half the sports divers in the world would love to pay a visit—long before you get to Florida."

"Thanks for the suggestion, Donald," said Parkinson amiably. "We'll certainly give it a thought."

"Well, now we've broken the ice—ha, ha!—let's get down to business. What I'd like you to do—Donald, Rupert—is for each of you to explain where your project stands at the moment. I don't expect you to give away any secrets, of course. Then I'll ask Jason to make any comments—if he wants to. As *C* comes before *P*, you go on first, Donald."

"Well—um—the problem with the stern is that it's so badly smashed up. Sealing it in ice is the most sensible way of handling it as a single unit. And, of course, ice *floats*—as Captain Smith apparently forgot in 1912.

"My friends in Japan have worked out a very efficient method of freezing water, using electric current. It's already at almost zero centigrade down there, so very little additional cooling is needed.

"We've manufactured the neutral-buoyancy cables and the thermoelectric elements, and our underwater robots will start installing them in a few days. We're still negotiating for the electricity, and hope to have contracts signed very soon."

"And when you've made your deep-sea iceberg, what then?"

"Ah—well—that's something I'd rather not discuss at the moment."

Though none of those present knew it, Donald was not stalling. He was genuinely ignorant—even baffled. What *had* Kato meant in their last conversation? Surely he must have been joking: really, it was not very polite to leave his partners in the dark. . . .

"Very well, Donald. Any comments, Jason?"

Bradley shook his head. "Nothing important. The scheme's audacious, but our scientists can't fault it. And, of course, it has—what do you say?—poetic justice."

"Rupert?"

"I agree. It's a lovely idea. I only *hope* it works."

Parkinson managed to convey a genuine sense of regret for

the failure he obviously expected. It was a masterly little performance.

"Well, it's your turn. Where do you stand?"

"We're using straightforward techniques—nothing exotic! Because air is compressed four hundred times at *Titanic*'s depth, it's not practical to pump it down to get lift. So we're using hollow glass spheres; they have the same buoyancy at any depth. They'll be packed—millions of them—in bundles of the appropriate size. Some may be put in the ship at strategic points, by small ROVs—sorry, Remote Operated Vehicles. But most of them will be attached to a lifting cradle we're lowering down to the hull."

"And just how," interjected Kilford, "are you going to attach the *hull* to the *cradle*?"

Kilford had obviously done his homework, Bradley thought admiringly. Most laymen would have taken such a matter for granted, as a point not worth special attention; but it was the key to the whole operation.

Rupert Parkinson smiled broadly. "Donald has his little secrets; so have we. But we'll be doing some tests very shortly, and Jason has kindly agreed to observe them—haven't you?"

"Yes—if the U.S. Navy can lend us *Marvin* in time. ISA doesn't have any deep subs of its own, alas. But we're working on it."

"One day I'd like to dive with you—I think," said Kilford. "Can you get a video link down to the wreck?"

"No problem, with fiber optics. We have several monitoring circuits already."

"Splendid. I'll start bullying my producer. Well, I see there are lots of lights flashing. Our first caller is Mr.—sorry, I guess that's Miss—Chandrika de Silva of Notting Hill Gate. Go ahead, Chandrika. . . ."

ICE

We're in a buyer's market," said Kato with undisguised glee. "The U.S. and USSR navies are trying to underbid each other. If we got tough, I think they'd both *pay* us to take their radioactive toys off their hands."

On the other side of the world, the Craigs were watching him through the latest marvel of communications technology. POLAR 1, opened with great fanfare only a few weeks ago, was the first fiber-optic cable to be laid under the Arctic ice cap. By eliminating the long haul up to the geostationary orbit, and its slight but annoying time delay, the global phone system had been noticeably improved; speakers no longer kept interrupting each other, or wasting time waiting for replies. As the Director-General of INTELSAT had said, smiling bravely through his tears, "Now we can devote comsats to the job God intended them for—providing service to airplanes and ships and automobiles—and *everyone* who likes to get out into the fresh air."

"Have you made a deal yet?" asked Donald.

"It will be wrapped up by the end of the week. One Russki, one Yank. Then they'll compete to see which will do the better job for us. Isn't that nicer than throwing nukes at each other?"

"Much nicer."

"The British and French are also trying to get into the act—that helps our bargaining position, of course. We may even rent one of theirs as a standby. Or in case we decide to speed up operations."

"Just to keep level with Parky and Company? Or to get our section up first?"

There was a brief silence—just about long enough for the question to have traveled to the Moon and back.

"Really, Edith!" said Kato. "I was thinking of unexpected snags. Remember, we're not in a race—perish the thought! We've both promised ISA to lift between seven and fifteen April '12. We want to make sure we can meet the schedule— that's all."

"And will you?"

"Let me show you our little home movie—I'd appreciate it if you'd exit RECORD mode. This isn't the final version, so I'd like your comments at this stage."

The Japanese studios, Donald recalled, had a long and well-deserved reputation for model work and special effects. (How many times had Tokyo been destroyed by assorted monsters?) The detail of ship and seabed was so perfect that there was no sense of scale; anyone who did not know that visibility underwater was never more than a hundred meters—at best—might have thought that this was the real thing.

Titanic's crumpled rear section—about a third of her total length—lay on a flat, muddy plain surrounded by the debris that had rained down when the ship tore in two. The stern itself was in fairly good shape, though the deck had been partly peeled away, but farther forward it looked as if a giant hammer had smashed into the wreck. Only half of the rudder protruded from the seabed; two of the three enormous propellers were completely buried. Extricating *them* would be a major problem in itself.

"Looks a mess, doesn't it?" said Kato cheerfully. "But watch."

A shark swam leisurely past, suddenly noticed the imaginary camera, and departed in alarm. A nice touch, thought Donald, silently saluting the animators.

Now time speeded up. Numbers indicating days flickered on the right of the picture, twenty-four hours passing in every second. Slim girders descended from the liquid sky, and assembled themselves into an open framework surrounding the wreckage. Thick cables snaked into the shattered hulk.

Day Four Hundred—more than a year had passed. Now the water, hitherto quite invisible, was becoming milky. First the upper portion of the wreck, then the twisted plating of the hull, then everything down to the seabed itself, slowly disappeared into a huge block of glistening whiteness.

"Day Six Hundred," said Kato proudly. "Biggest ice cube in the world—except that it isn't quite cube-shaped. Think of all the refrigerators *that's* going to sell."

Maybe in Asia, thought Donald. But not in the U.K.—especially in Belfast. . . . Already there had been protests, cries of "sacrilege!" and even threats to boycott everything Japanese. Well, that was Kato's problem, and he was certainly well aware of it.

"Day Six Hundred Fifty. By this time, the seabed will also have consolidated, right down to several meters below the triple screws. Everything will be sealed tight in one solid block. All we have to do is lift it up to the surface. The ice will only provide a fraction of the buoyancy we need. So . . ."

". . . so you'll ask Parky to sell you a few billion microspheres."

"Believe it or not, Donald, we *had* thought of making our own. But to copy Western technology? Perish the thought!"

"Then what *have* you invented instead?"

"Something very simple; we'll use a really hi-tech approach.

"Don't tell anyone yet—but we're going to bring the *Titanic* up with rockets."

JASON JUNIOR

There were times when the International Seabed Authority's deputy director (Atlantic) had no official duties, because both halves of the *Titanic* operation were proceeding smoothly. But Jason Bradley was not the sort of man who enjoyed inaction.

Because he did not have to worry about tenure—the income on his investments was several times his ISA salary—he regarded himself as very much a free agent. Others might be trapped in their little boxes on the authority's organization chart; Jason Bradley roved at will, visiting any departments that looked interesting. Sometimes he informed the D.G., sometimes not. And usually he was welcomed, because his fame had spread before him, and other department heads regarded him more as an exotic visitor than a rival.

The other four deputy directors (Pacific, Indian, Antarctic, Arctic) all seemed willing enough to show him what was happening in their respective ocean empires. They were, of course, now united against a common enemy—the global rise in the sea level. After more than a decade of often acrimonious argument, it was now agreed that this rise was between one and two centimeters a year.

Bluepeace and other environmental groups put the blame on man; the scientists were not so sure. It was true that the billions of tons of CO_2 from thermal power plants and automobiles made *some* contribution to the notorious "Greenhouse Effect," but Mother Nature might still be the principal culprit; mankind's most heroic efforts could not match the pollution produced by one large volcano. All these arguments sounded very academic to peoples whose homes might cease to exist within their own lifetimes.

ISA chief scientist Franz Zwicker was widely regarded as the world's leading oceanographer—an opinion he made little effort to discourage. The first item most visitors noticed when entering his office was the *Time* magazine cover, with its caption "Admiral of the Ocean Sea." And no visitor escaped without a lecture, or at least a commercial, for Operation NEPTUNE.

"It's a scandal," Zwicker was fond of saying. "We have photo coverage of the Moon and Mars showing everything down to the size of a small house—but most of *our* planet is still completely unknown! They're spending billions to map the human genome, in the hope of triggering advances in medicine—someday. I don't doubt it; but mapping the seabed down to one-meter resolution would pay off immediately. Why, with camera and magnetometer we'd locate *all* the wrecks that have ever happened, since men started to build ships!"

To those who accused him of being a monomaniac, he was fond of giving Edward Teller's famous reply: "That's simply not true. I have *several* monomanias."

There was no doubt, however, that Operation NEPTUNE was the dominant one, and after some months' exposure to Zwicker, Bradley had begun to share it—at least when he was not preoccupied with *Titanic*.

The result, after months of brainstorming and gigabytes of CADCAMing, was Experimental Long-Range Autonomous

Surveyor Mark I. The official acronym ELRAS survived only about a week; then, overnight, it was superseded. . . .

"He doesn't look much like his father," said Roy Emerson.

Bradley was getting rather tired of the joke, though for reasons which none of his colleagues—except the director-general—could have known. But he usually managed a sickly grin when displaying the lab's latest wonder to VVIPs. Mere VIPs were handled by the deputy director, Public Relations.

"No one will believe he's not named after me, but it's true. By pure coincidence, the U.S. Navy robot that made the first reconnaissance inside *Titanic* was called Jason Junior. So I'm afraid the name's stuck.

"But ISA's J.J. is very much more sophisticated—and completely independent. It can operate by itself, for days—or weeks—without any human intervention. Not like the first J.J., which was controlled through a cable; someone described it as a puppy on a leash. Well, we've slipped the leash; *this* J.J. can go hunting over all the world's ocean beds, sniffing at anything that looks interesting."

Jason Junior was not much larger than a man, and was shaped like a fat torpedo, with forward- and downward-viewing cameras. Main propulsion was provided by a single multibladed fan, and several small swivel jets gave attitude control. There were various streamlined bulges housing instruments, but none of the external manipulators found on most ROVs.

"What, no hands?" said Emerson.

"Doesn't need them—so we have a much cleaner design, with more speed and range. J.J.'s purely a surveyor; we can always go back later and look at anything interesting he finds on the seabed. Or under it, with his magnetometer and sonar."

Emerson was impressed; this was the sort of machine that appealed to his gadgeteering instincts. The short-lived fame that the Wave Wiper had brought him had long ago evaporated—though not, fortunately, the wealth that came with it.

He was, it seemed, a one-idea man; later inventions had all proved failures, and his well-publicized experiment to *drop* microspheres down to the *Titanic* in a hollow, air-filled tube had been an embarrassing debacle. Emerson's "hole in the sea" stubbornly refused to stay open; the descending spheres clogged it halfway, unless the flow was so small as to be useless.

The Parkinsons were quite upset, and had made poor Emerson feel uncomfortable at the last board meetings in ways that the English upper class had long perfected; for a few weeks, even his good friend Rupert had been distinctly cool.

But much worse was to come. A satirical Washington cartoonist had created a crazy "Thomas Alva Emerson" whose zany inventions would have put Rube Goldberg to shame. They had begun with the motorized zipper and proceeded via the digital toothbrush to the solar-powered pacemaker. By the time it had reached Braille speedometers for blind motorists, Roy Emerson had consulted his lawyer.

"Winning a libel action against a network," said Joe Wickram, "is about as easy as writing the Lord's Prayer on a rice grain with a felt pen. The defendant will plead fair comment, public interest, and quote at great length from the Bill of Rights. Of course," he added hopefully, "I'll be very happy to have a crack at it. I've always wanted to argue a case before the Supreme Court."

Very sensibly, Emerson had declined the offer, and at least something good had come out of the attack. The Parkinsons, to a man—and woman—felt it was unfair, and had rallied around him. Though they no longer took his engineering suggestions very seriously, they encouraged him to go on fact-finding missions like this one.

The authority's modest research and development center in Jamaica had no secrets, and was open to everybody. It was—in theory, at least—an impartial advisor to all who had dealings with the sea. The Parkinson and Nippon-Turner groups were now far and away the most publicly visible of these, and paid frequent visits to get advice on their own operations—and if possible, to check on the competition. They were careful to avoid scheduling conflicts, but sometimes there were slip-ups and polite "Fancy meeting *you* here!" exchanges. If Roy Emerson was not mistaken, he had noticed one of Kato's people in the departure lounge of Kingston Airport, just as he was arriving.

ISA, of course, was perfectly well aware of these undercurrents, and did its best to exploit them. Franz Zwicker was particularly adept at plugging his own projects—and getting other people to pay for them. Bradley was glad to cooperate, especially where J.J. was concerned, and was equally adept at giving little pep talks and handing out glossy brochures on Operation NEPTUNE.

". . . Once the software's been perfected," Bradley told Emerson, "so that he can avoid obstacles and deal with emergency situations, we'll let him loose. He'll be able to map the seabed in greater detail than anyone's ever done before. When the job's finished, he'll surface and we'll pick him up, recharge his batteries, and download his data. Then off he'll go again."

"Suppose he meets the great white shark?"

"We've even looked into that. Sharks seldom attack anything unfamiliar, and J.J. certainly doesn't look very appetizing. And his sonar and electromagnetic emissions will scare away most predators."

"Where do you plan to test him—and when?"

"Starting next month, on some well-mapped local sites. Then out to the Continental Shelf. And then—up to the Grand Banks."

"I don't think you'll find much new around *Titanic*. Both sections have been photographed down to the square millimeter."

"That's true; we're not really interested in them. But J.J. can probe at least twenty meters below the seabed—and no one's ever done that for the debris field. God knows what's still buried there. Even if we don't find anything exciting, it will show J.J.'s capabilities—and give a big boost to the project. I'm going up to *Explorer* next week to make arrangements. It's ages since I was aboard her—and Parky—Rupert—says he has something to show me."

"He has indeed," said Emerson with a grin. "I shouldn't tell you this—but we've found the *real* treasure of the *Titanic.* Exactly where it was supposed to be."

26

THE MEDICI GOBLET

I wonder if you realize," Bradley shouted, to make himself heard above the roar and rattle of machinery, "what a bargain you've got. She cost almost a quarter billion to build—and that was back when a billion dollars was real money."

Rupert Parkinson was wearing an immaculate yachtsman's outfit which, especially when crowned by a hard hat, seemed a little out of place down here beside *Glomar Explorer*'s moon pool. The oily rectangle of water—larger than a tennis court—was surrounded by heavy salvage and handling equipment, much of it showing its age. Everywhere there were signs of hasty repairs, dabs of anticorrosion paint, and ominous notices saying OUT OF ORDER. Yet enough seemed to be working; Parkinson claimed they were actually ahead of schedule.

It's hard to believe, Bradley told himself, that it's almost thirty-five years since I stood here, looking down into this same black rectangle of water. I don't *feel* thirty-five years older . . . but I don't remember much about the callow youngster who'd just signed up for his first big job. Certainly he could never have dreamed of the one I'm holding down now.

It had turned out better than he had expected. After decades of battling with U.N. lawyers and a whole alphabet stew of government departments and environmental authorities, Bradley was learning that they were a necessary evil.

The Wild West days of the sea were over. There had been a brief time when there was very little law below a hundred fathoms; now he was sheriff, and, rather to his surprise, he was beginning to enjoy it.

One sign of his new status—some of his old colleagues called it "conversion"—was the framed certificate from Bluepeace he now had hanging on the office wall. It was right beside the photo presented to him years ago by the famous extinguisher of oil-rig fires, "Red" Adair. That bore the inscription: "Jason—isn't it great not to be bothered by life-insurance salesmen? Best wishes—Red."

The Bluepeace citation was somewhat more dignified:

TO JASON BRADLEY—IN RECOGNITION OF YOUR HUMANE TREATMENT OF A UNIQUE CREATURE, *OCTOPUS GIGANTEUS VERRILL*

At least once a month Bradley would leave his office and fly to Newfoundland—a province that was once more living up to its name. Since operations had started, more and more of world attention had been turned toward the drama being played out on the Grand Banks. The countdown to 2012 had begun, and bets were already being placed on the winner of "The Race for the *Titanic*."

And there was another focus of interest, this time a morbid one. . . .

"What annoys me," said Parkinson, as they left the noisy and clamorous chaos of the moon pool, "are the ghouls who keep asking: 'Have you found any bodies yet?' "

"I'm always getting the same question. One day I'll answer: 'Yes—you're the first.' "

Parkinson laughed.

"Must try that myself. But here's the answer I give. You know that we're still finding boots and shoes lying on the seabed—in *pairs*, a few centimeters apart? Usually they're cheap and well worn, but last month we came across a beautiful example of the best English leatherwork. Looks as if they're straight from the cobbler—you can still read the label that says 'By Appointment to His Majesty.' Obviously one of the first-class passengers. . . .

"I've put them in a glass case in my office, and when I'm asked about bodies I point to them and say: 'Look—not even a scrap of bone left inside. It's a hungry world down there. The leather would have gone too, if it wasn't for the tannic acid.' That shuts them up very quickly."

Glomar Explorer had not been designed for gracious living, but Rupert Parkinson had managed to transform one of the aft staterooms, just below the helipad, into a fair imitation of a luxury hotel suite. It reminded Bradley of their first meeting, back in Piccadilly—ages ago, it now seemed. The room contained one item, however, which was more than a little out of place in such surroundings.

It was a wooden chest, about a meter high, and it appeared almost new. But as he approached, Bradley recognized a familiar and unmistakable odor—the metallic tang of iodine, proof of long immersion in the sea. Some diver—was it Cousteau?— had once used the phrase "The scent of treasure." Here it was, hanging in the air—and setting the blood pounding in his veins.

"Congratulations, Rupert. So you've got into Great Grandfather's suite."

"Yes. Two of the Deep ROVs entered a week ago and did a preliminary survey. This is the first item they brought out."

The chest still displayed, in stenciled lettering unfaded after a century in the abyss, a somewhat baffling inscription:

BROKEN ORANGE PEKOE
UPPER GLENCAIRN ESTATE
MATAKELLE

Parkinson raised the lid, almost reverently, and then drew aside the sheet of metal foil beneath it.

"Standard eighty-pound Ceylon tea chest," he said. "It happened to be the right size, so they simply repacked it. And I'd no idea they used aluminum foil, back in 1912! Of course, the B.O.P. wouldn't fetch a very good price at Colombo auction now—but it did its job. Admirably."

With a piece of stiff cardboard, Parkinson delicately cleared away the top layer of the soggy black mess; he looked, Bradley thought, exactly like an underwater archaeologist extracting a fragment of pottery from the seabed. This, however, was not twenty-five-century-old Greek amphora, but something far more sophisticated.

"The Medici Goblet," Parkinson whispered almost reverently. "No one has seen it for a hundred years; no one *ever* expected to see it again."

He exposed only the upper few inches, but that was enough to show a circle of glass inside which multicolored threads were embedded in a complex design.

"We won't remove it until we're on land," said Parkinson, "but this is what it looks like."

He opened a typical coffee-table art book, bearing the title *Glories of Venetian Glass.* The full-page photo showed what at first sight looked like a glittering fountain, frozen in midair.

"I don't believe it," said Bradley, after a few seconds of wide-eyed astonishment. "How could anyone actually drink from it? More to the point, how could anyone *make* it?"

"Good questions. First of all, it's purely ornamental—intended to be looked at, not used. A perfect example of Wilde's dictum: 'All art is quite useless.'

"And I wish I could answer your second question. *We just don't know.* Oh, of course we can guess at some of the techniques used—but how did the glassblower make those curlicues intertwine? And look at the way those little spheres are nested one inside the other! If I hadn't seen them with my own eyes, I'd have sworn that some of these pieces could only have been assembled in zero gravity."

"So *that's* why Parkinson's booked space on Skylab 3."

"What a ridiculous rumor; not worth contradicting."

"Roy Emerson told me he was looking forward to his first trip into space . . . and setting up a weightless lab."

"I'll fax Roy a polite note, telling him to keep his bloody mouth shut. But since you've raised the subject—yes, we think there are possibilities for zero-gee glassblowing. It may not start a revolution in the industry, like float glass back in the last century—but it's worth a try."

"This probably isn't a polite question, but how much is this goblet worth?"

"I assume you're not asking in your official capacity, so I won't give a figure I'd care to put in a company report. Anyway, you know how crazy the art business is—more ups and downs than the stock market! Look at those late twentieth-century megadollar daubs you can't give away now. And in this case there's the history of the piece—how can you put a value on *that?*"

"Make a guess."

"I'd be very disappointed at anything less than fifty M."

Bradley whistled.

"And how much more is down there?"

"Lots. Here's the complete listing, prepared for the exhibition the Smithsonian had planned. *Is* planning—just a hundred years late."

There were more than forty items on the list, all with highly technical Italianate descriptions. About half had question marks beside them.

"Bit of a mystery here," said Parkinson. "Twenty-two of the pieces are missing—but we *know* they were aboard, and we're sure G.G. had them in his suite, because he complained about the space they were taking up—he couldn't throw a party."

"So—going to blame the French again?"

It was an old joke, and rather a bitter one. Some of the French expeditions to the wreck, in the years following its 1985 discovery, had done considerable damage while attempting to recover artifacts. Ballard and his associates had never forgiven them.

"No. I guess they've a pretty good alibi; we're definitely the first inside. My theory is that G.G. had them moved out into an adjoining suite or corridor—I'm sure they're not far away—we'll find them sooner or later."

"I hope so; if your estimate is right—and after all, you're the expert—those boxes of glass will pay for this whole operation. And everything else will be a pure bonus. Nice work, Rupert."

"Thank you. We hope Phase Two goes equally well."

"The Mole? I noticed it down beside the moon pool. Anything since your last report—which was rather sketchy?"

"I know. We were in the middle of urgent mods when your office started making rude noises about schedules and deadlines. But now we're on top of the problem—I hope."

"Do you still plan to make a test first, on a stretch of open seabed?"

"No. We're going to go for broke; we're confident that all systems are okay, so why wait? Do you remember what happened in the Apollo Program, back in '68? One of the most daring technological gambles in history. . . . The big Saturn V had only flown twice—unmanned—and the second flight had been a partial failure. Yet NASA took a calculated risk; the next flight was not only manned—it went straight to the Moon!

"Of course, we're not playing for such high stakes, but if the

Mole doesn't work—or we lose it—we're in real trouble; our whole operation depends on it. The sooner we know about any real problems, the better.

"No one's ever tried something quite like this before; but our first run will be the real thing—and we'd like you to watch.

"Now, Jason—how about a nice cup of tea?"

INJUNCTION

Article 1
Use of terms and scope
1. For the purposes of this Convention:
   (1) "Area" means the seabed and ocean floor and subsoil thereof, beyond the limits of national jurisdiction;
   (2) "Authority" means the International Seabed Authority;

Article 145
Protection of the marine environment
Necessary measures shall be taken in accordance with this Convention with respect to activities in the Area to ensure effective protection for the marine environment from harmful effects which may arise from such activities. To this end the Authority shall adopt appropriate rules, regulations and procedures for *inter alia*:

   (a) the prevention, reduction and control of pollution and other hazards to the marine environment . . . particular attention being paid to the need for protection from harmful effects of such activities as drilling, dredging, disposal of waste, construction and operation or maintenance of installations, pipelines, and other devices related to such activities. (United Nations Convention on the Law of the Sea, 1982.)

"We're in deep trouble," said Kato, from his Toyko office, "and that's not meant to be funny."

"What's the problem?" asked Donald Craig, relaxing in the Castle garden. From time to time he liked to give his eyes a chance of focusing on something more than half a meter away, and this was an unusually warm and sunny afternoon for early spring.

"Bluepeace. They've lodged another protest with ISA—and this time I'm afraid they've got a case."

"I thought we'd settled all this."

"So did we; heads are rolling in our legal department. We can do everything we'd planned—except actually *raise* the wreck."

"It's a little late in the day to discover that, isn't it? And you've never told me how you intended to get the extra lift. Of course, I never took that crack about rockets seriously."

"Sorry about that—we'd been negotiating with Du Pont and Thiokol and Union Carbide and half a dozen others— didn't want to talk until we were certain of our supplier."

"Of what?"

"Hydrazine. Rocket monopropellant. So I wasn't economizing too greatly with the truth."

"Hydrazine? Now where— Of course! That's how Cussler brought her up, in *Raise the* Titanic!"

"Yes, and it's quite a good idea—it decomposes into pure nitrogen and hydrogen, plus lots of heat. But Cussler didn't have to cope with Bluepeace. They got wind of what we were doing—wish I knew how—and claim that hydrazine is a dangerous poison, and some is bound to be spilled, however carefully we handle it, and so on and so forth."

"*Is* it a poison?"

"Well, I'd hate to drink it. Smells like concentrated ammonia, and probably tastes worse."

"So what are you going to do?"

"Fight, of course. And think of alternatives. Parky will be laughing his head off."

MOLE

The three-man deep-sea submersible *Marvin* had been intended as the successor of the famous *Alvin*, which had played such a key role in the first exploration of the wreck. *Alvin*, however, showed no intention of retiring, though almost every one of its original components had long since been replaced.

Marvin was also much more comfortable than its progenitor, and had greater reserves of power. No longer was it necessary to spend a boring two and a half hours in free-fall to the seabed; with the help of its motors, *Marvin* could reach the *Titanic* in less than an hour. And in an emergency, by jettisoning all external equipment, the titanium sphere holding the crew could get back to the surface in minutes—an incompressible air bubble ascending from the depths.

For Bradley, this was a double first. He had never yet seen the *Titanic* with his own eyes, and though he had handled *Marvin* on test and training runs down to a few hundred meters, he had never taken it right down to the bottom. Needless to say, he was carefully watched by the submersible's usual pilot, who was doing his best not to be a backseat driver.

"Altitude two hundred meters. Wreck bearing one two zero."

Altitude! That was a word that sounded strangely in a diver's ear. But here inside *Marvin*'s life-support sphere, depth was almost irrelevant. What really concerned Bradley was his elevation above the seabed, and keeping enough clearance to avoid obstacles. He felt that he was piloting not a submarine but a low-flying aircraft—one searching for landmarks in a thick fog. . . .

"Searching," however, was hardly the right word, for he knew exactly where his target was. The brilliant echo on the sonar display was dead ahead, and now only a hundred meters away. In a moment the TV camera would pick it up, but Bradley wanted to use his own eyes. He was not a child of the video age, to whom nothing was quite real until it had appeared on a screen.

And there was the knife edge of the prow, looming up in the glare of *Marvin*'s lights. Bradley cut the motor, and let his little craft drift slowly toward the converging cliffs of steel.

Now he was separated from the *Titanic* by only a few centimeters of adamantine crystal, bearing a pressure that it was not wise to dwell upon. He was confronting the ghost that had haunted the Atlantic sea lanes for almost a century; it still seemed to be driving ahead under its own power, as if on a voyage that, even now, had only just begun.

The enormous anchor, half hidden by its drapery of weeds, was still patiently waiting to be lowered. It almost dwarfed *Marvin*, and its dangling tons of mass appeared so ominous that Bradley gave it a wide berth as he cruised slowly down the line of portholes, staring blankly into nothingness like the empty eye sockets of a skull.

He had almost forgotten the purpose of his mission, when the voice from the world above jolted him back to reality.

"*Explorer* to *Marvin*. We're waiting."

"Sorry—just admiring the view. She *is* impressive—cameras don't do her justice. You've got to see her for yourself."

This was an old argument, which as far as Bradley was concerned had been settled long ago. Though robots and their electronic sensors were invaluable—indeed, absolutely essential—both for reconnaissance and actual operations, they could never give the whole picture. "Telepresence" was marvelous, but it could sometimes be a dangerous illusion. You might believe you were experiencing a hundred percent of some remote reality but it was only ninety-five percent—and that remaining five percent could be vital: men had died because there was still no good way of transmitting those warning signals that only the sense of smell could detect. Although he had seen thousands of stills and videos of the wreck, only now did Bradley feel that he was beginning to understand it.

He was reluctant to tear himself away, and realized how frustrated Robert Ballard must have been when he had only seconds for *his* first sighting of the wreck. Then he actuated the bow thrusters, swung *Marvin* away from the towering metal cliff, and headed toward his real target.

The Mole was resting on a cradle about twenty meters from *Titanic*, pointing downward at a forty-five-degree angle. It looked rather like a spaceship headed in the wrong direction, and there had been many deplorable ethnic jokes about launchpads built by the engineers of certain small European countries.

The conical drilling head was already deeply buried in the sediment, and a few meters of the broad metal tape that was the Mole's "payload" lay stretched out on the seabed behind it. Bradley moved *Marvin* into position to get a good view, and switched the video recorders to high speed.

"We're ready," he reported to topside. "Start the countdown."

"We're holding at T minus ten seconds. Inertial guidance

running . . . seven . . . six . . . five . . . four . . . three . . . two . . . one . . . liftoff! Sorry—I mean, dig in!"

The drill had started to spin, and almost at once the Mole was hidden by clouds of silt. However, Bradley could see that it was disappearing with surprising speed; in only a matter of seconds it had vanished into the seabed.

"You've cleared the tower," he reported, keeping the spirit of the occasion. "Can't see anything—the launchpad's hidden by smoke. Well, mud. . . .

"Now it's settling. The Mole's vanished. Just a little crater, slowly filling in. We'll head around the other side to meet it."

"Take your time. Quickest estimate is thirty minutes. Longest is fifty. Quite a few bets riding on this baby."

And quite a few million dollars as well, thought Bradley, as he piloted *Marvin* toward *Titanic's* prow. If the Mole gets stuck before it can complete its mission, Parky and company will have to go back to the drawing board.

He was waiting on the port side when the Mole resurfaced after forty-five minutes. It was not attempting any speed records; its maiden voyage had been a complete success.

Now the first of the planned thirty belts, each capable of lifting a thousand tons, had been safely emplaced. When the operation had been completed, *Titanic* could be lifted off the ocean floor, like a melon in a string bag.

That was the theory, and it seemed to be working. Florida was still a long way off, but now it had come just a little closer.

SARCOPHAGUS

W e've found it!"

Roy Emerson had never seen Rupert Parkinson in so exuberant a mood; it was positively un-English.

"Where?" he asked. "Are you sure?"

"Ninety-nine—well, ninety-five percent. Just where I expected. There was an unoccupied suite—wasn't ready in time for the voyage. On the same deck as G.G. and only a few yards away. Both doors are jammed so we'll have to cut our way in. The ROV's going down now to have a crack at it. You should have been here."

Perhaps, thought Emerson. But this is a family affair, and he would feel an interloper. Besides, it might be a false alarm—like most rumors of sunken treasure.

"How long before you get inside?"

"Shouldn't take more than an hour—it's fairly thin steel, and we'll be through it in no time."

"Well, good luck. Keep me in the picture."

Roy Emerson went back to what he pretended was work. He felt guilty when he was not inventing something, which was now most of the time. Trying to reduce the electronic chaos of his data banks by rearranging and reclassifying did give the illusion of useful employment.

And so he missed all the excitement.

The little group in Rupert's suite aboard *Glomar Explorer* was so intent upon the monitor screen that their drinks were virtually ignored—no great hardship, because according to long tradition on such vessels, they were nonalcoholic.

A record number of Parkinsons—almost a quorum, someone had pointed out—had assembled for this occasion. Though few shared Rupert's confidence, it had been a good excuse to visit the scene of operations. Only George had been here before; William, Arnold, and Gloria were all newcomers. The rest of the group watching ROV 3 gliding silently across *Titanic*'s deck were ship's officers and senior engineers, recruited from half a dozen ocean-oriented firms.

"Have you noticed," somebody whispered, "how the weeds have grown? Must be due to our lights—she wasn't like this when we started ops—bridge looks like the Hanging Gardens of Babylon. . . ."

There was very little other comment, still less any conversation, as ROV 3 dropped down into the yawning cavity of the grand staircase. A century ago, elegant ladies and their sleek escorts had strolled up and down the thick-piled carpet, never dreaming of their fate—or imagining that in little more than two years the guns of August would put an end to the gilded Edwardian Age they so perfectly epitomized.

ROV 3 turned into the main starboard corridor on the promenade deck, past the rows of first-class staterooms. It was moving very slowly in these confined quarters, and the TV image was now limited to freeze-frame black and white, with a new picture every two seconds.

All data and control signals were now being relayed over an ultrasonic link through a repeater placed on the deck. From time to time there were annoying holdups, when the screen went blank and the only indication of ROV 3's continued existence was a high-pitched whistle. Some obstacle was absorbing the carrier wave, causing a momentary break in the connection. There would be a brief interval of electronic "handshaking" and error correction; then the picture would return and ROV 3's pilot, four kilometers above, could resume progress. These interruptions did nothing to lessen the suspense; it had been several minutes before anyone in Parkinson's suite had said a word.

There was a universal sigh of relief as the robot came to rest outside a plain, unmarked door, its white paint blindingly brilliant in ROV 3's floodlights. The decorators might have left only yesterday; apart from a few flakes that had peeled away, almost all the paint was still intact.

Now ROV 3 began the tricky but essential task of anchoring itself to the job—a procedure just as important underwater as in space. First it blasted two explosive bolts through the door, and clamped itself on to them, so it was rigidly attached to the working area.

The glare of the oxy-arc thermal lance flooded the corridor, making ROV 3's own lights seem feeble in comparison. The thin metal of the door offered no resistance as the incandescent knife—favorite tool of generations of safecrackers—sliced through it. In less than five minutes, a circle almost a meter wide had been carved out, and fell slowly forward, knocking up a small cloud of silt as it hit the floor.

ROV 3 unclamped itself, and rose a few centimeters so it could peer into the hole. The image flickered, then stabilized as the automatic exposure adjusted to the new situation.

Almost at once, Rupert Parkinson gave a hoot of delight.

"There they are!" he cried. "Just as I said—one . . . two . . . three-four-five . . . swing the camera over to the right—six . . . seven—a little higher . . . *My God—what's that?*"

No one ever remembered who screamed first.

PIETÀ

Jason Bradley had seen something like this before, in a space movie whose name he couldn't recall. There had been a dead astronaut cradled in mechanical arms, being carried toward the stars. . . . But this robot pietà was rising from the Atlantic depths, toward the circling inflatable boats waiting to receive it.

"That's the last one," said Parkinson somberly. "The girl. We still don't know her name."

Just like those Russian sailors, thought Bradley, who had been laid out on this very same deck, more than thirty years ago. He could not avoid it; the silly cliché flashed into his mind: "This is where I came in."

And, like many of the sailors brought up in Operation JENNIFER, these dead also appeared to be only sleeping. That was the most amazing—indeed, uncanny—aspect of the whole matter, which had seized the imagination of the world. After all the trouble we went to, explaining why there couldn't possibly be even a scrap of bone. . . .

"I'm surprised," he said to Parkinson, "that you were able to identify any of them, after all these years."

"Contemporary newspapers—family albums—even poor

Irish immigrants usually had at least one photo taken during their lifetime. Especially when they were leaving home forever. I don't think there's an attic in Ireland the media haven't ransacked in the last couple of days."

ROV 3 had handed over its burden to the rubber-suited divers circling in their inflatables. They lifted it carefully—tenderly—into the cradle suspended over the side from one of *Explorer's* cranes. It was obviously very light; one man was able to handle it easily.

With a common, unspoken impulse both Parkinson and Bradley moved away from the rail; they had seen enough of this sad ritual. During the past forty-eight hours, five men and one woman had been brought out of the tomb in which they had been lying for almost a century—apparently beyond the reach of time.

When they were together in Parkinson's suite, Bradley handed over a small computer module. "It's all there," he said. "The ISA lab's been working overtime. There are still some puzzling details, but the general picture seems clear.

"I don't know if you ever heard the story about *Alvin*—in the early days of its career, it was lost in deep water. The crew just managed to scramble out—leaving their lunch behind.

"When the sub was salvaged a couple of years later, the crew's lunch was *exactly* as they'd left it. That was the first hint that in cold water, with low oxygen content, organic decay can be vanishingly slow.

"And they've recovered bodies from wrecks in the Great Lakes that look absolutely fresh after decades—you can still see the expressions of surprise on the sailors' faces!

"So," continued Bradley, "the first requirement is that the corpse be in a sealed environment, where marine organisms can't get at it. That's what happened here; these people were trapped when they tried to find a way out—poor devils, they must have been lost in first-class territory! They'd broken the lock on the other door of the suite—but couldn't open the other before the water reached them. . . .

"But there's more to it than cold, stagnant water—and this is the really fascinating part of the story. Have you ever heard of bog people?"

"No," said Parkinson.

"Neither had I, until yesterday. But from time to time Danish archaeologists keep finding almost perfectly preserved corpses—victims of sacrifices, apparently—more than a *thousand* years old. Every wrinkle, every hair intact—they look like incredibly detailed sculptures. The reason? They were buried in peat bogs, and the tannin protected them from decay. Remember the boots and shoes found scattered around the wreck—all the leather untouched?"

Parkinson was no fool, though he sometimes pretended to be a character out of P. G. Wodehouse; it took him only seconds to make the connection.

"Tannin? But how? Of course—the tea chests!"

"Exactly; several of them had been breached by the impact. But our chemists say tannin may be only part of the story. The ship had been newly painted, of course—so the water samples we've analyzed show considerable amounts of arsenic and lead. A mighty unhealthy environment for any bacteria."

"I'm sure that's the answer," said Parkinson. "What an extraordinary twist of fate! That tea did a lot better than anyone ever imagined—or *could* imagine. . . . And I'm afraid G.G. has brought us some very bad luck. Just when things were going smoothly."

Bradley knew exactly what he meant. To the old charge of desecrating a historic shrine had now been added that of grave robbing. And, by a strange paradox, an apparently fresh grave at that.

The long-forgotten Thomas Conlin, Patrick Dooley, Martin Gallagher, and their three as-yet-still-anonymous companions had transformed the whole situation.

It was a paradox which, surely, would delight any true Irishman. With the discovery of her dead, *Titanic* had suddenly come alive.

A MATTER OF MEGAWATTS

W e have the answer," said a tired but triumphant Kato.

"I wonder if it matters now," answered Donald Craig.

"Oh, all that hysteria isn't going to last. Our P.R. boys are already hard at work—and so are Parky's. We've had a couple of summit meetings to plan a joint strategy. We may even turn it to our mutual advantage."

"I don't see—"

"Obvious! Thanks to *our*—well, Parky's—careful exploring, these poor folk will at last get a Christian burial, back in their own country. The Irish will love it. Don't tell anyone, but we're already talking to the Pope."

Donald found Kato's flippant approach more than a little offensive. It would certainly upset Edith, who seemed fascinated by the lovely child-woman the world had named Colleen.

"You'd better be careful. Some of them may be Protestant."

"Not likely. They all boarded in the deep south, didn't they?"

"Yes—at Queenstown. You won't find it on the map, though—a name like that wasn't popular after Independence. Now it's called Cobh."

"How do you spell that?"

"C-O-B-H."

"Well, we'll talk to the archbishops, or whoever, as well as the cardinals, just to cover all bases. But let me tell you what our engineers have cooked up. If it works, it will be a lot better than hydrazine. And it should even start Bluepeace shouting slogans for *us*."

"That'll be a nice change. In fact, a miracle."

"Miracles are our business—didn't you know?"

"What are the specs of this particular one?"

"First, we're making our iceberg larger, to get more lift. As a result, we'll only need about ten k-tons of extra buoyancy. We *could* go Parky's route for that, and at first we were afraid we might have to. But there's a neater—and cleaner—way of getting gas down there. *Electrolysis.* Splitting the water into oxygen and hydrogen."

"That's an old idea. Won't it take enormous amounts of current? And what about the risk of an explosion?"

"Silly question, Donald. The gases will go to separate electrodes, and we'll have a membrane to keep them apart. But you're right about the current. Gigawatt-hours! But we've got them—when our nuclear subs have done their thing with the Peltier cooling elements, we'll switch to electrolysis. May have to rent another boat, though—why are subs always called boats? I told you that the Brits and the French would like to get into the act, so *that's* no problem."

"Very elegant," said Donald. "And I see what you mean about pleasing Bluepeace. Everyone's in favor of oxygen."

"Exactly—and when we vent the balloons on the way up,

the whole world will breathe a little easier. At least, that's what P.R. will be saying."

"And the hydrogen will go straight up to the stratosphere without bothering anyone. Oh—what about the poor old ozone layer? Any danger of making more holes?"

"We've checked that, of course. Won't be any worse off than it is now. Which, I admit, isn't saying a great deal."

"Would it make sense to *bottle* the gases on the way up? You're starting with hundreds of tons of oxy-hydrogen, at four hundred atmospheres. That must be quite valuable; why throw it away?"

"Yes—we've even looked into that. It's marginal—increased complexity, cost of shipping tanks, and so on. Might be worth a try on a test basis—and gives us a fall-back position if the environment lobby gets nasty again."

"You've thought of everything, haven't you?" said Donald with frank admiration.

Kato shook his head slowly.

"Our friend Bradley once told me: 'When you've thought of everything—the sea will think of something else.' Words of wisdom, and I've never forgotten them. . . . Must hang up now— Oh—give my love to Edith."

OPERATIONS

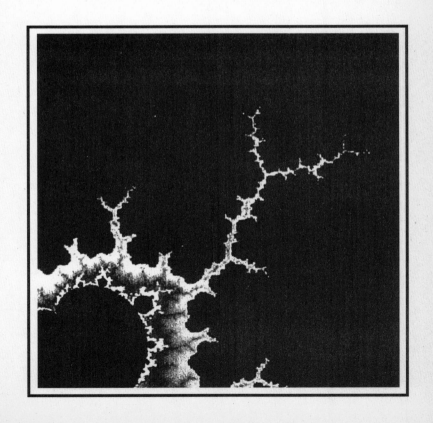

NOBODY HERE BUT US ROBOTS

Until the first decade of the new century, the great wreck and the debris surrounding it had remained virtually unchanged, though not untouched. Now, as 2010 approached, it was a hive of activity—or, rather, two hives, a thousand meters apart.

The framework of scaffolding around the bow section was almost complete, and the Mole had successfully laid twenty-five of the massive straps under the hull; there were only five to go. Most of the mud that had piled up around the prow when it drove into the seabed had been blasted away by powerful water jets, and the huge anchors were no longer half buried in silt.

More than twenty thousand tons of buoyancy had already been provided by as many cubic meters of packaged microspheres, strategically placed around the framework, and at the few places inside the wreck where the structure could safely take the strain. But *Titanic* had not stirred from her resting place—nor was she supposed to. Another ten thousand tons of lift would be needed to get her out of the mud, and to start her on the long climb to the surface.

As for the shattered stern—that had already disappeared inside a slowly accreting block of ice. The media were fond of quoting Hardy's "In shadowy silent distance grew the Iceberg too"—even though the poet could never have imagined this application of his words.

The penultimate verse was also quoted widely, and equally out of context. Both the Parkinson and Nippon-Turner consortia were rather tired of being told that

> They were bent
> By paths coincident
> On being anon twin halves of one august event

They hoped that it would be "august"—but not, if they could possibly help it, coincident.

Virtually all the work on both portions of the wreck had been carried out by remote control from the surface; only in critical cases were human beings actually required on the site. During the past decade, underwater robot technology had been pushed far beyond even the remarkable achievements of the previous century's offshore oil operations. The payoff would be enormous—although, as Rupert Parkinson often wryly remarked, most of it would go to other people.

There had, of course, been problems, mishaps—even accidents, though none involving loss of life. During one severe winter storm, *Explorer* had been forced to abandon station, much to the disgust of her captain, who considered this a professional insult. His vomitous passengers did not altogether appreciate his point of view.

Even this display of North Atlantic ferocity, however, had not interrupted operations on the stern. Two hundred meters down, the demobilized nuclear submarines, now rechristened, after a pioneer oceanographer and a famous shipbuilder, *Matthew Fontaine Maury* and *Peter the Great*, were scarcely aware of the storm. Their reactors continued steadily pouring megawatt upon megawatt of low-voltage current down to the seabed—creating a rising column of warm water in the process, as heat was pumped out of the wreck.

This artificial upwelling had produced an unexpected bonus, by bringing to the surface nutrients that would otherwise have been trapped on the seabed. The resulting plankton bloom was much appreciated by the local fish population, and the last cod harvest had been a record one. The government of Newfoundland had formally requested the submarines to remain on station, even when they had fulfilled their contract with Nippon-Turner.

Quite apart from all this activity off the Grand Banks, a great deal of money and effort was being expended thousands of kilometers away. Down in Florida, not far from the launch-pads that had seen men leave for the Moon—and were now seeing them prepare to go to Mars—dredging and construction for the *Titanic* Underwater Museum was well under way. And on the other side of the globe, Tokyo-on-Sea was preparing an even more elaborate display, with transparent viewing corridors for visitors and, of course, continuous performances of what was hoped would be a truly spectacular movie.

Vast sums of money were also being gambled elsewhere— especially in the land once more called Russia. Thanks to *Peter the Great*, share dealings in *Titanic* spinoff companies were very popular on the Moscow Stock Exchange.

SOLAR MAX

Another of my monomanias," said Franz Zwicker, "is the sunspot cycle. Especially the current one."

"What's particular about it?" asked Bradley, as they walked down to the lab together.

"First of all, it will peak in—you guessed it!—2012. It's already way past the 1990 maximum, and getting close to the 2001 record."

"So?"

"Well, between you and me, I'm scared. So many cranks have tried to correlate events with the eleven-year cycle—which isn't always eleven years anyway!—that sunspot counting sometimes gets classed with astrology. But there's no doubt that the Sun influences practically everything on Earth. I'm sure it's responsible for the weird weather we've been having during the last quarter century. To some extent, anyway; we can't put *all* the blame on the human race, much as Bluepeace and Company would like to."

"I thought you were supposed to be on their side!"

"Only on Mondays, Wednesdays, and Fridays. The rest of the week I keep a wary eye on Mother Nature. And the weather patterns aren't the only abnormality. Seismic activity seems to be increasing. Look at California. Why do people *still* build houses in San Francisco? Wasn't 2002 bad enough? And we're *still* waiting for the Big One. . . ."

Jason felt privileged to share the scientist's thoughts; the two men, so different in background and character, had grown to respect each other.

"And there's something else, that occasionally gives me nightmares. Deep-water blowouts—perhaps triggered by earthquakes. Or even by man."

"I've known several. A big one in '98, in the Louisiana Field. Wrote off a whole rig."

"Oh, that was just a mild burp! I'm talking about the real thing—like that crater the Shell Oil scientists found two kilometers down in the Gulf, back in the eighties. Imagine the explosion that caused *that*—three million tons of seabed scooped out! Equivalent to a good-sized atomic bomb."

"And you think that could happen again?"

"I *know* it will—but not when and where. I keep warning the people up at Hibernia that they're tickling the dragon's tail. If Tommy Gold is right—and he was right about neutron stars, even if he struck out on moondust and the Steady State!— we've barely scratched the Earth's crust. Everything we've tapped so far is just minor leakage from the *real* hydrocarbon reservoirs, ten or more kilometers down."

"Some leak! It's been running our civilization for the last couple of centuries."

"Did you say running—or ruining? Well, here's your prize pupil. How's class going?"

J.J. lay in a transporter cradle, very much a fish out of water. It was attached to a bank of computers by what seemed to Bradley to be an absurdly thin cable. Having grown up with copper wiring, he had never become quite accustomed to the fiber-optic revolution.

Nothing seemed to be happening; the technician in charge

hastily concealed the microbook she was viewing, and quickly scanned the monitor display.

"Everything fine, Doctor," she said cheerfully. "Just verifying the expert system databases."

That's part of *me,* thought Jason. He had spent hours in dive simulators, while computer programmers tried to codify and record his hard-won skills—the very essence of veteran ocean engineer J. Bradley. He was beginning to feel more and more that, at least in a psychological sense, J.J. was becoming a surrogate son.

That feeling became strongest when they were engaged in a direct conversation. It was an old joke in the trade that divers had a vocabulary of only a couple of hundred words—which was all they needed for their work. J.J. had enough artificial intelligence to exceed this by a comfortable margin.

The lab had hoped to surprise Jason by using his voice as a template for J.J.'s speech synthesizer, but his reaction had been disappointing. The pranksters had forgotten that few people can recognize their own recorded voice, especially if it is uttering sentences that they have never spoken themselves. Jason had not caught on until he had noticed the grinning faces around him.

"Any reason, Anne, why we can't start the wet run on schedule?" Zwicker asked.

"No, Doctor. The emergency recall algorithm still doesn't seem to be working properly, but of course we won't need it for the tests."

Although the sound transducers were not designed to function in air, Jason could not resist a few words with Junior.

"Hello, J.J. Can you hear me?"

"I can hear you."

The words were badly distorted, but quite recognizable. Underwater, the speech quality would be much better.

"Do you recognize me?"

There was a long silence. Then J.J. replied.

"Question not understood."

"Walk closer, Mr. Bradley," the technician advised. "He's very deaf out of water."

"Do you recognize me?"

"Yes. You are John Maxwell."

"Back to the drawing board," muttered Zwicker.

"And who," asked Bradley, more amused than annoyed, "is John Maxwell?"

The girl was quite embarrassed.

"He's section chief, Voice Recognition. But there's no problem—this isn't a fair test. Underwater he'll know you from half a kilometer away."

"I hope so. Goodbye, J.J. See you later—when you're not quite so deaf. Let's see if Deep Jeep is in better shape."

Deep Jeep was the lab's other main project, in some ways almost equally demanding. The reaction of most visitors at first viewing was: "Is it a submarine or a diving suit?" And the answer was always, "Both."

Servicing and operating three-man deep submersibles like *Marvin* was an expensive business: a single dive could cost a hundred thousand dollars. But there were many occasions when a much less elaborate, one-man vehicle would be adequate.

Jason Bradley's secret ambition was already well known to the entire lab. He hoped Deep Jeep would be ready in time to take him down to *Titanic*—while the wreck still lay on the ocean floor.

STORM

I t would be decades before the meteorologists could prove
that the great storm of 2010 was one of the series that had
begun in the 1980s, heralding the climatic changes of the
next millennium. Before it exhausted its energies battering
against the western ramparts of the Alps, Gloria did twenty billion dollars' worth of damage and took more than a thousand
lives.

The weather satellites, of course, gave a few hours' warning—otherwise the death toll would have been even greater.
But, inevitably, there were many who did not hear the fore-
casts, or failed to take them seriously. Especially in Ireland,
which was the first to receive the hammerblow from the heavens.

Donald and Edith Craig were editing the latest footage
from Operation DEEP FREEZE when Gloria hit Conroy Castle. They heard and felt nothing deep inside the massive
walls—not even the crash when the camera obscura was swept
off the battlements.

Ada now cheerfully admitted that she was hopeless at *pure*
mathematics—the kind which, in G. H. Hardy's famous toast,

would never be of any use to anyone. Unknown to him—because the secrets of ENIGMA's code-breaking were not revealed until decades later—Hardy had been proved spectacularly wrong during his own lifetime. In the hands of Alan Turing and his colleagues, even something as abstract as number theory could win a war.

Most of calculus and higher trigonometry, and virtually all of symbolic logic, were closed books to Ada. She simply wasn't interested; her heart was in geometry and the properties of space. Already she was trifling with five dimensions, four having proved too simple. Like Newton, much of the time she was "sailing strange seas of thought—alone."

But today, she was back in ordinary three-space, thanks to the present that "Uncle" Bradley had just sent her. Thirty years after its first appearance, Rubik's Cube had made a comeback—in a far more deadly mutation.

Because it was a purely mechanical device, the original cube had one weakness, for which its addicts were sincerely thankful. Unlike all their neighbors, the six *center* squares on each face were fixed. The other forty-eight squares could orbit around them, to create a possible 43252 00327 44898 56000 distinct patterns.

The Mark II had no such limitations; all the fifty-four squares were capable of movement, so there were no fixed centers to give reference points to its maddened manipulators. Only the development of microchips and liquid crystal displays had made such a prodigy possible; nothing *really* moved, but the multicolored squares could be dragged around the face of the cube merely by touching them with a fingertip.

Relaxing in her little boat with Lady, engrossed with her new toy, Ada had been slow to notice the darkening sky. The storm was almost upon her before she started the electric motor and headed for shelter. That there could be any danger never occurred to her; after all, Lake Mandelbrot was only three feet deep. But she disliked getting wet—and Lady *hated* it.

By the time she had reached the lake's first western lobe, the roar of the gale was almost deafening. Ada was thrilled; this was really exciting! But Lady was terrified, and tried to hide herself under the seat.

Heading down the Spike, between the avenue of cypresses, she was partly sheltered from the full fury of the gale. But for the first time, she became alarmed; the great trees on either side were swaying back and forth like reeds.

She was only a dozen meters from the safety of the boathouse, far into the Utter West of the M-Set and nearing the infinity border post at minus 1.999, when Patrick O'Brian's fears about the transplanted cypress trees were tragically fulfilled.

ARTIFACT

One of the most moving archaeological discoveries ever made took place in Israel in 1976, during a series of excavations carried out by scientists from the Hebrew University and the French Center for Prehistoric Research in Jerusalem.

At a 10,000-year-old campsite, they uncovered the skeleton of a child, one hand pressed against its cheek. In that hand is another tiny skeleton: that of a puppy about five months old.

This is the earliest example we know of man and dog sharing the same grave. There must be many, many later ones.

(From Friends of Man *by Roger Caras: Simon & Schuster, 2001.)*

Y ou may be interested to know," said Dr. Jafferjee with that clinical detachment which Donald found annoying (though how else could psychiatrists stay sane?) "that Edith's case isn't unique. Ever since the M-Set was discovered in 1980, people have managed to become obsessed with it. Usually they are computer hackers, whose grip on reality is often rather tenuous. There are no less than sixty-three examples of Mandelmania now in the data banks."

"And is there any cure?"

Dr. Jafferjee frowned. "Cure" was a word he seldom used. "Adjustment" was the term he preferred.

"Let's say that in eighty percent of the cases, the subject has been able to resume an—ah—normal life, sometimes with the help of medication or electronic implants. Quite an encouraging figure."

Except, thought Donald, for the twenty percent. Which category does Edith belong to?

For the first week after the tragedy, she had been unnaturally calm; after the funeral, some of their mutual friends had been shocked by her apparent lack of emotion. But Donald knew how badly she had been wounded, and was not surprised when she began to behave irrationally. When she started to wander around the castle at night, searching through the empty rooms and dank passageways that had never been renovated, he realized that it was time to get medical advice.

Nevertheless, he kept putting it off, hoping that Edith would make the normal recovery from the first stages of grief. Indeed, this seemed to be happening. Then Patrick O'Brian died.

Edith's relationship with the old gardener had always been a prickly one, but they had respected each other and shared a mutual love for Ada. The child's death had been as devastating a blow to Pat as to her parents; he also blamed himself for the tragedy. If only he had refused to transplant those cypresses— if only . . .

Pat began drinking heavily again, and was now seldom sober. One cold night, after the landlord of the Black Swan had gently ejected him, he managed to lose his way in the village where he had spent his entire life, and was found frozen to death in the morning. Father McMullen considered that the verdict should have been suicide rather than misadventure; but if it was a sin to give Pat a Christian burial, he would argue that out with God in due course. As, also, the matter of the tiny bundle that Ada held cradled in her arms.

The day after the second funeral, Donald had found Edith sitting in front of a high-resolution monitor, studying one of the infinite miniature versions of the set. She would not speak to him, and presently he realized, to his horror, that she was searching for Ada.

In later years, Donald Craig would often wonder about the relationship that had developed between himself and Jason Bradley. Though they had met only half a dozen times, and then almost always on business, he had felt that bond of mutual sympathy that sometimes grows between two men, and can be almost as strong as a sexual one, even when it has absolutely no erotic content.

Perhaps Donald reminded Bradley of his lost partner Ted Collier, of whom he often spoke. In any event, they enjoyed each other's company, and met even when it was not strictly necessary. Though Kato and the Nippon-Turner syndicate might well have been suspicious, Bradley never compromised his ISA neutrality. Still less did Craig try to exploit it; they might exchange personal secrets, but not professional confidences. Donald never learned what role, if any, Bradley had played in the authority's decision to ban hydrazine.

After Ada's funeral—which Bradley had flown halfway around the world to attend—they had an even closer link. Both had lost a wife and child; though the circumstances were different, the effects were much the same. They became even more intimate, sharing secrets and vulnerabilities that neither had revealed to any other person.

Later, Donald wondered why he did not think of the idea himself; perhaps he was so close to it that he couldn't see the picture for the scan lines.

The fallen cypresses had been cleared away, and the two men were walking by the side of Lake Mandelbrot—for the last time, as it turned out, for both of them—when Bradley outlined the scenario. "It's not *my* idea," he explained, rather apologetically. "I got it from a psychologist friend."

It was a long time before Donald discovered who the "friend" was, but he saw the possibilities at once.

"Do you really think it will work?" he asked.

"That's something you'll have to discuss with Edith's psychiatrist. Even if it *is* a good idea, he may not be willing to go along with it. The NIH syndrome, you know."

"National Institutes of Health?"

"No—Not Invented Here."

Donald laughed, without much humor.

"You're right. But first, I must see if I can do my part. It won't be easy."

That had been an understatement; it was the most difficult task he had ever undertaken in his life. Often he had to stop work, blinded by tears.

And then, in their own mysterious way, the buried circuits of his subconscious triggered a memory that enabled him to continue. Somewhere, years ago, he had come across the story of a surgeon in a third world country who ran an eye-bank which restored sight to poor people. To make a graft possible corneas had to be removed from the donor within minutes of death.

That surgeon must have had a steady hand, as he sliced into his own mother's eyes. I can do no less, Donald told himself grimly, as he went back to the editing table where he and Edith had spent so many hours together.

Dr. Jafferjee had proved surprisingly receptive. He had asked in a mildly ironic but quite sympathetic manner: "Where did you get the idea? Some pop-psych video-drama?"

"I know it sounds like it. But it seems worth a try—if you approve."

"You've already made the disk?"

"Capsule. I'd like to run it now—I see you've got a hybrid viewer in your outer office."

"Yes. It will even show VHS tapes! I'll call Dolores—I rely on her a good deal." He hesitated, and looked thoughtfully at Donald as if he was going to add something. Instead, he pressed a switch and said softly into the clinic's paging system: "Nurse Dolores—will you please come to my office? Thank you."

Edith Craig is still *somewhere* inside that skull, thought Donald as he sat with Dr. Jafferjee and Nurse Dolores, watching the figure sitting stiffly at the big monitor. Can I smash the invisible yet unyielding barrier that grief has erected, and bring her back to the world of reality?

The familiar black, beetle-shaped image floated on the screen, radiating tendrils that connected it to the rest of the Mandelbrot universe. There was no way of even guessing at the scale, but Donald had already noted the coordinates that defined the size of this particular version. If one could imagine the whole set, stretching out beyond this monitor, it was already larger than the Cosmos that even the Hubble Space Telescope had yet revealed.

"Are you ready?" asked Dr. Jafferjee.

Donald nodded. Nurse Dolores, sitting immediately behind Edith, glanced toward their camera to indicate that she had heard him.

"Then go ahead."

Donald pressed the EXECUTE key, and the subroutine took over.

The ebon surface of the stimulated Lake Mandelbrot seemed to tremble. Edith gave a sudden start of surprise.

"Good!" whispered Dr. Jafferjee. "She's reacting!"

The waters parted. Donald turned away; he could not bear to watch again this latest triumph of his skills. Yet he could still see Ada's image as her voice said gently: "I love you, mother—

but you cannot find me here. I exist only in your memories—
and I shall always be there. Goodbye. . . ."

Dolores caught Edith's falling body, as the last syllable died
away into the irrevocable past.

THE LAST LUNCH

I t was a charming idea, though not everyone agreed that it really worked. The decor for the interior of the world's only deep-diving tourist submarine had been borrowed straight from Disney's classic *20,000 Leagues Under the Sea.*

Passengers who boarded the *Piccard* (port of registry, Geneva) found themselves in a plush, though rather oddly proportioned, mid-Victorian drawing room. This was supposed to provide instant reassurance, and divert all thoughts from the several hundred tons pressing on each of the little windows which gave a rather restricted view of the outside world.

The greatest problems that *Piccard*'s builders had had to face were not engineering, but legal ones. Only Lloyd's of London would insure the hull; no one would insure the passengers, who tended to be VIPs with astronomical credit ratings. So before every dive, notarized waivers of liability were collected, as discreetly as possible.

The ritual was only slightly more unsettling than the cabin steward's cheerful litany of possible disasters that passengers on transocean flights had endured for decades. NO SMOKING signs, of course, were no longer necessary; nor did *Piccard* have seat belts and life jackets—which would have been about as useful as parachutes on commercial airliners. Its numerous built-in safety features were unobtrusive and automatic. If worst came to worst, the independent two-man crew capsule would separate from the passenger unit, and each would make a free ascent to the surface, ultrasonic beacons pinging frantically.

This particular dive was the last one of the season: it was getting late in the year, and *Piccard* would soon be airlifted back to calmer seas in the southern hemisphere. Although at the depths the submarine operated, winter and summer made no more difference than day and night, bad weather on the surface could make passengers very, very unhappy.

During the thirty-minute free-fall to the wreck site, *Piccard*'s distinguished guests watched a short video showing the current status of operations, and a map of the planned dive. There was nothing else to see during the descent into darkness, except for the occasional luminous fish attracted to this strange invader of its domain.

Then, abruptly, it seemed that a ghostly dawn was spreading far below. All but the faint red emergency lights in *Piccard* were switched off, as *Titanic*'s prow loomed up ahead.

Almost everyone who saw her now was struck by the same thought: She must have looked much like this, in the Harland and Wolff Shipyard, a hundred years ago. Once again she was surrounded by an elaborate framework of steel scaffolding, while workers swarmed over her. The workers, however, were no longer human.

Visibility was excellent, and the pilot maneuvered *Piccard* so that the passengers on both sides of the cabin could get the best possible view through the narrow portholes. He was extemely careful to avoid the busy robots, who ignored the submarine completely. It was no part of the universe they had been trained to deal with.

"If you look out on the right," said the tour guide—a young Woods Hole graduate, making a little money in his vacation—"you'll see the 'down' cable, stretching up to *Explorer*.

And there's a module on the way right now, with its counter-weight. Looks like a two-ton unit—

"And there's a robot going to meet it—now the module's unhooked—you see it's got neutral buoyancy, so it can be moved around easily. The robot will carry it over to its attach-ment point on the lifting cradle, and hook it on. Then the two-ton counterweight that brought it down will be shuttled over to the 'up' cable, and sent back to *Explorer* to be reused. After that's been done ten thousand times, they can lift *Titanic*. This section of her, anyway."

"Sounds a very roundabout way of doing things," com-mented one of the VIPs. "Why can't they just use compressed air?"

The guide had heard this a dozen times, but had learned to answer all such questions politely. (The pay was good, and so were the fringe benefits.)

"It's possible, ma'am, but much too expensive. The pressure here is *enormous*. I imagine you're all familiar with the standard scuba bottles—they're usually rated at two hundred atmo-spheres. Well, if you opened one of these down here, the air wouldn't come out. The water would rush *in*—and fill half the bottle!"

Perhaps he'd overdone it; some of the passengers were look-ing a little worried. So he continued hastily, hoping to divert their thoughts.

"We *do* use some compressed air for trimming and fine control. And in the final stages of the ascent, it will play a major role.

"Now, the skipper is going to fly us toward the stern, along the promenade deck. Then he'll do a reverse run, so you'll all have an equally good view. I won't do any more talking for a while—"

Very slowly, *Piccard* moved the length of the great shadowy hulk. Much of it was in darkness, but some open hatches spilled dramatic fans of light where robots were at work in the interior, fixing buoyancy modules wherever lifting forces could be tolerated.

No one spoke a word as the weed-festooned walls of steel glided by. It was still very hard to grasp the scale of the wreck—still, after a hundred years, one of the largest passenger ships ever built. And the most luxurious, if only for reasons of pure economics. *Titanic* had marked the end of an era; after the war that was coming, no one would ever again be able to afford such opulence. Nor, perhaps, would anyone care to risk it, lest such arrogance once again provoke the envy of the gods.

The mountain of steel faded into the distance; for a while, the nimbus of light surrounding it was still faintly visible. Then there was only the barren seabed drifting below *Piccard*, appearing and disappearing in the twin ovals of its forward lights.

Though it was barren, it was not featureless; it was pitted and gouged, and crisscrossed with trenches and the scars of deep-sea dredges.

"This is the debris field," said the guide, breaking his silence at last. "It was covered with pieces of the ship—crockery, furniture, kitchen utensils, you name it. They were all collected while Lloyd's and the Canadian government were still arguing in the World Court. When the ruling came, it was too late—"

"What's *that?*" one of the passengers suddenly asked. She had caught a glimpse of movement through her little window.

"Where— Let me see— Oh, that's J.J."

"Who?"

"Jason Junior. ISA—sorry, International Seabed Authority's—latest toy. It's being tested out—it's an automatic surveying robot. They hope to have a small fleet of them, so that all the seabeds can be mapped down to one-meter resolution. Then we'll know the ocean as well as we know the Moon. . . ."

Another oasis of light was appearing ahead, and presently resolved itself into a spectacle that was still hard to believe, no matter how many times one had seen it in photos or video displays.

Nothing of the stern portion of the wreck was now visible: it was all buried deep inside the huge, irregular block of ice sitting on the seabed. Protruding out of the ice were dozens of girders, to many of which half-inflated balloons had been attached by cables of varying length.

"It's a *very* tricky job," the young guide said, with obvious admiration. "The big problem is to stop the ice from breaking off and floating up by itself. So there's a lot of internal structure that you can't see. As well as a kind of roof up there on top."

One of the passengers, who obviously hadn't paid attention to the briefing, asked: "Those balloons—didn't you say they couldn't pump air down to this depth?"

"Not enough to lift masses like this. But that's not air. Those flotation bags contain H_2 and O_2—hydrogen and oxygen released by electrolysis. See those cables? They're bringing down millions—no, *billions* of amp-hours from the two nuclear subs four kilometers above us. Enough electricity to run a small township."

He looked at his watch.

"Not so much to see here, I'm afraid. We'll do one circuit in each direction, then start home."

Piccard dumped its excess weights—they would be collected later—and was sent back along the "up" elevator cable at *Titanic*'s bow. It was time to start autographing the souvenir brochure; and that, to most of the passengers, would be quite a surprise. . . .

D.S.V. "PICCARD"   R.M.S. "TITANIC"
October 14, 2011   *April 14, 1912*

LUNCHEON
Consommé Fermier Cockie Leekie
Fillets of Brill

Egg à l'Argenteuil
Chicken à la Maryland
Corned Beef, Vegetables, Dumplings

FROM THE GRILL

Grilled Mutton Chops
Mashed, Fried and Baked Jacket Potatoes

Custard Pudding
Apple Meringue   Pastry

BUFFET

Salmon Mayonnaise   Potted Shrimps
Norwegian Anchovies   Soused Herrings
Plain & Smoked Sardines
Roast Beef
Round of Spiced Beef
Veal & Ham Pie
Virginia & Cumberland Ham
Bologna Sausage   Brawn
Galantine of Chicken
Corned Ox Tongue
Lettuce   Beetroot   Tomatoes

CHEESE

Cheshire, Stilton, Gorgonzola, Edam
Camembert, Roquefort, St. Ivel, Cheddar

Iced draught Munich Lager Beer 3d. & 6d. a Tankard

"I'm afraid quite a few items are off the menu," said the
young guide, in tones of mock apology. "*Piccard*'s catering
arrangements are rather limited. We don't even run a mi-
crowave—would take too much power. So please ignore the
grill; I can assure you that the cold buffet is delicious. We also
have *some* of the cheeses—but only the milder ones. Gorgonzola didn't seem a very good idea in these confined quarters. . . .

"Oh yes—the lager—it's genuine, straight from Munich!

And it cost us rather more than three pence per tankard. Even more than six.

"Enjoy yourselves, ladies and gentlemen. We'll be topside in just one hour."

37

RESURRECTION

t had not been easy to arrange, and had taken months of arguing across the border. However, the joint funeral services had gone smoothly enough; for once, sharing the same tragedy, Christian could talk politely to Christian. The fact that one of the dead had come from Northern Ireland helped a good deal; coffins could be lowered into the ground simultaneously in Dublin and Belfast.

As the "Lux aeterna" of Verdi's *Requiem Mass* ebbed softly away, Edith Craig turned to Dolores and asked: "Should I tell Dr. Jafferjee now? Or will he think I'm crazy again?"

Dolores frowned, then answered in that lilting Caribbean accent that had once helped to reach the far place where Edith's mind was hiding:

"Please, dear, *don't* use that word. And yes, I think you should. It's about time we spoke to him again—he'll be getting worried. He's not like some doctors I could mention—he keeps track of his patients. They're not just case numbers to him."

Dr. Jafferjee was indeed pleased to receive Edith's call; he wondered where it was coming from, but she did not enlighten him. He could see that she was sitting in a large room with

cane furniture (ah, probably the tropics—Dolores' home island?) and was happy to note that she seemed completely relaxed. There were two large photographs on the wall behind
her, and he recognized both—Ada, and "Colleen."

Physician and ex-patient greeted each other with warmth;
then Edith said, a little nervously: "You may think I'm starting
on another hopeless quest—and you may be right. But at least
this time I know what I'm doing—and I'll be working with
some of the world's top scientists. The odds may be a million
to one against success. But that's infinitely—and I *mean* infinitely—better than . . . than . . . finding what you need in the
M-Set."

Not what you need, thought Dr. Jafferjee: what you *want*.
But he merely said, rather cautiously: "Go ahead, Edith. I'm
intrigued—and completely in the dark."

"What do you know about cryonics?"

"Not much. I know a lot of people have been frozen, but
it's never been proved that they can be— Oh! I see what you're
driving at! What a fantastic idea!"

"But not a ridiculous one?"

"Well, your million-to-one odds may be optimistic. But for
such a payoff—no, I wouldn't say it was ridiculous. And if
you're worried that I'll ask Dolores to put you on the first plane
back to the clinic, you needn't be. Even if your project doesn't
succeed, it could be the best possible therapy."

But only if, Jafferjee thought, you aren't overwhelmed by
the almost inevitable failure. Still, that would be years
ahead. . . .

"I'm so glad you feel that way. As soon as I heard that they
were going to keep Colleen in the hope of identifying her, I
knew what I had to do. I don't believe in destiny—or fate—but
how could I possibly turn down the chance?"

How could you, indeed? thought Jafferjee. You have lost
one daughter; you hope to gain another. A Sleeping Beauty, to
be awakened not by a young prince, but an aging princess.

No—a witch—a good one, this time!—possessing powers utterly beyond the dreams of any Irish lass born in the nineteenth century.

If—*if!*—it works, what a strange new world Colleen will face! *She* would be the one to need careful psychological counseling. But this was all the wildest extrapolation.

"I don't wish to pour cold water on the idea," Jafferjee said. "But surely, even if you can revive the body—won't there be irreversible brain damage after a hundred years?"

"That's exactly what I was afraid of, when I started thinking about it. But there's a great deal of research that makes it very plausible—I've been quite surprised. More than that—impressed. Have you ever heard of Professor Ralph Merkle?"

"Vaguely."

"More than thirty years ago, he and a couple of other young mathematicians revolutionized cryptography by inventing the public-key system—I won't bother to explain that, but it made every cipher machine in the world, and a lot of spy networks, obsolete overnight.

"Then, in 1990—sorry, 1989—he published a classic paper called 'Molecular Repair of the Brain'—"

"Oh, *that* fellow!"

"Good—I was sure you must have heard of his work. He pointed out that even if there had been gross damage to the brain, it could be repaired by the molecule-sized machines he was quite certain would be invented in the next century. *Now.*"

"And have they been?"

"Many of them. Look at the computer-controlled microsubs the surgeons are using now, to ream out the arteries of stroke victims. You can't watch a science channel these days without seeing the latest achievements of nanotechnology."

"But to repair a whole brain, molecule by molecule! Think of the sheer numbers involved!"

"About ten to the twenty-third. A trivial number."

"Indeed." Jafferjee was not quite sure whether Edith was joking; no—she was perfectly serious.

"Very well. Suppose you *do* repair a brain, right down to the last detail. Would that bring the person back to life? Complete with memories? Emotions? And everything else—whatever it is—that makes a specific, self-conscious individual?"

"Can you give me a good reason why it wouldn't? I don't believe the brain is any more mysterious than the rest of the body—and we know how *that* works, in principle if not in detail. Anyway, there's only one way to find out—and we'll learn a lot in the process."

"How long do you think it will take?"

"Ask me in five years. Then I may know if we'll need another decade—or a century. Or forever."

"I can only wish you luck. It's a fascinating project—and you're going to have lots of problems beside the purely technical ones. Her relations, for example, if they're ever located."

"It doesn't seem likely. The latest theory is that she was a stowaway, and so not on the passenger list."

"Well, the church. The media. Thousands of sponsors. Ghost writers who want to do her autobiography. I'm beginning to feel sorry for that poor girl already."

And he could not help thinking, though he did not say it aloud: I hope Dolores won't be jealous.

Donald, of course, had been both astonished and indignant: husbands (and wives) always were on such occasions.

"She didn't even leave any message?" he said unbelievingly.

Dr. Jafferjee shook his head.

"There's no need to worry. She'll contact you as soon as she's settled down. It will take her a while to adjust. Give her a few weeks."

"Do you know where she's gone?"

The doctor did not answer, which was answer enough.

"Well, are you quite sure she's safe?"

"No doubt of it; she's in extremely good hands." The psychiatrist made one of those lengthy pauses which were part of his stock-in-trade.

"You know, Mr. Craig, I should be quite annoyed with you."

"Why?" asked Donald, frankly astonished.

"You've cost me the best member of my staff—my right-hand woman."

"Nurse Dolores? I wondered why I'd not seen her—I wanted to thank her for all she'd done."

Another of those calculated pauses; then Dr. Jafferjee said: "She's helped Edith more than you imagine. Obviously, you've never guessed, and this may be a shock to you. But I owe you the truth—it will help you with your own adjustment.

"Edith's prime orientation isn't toward men—and Dolores actively disliked them, though she was sometimes kind enough to make an exception in my case. . . .

"She was able to contact Edith on the physical level even before we connected on the mental one. They will be very good for each other. But I'll miss her, dammit."

Donald Craig was speechless for a moment. Then he blurted out: "You mean—they were having an affair? And you *knew* it?"

"Of course I did; my job as a physician is to help my patients in any way I can. You're an intelligent man, Mr. Craig—I'm surprised that seems to shock you."

"Surely it's . . . *unprofessional* conduct!"

"What nonsense! Just the reverse—it's highly professional. Oh, back in the barbarous twentieth century many people would have agreed with you. Can you believe it was a *crime* in those days for the staff of institutions to have any kind of sex with patients under their care, even though that would often have been the best possible therapy for them?

"One good thing did come out of the AIDS epidemic—it forced people to be honest: it wiped out the last remnants of the Puritan aberration. My Hindu colleagues—with their temple prostitutes and erotic sculpture—had the right idea all the time. Too bad it took the West three thousand years of misery to catch up with them."

Dr. Jafferjee paused for breath, giving Donald Craig time to marshal his own thoughts. He could not help feeling that the doctor had lost some of his professional detachment. Had he been erotically interested in the inaccessible Nurse Dolores? Or did he have deeper problems?

But, of course, everyone knew just why people became psychiatrists in the first place. . . .

With luck, you could cure yourself. And even if you failed, the work was interesting—and the pay was excellent.

FINALE

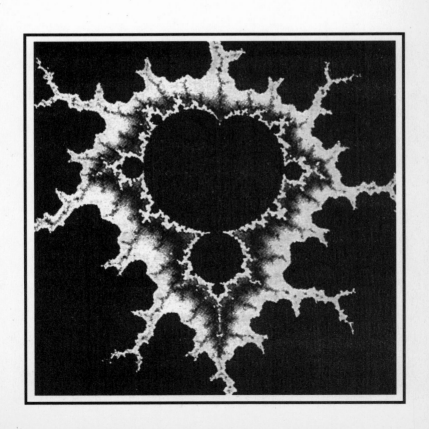

38

RICHTER EIGHT

Jason Bradley was on the bridge of *Glomar Explorer*, monitoring J.J.'s progress on the seabed, when he felt the sudden sharp hammerblow. The two electronics technicians watching the displays never even noticed; they probably thought it was some change in the incessant rhythm of the ship's machinery. Yet for a chilling instant Jason was reminded of a moment almost a century ago, equally unnoticed by most of the passengers. . . .

But, of course, *Explorer* was at anchor (in four kilometers of water, and how *that* would have astonished Captain Smith!) and no iceberg could possibly creep undetected through her radar. Nor, at drifting speed, would it do much worse than scrape off a little paint.

Before Jason could even call the communications center, a red star began to flash on the satfax screen. In addition, a piercing audio alarm, guaranteed to set teeth on edge as it warbled up and down through a kilocycle range, sounded on the unit's seldom-used speaker. Jason punched the audio cutoff, and concentrated on the message. Even the two landlubbers beside him now realized that *something* was wrong.

"What is it?" one of them asked anxiously.

"Earthquake—and a big one. Must have been close."

"Any danger?"

"Not to *us*. I wonder where the epicenter is. . . ."

Bradley had to wait a few minutes for the seismograph-computer networks to do their calculations. Then a message appeared on the fax screen:

SUBSEA EARTHQUAKE ESTIMATED RICHTER 7
EPICENTER APPROX 55 W 44 N.
ALERT ALL ISLANDS AND COASTAL AREAS
NORTH ATLANTIC

Nothing else happened for a few seconds; then another line appeared:

CORRECTION: UPDATE TO RICHTER 8

Four kilometers below, J.J. was patiently and efficiently going about its business, gliding over the seabed at an altitude of ten meters and a speed of a comfortable eight knots. (Some nautical traditions refused to die; knots and fathoms still survived into the metric age.) Its navigation program had been set so that it scanned overlapping swaths, like a plowman driving back and forth across a field being prepared for the next harvest.

The first shock wave bothered J.J. no more than it had the *Explorer*. Even the two nuclear submarines had been completely unaffected; they had been designed to withstand far worse—though their commanders had spent a few anxious seconds speculating about depth charges.

J.J. continued its automatic quest, collecting and recording megabytes of information every second. Ninety-nine percent of this would never be of the slightest interest to anyone—and it might be centuries before scientific gold was found in the residue.

To eye or video camera, the seabed here appeared almost completely featureless, but it had been chosen with care. The original "debris field" around the severed stern section had long ago been cleared of all interesting items; even the lumps of coal spilled from the bunkers had been salvaged and made into souvenirs. However, only two years ago a magnetometer search had revealed anomalies near the bow which might be worth investigating. J.J. was just the entity for the job; in another few hours it would have completed the survey, and would return to its floating base.

"It looks like 1929 all over again," said Bradley.

Back in the ISA lab, Dr. Zwicker shook his head.

"No—much worse, I'm afraid."

In Tokyo, at another node of the hastily arranged conference, Kato asked: "What happened in 1929?"

"The Grand Banks earthquake. It triggered a turbidity current—call it an underwater avalanche. Snapped the telegraph cables one after the other, like cotton, as it raced across the seabed. That's how its speed was calculated—sixty kilometers an hour. Perhaps more."

"Then it could reach us in—my God—three or four hours. What's the likelihood of damage?"

"Impossible to say at this stage. Best case—very little. The 1929 quake didn't touch *Titanic*, though many people thought she'd been buried; luckily, it was a couple of hundred kilometers to the west. Most of the sediment was diverted into a canyon, and missed the wreck completely."

"Excuse me," interrupted Rupert Parkinson, from his London office. "We've just heard that one of our flotation modules has surfaced. Jumped twenty meters out of the water. And we've lost telemetry to the wreck. How about you, Kato?"

Kato hesitated only a moment; then he called out something in Japanese to an associate off-screen.

"I'll check with *Peter* and *Maury.* Dr. Zwicker—what's your worst-case analysis?"

"Our first quick look suggests a few meters of sediment. We'll have a better computer modeling within the hour."

"A meter wouldn't be too bad."

"It could wreck our schedule, dammit."

"A report from *Maury,* gentlemen," said Kato. "No problem—everything normal."

"But for how long? If that . . . avalanche . . . really is racing toward us, we should pull up whatever equipment we can. What do *you* advise, Dr. Zwicker?"

The scientist was just about to speak when Bradley whispered urgently in his ear. Zwicker looked startled, then glum—then nodded in reluctant agreement.

"I don't think I should say any more, gentlemen. Mr. Bradley is more experienced in this area than I am. Before I give any *specific* advice, I should consult our legal department."

There was a shocked silence; then Rupert Parkinson said quickly: "We're all men of the world; we can understand that ISA doesn't want to get involved in lawsuits. So let's not waste time. We're pulling up what we can. And I advise you to do the same, Kato—just in case Dr. Zwicker's *worst* case is merely the bad one."

That was precisely what the scientist had feared. A submarine seaquake was impressive enough; but—as a fission bomb serves as detonator for a fusion one—it might merely act as a trigger to release even greater forces.

Millions of years of solar energy had been stored in the petrochemicals beneath the bed of the Atlantic; barely a century's worth had been tapped by man.

The rest was still waiting.

PRODIGAL SON

O n the bed of the Atlantic, a billion dollars' worth of robots downed tools and started to float up to the surface. There was no great hurry; no lives were at stake, even though fortunes were. *Titanic* shares were already plunging on the world's stock exchanges, giving media humorists an opportunity for all-too-obvious jokes.

The great offshore oil fields were also playing it safe. Although Hibernia and Avalon, in relatively shallow water, had little to fear from turbidity currents, they had suspended all operations, and were doubly and triply checking their emergency and backup systems. Now there was nothing to do but to wait—and to admire the superb auroral displays that had already made this sunspot cycle the most spectacular ever recorded.

Just before midnight—no one was getting much sleep—Bradley was standing on *Explorer*'s helicopter pad, watching the great curtains of ruby and emerald fire being drawn across the northern sky. He was not a member of the crew; if the skipper or anyone else wanted him, he would be available in seconds. Busy people, especially in emergencies, did not care to have observers standing behind their backs—however well intentioned or highly qualified they might be.

And the summons, when it did come, was not from the bridge, but the operations center.

"Jason? Ops here. We have a problem. J.J. won't acknowledge our recall signal."

Bradley felt a curious mix of emotions. First there was concern at losing one of the lab's most promising—and expensive—pieces of equipment. Then there was the inevitable mental question mark—"What could have gone wrong?"—followed immediately by: "What can we do about it?"

But there was also something deeper. J.J. represented an enormous personal investment of time, effort, thought . . . even devotion. He recalled all those jokes about the robot's paternity; there was some truth in them. Creating a real son (what had happened to the flesh-and-blood J.J.?) had required very much less energy. . . .

Hell, Jason told himself, it's only a machine! It could be rebuilt; we still have all the programs. Nothing would be lost except the information collected on the present mission.

No—a great deal would be lost. It was even possible that the whole project might be abandoned; developing J.J. had stretched ISA's funding and resources to the limit. At the very least, Operation NEPTUNE would be delayed for years—probably beyond Zwicker's lifetime. The scientist was a prickly old S.O.B., but Jason liked and admired him. Losing J.J. would break his heart. . . .

Even as he hurried toward the ops center, Bradley was collecting and analyzing reports over his wristcom.

"You're sure J.J.'s operating normally?"

"Yes—beacon's working fine—last housekeeping report fifteen minutes ago said all systems nominal—continuing with search pattern. But it just won't respond to the recall signal."

"Damn! The lab told me that algorithm had been fixed. Just

keep trying. . . . Boost your power as much as you can. What's the latest on the quake?"

"Bad—Mount Pelée is rumbling—they're evacuating Martinique. And tsunami warnings have been sent out all over, of course."

"But what about the Grand Banks? Any sign of that avalanche starting yet?"

"The seismographs are all jangling—no one's quite sure what the hell's happening. Just a minute while I get an update—

"—ah, here's something. The Navy antisubmarine network—didn't know it was still running!—is getting chopped up. So are the Atlantic cables—just like '29. . . . Yes—it's heading this way."

"How long before it hits us?"

"If it doesn't run out of steam, a good three hours. Maybe four."

Time enough, thought Bradley. He knew exactly what he had to do.

"Moon pool?" he called. "Open up Deep Jeep. I'm going down."

I'm really enjoying this, Bradley told himself. For the first time, I have an ironclad excuse to take Deep Jeep down to the wreck, without having to make application through channels, in triplicate. There'll be plenty of time later to do the paperwork—or to input the electronic memos. . . .

To speed the descent, Deep Jeep was heavily overweighted; this was no time to worry about littering the seabed with discarded ballast. Only twenty minutes after the brilliant auroral glow had faded in the waters above him, Bradley saw the first phosphorescent nimbus around *Titanic*'s prow. He did not need it, of course, because he knew his exact location, and the wreck was not even his target; but he was glad that the lights had been switched on again for his exclusive benefit.

J.J. was only half a kilometer away, going about its business with simpleminded concentration and devotion to duty. The monotonous *ping . . . ping-ping* call sign of its beacon filled Deep Jeep's tiny bubble of air every ten seconds, and it was also clearly visible on the search sonar.

Without much hope, Bradley retransmitted the emergency recall sequence, and continued to do so as he approached the recalcitrant robot. He was not surprised, or disappointed, at the total lack of response. Not to worry, he told himself; I've lots of other tricks up my sleeve.

He saved the next one until they were only ten meters apart. Deep Jeep could easily outrun J.J., and Bradley had no difficulty in placing his vehicle athwart the robot's precomputed track. Such underwater confrontations had often been arranged, to test J.J.'s obstacle avoidance algorithms—and these, at least, now operated exactly as planned.

J.J. came to a complete halt, and surveyed the situation. At this point-blank range Bradley could just detect, with his unaided ears, a piccololike subharmonic as the robot scanned the obstacle ahead, and tried to identify it.

He took this opportunity of sending out the recall command once more; no luck. It was pointless to try again; the problem must be in the software.

J.J. turned ninety degrees left, and headed off at right angles to its original course. It went only ten meters, then swung back to its old bearing, hoping to avoid the obstruction. But Bradley was there already.

While J.J. was thinking this over, Bradley tried a new gambit. He switched on the external sound transducer.

"J.J.," he said. "Can you hear me?"

"Yes," the robot answered promptly.

"Do you recognize me?"

"Yes, Mr. Bradley."

Good, thought Bradley. We're getting somewhere. . . .

"Do you have any problems?"

"No. All systems are normal."

"We have sent you a recall—Subprogram 999. Have you received it?"

"No. I have not received it."

Well, thought Bradley, whatever science fiction writers may have pretended, robots won't lie—unless they're programmed to do so. And no one's played that dirty trick on J.J.—I hope. . . .

"One has been sent out. I repeat: Obey Code 999. Acknowledge."

"I acknowledge."

"Then execute."

"Command not understood."

Damn. We're going around in circles, Bradley realized. And we could do that, literally, until we both run out of power—or patience.

While Bradley was considering his next step, *Explorer* interrupted the dialogue.

"Deep Jeep—sorry you're having no luck so far. But we've an update for you—and a message from the Prof."

"Go ahead."

"You're missing some real fireworks. There's been a—well, *blowout*'s the only word—around forty west, fifty north. Much too deep to do any serious damage to the offshore rigs, luckily—but hydrocarbon gas is bubbling up by the millions of cubic meters. *And it's ignited*—we can see the glare from here—forget the aurora! You should see the Earthsat images: looks as if the North Atlantic's on fire."

I'm sure it's very spectacular, thought Bradley. But how does it affect *me*?

"What's that about a message from Dr. Zwicker?"

"He asked us to tell you Tommy Gold was right. Said you'd understand."

"Frankly, I'm not interested in proving scientific theories at the moment. How long before I must come up?"

Bradley felt no sense of alarm—only of urgency. He could drop his remaining ballast and blow his tanks in a matter of seconds, and be safely on his way up long before any submarine avalanche could overwhelm him. But he was determined to complete his mission, for reasons which were now as much personal as professional.

"Latest estimate is one hour—you may have more. Plenty of time before it gets here—if it does."

An hour was ample; five minutes might be enough.

"J.J.," he commanded. "I am giving you a new program. Command Five Two Seven."

That was main power cutoff, which should leave only the backup systems running. Then J.J. would have no choice but to surface.

"Command Five Two Seven accepted."

Good—it had worked! J.J.'s external lights flickered, and the little attitude-control propellers idled to a halt. For a moment, J.J. was dead in the water. Hope I haven't overdone it, Bradley thought.

Then the lights came on again, and the props started to spin once more.

Well, it was a nice try. Nothing had gone wrong this time, but it was impossible to remember everything, in a system as complex as J.J.'s. Bradley had simply forgotten one small detail. Some commands only worked in the lab; they were disabled on operational missions. The override had been automatically overridden.

That left only one option. If gentle persuasion had failed, he would have to use brute force. Deep Jeep was much stronger than J.J.—which in any case had no limbs with which to defend itself. Any wrestling match would be very one-sided.

But it would also be undignified. There was a better way.

Bradley put Deep Jeep into reverse, so that the submersible no longer blocked J.J. The robot considered the new situation for a few seconds, then set off again on its rounds. Such dedication was indeed admirable, but it could be overdone. Was it true that archaeologists had found a Roman sentry still at his post in Pompeii, overwhelmed by the ashes of Vesuvius because no officer had come to relieve him of his duty? That was very much what J.J. now seemed determined to do.

"Sorry about this," Bradley muttered as he caught up with the unsuspecting machine.

He jammed Deep Jeep's manipulator arm into the main prop, and pieces of metal flew off in all directions. The auxiliary fans spun J.J. in a half circle, then slowed to rest.

There was only one way out of this situation, and J.J. did not stop to argue.

The intermittent beacon signal switched over to the continuous distress call—the robot Mayday—which meant "Come and get me!"

Like a bomber dropping its payload, J.J. released the iron ballast weight which gave it neutral buoyancy, and started its swift rise to the surface.

"J.J.'s on the way up," Bradley reported to *Explorer*. "Should be there in twenty minutes."

Now the robot was safe; it would be tracked by half a dozen systems as soon as it broke water, and would be back in the moon pool well before Deep Jeep.

"I hope you realize," Bradley muttered as J.J. disappeared into the liquid sky above, "that hurt me much more than it hurt you."

TOUR OF INSPECTION

Jason Bradley was just preparing to drop his own ballast and follow J.J. up to the surface when *Explorer* called again.

"Nice work, Jason—we're tracking J.J. on the way up. The inflatables are already waiting for him.

"But don't drop your weights yet. There's a small job the N-T group would like you to do—it will only take a minute or five."

"Do I have that long?"

"No problem, or we wouldn't ask. A good forty minutes before the thing hits—it looks like a weather front on our computer simulations. We'll give you plenty of warning."

Bradley considered the situation. Deep Jeep could easily reach the Nippon-Turner site within five minutes, and he would like to have one last look at *Titanic*—both sections, if possible. There was no risk; even if the arrival estimate was wildly in error, he would still have several minutes of warning time and could be a thousand meters up before the avalanche swept past below.

"What do they want me to do?" he asked, swinging Deep Jeep around so that the ice-shrouded stern was directly ahead on his sonar scan.

"*Maury* has a problem with its power cables—can't haul them up. May be snagged somewhere. Can you check?"

"Will do."

It was a reasonable request, since he was virtually on the spot. The massive, neutral-buoyancy conductors which had carried down their enormous amperages to the wreck cost millions of dollars; no wonder the submarines were trying to winch them up. He assumed that *Peter the Great* had already succeeded.

He had only Deep Jeep's own lights to illuminate the ice mountain still tethered to the seabed, awaiting a moment of release that now might never come. Moving cautiously, to avoid the wires linking it with the straining oxy-hydrogen balloons, he skirted the mass until he came to the pair of thick power cables running up to the submarine far above.

"Can't see anything wrong," he said. "Just give another good pull."

Only seconds later, the great cables vibrated majestically, like the strings of some gigantic musical instrument. It seemed to Bradley that he should feel the wave of infrasound spreading out from them.

But the cables remained defiantly taut.

"Sorry," he said. "Nothing I can do. Maybe the shock wave jammed the release mechanism."

"That's the feeling up here. Well, many thanks. Better come home—you've still plenty of time, but the latest estimate is that half a billion tons of mud is heading your way. They say it's like the Mississippi in full spate."

"How many minutes before it gets here?"

"Twenty—no, fifteen."

I'd like to visit the prow, Bradley thought wistfully, but I won't press my luck. Even if I do miss the chance of being the very last man ever to set eyes on *Titanic*.

Reluctantly, he jettisoned Number 1 ballast weight, and Deep Jeep started to rise. He had one final glimpse of the immense ice-encrusted framework as he lifted away from it; then he concentrated on the pair of cables glimmering in his forward lights. Just as the anchor chain of his boat gives reassurance to a scuba diver, they also provided Bradley with a welcoming link to the world far above.

He was just about to drop the second weight, and increase his rate of ascent, when things started to go wrong.

Maury was still hopefully jerking on the cables, trying to retrieve its expensive hardware, when something finally gave way. But not, unfortunately, what was intended.

There was a loud *ping* from the anticollision sonar, then a crash that shook Deep Jeep and threw Bradley against his seat belt. He had a brief glimpse of a huge white mass soaring past him, and up into the heights above.

Deep Jeep started to sink. Bradley dropped the remaining two ballast weights.

His rate of descent dropped, almost to zero. But not quite; he was still sinking, very slowly, toward the seabed.

Bradley sat in silence for a few minutes. Then, despite himself, he began to laugh. He was in no immediate danger, and it really *was* quite funny.

"*Explorer*," he said. "You're not going to believe this. I've just been hit by an iceberg."

FREE ASCENT

E ven now, Bradley did not consider himself to be in real jeopardy; he was more annoyed than alarmed. Yet on the face of it, the situation seemed dramatic enough. He was stranded on the seabed, his buoyancy lost. The glancing blow from the ascending mini-iceberg must have sheared away some of Deep Jeep's flotation modules. And as if that were not enough, the biggest underwater avalanche ever recorded was bearing down upon him, and now due to arrive in ten or fifteen minutes. He could not help feeling like a character in an old Steven Spielberg movie.

First step, he thought: see if Deep Jeep's propulsion system can provide enough lift to get me out of this. . . .

The submarine stirred briefly, and blasted up a cloud of mud which filled the surrounding water with a dazzling cloud of reflected light. Deep Jeep rose a few meters, then settled back. The batteries would be flat long before he could reach the surface.

I hate to do this, he told himself. A couple of million bucks down the drain—or at least on the seabed. But maybe we can salvage the rest of Deep Jeep when this is all over—just as they did with good old *Alvin*, long ago.

Bradley reached for the "chicken switch," and unlatched the protective cover.

"Deep Jeep calling *Explorer*. I've got to make a free ascent; you won't hear from me until I reach the surface. Keep a good sonar lookout—I'll be coming up fast. Get your thrusters started, in case you have to sidestep me."

Calculations had shown—and tests had confirmed—that shorn of its surrounding equipment Deep Jeep's buoyant life-support sphere would hit forty klicks, and jump high enough out of the water to land on the deck of any ship that was too close. Or, of course, hole it below the water line, if it was un-lucky enough to score a direct hit.

"We're ready, Jason. Good luck."

He turned the little red key, and the lights flickered once as the heavy current pulsed through the detonators.

There are some engineering systems which can never be fully checked out, before the time when they are needed. Deep Jeep had been well designed, but testing the escape mechanism at four hundred atmospheres pressure would have required most of ISA's budget.

The twin explosive charges separated the buoyant life-support sphere from the rest of the vehicle, exactly as planned.

But, as Jason had often said, the sea could always think of something else. The titanium hull was already stressed to its maximum safe value; and the shock waves, relatively feeble though they were, converged and met at the same spot.

It was too late for fear or regret; in the fraction of a second that was left to him before the sphere imploded, Jason Bradley had time for only a single thought: This is a good place to die.

THE VILLA, AT SUNSET

As he drove his hired car past the elaborate iron gates, the beautifully manicured trees and flowerbeds triggered a momentary flashback. With a deliberate effort of will, Donald Craig forced down the upwelling memories of Conroy Castle. He would never see it again; that chapter of his life was over.

The sadness was still there, and part of it would always be with him. And yet he also felt a sense of liberation; it was not too late—what was Milton's most misquoted phrase?—to seek fresh woods and pastures new. I'm trying to reprogram myself, Donald thought wryly. Open a new file. . . .

There was a parking space waiting for him a few meters from the elegant Georgian house; he locked the hired car, and walked to the front door. There was a very new brass plate at eye level, just above the bell push and speaker grill. Though Donald could not see any camera lens, he did not doubt that one was observing him.

The plate carried a single line, in bold lettering:

Dr. Evelyn Merrick, Ph.D. (Psych)

Donald looked at it thoughtfully for a few seconds, then smiled and reached for the bell push. But the door anticipated him.

There was a faint click as it swung open; then Dame Eva said, in that probing yet sympathetic voice that would often remind him of Dr. Jafferjee: "Welcome aboard, Mr. Craig. Any friend of Jason's is a friend of mine."

43

EXORCISM

2012 April 15, 2:00 A.M.

It was a bad time for the media networks—too early for the Americas, not late enough for the evening Euronews. In any case, it was a story that had peaked; few were now interested in a race that had been so well and truly lost.

Every year, for a century now, the U.S. Coast Guard had dropped a wreath at this same spot. But *this* centennial was a very special one: the focus of so many vanished hopes and dreams—and fortunes.

Glomar Explorer had been swung into the wind, so that her forward deckhouse gave her distinguished guests some protection from the icy gusts from the north. Yet it was not as cold as it had been on that immaculate night a hundred years ago, when the whole North Atlantic had lain all Danaë to the stars.

There was no one aboard who had been present the last time *Explorer* had paid its tribute to the dead, but many must have recalled that secret ceremony on the other side of the world, in a bloodstained century that now seemed to belong to another age. The human race had matured a little, but still had far to go before it could claim to be civilized.

The slow movement of Elgar's Second Symphony ebbed

into silence. No music could have been more appropriate than this haunting farewell to the Edwardian Era, composed during the very years that *Titanic* grew in the Belfast shipyard.

All eyes were on the tall, gray-haired man who picked up the single wreath and dropped it gently over the side. For a long time he stood in silence; though all his companions on the windswept deck could share his emotions, for some they were especially poignant. They had been with him aboard the *Knorr*, when the TV monitor had shown the first wreckage on the morning of 1 September 1985. And there was one whose dead wife's wedding ring had been cast into these same waters, a quarter of a century ago.

This time, *Titanic* was lost forever to the race that had conceived and built her; no human eyes would look upon her scattered fragments again.

More than a few men were free at last, from the obsessions of a lifetime.

44

EPILOGUE:
THE DEEPS OF TIME

The star once called the Sun had changed little since the far-off days when men had worshiped it.

Two planets had gone—one by design, one by accident—and Saturn's rings had lost much of their glory. But on the whole, the Solar System had not been badly damaged during its brief occupancy by a space-faring species.

Indeed, some regions still showed signs of past improvements. The Martian oceans had dwindled to a few shallow lakes, but the great forests of mutated pines still survived along the equatorial belt. For ages to come, they would maintain and protect the ecology they had been designed to create.

Venus—once called New Eden—had reverted to its former Hell. And of Mercury, nothing remained. The System's mother lode of heavy metals had been whittled away through millennia of astroengineering. The last remnant of the core—with its unexpected and providential bonus of magnetic monopoles—had been used to build the worldships of the Exodus Fleet.

And Pluto, of course, had been swallowed by the fearsome singularity which the best scientists of the human race were still vainly struggling to comprehend, even as they fled in search of safer suns. There was no trace of this ancient tragedy, when the Seeker fell earthward out of deep space, following an invisible trail.

The interstellar probe that Man had launched toward the Galactic core had reconnoitered a dozen stars before its signals had been intercepted by another civilization. The Seeker knew, to within a few dozen light-years, the origin of the primitive machine whose trajectory it was retracing. It had explored almost a hundred solar systems, and had discovered much. The planet it was approaching now was little different from many others it had inspected; there was no cause for excitement, even if the Seeker had been capable of such an emotion.

The radio spectrum was silent, except for the hiss and crash of the cosmic background. There were none of the glittering networks which covered the nightlands of most technologically developed worlds. Nor, when it entered atmosphere, did the Seeker find the chemical traces of industrial development.

Automatically, it went into the standard search routine. It dissolved into a million components, which scattered over the face of the planet. Some would never return, but would merely send back information. No matter; the Seeker could always create others to replace them. Only its central core was indispensable—and there were backup copies of that, safely stored at right angles to all three dimensions of normal space.

Earth had orbited the Sun only a few times before the Seeker had gathered all the easily accessible information about the abandoned planet. It was little enough; megayears of winds and rains had wiped away all man's cities, and the slow grinding of the tectonic plates had completely changed the patterns of land and sea. Continents had become oceans; seabeds had become plains, which had then been wrinkled into mountains. . . .

... The anomaly was the faintest of echoes on a neutrino scan, but it attracted immediate attention. Nature abhorred straight lines, right angles, repeated patterns—except on the scale of crystals and snowflakes. This was millions of times larger; indeed, it dwarfed the Seeker. It could only be the work of intelligence.

The object lay in the heart of a mountain, beneath kilometers of sedimentary rock. To reach it would require only seconds; to excavate it without doing any damage, and to learn all its secrets, might require months or years.

The scan was repeated, at higher resolution. Now it was observed that the object was made from ferrous alloys of an extremely simple type. No civilization that could build an interstellar probe would have used such crude materials. The Seeker almost felt disappointment. . . .

Yet, primitive though this object was, no other artifact of comparable size or complexity had been found. It might, after all, be worth the trouble of recovering.

The Seeker's high-level systems considered the problem for many, many microseconds, analyzing all the possibilities that might arise. Presently the Master Correlator made its decision.

"Let us begin."

Sources and Acknowledgments

R M.S. *Titanic* has haunted me all my life, as is amply demonstrated by this extract from *Arthur C. Clarke's Chronices of the Strange and Mysterious* (Collins, 1987):

> My very first attempt at a full-length science-fiction story (fortunately long since destroyed) concerned that typical disaster of the spaceways, the collision between an interplanetary liner and a large meteorite—or small comet, if you prefer. I was quite proud of the title, *Icebergs of Space*—never dreaming at the time that such things really existed. I have always been a little too fond of surprise endings. In the last line I revealed the name of the wrecked spaceship. It was—wait for it—*Titanic*.

More than four decades later, I returned to the subject in *Imperial Earth* (1976), bringing the wreck to New York to celebrate the 2276 Quincentennial. At the time of writing, of course, no one knew that the ship was in two badly damaged portions.

Meanwhile I had grown to know Bill MacQuitty, the Irish movie maker (and much else) to whom this book is dedicated. Following the success of his superb *A Night to Remember*

(1958), Bill was determined to film my 1961 novel *A Fall of Moondust*; however, the Rank Organization refused to dabble in fantasy (men on the Moon, indeed!) and the project was turned down. I am happy to say that the novel is now being turned into a TV mini-series by another close friend, Michael Deakin. If you wonder how we manage to find seas of dust on the Moon, stay tuned.

I am also indebted to Bill MacQuitty for photographs, plans, drawings, and documents on R.M.S. *Titanic*—especially the menu reproduced in Chapter 36, "The Last Lunch." Bill's beautiful book *Irish Gardens* (text by Edward Hyams; Macdonald, London, 1967) also provided much inspiration.

It is pleasant to record that Bill's director of photography was Geoffrey Unsworth—who, a decade later, also filmed *2001: A Space Odyssey*. I can still remember Geoffrey wandering round the set with a slightly bemused expression, telling all and sundry: "I've been in this business for forty years—and Stanley's just taught me something I didn't know." Michael Crichton has reminded me that *Superman* was dedicated to Geoffrey, who died during its production, much mourned by all those who had worked with him.

This novel would not have been possible, of course, without inputs from the two classic books on the subject, Walter Lord's *A Night to Remember* (Allen Lane, 1976) and Robert Ballard's *The Discovery of the Titanic* (Madison Press Books, 1987), both of which are beyond praise. Two other books I have also found very valuable are Walter Lord's recent "sequel" *The Night Lives On* (William Morrow, 1986) and Charles Pellegrino's *Her Name, Titanic* (Avon, 1990). I am also extremely grateful to Charlie (who appears in Chapter 43) for a vast amount of technical information about "Bringing up Baby"— an enterprise which we both regard with very mixed feelings.

Martin Gardner's book *The Wreck of the Titanic Foretold?* (Prometheus Books, 1986) reprints the extraordinary Morgan Robertson novel, *The Wreck of the Titan* (1898!), which Lord

Aldiss refers to in Chapter 9. Martin makes a good case for intelligent anticipation on Robertson's part; nevertheless, I cannot blame anyone who thinks there must have been *some* feedback from 1912. . . .

Since many of the events in this novel have already occurred—or are about to do so—it has often been necessary to refer to real individuals. I hope they will enjoy my occasional extrapolation of their activities.

"The Century Syndrome" (Chapter 4) already has many people worried, though we will have to wait until 1/1/00 to see whether matters are as bad as I suggest. While I was writing this book, my most long-standing American friend, Dr. Charles Fowler (GCA, 1942—though neither of us can quite believe it), sent me an article from the *Boston Globe* entitled "Mainframes have a problem with the year 2000." According to this, the joke in the trade is that everyone will retire in 1999. We'll see. . . .

This problem will not, of course, arise in 2099. By then, computers will be able to take care of themselves (as well as H. Sap., if he/she is still around).

I have not invented the unusually large mollusk in Chapter 12. Details (with photographs) of this awesome beast will be found in *Arthur C. Clarke's Mysterious World* (Collins, 1980). *Octopus giganteus* was first positively identified by F. G. Wood and Dr. Joseph Gennaro (*Natural History*, March 1971), both of whom I was happy to get on camera for my *Mysterious World* TV series.

The useful hint on octopus allergies (e.g., what to do if you find one in the toilet) comes from Jacques-Yves Cousteau and Philippe Diole's *Octopus and Squid: The Soft Intelligence* (Cassell, 1973).

And here I must put on record something that has mystified me for many years. In this book, Jacques asserts that though his divers have played with octopuses (very well: octopodes) hundreds of times, they have never once been bit-

ten—and have never even heard of such an incident. Well . . .
the *only* time I caught one, off the eastern coast of Australia, it
bit me! (see *The Coast of Coral*, Harper & Row, 1956). I am
quite unable to explain this total breakdown of the laws of
probability.

According to *Omni* magazine, the question described in
Chapter 13 was actually set in a high school intelligence test,
and only one genius-type pupil spotted that the printed answer
was wrong. I still find this amazing; skeptics may profitably
spend a few minutes with scissors and cardboard. The even
more incredible story of Srinivasa Ramanujan, mentioned *passim* in the same chapter, will be found in G. H. Hardy's small
classic, *A Mathematician's Apology*, and more conveniently in
Volume 1 of James Newman's *The World of Mathematics*.

For a crash course in offshore oil drilling operations, I must
thank my longtime Sri Lankan friend Cuthbert Charles and
his colleagues Walter Jackson and Danny Stephens (all with
Brown & Root Vickers Ltd.) and Brian Redden (Technical
Services Division Manager, Wharton Williams). They prevented me from making (I hope) too many flagrant errors, and
they are in no way responsible for my wilder extrapolations of
their truly astonishing achievements—already comparable to
much that we will be doing in space during the next century.
I apologize for awarding their kindness by sabotaging so much
of their handiwork.

The full story of 1974's "Operation JENNIFER" has never
been told, and probably never will be. To my surprise, its director turned out to be an old acquaintance, and I am grateful
to him for his evasive but not unhelpful replies to my queries.
On the whole, I would prefer not to know too much about the
events of that distant summer, so that I am not handicapped
by mere facts.

While writing this novel, I was amused to encounter another work of fiction using the *Glomar Explorer*, though (luckily!) for a very different purpose: *Ship of Gold*, by Thomas Allen and Norman Polmar (Macmillan, 1987).

My thanks also to sundry CIA and KGB acquaintances, who would prefer to remain anonymous.

One informant I am happy to identify is Professor William Orr, Dept. of Geological Science, University of Oregon, my erstwhile shipmate on the floating campus SS *Universe*. The plans and documentation he provided on *Glomar Explorer* (now languishing in Suisun Bay, California, between Vallejo and Martinez—you can see her from Highway 680) were essential inputs.

The discovery of major explosive events on the seabed, referred to in Chapter 33, was reported by David B. Prior, Earl H. Doyle, and Michael J. Kaluza in *Science*, vol. 243, pp. 517–9, 27 January 1989, under the title "Evidence for Sediment Eruption on Deep Sea Floor, Gulf of Mexico."

On the very day I was making the final corrections to this manuscript, I learned that there is now strong evidence that oil drilling *can* cause earthquakes. The October 28, 1989, *Science News* cites a paper by Paul Segall of the U.S. Geological Survey, making this claim in the October 1989 issue of *Geology*.

The report on the Neolithic grave quoted in Chapter 34 will be found in *Nature*, *276*, 608, 1978.

Ralph C. Merkle's truly mind-boggling paper "Molecular Repair of the Brain" first appeared in the October 1989 issue of *Cryonics* (published by ALCOR, 12327, Doherty St., Riverside, CA, 92503) to whom I am grateful for an advance copy.

My thanks to Kumar Chitty for information on the U.N. Law of the Sea Convention, directed for many years by the late Ambassador Shirley Hamilton Amarasinghe. It is a great tragedy that Shirley (the hospitality of whose Park Avenue apartment I often enjoyed in the '70s) did not see the culmination of his efforts. He was a wonderful persuader, and had he lived might even have prevented the U.S. and U.K. delegations from shooting themselves in the foot.

I am particularly grateful to my collaborator Gentry Lee (*Cradle*, the *Rama* trilogy) for arranging his schedule so that I could concentrate all my energies on the latest of my "last" novels. . . .

Very special thanks to Navam and Sally Tambayah—not to mention Tasha and Cindy—for hospitality, WORDSTAR, and faxes. . . .

And, finally: a tribute to my dear friend the late Reginald Ross, who besides many other kindnesses introduced me to Rachmaninoff and Elgar half a century ago, and who died at the age of 91 while this book was being written.

Mandelmemo

The literature on the Mandelbrot Set, first introduced to the non-IBM world in A. K. Dewdney's "Computer Recreations" (*Scientific American*, Aug. 1985, 16–25), is now enormous. The master's own book, *The Fractal Geometry of Nature* (W. H. Freeman, 1982), is highly technical, and much is inaccessible even to those with delusions of mathematical ability. Nevertheless, a good deal of the text is informative and witty, so it is well worth skimming. However, it contains only the briefest references to the M-Set, the exploration of which was barely beginning in 1982.

The Beauty of Fractals (H-O. Peitgen and P. H. Richter, Springer-Verlag, 1986) was the first book to show the M-Set in glorious Technicolor, and contains a fascinating (and often amusing) essay by Dr. M. himself on its origins and discovery (invention?). He describes later developments in *The Science of Fractal Images* (edited by H-O. Peitgen and Dietmar Saupe, Springer-Verlag, 1988). Both these books are highly technical.

Much more accessible to the general—though determined—reader is A. K. Dewdney's *The Armchair Universe* (W. H. Freeman, 1988). This contains the original 1985 *Scientific American* article, with updates and information on software available for personal computers. I have been very happy with MandFXP, from Cygnus Software (1215 Davie St., P.O. Box 363, Vancouver BC, V6E 1N4, Canada), and have used this extensively on my AMIGA 2000. While making a TV documentary, "God, the Universe, and Everything Else" for U.K.'s Channel 4, I had the rare privilege of showing Stephen Hawking some beautiful "black holes" I had discovered, while expanding the set until it would have filled the orbit of Mars. Another supplier of M-Set software (for MAC and IBM) is Sintar Software (1001 4th Ave., Suite 3200, Seattle, WA 98154).

Needless to say, there are Mandelbrot "fan magazines," containing hints on speeding up programs, notes from explorers in far-off regions of the set—and even samples of a new literary genre, Fractalfiction. The newsletter of the field is *Amygdala*, edited by Rollo Silver, who also supplies software (Box 111, San Cristobal, NM 87564).

Undoubtedly the best way of appreciating the set is through the videotapes that have been made of it, usually with accompanying music. Most celebrated is "Nothing But Zooms" from Art Matrix (P.O. Box 880, Ithaca, NY 14851). I have also enjoyed "A Fractal Ballet" (The Fractal Stuff Company, P.O. Box 5202, Spokane, WA 99205-5202).

Strictly speaking, the "Utter West" of the M-Set is at exactly -2, not -1.999 . . . to infinity, as stated in Chapter 18. Anyone care to split the difference?

I do not know if there have been any cases of Mandelmania in real life, but I expect to receive reports as soon as this book appears—and waive all responsibility in advance.

APPENDIX: THE COLORS OF INFINITY

In November 1989, when receiving the Association of Space Explorers Special Achievement Award in Riyadh, Saudi Arabia, I had the privilege of addressing the largest gathering of astronauts and cosmonauts ever assembled at one place. (More than fifty, including Apollo 11's Buzz Aldrin and Mike Collins, and the first "space walker" Alexei Leonov, who is no longer embarrassed at sharing the dedication of *2010: Odyssey Two* with Andrei Sakharov.) I decided to expand their horizons by introducing them to something *really* large, and, with astronaut Prince Sultan bin Salman bin Abdul Aziz in the chair, delivered a lavishly illustrated lecture "The Colors of Infinity: Exploring the Fractal Universe."

The material that follows is extracted from my speech; another portion appears at the beginning of Chapter 15. I'm only sorry that I cannot illustrate it with the gorgeous 35-millimeter slides—and videos—I used at Riyadh.

Today, everybody is familiar with graphs—especially the one with time along the horizontal axis, and the cost of living climbing steadily up the vertical one. The idea that any point on a plane can be expressed by two numbers, usually written x

and *y*, now appears so obvious that it seems quite surprising that the world of mathematics had to wait until 1637 for Descartes to invent it.

We are still discovering the consequences of that apparently simple idea, and the most amazing is now just ten years old. It's called the Mandelbrot Set (from now on, the M-Set) and you're soon going to meet it everywhere—in the design of fabrics, wallpaper, jewelry, and linoleum. And, I'm afraid, it will be popping out of your TV screen in every other commercial.

Yet the most astonishing feature of the M-Set is its basic *simplicity.* Unlike almost everything else in modern mathematics, any schoolchild can understand how it is produced. Its generation involves nothing more advanced than addition and multiplication; there's no need for such complexities as subtraction and—heaven forbid!—division, let alone any of the more exotic beasts from the mathematical menagerie.

There can be few people in the civilized world who have not encountered Einstein's famous $E = mc^2$, or who would consider it too hopelessly complicated to understand. Well, the equation that defines the M-Set contains the same number of terms, and indeed looks very similar. Here it is.

$$Z = z^2 + c$$

Not very terrifying, is it? Yet the lifetime of the Universe would not be long enough to explore all its ramifications.

The *z*'s and the *c* in Mandelbrot's equation are all *numbers,* not (as in Einstein's) physical quantities like mass and energy. They are the coordinates which specify the position of a point, and the equation controls the way in which it moves, to trace out a pattern.

There's a very simple analog familiar to everyone—those children's books with blank pages sprinkled with numbers, which when joined up in the right order reveal hidden—and

often surprising—pictures. The image on a TV screen is produced by a sophisticated application of the same principle.

In theory, anyone who can add and multiply could plot out
the M-Set with pen or pencil on a sheet of squared paper. However, as we'll see later, there are certain practical difficulties—
notably the fact that a human life span is seldom more than a
hundred years. So the set is invariably computer-generated, and
usually shown on a visual display unit.

Now, there are two ways of locating a point in space. The
more common employs some kind of grid reference—west-
east, north-south, or on squared graph paper, a horizontal X-
axis and a vertical Y-axis. But there's also the system used in
radar, now familiar to most people thanks to countless movies.
Here the position of an object is given by (1) its distance from
the origin, and (2) its direction, or compass bearing. Incidentally, this is the *natural* system—the one you use automatically
and unconsciously when you play any ball game. Then you're
concerned with distances and angles, with yourself as the origin.

So think of a computer's VDU as a radar screen, with a single blip on it, whose movements are going to trace out the M-
Set. However, before we switch on our radar, I want to make
the equation even simpler, to:

$$Z = z^2$$

I've thrown c away, for the moment, and left only the z's.
Now let me define them more precisely.

Small z is the initial range of the blip—the distance at
which it starts. Big Z is its final distance from the origin. Thus
if it was initially 2 units away, by obeying this equation it
would promptly hop to a distance of 4.

Nothing to get very excited about, but now comes the mod-
ification that makes all the difference:

$$Z \rightleftharpoons z^2$$

That double arrow is a two-way traffic sign, indicating that the numbers flow in both directions. This time, we don't stop at $Z = 4$; we make *that* equal to a new z—which promptly gives us a second Z of 16, and so on. In no time we've generated the series

$$256, \quad 65536, \quad 4294967296 \ldots$$

and the spot that started only 2 units from the center is heading toward infinity in giant steps of ever-increasing magnitude.

This process of going around and around a loop is called "iteration." It's like a dog chasing its own tail, except that a dog doesn't get anywhere. But mathematical iteration can take us to some very strange places indeed—as we shall soon discover.

Now we're ready to turn on our radar. Most displays have range circles at 10, 20 . . . 100 kilometers from the center. We will require only a single circle, at a range of 1. There's no need to specify any units, as we're dealing with pure numbers. Make them centimeters or light-years, as you please.

Let's suppose that the initial position of our blip is anywhere on this circle—the bearing doesn't matter. So z is 1.

And because 1 squared is still 1, so is Z. And it remains at that value, because no matter how many times you square 1, it always remains exactly 1. The blip may hop around and around the circle, *but it always stays on it.*

Now consider the case where the initial z is greater than 1. We've already seen how rapidly the blip shoots off to infinity if z equals 2—but the same thing will happen sooner or later, even if it's only a microscopic shade more than 1—say 1.00000000000000000001. Watch:

At the first squaring, Z becomes

$$1.00000000000000000002$$

then

1.000000000000000000004
1.000000000000000000008
1.000000000000000000016
1.000000000000000000032

and so on for pages of printout. For all practical purposes, the value is still exactly 1. The blip hasn't moved visibly outward or inward; it's still on the circle at range 1.

But those zeros are slowly being whittled away, as the digits march inexorably across from the right. Quite suddenly, something appears in the third, second, first decimal place—and the numbers explode after a very few additional terms, as this example shows:

1.001 1.002 1.004 1.008 1.016 1.032

1.066 1.136 1.292 1.668 2.783 7.745

59.987 3598.467 12948970

167675700000000

28115140000000000000000000000

(Overflow)

There could be a million—a billion—zeros on the right-hand side, and the result would still be the same. Eventually the digits would creep up to the decimal point—and then Z would take off to infinity.

Now let's look at the other case. Suppose z is a microscopic amount *less* than 1—say something like

.99999999999999999999

As before, nothing much happens for a long time as we go around the loop, except that the numbers on the far right get steadily smaller. But after a few thousand or million iterations—catastrophe! Z suddenly shrinks to nothing, dissolving in an endless string of zeros. . . .

Check it out on your computer. It can only handle twelve digits? Well, no matter how many you had to play with, you'd still get the same answer. Trust me. . . .

The results of this "program" can be summarized in three laws that may seem too trivial to be worth formulating. But no mathematical truth is trivial, and in a few more steps these laws will take us into a universe of mind-boggling wonder and beauty.

Here are the three laws of the "Squaring" Program:

1. If the input z is exactly *equal* to 1, the output Z always remains 1.
2. If the input is *more than* 1, the output eventually becomes infinite.
3. If the input is *less than* 1, the output eventually becomes zero.

That circle of radius 1 is therefore a kind of map—or, if you like, fence—dividing the plane into two distinct territories. Outside it, numbers which obey the squaring law have the freedom of infinity; numbers inside it are prisoners, trapped and doomed to ultimate extinction.

At this point, someone may say: "You've only talked about *ranges*—distances from the origin. To fix the blip's position, you have to give its bearing as well. What about that?"

Very true. Fortunately, in this selection process—this division of the z's into two distinct classes—bearings are irrelevant; the same thing happens whichever direction r is pointing. For this simple example—let's call it the S-set—we can ignore them. When we come on to the more complicated case of the M-Set, where the bearing *is* important, there's a very neat mathematical trick which takes care of it, by using complex or imaginary numbers (which really aren't at all complex, still less imaginary). But we don't need them here, and I promise not to mention them again.

The S-set lies inside a *map*, and its frontier is the circle enclosing it. That circle is simply a continuous line with no thickness. If you could examine it with a microscope of infinite power, it would always look exactly the same. You could expand the S-set to the size of the Universe; its boundary would still be a line of zero thickness. Yet there are no holes in it; it's an absolutely impenetrable barrier, forever separating the z's less than one from those greater than one.

Now, at last, we're ready to tackle the M-Set, where these commonsense ideas are turned upside down. Fasten your seat belts.

During the 1970s, the French mathematician Benoit Mandelbrot, working at Harvard and IBM, started to investigate the equation which has made him famous, and which I will now write in the dynamic form:

$$Z \rightleftharpoons z^2 + c$$

The only difference between this and the equation we have used to describe the S-set is the term c. This—not z—is now the starting point of our mapping operation. The first time around the loop, z is put equal to zero.

It seems a trifling change, and no one could have imagined the universe it would reveal. Mandelbrot himself did not obtain the first crude glimpses until the spring of 1980, when vague patterns started to emerge on computer printouts. He had begun to peer through Keats'

Charm'd magic casements, opening on the foam
Of perilous seas, in faery lands forlorn . . .

As we shall learn later, that word "foam" is surprisingly appropriate.

The new equation asks and answers the same question as the earlier one: What shape is the "territory" mapped out when we put numbers into it? For the S-set it was a circle with radius 1. Let's see what happens when we start with this value in the M-equation. You should be able to do it in your head—for the first few steps. After a few dozen, even a supercomputer may blow a gasket.

> For starters, $z = 0$, $c = 1$. So $Z = 1$
> First loop: $Z = 1^2 + 1 = 2$
> Second loop: $Z = 2^2 + 1 = 5$
> Third loop: $Z = 5^2 + 1 = 26$
> Fourth loop: $Z = 26^2 + 1$ . . . and so on.

I once set my computer to work out the higher terms (about the limit of my programming ability) and it produced only two more values before it had to start approximating:

$$1, 2, 5, 26, 677, 458330,$$
$$21006640000$$
$$4412789000000000000000$$

At that point it gave up, because it doesn't believe there are any numbers with more than 38 digits.

However, even the first two or three terms are quite enough to show that the M-Set must have a very different shape from the perfectly circular S-set. A point at distance 1 is in the S-set; indeed, it defines its boundary. A point at that same distance may be outside the boundary of the M-set.

Note that I say "may," not "must." It all depends on the initial *direction*, or bearing, of the starting point, which we have been able to ignore hitherto because it did not affect our discussion of the (perfectly symmetrical) S-set. As it turns out, the M-set is only symmetrical about the X, or horizontal, axis.

One might have guessed that, from the nature of the equation. But no one could possibly have intuited its real appearance. If the question had been put to me in virginal pre-Mandelbrot days, I would probably have hazarded: "Something like an ellipse, squashed along the Y-axis." I might even (though I doubt it) have correctly guessed that it would be shifted toward the left, or minus, direction.

At this point, I would like to try a thought experiment on you. The M-Set being literally indescribable, here's my attempt to describe it:

Imagine you're looking straight down on a rather plump turtle, swimming westward. It's been crossed with a swordfish, so has a narrow spike pointing ahead of it. Its entire perimeter is festooned with bizarre marine growths—and with baby turtles of assorted sizes, which have smaller weeds growing on them. . . .

I defy you to find a description like *that* in any math textbook. And if you think you can do better when you've seen the real beast, you're welcome to try. (I suspect that the insect world might provide better analogies; there may even be a Mandelbeetle lurking in the Brazilian rain forests. Too bad we'll never know.)

Here is the first crude approximation, shorn of details— much like Conroy Castle's "Lake Mandelbrot" (Chapter 18). If you like to fill its blank spaces with the medieval cartographers' favorite "Here be dragons" you will hardly be exaggerating.

First of all, note that—as I've already remarked—it's shifted to the left (or west, if you prefer of the S-set, which of course extends from +1 to −1 along the X-axis. The M-Set only gets to 0.25 on the right along the axis, though above and below the axis it bulges out to just beyond 0.4.

On the left-hand side, the map stretches to about −1.4, and then it sprouts a peculiar spike—or antenna—which reaches out to exactly –2.0. As far as the M-Set is concerned, there is *nothing* beyond this point; it is the edge of the Universe. Mandelbrot fans call it the "Utter West," and you might like to see what happens when you make *c* equal to –2. *Z* doesn't converge to zero—but it doesn't escape to infinity either, so the point belongs to the set—*just*. But if you make *c* the slightest bit larger, say –2.00000 . . . 000001, before you know it you're passing Pluto and heading for Quasar West.

Now we come to the most important distinction between the two sets. The S-set has a nice, clean line for its boundary. The frontier of the M-Set is, to say the least, fuzzy. Just how fuzzy you will begin to understand when we start to "zoom" into it; only then will we see the incredible flora and fauna which flourish in that disputed territory.

The boundary—if one can call it that—of the M-Set is not a simple line; it is something which Euclid never imagined, and for which there is no word in ordinary language. Mandelbrot, whose command of English (and American) is awesome, has ransacked the dictionary for suggestive nouns. A few ex-

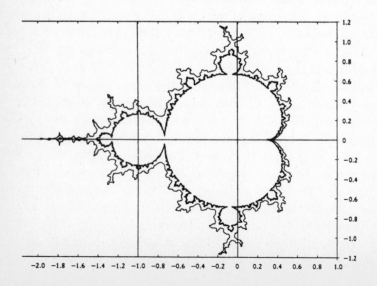

amples: foams, sponges, dusts, webs, nets, curds. He himself coined the technical name *fractal*, and is now putting up a spirited rearguard action to stop anyone from defining it too precisely.

Computers can easily make "snapshots" of the M-Set at any magnification, and even in black and white they are fascinating. However, by a simple trick they can be colored, and transformed into objects of amazing, even surreal, beauty.

The original equation, of course, is no more concerned with color than is Euclid's *Elements of Geometry*. But if we instruct the computer to color any given region in accordance with the number of times z goes around the loop before it decides *whether or not* it belongs to the M-Set, the results are gorgeous.

Thus the colors, though arbitrary, are not meaningless. An exact analogy is found in cartography. Think of the contour lines on a relief map, which show elevations above sea level. The spaces between them are often colored so that the eye can more easily grasp the information conveyed. Ditto with bathymetric charts; the deeper the ocean, the darker the blue. The mapmaker can make the colors anything he likes, and is guided by aesthetics as much as geography.

It's just the same here—except that *these* contour lines are set automatically by the speed of the calculation—I won't go into details. I have not discovered what genius first had this idea—perhaps Monsieur M. himself—but it turns them into fantastic works of art. And you should see them when they're animated. . . .

One of the many strange thoughts that the M-Set generates is this. In principle, it could have been discovered as soon as the human race learned to count. In practice, since even a "low magnification" image may involve *billions* of calculations, there was no way in which it could even be glimpsed before computers were invented! And such movies as Art Matrix' *Nothing But Zooms* would have required the entire present world population to calculate night and day for years—without making a *single* mistake in multiplying together trillions of hundred-digit numbers. . . .

I began by saying that the Mandelbrot Set is the most extraordinary discovery in the history of mathematics. For who could have possibly imagined that so absurdly simple an equation could have generated such—literally—infinite complexity, and such unearthly beauty?

The Mandelbrot Set is, as I have tried to explain, essentially a map. We've all read those stories about maps which reveal the location of hidden treasure.

Well, in this case—the map *is* the treasure!

Colombo, Sri Lanka
1990 February 28

THE DEEP RANGE

AUTHOR'S NOTE

I n this novel I have made certain assumptions about the maximum size of various marine animals which may be challenged by some biologists. I do not think, however, that they will meet much criticism from underwater explorers, who have often encountered fish *several times* the size of the largest recorded specimens.

For an account of Heron Island as it is today, seventy-five years before the opening of this story, I refer the reader to *The Coast of Coral*, and I hope that the University of Queensland will appreciate my slight extrapolation of its existing facilities.

1956

INTRODUCTION

The Deep Range began its existence as a 3,500-word story written in November 1953, first published in Frederik Pohl's Star Science Fiction series (Number 3, 1954). I had just become seriously addicted to underwater exploration, and soon afterward bought my first scuba set. Like a motorist in those pioneering days before any interfering bureaucrat had dreamed of driving licenses, I simply ordered it from Abercrombie and Fitch, strapped it on, and plunged into the nearest convenient body of water.

This happened to be Florida's famed Weeki-Wachi Springs, the crystal clarity of which must be unmatched anywhere in the world. I was carrying with me my first underwater camera—a Leica, in a cylindrical plastic case I'd purchased from a *LIFE* magazine photographer—loaded with Kodachrome (a torpid ASA 10 or so in those days, if I remember correctly).

The camera worked fine, and when I dived into Weeki-Wachi Springs the first subject I encountered was a fair-sized alligator, hanging languidly in a vertical position with its nostrils just breaking the surface. I'd never met one before and assumed (correctly) that it wouldn't attack a strange, bubble-blowing creature heading confidently toward it. So I got half a dozen excellent shots before it became camera shy and fled up the nearest creek.

The remainder of the roll wasn't so exciting: It merely showed a lot of fish apparently suspended in midair. The trouble with Weeki-Wachi (visibility approx. 200 feet) is that you can't see the water, which explains a comment by the late Alfred Bester (*The Demolished Man, The Stars My Destination,* etc.): "Damn it, Arthur, these aren't underwater shots. You took them in an aquarium. I can see the reflection in the plate glass."

In December 1954, I left the Northern Hemisphere for the Great Barrier Reef, where I encountered my first whales, as well as the justly famed Australian sharks. After completing *The Coast of Coral* (1956), I realized that I now had the background for a whole novel, which was written in Ceylon during 1956 and published the next year. Still later, I used the same Heron Island background for another book, *Dolphin Island* (1963). Both novels have been purchased by optimistic movie makers. I wish them luck with their casting problems.

Back in 1957 (the year the Space Age opened!), only a few people were interested in whales, and the idea of ranching them was still quite novel, though not original: I suspect I got it from Jacques Cousteau. Now they—and cetaceans in general—are among mankind's most favorite animals, and the ecological points I attempted to make almost half a century ago are widely accepted (vide *Free Willy!*).

When I wrote *Dolphin Island* back in 1962, I felt I was risking ridicule by having my hero actually ride a killer whale. Now it's a regular act in oceanaria, and the trainer even puts his—often her—head inside the animal's mouth, between those huge teeth. I once saw a hair-raising television film in which a girl trainer was grabbed by a killer whale, who wouldn't let her go until her colleagues had prised open his jaws. He was just lonely and didn't want her to leave! I'm happy to say that the brave girl was back in the tank the next day.

There has certainly been a revolution in public attitudes toward marine mammals, as a direct result of underwater movies

like Jacques Cousteau's famous films, the popularity of oceanaria, and the explosion of interest in diving as a sport or
hobby. I often wonder what Herman Melville would have
thought of today's campaign to save the whales—especially
sperm whales, the ferocious monster he described so vividly in
Moby Dick. I suspect he'd now agree with the ironic saying:
"This animal is very vicious—when attacked, it defends itself."

How is it that we can so easily make friends with large and
powerful carnivores in the sea—when we wouldn't dream of
doing so on land? Anyone who behaved toward a lion, a tiger,
or polar bear as divers have done countless times toward sperm
whales, killer whales, and dolphins wouldn't come back to tell
the tale. I've never seen an answer to this question.

An even greater enigma is presented by the musical repertoire of the humpback whales, something unique in nature. By
comparison, all bird songs are simple: They last only seconds
and are repeated mechanically year by year (though there are
regional variations—perhaps the equivalent of human di-
alects). But whale songs last up to half an hour, and they
change style in successive years.

The amount of information contained in one of these songs
must be considerable: at a rough estimate, the capacity of a
small computer. How is it stored? What is its purpose? If they
are intended merely for location, identification, warning, mating, these songs seem far more elaborate than necessity would
warrant. After all, the birds manage rather well with a much
simpler repertoire.

And it's a strange thought that the songs of the humpback
whales are now, literally, on the way to the stars. The two *Voy-
ager* spacecraft that flew by Jupiter and Saturn in 1979 carried
with them gold-plated records on which were stored many of
the characteristic sounds of Earth and messages in many lan-
guages.

In the benign and changeless environment of space, these
records will still exist when all the other artifacts of man have

been eroded by time, and even the Earth itself has been consumed by the Sun when it goes nova at the end of its evolutionary sequence. So perhaps these songs will be heard again, by creatures we cannot imagine, when they encounter our primitive space probe. How ironic it will be, if extraterrestrials a billion years hence grasp a message from fellow Earthlings that has been incomprehensible to us.

Colombo, Sri Lanka

I

THE APPRENTICE

CHAPTER

There was a killer loose on the range. The South Pacific air patrol had seen the great corpse staining the sea crimson as it wallowed in the waves. Within seconds, the intricate warning system had been alerted; from San Francisco to Brisbane, men were moving counters and drawing range circles on the charts. And Don Burley, still rubbing the sleep from his eyes, was hunched over the control board of Scoutsub 5 as it dropped down to the twenty-fathom line.

He was glad that the alert was in his area; it was the first real excitement for months. Even as he watched the instruments on which his life depended, his mind was ranging far ahead. What could have happened? The brief message had given no details; it had merely reported a freshly killed right whale lying on the surface about ten miles behind the main herd, which was still proceeding north in panic-stricken flight. The obvious assumption was that, somehow, a pack of killer whales had managed to penetrate the barriers protecting the range. If that was so, Don and all his fellow wardens were in for a busy time.

The pattern of green lights on the telltale board was a glowing symbol of security. As long as that pattern was unchanged, as long as none of those emerald stars winked to red, all was

well with Don and his tiny craft. Air—fuel—power—this was
the triumvirate that ruled his life. If any one of these failed, he
would be sinking in a steel coffin down toward the pelagic
ooze, as Johnnie Tyndall had done the season before last. But
there was no reason why they should fail, and the accidents
one foresaw, Don told himself reassuringly, were never those
that happened.

He leaned across the tiny control board and spoke into the
mike. Sub 5 was still close enough to the mother ship for radio
to work, but before long he'd have to switch to the ultrasonics.

"Setting course 255, speed 50 knots, depth 20 fathoms,
full sonar coverage. Estimated time to target area 40 minutes.
Will report at ten-minute intervals until contact is made. That
is all. Out."

The acknowledgment from the *Rorqual* was barely audible,
and Don switched off the set. It was time to look around.

He dimmed the cabin lights so that he could see the scanner screen more clearly, pulled the Polaroid glasses down over
his eyes, and peered into the depths. It took a few seconds for
the two images to fuse together in his mind; then the 3-D display sprang into stereoscopic life.

This was the moment when Don felt like a god, able to
hold within his hands a circle of the Pacific twenty miles
across, and to see clear down to the still largely unexplored
depths two thousand fathoms below. The slowly rotating beam
of inaudible sound was searching the world in which he
floated, seeking out friend and foe in the eternal darkness
where light could never penetrate. The pattern of soundless
shrieks, too shrill even for the hearing of the bats who had invented sonar millions of years before man, pulsed out into the
watery night; the faint echoes came tingling back, were captured and amplified, and became floating, blue-green flecks on
the screen.

Through long practice, Don could read their message with
effortless ease. Five hundred feet below, stretching out to the

limits of his submerged horizon, was the Scattering Layer—the blanket of life that covered half the world. The sunken meadow of the sea, it rose and fell with the passage of the Sun, hovering always at the edge of darkness. During the night it had floated nearly to the surface, but the dawn was now driving it back into the depths.

It was no obstacle to his sonar. Don could see clear through its tenuous substance to the ooze of the Pacific floor, over which he was driving high as a cloud above the land. But the ultimate depths were no concern of his; the flocks he guarded, and the enemies who ravaged them, belonged to the upper levels of the sea.

Don flicked the switch of the depth selector, and his sonar beam concentrated itself into the horizontal plane. The glimmering echoes from the abyss vanished, and he could see more clearly what lay around him here in the ocean's stratospheric heights. That glowing cloud two miles ahead was an unusually large school of fish; he wondered if Base knew about it, and made an entry in his log. There were some larger blips at the edge of the school—the carnivores pursuing the cattle, ensuring that the endlessly turning wheel of life and death would never lose momentum. But this conflict was no affair of Don's; he was after bigger game.

Sub 5 drove on toward the west, a steel needle swifter and more deadly than any other creature that roamed the seas. The tiny cabin, now lit only by the flicker of lights from the instrument board, pulsed with power as the spinning turbines thrust the water aside. Don glanced at the chart and noted that he was already halfway to the target area. He wondered if he should surface to have a look at the dead whale; from its injuries he might be able to learn something about its assailants. But that would mean further delay, and in a case like this time was vital.

The long-range receiver bleeped plaintively, and Don switched over to Transcribe. He had never learned to read code by ear, as some people could do, but the ribbon of paper emerging from the message slot saved him the trouble.

AIR PATROL REPORTS SCHOOL 50-100 WHALES HEADING 95 DEGREES GRID REF X186593 Y432011 STOP MOVING AT SPEED AFTER CHANGE OF COURSE STOP NO SIGN OF ORCAS BUT PRESUME THEY ARE IN VICINITY STOP RORQUAL

Don considered this last piece of deduction highly unlikely. If the orcas—the dreaded killer whales—had indeed been responsible, they would surely have been spotted by now as they surfaced to breathe. Moreover, they would never have let the patrolling plane scare them away from their victim, but would have remained feasting on it until they had gorged themselves.

One thing was in his favor; the frightened herd was now heading almost directly toward him. Don started to set the coordinates on the plotting grid, then saw that it was no longer necessary. At the extreme edge of his screen, a flotilla of faint stars had appeared. He altered course slightly, and drove head on to the approaching school.

Part of the message was certainly correct; the whales were moving at unusually high speed. At the rate they were traveling, he would be among them in five minutes. He cut the motors and felt the backward tug of the water bringing him swiftly to rest.

Don Burley, a knight in armor, sat in his tiny, dim-lit room a hundred feet below the bright Pacific waves, testing his weapons for the conflict that lay ahead. In these moments of poised suspense, before action began, he often pictured himself thus, though he would have admitted it to no one in the world. He felt, too, a kinship with all shepherds who had guarded their flocks back to the dawn of time. Not only was he Sir Lancelot, he was also David, among ancient Palestinian hills, alert for the mountain lions that would prey upon his father's sheep.

Yet far nearer in time, and far closer in spirit, were the men who had marshaled the great herds of cattle on the American plains, scarcely three lifetimes ago. They would have understood his work, though his implements would have been magic to them. The pattern was the same; only the scale of things had altered. It made no fundamental difference that the beasts Don herded weighed a hundred tons and browsed on the endless savannas of the sea.

The school was now less than two miles away, and Don checked his scanner's steady circling to concentrate on the sector ahead. The picture on the screen altered to a fan-shaped wedge as the sonar beam started to flick from side to side; now he could count every whale in the school, and could even make a good estimate of its size. With a practiced eye, he began to look for stragglers.

Don could never have explained what drew him at once toward those four echoes at the southern fringe of the school. It was true that they were a little apart from the rest, but others had fallen as far behind. There is some sixth sense that a man acquires when he has stared long enough into a sonar screen—some hunch which enables him to extract more from the moving flecks than he has any right to do. Without conscious thought, Don reached for the controls and started the turbines whirling once more.

The main body of the whale pack was now sweeping past him to the east. He had no fear of a collision; the great animals, even in their panic, could sense his presence as easily as he could detect theirs, and by similar means. He wondered if he should switch on his beacon. They might recognize its sound pattern, and it would reassure them. But the still unknown enemy might recognize it too, and would be warned.

The four echoes that had attracted his attention were almost at the center of the screen. He closed for an interception, and hunched low over the sonar display as if to drag from it by sheer willpower every scrap of information the scanner could give. There were two large echoes, some distance apart, and one was accompanied by a pair of smaller satellites. Don wondered if he was already too late; in his mind's eye he could picture the death struggle taking place in the water less than a mile ahead. Those two fainter blips would be the enemy, worrying a whale while its mate stood by in helpless terror, with no weapons of defense except its mighty flukes.

Now he was almost close enough for vision. The TV camera in Sub 5's prow strained through the gloom, but at first could show nothing but the fog of plankton. Then a vast, shadowy shape appeared in the center of the screen, with two smaller companions below it. Don was seeing, with the greater precision but hopelessly limited range of light, what the sonar scanners had already told him.

Almost at once he saw his incredible mistake: The two satellites were calves. It was the first time he had ever met a whale with twins, although multiple births were not uncommon. In normal circumstances, the sight would have fascinated him, but now it meant that he had jumped to the wrong conclusion and had lost precious minutes. He must begin the search again.

As a routine check, he swung the camera toward the fourth blip on the sonar screen—the echo he had assumed, from its size, to be another adult whale. It is strange how a preconceived idea can affect a man's understanding of what he sees; seconds passed before Don could interpret the picture before his eyes—before he knew that, after all, he had come to the right place.

"Jesus!" he said softly. "I didn't know they grew that big." It was a shark, the largest he had ever seen. Its details were still obscured, but there was only one genus it could belong to. The whale shark and the basking shark might be of comparable size, but they were harmless herbivores. This was the king of all selachians—*Carcharodon*—the Great White Shark. Don tried to recall the figures for the largest known specimen. In 1990, or thereabouts, a fifty-footer had been killed off New Zealand, but this one was half as big again.

These thoughts flashed through his mind in an instant, and in that same moment he saw that the great beast was already maneuvering for the kill. It was heading for one of the calves, and ignoring the frantic mother. Whether this was cowardice or common sense there was no way of telling; perhaps such distinctions were meaningless to the shark's tiny and utterly alien mind.

There was only one thing to do. It might spoil his chance of a quick kill, but the calf's life was more important. He punched the button of the siren, and a brief, mechanical scream erupted into the water around him.

Shark and whales were equally terrified by the deafening shriek. The shark jerked round in an impossibly tight curve, and Don was nearly jolted out of his seat as the autopilot snapped the sub onto a new course. Twisting and turning with an agility equal to that of any other sea creature of its size, Sub 5 began to close in upon the shark, its electronic brain automatically following the sonar echo and thus leaving Don free to concentrate on his armament. He needed that freedom; the next operation was going to be difficult unless he could hold a steady course for at least fifteen seconds. At a pinch he could use his tiny rocket torps to make a kill; had he been alone and faced with a pack of orcas, he would certainly have done so. But that was messy and brutal, and there was a neater way. He had always preferred the technique of the rapier to that of the hand grenade.

Now he was only fifty feet away, and closing rapidly. There might never be a better chance. He punched the launching stud.

From beneath the belly of the sub, something that looked like a sting ray hurtled forward. Don had checked the speed of his own craft; there was no need to come any closer now. The tiny, arrow-shaped hydrofoil, only a couple of feet across, could move far faster than his vessel and would close the gap in seconds. As it raced forward, it spun out the thin line of the control wire, like some underwater spider laying its thread. Along that wire passed the energy that powered the sting, and the signals that steered the missile to its goal. It responded so instantly to his orders that Don felt he was controlling some sensitive, high-spirited steed.

The shark saw the danger less than a second before impact. The resemblance of the sting to an ordinary ray confused it, as the designers had intended. Before the tiny brain could realize that no ray behaved like this, the missile had struck. The steel hypodermic, rammed forward by an exploding cartridge, drove through the shark's horny skin, and the great fish erupted in a frenzy of terror. Don backed rapidly away, for a blow from that tail would rattle him around like a pea in a can and might even damage the sub. There was nothing more for him to do, except to wait while the poison did its work.

The doomed killer was trying to arch its body so that it could snap at the poisoned dart. Don had now reeled the sting back into its slot amidships, pleased that he had been able to retrieve the missile undamaged. He watched with awe and a dispassionate pity as the great beast succumbed to its paralysis.

Its struggles were weakening. It was now swimming aimlessly back and forth, and once Don had to sidestep smartly to avoid a collision. As it lost control of buoyancy, the dying shark drifted up to the surface. Don did not bother to follow; that could wait until he had attended to more important business.

He found the cow and her two calves less than a mile away, and inspected them carefully. They were uninjured, so there was no need to call the vet in his highly specialized two-man sub which could handle any cetological crisis from a stomachache to a Caesarean.

The whales were no longer in the least alarmed, and a check on the sonar had shown that the entire school had ceased its panicky flight. He wondered if they already knew what had happened; much had been learned about their methods of communication, but much more was still a mystery.

"I hope you appreciate what I've done for you, old lady," he muttered. Then, reflecting that fifty tons of mother love was a slightly awe-inspiring sight, he blew his tanks and surfaced.

It was calm, so he opened the hatch and popped his head out of the tiny conning tower. The water was only inches below his chin, and from time to time a wave made a deter-mined effort to swamp him. There was little danger of this happening, for he fitted the hatch so closely that he was quite an effective plug.

Fifty feet away, a long gray mound, like an overturned boat, was rolling on the surface. Don looked at it thoughtfully, won-dering how much compressed air he'd better squirt into the corpse to prevent it sinking before one of the tenders could reach the spot. In a few minutes he would radio his report, but for the moment it was pleasant to drink the fresh Pacific breeze, to feel the open sky above his head, and to watch the Sun begin its long climb toward noon.

Don Burley was the happy warrior, resting after the one battle that man would always have to fight. He was holding at bay the specter of famine which had confronted all earlier ages, but which would never threaten the world again while the great plankton farms harvested their millions of tons of pro-tein, and the whale herds obeyed their new masters. Man had come back to the sea, his ancient home, after aeons of exile; until the oceans froze, he would never be hungry again. . . .

Yet that, Don knew, was the least of his satisfactions. Even if what he was doing had been of no practical value, he would still have wished to do it. Nothing else that life could offer matched the contentment and the calm sense of power that filled him when he set out on a mission such as this. Power? Yes, that was the right word. But it was not a power that would ever be abused; he felt too great a kinship with all the creatures who shared the seas with him—even those it was his duty to destroy.

To all appearances, Don was completely relaxed, yet had any one of the many dials and lights filling his field of view called for attention he would have been instantly alert. His mind was already back on the *Rorqual*, and he found it increasingly hard to keep his thoughts away from his overdue breakfast. In order to make the time pass more swiftly, he started mentally composing his report. Quite a few people, he knew, were going to be surprised by it. The engineers who maintained the invisible fences of sound and electricity which now divided the mighty Pacific into manageable portions would have to start looking for the break; the marine biologists who were so confident that sharks never attacked whales would have to think up excuses. Both enterprises, Don was quite sure, would be successfully carried out, and then everything would be under control again, until the sea contrived its next crisis.

But the crisis to which Don was now unwittingly returning was a man-made one, organized without any malice toward him at the highest official levels. It had begun with a suggestion in the Space Department, duly referred up to the World Secretariat. It had risen still higher until it reached the World Assembly itself, where it had come to the approving ears of the senators directly interested. Thus converted from a suggestion to an order, it had filtered down through the Secretariat to the World Food Organization, thence to the Marine Division, and finally to the Bureau of Whales. The whole process had taken the incredibly short time of four weeks.

Don, of course, knew nothing of this. As far as he was concerned, the complicated workings of global bureaucracy resolved themselves into the greeting his skipper gave him when he walked into the *Rorqual*'s mess for his belated breakfast.

"Morning, Don. Headquarters wants you to run over to Brisbane—they've got some job for you. Hope it doesn't take too long; you know how shorthanded we are."

"What kind of a job?" asked Don suspiciously. He remembered an unfortunate occasion when he had acted as a guide to a permanent undersecretary who had seemed to be a bit of a fool, and whom he had treated accordingly. It had later turned out that the P.U.—as might have been guessed from his position—was a very shrewd character indeed and knew exactly what Don was doing.

"They didn't tell me," said the skipper. "I'm not quite sure they know themselves. Give my love to Queensland, and keep away from the casinos on the Gold Coast."

"Much choice I have, on *my* pay," snorted Don. "Last time I went to Surfer's Paradise, I was lucky to get away with my shirt."

"But you brought back a couple of thousand on your first visit."

"Beginner's luck—it never happened again. I've lost it all since then, so I'll stop while I still break even. No more gambling for me."

"Is that a bet? Would you put five bucks on it?"

"Sure."

"Then pay over—you've already lost by accepting."

A spoonful of processed plankton hovered momentarily in mid-air while Don sought for a way out of the trap.

"Just try and get me to pay," he retorted. "You've got no witnesses, and I'm no gentleman." He hastily swallowed the last of his coffee, then pushed aside his chair and rose to go.

"Better start packing, I suppose. So long, Skipper—see you later."

The captain of the *Rorqual* watched his first warden sweep out of the room like a small hurricane. For a moment the sound of Don's passage echoed back along the ship's corridors; then comparative silence descended again.

The skipper started to head back to the bridge. "Look out, Brisbane," he muttered to himself; then he began to rearrange the watches and to compose a masterly memorandum to HQ asking how he was expected to run a ship when thirty per cent of her crew were permanently absent on leave or special duty. By the time he reached the bridge, the only thing that had stopped him from resigning was the fact that, try as he might, he couldn't think of a better job.

CHAPTER

Though he had been kept waiting only a few minutes, Walter Franklin was already prowling impatiently around the reception room. Swiftly he examined and dismissed the deep-sea photographs hanging on the walls; then he sat for a moment on the edge of the table, leafing through the pile of magazines, reviews, and reports which always accumulated in such places. The popular magazines he had already seen—for the last few weeks he had had little else to do but read—and few of the others looked interesting. Somebody, he supposed, had to go through these lavishly electroprinted food-production reports as part of their job; he wondered how they avoided being hypnotized by the endless columns of statistics. *Neptune*, the house organ of the Marine Division, seemed a little more promising, but as most of the personalities discussed in its columns were unknown to him he soon became bored with it. Even its fairly lowbrow articles were largely over his head, assuming a knowledge of technical terms he did not possess.

The receptionist was watching him—certainly noticing his impatience, perhaps analyzing the nervousness and insecurity that lay behind it. With a distinct effort, Franklin forced himself to sit down and to concentrate on yesterday's issue of the

Brisbane *Courier*. He had almost become interested in an editorial requiem on Australian cricket, inspired by the recent Test results, when the young lady who guarded the director's office smiled sweetly at him and said: "Would you please go in now, Mr. Franklin?"

He had expected to find the director alone, or perhaps accompanied by a secretary. The husky young man sitting in the other visitor's chair seemed out of place in this orderly office, and was staring at him with more curiosity than friendliness. Franklin stiffened at once; they had been discussing him, he knew, and automatically he went on the defensive.

Director Cary, who knew almost as much about human beings as he did about marine mammals, sensed the strain immediately and did his best to dispel it.

"Ah, there you are, Franklin," he said with slightly excessive heartiness. "I hope you've been enjoying your stay here. Have my people been taking care of you?"

Franklin was spared the trouble of answering this question, for the director gave him no time to reply.

"I want you to meet Don Burley," he continued. "Don's first warden on the *Rorqual*, and one of the best we've got. He's been assigned to look after you. Don, meet Walter Franklin."

They shook hands warily, weighing each other. Then Don's face broke into a reluctant smile. It was the smile of a man who had been given a job he didn't care for but who had decided to make the best of it.

"Pleased to meet you, Franklin," he said. "Welcome to the Mermaid Patrol."

Franklin tried to smile at the hoary joke, but his effort was not very successful. He knew that he should be friendly, and that these people were doing their best to help him. Yet the knowledge was that of the mind, not the heart; he could not relax and let himself meet them halfway. The fear of being pitied and the nagging suspicion that they had been talking about him behind his back, despite all the assurances he had been given, paralyzed his will for friendliness.

Don Burley sensed nothing of this. He only knew that the director's office was not the right place to get acquainted with a new colleague, and before Franklin was fully aware of what had happened he was out of the building, buffeting his way through the shirt-sleeved crowds in George Street, and being steered into a minute bar opposite the new post office.

The noise of the city subsided, though through the tinted glass walls Franklin could see the shadowy shapes of the pedestrians moving to and fro. It was pleasantly cool here after the torrid streets; whether or not Brisbane should be air-conditioned—and if so, who should have the resulting multimillion-dollar contract—was still being argued by the local politicians, and meanwhile the citizens sweltered every summer.

Don Burley waited until Franklin had drunk his first beer and called for replacements. There was a mystery about his new pupil, and as soon as possible he intended to solve it. Someone very high up in the division—perhaps even in the World Secretariat itself—must have organized this. A first warden was not called away from his duties to wet-nurse someone who was obviously too old to go through the normal training channels. At a guess he would say that Franklin was the wrong side of thirty; he had never heard of anyone that age getting this sort of special treatment before.

One thing was obvious about Franklin at once, and that only added to the mystery. He was a spaceman; you could tell them a mile away. That should make a good opening gambit. Then he remembered that the director had warned him, "Don't ask Franklin too many questions. I don't know what his background is, but we've been specifically told not to talk about it with him."

That might make sense, mused Don. Perhaps he was a space pilot who had been grounded after some inexcusable lapse, such as absent-mindedly arriving at Venus when he should have gone to Mars.

"Is this the first time," Don began cautiously, "that you've been to Australia?" It was not a very fortunate opening, and the conversation might have died there and then when Franklin replied: "I was born here."

Don, however, was not the sort of person who was easily abashed. He merely laughed and said, half-apologetically, "Nobody ever tells me anything, so I usually find out the hard way. I was born on the other side of the world—over in Ireland—but since I've been attached to the Pacific branch of the bureau I've more or less adopted Australia as a second home. Not that I spend much time ashore! On this job you're at sea eighty per cent of the time. A lot of people don't like that, you know."

"It would suit me," said Franklin, but left the remark hanging in the air. Burley began to feel exasperated—it was such hard work getting anything out of this fellow. The prospect of working with him for the next few weeks began to look very uninviting, and Don wondered what he had done to deserve such a fate. However, he struggled on manfully.

"The superintendent tells me that you've a good scientific and engineering background, so I can assume that you'll know most of the things that our people spend the first year learning. Have they filled you in on the administrative background?"

"They've given me a lot of facts and figures under hypnosis, so I could lecture you for a couple of hours on the Marine Division—its history, organization, and current projects, with particular reference to the Bureau of Whales. But it doesn't *mean* anything to me at present."

Now we seem to be getting somewhere, Don told himself. The fellow can talk after all. A couple more beers, and he might even be human.

"That's the trouble with hypnotic training," agreed Don.

"They can pump the information into you until it comes out of your ears, but you're never quite sure how much you really know. And they can't teach you manual skills, or train you to have the right reactions in emergencies. There's only one way of learning anything properly—and that's by actually doing the job."

He paused, momentarily distracted by a shapely silhouette parading on the other side of the translucent wall. Franklin noticed the direction of his gaze, and his features relaxed into a slight smile. For the first time the tension lifted, and Don began to feel that there was some hope of establishing contact with the enigma who was now his responsibility.

With a beery forefinger, Don started to trace maps on the plastic table top.

"This is the setup," he began. "Our main training center for shallow-water operations is here in the Capricorn Group, about four hundred miles north of Brisbane and forty miles out from the coast. The South Pacific fence starts here, and runs on east to New Caledonia and Fiji. When the whales migrate north from the polar feeding grounds to have their calves in the tropics, they're compelled to pass through the gaps we've left here. The most important of these gates, from our point of view, is the one right here off the Queensland coast, at the southern entrance to the Great Barrier Reef. The reef provides a kind of natural channel, averaging about fifty miles wide, almost up to the equator. Once we've herded the whales into it, we can keep them pretty well under control. It didn't take much doing; many of them used to come this way long before we appeared on the scene. By now the rest have been so well conditioned that even if we switched off the fence it would probably make no difference to their migratory pattern."

"By the way," interjected Franklin, "is the fence purely electrical?"

"Oh no. Electric fields control fish pretty well but don't work satisfactorily on mammals like whales. The fence is

largely ultrasonic—a curtain of sound from a chain of generators half a mile below the surface. We can get fine control at
the gates by broadcasting specific orders; you can set a whole
herd stampeding in any direction you wish by playing back a
recording of a whale in distress. But it's not very often we have
to do anything drastic like that; as I said, nowadays they're too
well trained."

"I can appreciate that," said Franklin. "In fact, I heard
somewhere that the fence was more for keeping other animals
out than for keeping the whales in."

"That's partly true, though we'd still need some kind of
control for rounding up our herds at census or slaughtering.
Even so, the fence isn't perfect. There are weak spots where
generator fields overlap, and sometimes we have to switch off
sections to allow normal fish migration. Then, the really big
sharks, or the killer whales, can get through and play hell. The
killers are our worst problem; they attack the whales when they
are feeding in the Antarctic, and often the herds suffer ten per
cent losses. No one will be happy until the killers are wiped
out, but no one can think of an economical way of doing it.
We can't patrol the entire ice pack with subs, though when I've
seen what a killer can do to a whale I've often wished we
could."

There was real feeling—almost passion—in Burley's voice,
and Franklin looked at the warden with surprise. The "whale-
boys," as they had been inevitably christened by a nostalgically
minded public in search of heroes, were not supposed to be
much inclined either to thought or emotions. Though Franklin
knew perfectly well that the tough, uncomplicated characters
who stalked tight lipped through the pages of contemporary
submarine sagas had very little connection with reality, it was
hard to escape from the popular clichés. Don Burley, it was
true, was far from tight lipped, but in most other respects he
seemed to fit the standard specification very well.

Franklin wondered how he was going to get on with his

new mentor—indeed, with his new job. He still felt no enthusiasm for it; whether that would come, only time would show. It was obviously full of interesting and even fascinating problems and possibilities, and if it would occupy his mind and give him scope for his talents, that was as much as he could hope for. The long nightmare of the last year had destroyed, with so much else, his zest for life—the capacity he had once possessed for throwing himself heart and soul into some project.

It was difficult to believe that he could ever recapture the enthusiasm that had once taken him so far along paths he could never tread again. As he glanced at Don, who was still talking with the fluent lucidity of a man who knows and loves his job, Franklin felt a sudden and disturbing sense of guilt. Was it fair to Burley to take him away from his work and to turn him, whether he knew it or not, into a cross between a nursemaid and kindergarten teacher? Had Franklin realized that very similar thoughts had already crossed Burley's mind, his sympathy would have been quenched at once.

"Time we caught the shuttle to the airport," said Don, looking at his watch and hastily draining his beer. "The morning flight leaves in thirty minutes. I hope all your stuff's already been sent on."

"The hotel said they'd take care of it."

"Well, we can check at the airport. Let's go."

Half an hour later Franklin had a chance to relax again. It was typical of Burley, he soon discovered, to take things easily until the last possible moment and then to explode in a burst of activity. This burst carried them from the quiet bar to the even more efficiently silenced plane. As they took their seats, there was a brief incident that was to puzzle Don a good deal in the weeks that lay ahead.

"You take the window seat," he said. "I've flown this way dozens of times."

He took Franklin's refusal as ordinary politeness, and

started to insist. Not until Franklin had turned down the offer several times, with increasing determination and even signs of annoyance, did Burley realize that his companion's behavior had nothing to do with common courtesy. It seemed incredible, but Don could have sworn that the other was scared stiff. What sort of man, he wondered blankly, would be terrified of taking a window seat in an ordinary aircraft? All his gloomy premonitions about his new assignment, which had been partly dispelled during their earlier conversation, came crowding back with renewed vigor.

The city and the sunburned coast dropped below as the lifting jets carried them effortlessly up into the sky. Franklin was reading the paper with a fierce concentration that did not deceive Burley for a moment. He decided to wait for a while, and apply some more tests later in the flight.

The Glasshouse Mountains—those strangely shaped fangs jutting from the eroded plain—swept swiftly beneath. Then came the little coastal towns, through which the wealth of the immense farm lands of the interior had once passed to the world in the days before agriculture went to sea. And then— only minutes, it seemed, after take-off—the first islands of the Great Barrier Reef appeared like deeper shadows in the blue horizon mists.

The Sun was shining almost straight into his eyes, but Don's memory could fill in the details which were lost in the glare from the burning waters. He could see the low, green islands surrounded by their narrow borders of sand and their immensely greater fringes of barely submerged coral. Against each island's private reef the waves of the Pacific would be marching forever, so that for a thousand miles into the north snowy crescents of foam would break the surface of the sea.

A century ago—fifty years, even—scarcely a dozen of these hundreds of islands had been inhabited. Now, with the aid of universal air transport, together with cheap power and water-purification plants, both the state and the private citizen had invaded the ancient solitude of the reef. A few fortunate individuals, by means that had never been made perfectly clear, had managed to acquire some of the smaller islands as their personal property. The entertainment and vacation industry had taken over others, and had not always improved on Nature's handiwork. But the greatest landowner in the reef was undoubtedly the World Food Organization, with its complicated hierarchy of fisheries, marine farms, and research departments, the full extent of which, it was widely believed, no merely human brain could ever comprehend.

"We're nearly there," said Burley. "That's Lady Musgrave Island we've just passed—main generators for the western end of the fence. Capricorn Group under us now—Masthead, One Tree, North-West, Wilson—and Heron in the middle, with all those buildings on it. The big tower is Administration—the aquarium's by that pool—and look, you can see a couple of subs tied up at that long jetty leading out to the edge of the reef."

As he spoke, Don watched Franklin out of the corner of his eye. The other had leaned toward the window as if following his companion's running commentary, yet Burley could swear that he was not looking at the panorama of reefs and islands spread out below. His face was tense and strained; there was an indrawn, hooded expression in his eyes as if he was forcing himself to see nothing.

With a mingling of pity and contempt, Don understood the symptoms if not their cause. Franklin was terrified of heights; so much, then, for the theory that he was a spaceman. Then what was he? Whatever the answer, he hardly seemed the sort of person with whom one would wish to share the cramped quarters of a two-man training sub. . . .

The plane's shock absorbers touched down on the rectangle of scorched and flattened coral that was the Heron Island landing platform. As he stepped out into the sunlight, blinking in the sudden glare, Franklin seemed to make an abrupt recovery.

Don had seen seasick passengers undergo equally swift transformations on their return to dry land. If Franklin is no better as a sailor than an airman, he thought, this crazy assignment won't last more than a couple of days and I'll be able to get back to work. Not that Don was in a great rush to return immediately; Heron Island was a pleasant place where you could enjoy yourself if you knew how to deal with the red tape that always entangled headquarters establishments.

A light truck whisked them and their belongings along a road beneath an avenue of Pisonia trees whose heavily leafed branches blocked all direct sunlight. The road was less than a quarter of a mile long, but it spanned the little island from the jetties and maintenance plants on the west to the administration buildings on the east. The two halves of the island were partly insulated from each other by a narrow belt of jungle which had been carefully preserved in its virgin state and which, Don remembered sentimentally, was full of interesting tracks and secluded clearings.

Administration was expecting Mr. Franklin, and had made all the necessary arrangements for him. He had been placed in a kind of privileged limbo, one stage below the permanent staff like Burley, but several stages above the ordinary trainees under instruction. Surprisingly, he had a room of his own—something that even senior members of the bureau could not always expect when they visited the island. This was a great relief to Don, who had been afraid he might have to share quarters with his mysterious charge. Quite apart from any other factors, that would have interfered badly with certain romantic plans of his own.

He saw Franklin to his small but attractive room on the second floor of the training wing, looking out across the miles of coral which stretched eastward all the way to the horizon. In the courtyard below, a group of trainees, relaxing between classes, was chatting with a second warden instructor whom Don recognized from earlier visits but could not name. It was a pleasant feeling, he mused, going back to school when you already knew all the answers.

"You should be comfortable here," he said to Franklin, who was busy unpacking his baggage. "Quite a view, isn't it?"

Such poetic ecstasies were normally foreign to Don's nature, but he could not resist the temptation of seeing how Franklin would react to the leagues of coral-dappled ocean that lay before him. Rather to his disappointment, the reaction was quite conventional; presumably Franklin was not worried by a mere thirty feet of height. He looked out of the window, taking his time and obviously admiring the vista of blues and greens which led the eye out into the endless waters of the Pacific.

Serve you right, Don told himself—it's not fair to tease the poor devil. Whatever he's got, it can't be fun to live with.

"I'll leave you to get settled in," said Don, backing out through the door. "Lunch will be coming up in half an hour over at the mess—that building we passed on the way in. See you there."

Franklin nodded absently as he sorted through his belongings and piled shirts and underclothes on the bed. He wanted to be left alone while he adjusted himself to the new life which, with no particular enthusiasm, he had now accepted as his own.

Burley had been gone for less than ten minutes when there was a knock on the door and a quiet voice said, "Can I come in?"

"Who's there?" asked Franklin, as he tidied up the debris and made his room look presentable.

"Dr. Myers."

The name meant nothing to Franklin, but his face twisted into a wry smile as he thought how appropriate it was that his very first visitor should be a doctor. What kind of a doctor, he thought he could guess.

Myers was a stocky, pleasantly ugly man in his early forties, with a disconcertingly direct gaze which seemed somewhat at variance with his friendly, affable manner.

"Sorry to butt in on you when you've only just arrived," he said apologetically. "I had to do it now because I'm flying out to New Caledonia this afternoon and won't be back for a week. Professor Stevens asked me to look you up and give you his best wishes. If there's anything you want, just ring my office and we'll try to fix it for you."

Franklin admired the skillful way in which Myers had avoided all the obvious dangers. He did *not* say—true though it undoubtedly was—"I've discussed your case with Professor Stevens." Nor did he offer direct help; he managed to convey the assumption that Franklin wouldn't need it and was now quite capable of looking after himself.

"I appreciate that," said Franklin sincerely. He felt he was going to like Dr. Myers, and made up his mind not to resent the surveillance he would undoubtedly be getting. "Tell me," he added, "just what do the people here know about me?"

"Nothing at all, except that you are to be helped to qualify as a warden as quickly as possible. This isn't the first time this sort of thing has happened, you know—there have been high-pressure conversion courses before. Still, it's inevitable that there will be a good deal of curiosity about you; that may be your biggest problem."

"Burley is dying of curiosity already."

"Mind if I give you some advice?"

"Of course not—go ahead."

"You'll be working with Don continually. It's only fair to him, as well as to yourself, to confide in him when you feel you can do so. I'm sure you'll find him quite understanding. Or if you prefer, I'll do the explaining."

Franklin shook his head, not trusting himself to speak. It was not a matter of logic, for he knew that Myers was talking sense. Sooner or later it would all have to come out, and he might be making matters worse by postponing the inevitable.

Yet his hold upon sanity and self-respect was still so precarious that he could not face the prospect of working with men who knew his secret, however sympathetic they might be.

"Very well. The choice is yours and we'll respect it. Good luck—and let's hope all our contacts will be purely social."

Long after Myers had gone, Franklin sat on the edge of the bed, staring out across the sea which would be his new domain. He would need the luck that the other had wished him, yet he was beginning to feel a renewed interest in life. It was not merely that people were anxious to help him; he had received more than enough help in the last few months. At last he was beginning to see how he could help himself, and so discover a purpose for his existence.

Presently he jolted himself out of his daydream and looked at his watch. He was already ten minutes late for lunch, and that was a bad start for his new life. He thought of Don Burley waiting impatiently in the mess and wondering what had happened to him.

"Coming, teacher," he said, as he put on his jacket and started out of the room. It was the first time he had made a joke with himself for longer than he could remember.

CHAPTER

When Franklin first saw Indra Langenburg she was covered with blood up to her elbows and was busily hacking away at the entrails of a ten-foot tiger shark she had just disemboweled. The huge beast was lying, its pale belly upturned to the Sun, on the sandy beach where Franklin took his morning promenade. A thick chain still led to the hook in its mouth; it had obviously been caught during the night and then left behind by the falling tide.

Franklin stood for a moment looking at the unusual combination of attractive girl and dead monster, then said thoughtfully: "You know, this is not the sort of thing I like to see before breakfast. Exactly what are you doing?"

A brown, oval face with very serious eyes looked up at him. The foot-long, razor-sharp knife that was creating such havoc continued to slice expertly through gristle and guts.

"I'm writing a thesis," said a voice as serious as the eyes, "on the vitamin content of shark liver. It means catching a lot of sharks; this is my third this week. Would you like some teeth? I've got plenty, and they make nice souvenirs."

She walked to the head of the beast and inserted her knife in its gaping jaws, which had been propped apart by a block of wood. A quick jerk of her wrist, and an endless necklace of deadly ivory triangles, like a band saw made of bone, started to emerge from the shark's mouth.

"No thanks," said Franklin hastily, hoping she would not be offended. "Please don't let me interrupt your work."

He guessed that she was barely twenty, and was not surprised at meeting an unfamiliar girl on the little island, because the scientists at the Research Station did not have much contact with the administrative and training staff.

"You're new here, aren't you?" said the bloodstained biologist, sloshing a huge lump of liver into a bucket with every sign of satisfaction. "I didn't see you at the last HQ dance."

Franklin felt quite cheered by the inquiry. It was so pleasant to meet someone who knew nothing about him, and had not been speculating about his presence here. He felt he could talk freely and without restraint for the first time since landing on Heron Island.

"Yes—I've just come for a special training course. How long have you been here?"

He was making pointless conversation just for the pleasure of the company, and doubtless she knew it.

"Oh, about a month," she said carelessly. There was another slimy, squelching noise from the bucket, which was now nearly full. "I'm on leave here from the University of Miami."

"You're American, then?" Franklin asked. The girl answered solemnly: "No; my ancestors were Dutch, Burmese, and Scottish in about equal proportions. Just to make things a little more complicated, I was born in Japan."

Franklin wondered if she was making fun of him, but there was no trace of guile in her expression. She seemed a really nice kid, he thought, but he couldn't stay here talking all day. He had only forty minutes for breakfast, and his morning class in submarine navigation started at nine.

He thought no more of the encounter, for he was continually meeting new faces as his circles of acquaintances steadily expanded. The high-pressure course he was taking gave him no time for much social life, and for that he was grateful. His mind was fully occupied once more; it had taken up the load with a smoothness that both surprised and gratified him. Perhaps those who had sent him here knew what they were doing better than he sometimes supposed.

All the empirical knowledge—the statistics, the factual data, the ins and outs of administration—had been more or less painlessly pumped into Franklin while he was under mild hypnosis. Prolonged question periods, where he was quizzed by a tape recorder that later filled in the right answers, then confirmed that the information had really taken and had not, as sometimes happened, shot straight through the mind leaving no permanent impression.

Don Burley had nothing to do with this side of Franklin's training, but, rather to his disgust, had no chance of relaxing when Franklin was being looked after elsewhere. The chief instructor had gleefully seized this opportunity of getting Don back into his clutches, and had "suggested," with great tact and charm, that when his other duties permitted Don might like to lecture to the three courses now under training on the island. Outranked and outmaneuvered, Don had no alternative but to acquiesce with as good grace as possible. This assignment, it seemed, was not going to be the holiday he had hoped.

In one respect, however, his worst fears had not materialized. Franklin was not at all hard to get on with, as long as one kept completely away from personalities. He was very intelligent and had clearly had a technical training that in some ways was much better than Don's own. It was seldom necessary to explain anything to him more than once and long before they had reached the stage of trying him out on the synthetic trainers, Don could see that his pupil had the makings of a good pilot. He was skillful with his hands, reacted quickly and accurately, and had that indefinable poise which distinguishes the first-rate pilot from the merely competent one.

Yet Don knew that knowledge and skill were not in themselves sufficient. Something else was also needed, and there was no way yet of telling if Franklin possessed it. Not until Don had watched his reactions as he sank down into the depths of the sea would he know whether all this effort was to be of any use.

There was so much that Franklin had to learn that it seemed impossible that anyone could absorb it all in two months, as the program insisted. Don himself had taken the normal six months, and he somewhat resented the assumption that anyone else could do it in a third of the time, even with the special coaching he was giving. Why, the mechanical side of the job alone—the layout and design of the various classes of subs—took at least two months to learn, even with the best of instructional aids. Yet at the same time he had to teach Franklin the principles of seamanship and underwater navigation, basic oceanography, submarine signaling and communication, and a substantial amount of ichthyology, marine psychology, and, of course, cetology. So far Franklin had never even seen a whale, dead or alive, and that first encounter was something that Don looked forward to witnessing. At such a moment one could learn all that one needed to know about a man's fitness for this job.

They had done two weeks' hard work together before Don first took Franklin under water. By this time they had established a curious relationship which was at once friendly and remote. Though they had long since ceased to call each other by their surnames. "Don" and "Walt" was as far as their intimacy went. Burley still knew absolutely nothing about Franklin's past, though he had evolved a good many theories. The one which he most favored was that his pupil was an extremely talented criminal being rehabilitated after total therapy. He wondered if Franklin was a murderer, which was a stimulating thought, and half hoped that this exciting hypothesis was true.

Franklin no longer showed any of the obvious peculiarities

he had revealed on their first meeting, though he was undoubtedly more nervous and highly strung than the average. Since this was the case with many of the best wardens, it did not worry Don. Even his curiosity about Franklin's past had somewhat lessened, for he was far too busy to bother about it. He had learned to be patient when there was no alternative, and he did not doubt that sooner or later he would discover the whole story. Once or twice, he was almost certain, Franklin had been on the verge of some revelation, but then had drawn back. Each time Don had pretended that nothing had happened, and they had resumed their old, impersonal relationship.

It was a clear morning, with only a slow swell moving across the face of the sea, as they walked along the narrow jetty that stretched from the western end of the island out to the edge of the reef. The tide was in, but though the reef flat was completely submerged the great plateau of coral was nowhere more than five or six feet below the surface, and its every detail was clearly visible through the crystal water. Neither Franklin nor Burley spared more than a few glances for the natural aquarium above which they were walking. It was too familiar to them both, and they knew that the real beauty and wonder of the reef lay in the deeper waters farther out to sea.

Two hundred yards out from the island, the coral landscape suddenly dropped off into the depths, but the jetty continued upon taller stilts until it ended in a small group of sheds and offices. A valiant, and fairly successful, attempt had been made to avoid the grime and chaos usually inseparable from dockyards and piers; even the cranes had been designed so that they would not offend the eye. One of the terms under which the Queensland government had reluctantly leased the Capricorn Group to the World Food Organization was that the beauty of the islands would not be jeopardized. On the whole, this part of the agreement had been well kept.

"I've ordered two torpedoes from the garage," said Burley as they walked down the flight of stairs at the end of the jetty and passed through the double doors of a large air lock. Franklin's ears gave the disconcerting internal "click" as they adjusted themselves to the increased pressure; he guessed that he was now about twenty feet below the water line. Around him was a brightly lighted chamber crammed with various types of underwater equipment, from simple lungs to elaborate propulsion devices. The two torpedoes that Don had requisitioned were lying in their cradles on a sloping ramp leading down into the still water at the far end of the chamber. They were painted the bright yellow reserved for training equipment, and Don looked at them with some distaste.

"It's a couple of years since I used one of these things," he said to Franklin. "You'll probably be better at it than I am. When I get myself wet, I like to be under my own power."

They stripped to swim trunks and pull-overs, then fastened on the harness of their breathing equipment. Don picked up one of the small but surprisingly heavy plastic cylinders and handed it to Franklin.

"These are the high-pressure jobs that I told you about," he said. "They're pumped to a thousand atmospheres, so the air in them is denser than water. Hence these buoyancy tanks at either end to keep them in neutral. The automatic adjustment is pretty good; as you use up your air the tanks slowly flood so that the cylinder stays just about weightless. Otherwise you'd come up to the surface like a cork whether you wanted to or not."

He looked at the pressure gauges on the tanks and gave a satisfied nod.

"They're nearly half charged," he said. "That's far more than we need. You can stay down for a day on one of these tanks when it's really pumped up, and we won't be gone more than an hour."

They adjusted the new, full-face masks that had already

been checked for leaks and comfortable fitting. These would be as much their personal property as their toothbrushes while they were on the station, for no two people's faces were exactly the same shape, and even the slightest leak could be disastrous.

When they had checked the air supply and the short-range underwater radio sets, they lay almost flat along the slim torpedoes, heads down behind the low, transparent shields which would protect them from the rush of water sweeping past at speeds of up to thirty knots. Franklin settled his feet comfortably in the stirrups, feeling for the throttle and jet reversal controls with his toes. The little joy stick which allowed him to "fly" the torpedo like a plane was just in front of his face, in the center of the instrument board. Apart from a few switches, the compass, and the meters giving speed, depth, and battery charge, there were no other controls.

Don gave Franklin his final instructions, ending with the words: "Keep about twenty feet away on my right, so that I can see you all the time. *If* anything goes wrong and you do have to dump the torp, for heaven's sake remember to cut the motor. We don't want it charging all over the reef. All set?"

"Yes—I'm ready," Franklin answered into his little microphone.

"Right—here we go."

The torpedoes slid easily down the ramps, and the water rose above their heads. This was no new experience to Franklin; like most other people in the world, he had occasionally tried his hand at underwater swimming and had sometimes used a lung just to see what it was like. He felt nothing but a pleasant sense of anticipation as the little turbine started to whir beneath him and the walls of the submerged chamber slid slowly past.

The light strengthened around them as they emerged into the open and pulled away from the piles of the jetty. Visibility was not very good—thirty feet at the most—but it would improve as they came to deeper water. Don swung his torpedo at right angles to the edge of the reef and headed out to sea at a leisurely five knots.

"The biggest danger with these toys," said Don's voice from the tiny loudspeaker by Franklin's ear, "is going too fast and running into something. It takes a lot of experience to judge underwater visibility. See what I mean?"

He banked steeply to avoid a towering mass of coral which had suddenly appeared ahead of them. If the demonstration had been planned, thought Franklin, Don had timed it beautifully. As the living mountain swept past, not more than ten feet away, he caught a glimpse of a myriad brilliantly colored fish staring at him with apparent unconcern. By this time, he assumed, they must be so used to torpedoes and subs that they were quite unexcited by them. And since this entire area was rigidly protected, they had no reason to fear man.

A few minutes at cruising speed brought them out into the open water of the channel between the island and the adjacent reefs. Now they had room to maneuver, and Franklin followed his mentor in a series of rolls and loops and great submarine switchbacks that soon had him hopelessly lost. Sometimes they shot down to the seabed, a hundred feet below, then broke surface like flying fish to check their position. All the time Don kept up a running commentary, interspersed with questions designed to see how Franklin was reacting to the ride.

It was one of the most exhilarating experiences he had ever known. The water was much clearer out here in the channel, and one could see for almost a hundred feet. Once they ran into a great school of bonitos, which formed an inquisitive escort until Don put on speed and left them behind. They saw no sharks, as Franklin had half expected, and he commented to Don on their absence.

"You won't see many while you're riding a torp," the other replied. "The noise of the jet scares them. If you want to meet the local sharks, you'll have to go swimming in the old-fashioned way—or cut your motor and wait until they come to look at you."

A dark mass was looming indistinctly from the seabed, and they reduced speed to a gentle drift as they approached a little range of coral hills, twenty or thirty feet high.

"An old friend of mine lives around here," said Don. "I wonder if he's home? It's been about four years since I saw him last, but that won't seem much to him. He's been around for a couple of centuries."

They were now skirting the edge of a huge green-clad mushroom of coral, and Franklin peered into the shadows beneath it. There were a few large boulders there, and a pair of elegant angelfish which almost disappeared when they turned edge on to him. But he could see nothing else to justify Burley's interest.

It was very unsettling when one of the boulders began to move, fortunately not in his direction. The biggest fish he had ever seen—it was almost as long as the torpedo, and very much fatter—was staring at him with great bulbous eyes. Suddenly it opened its mouth in a menacing yawn, and Franklin felt like Jonah at the big moment of his career. He had a glimpse of huge, blubbery lips enclosing surprisingly tiny teeth; then the great jaws snapped shut again and he could almost feel the rush of displaced water.

Don seemed delighted at the encounter, which had obviously brought back memories of his own days as a trainee here.

"Well, it's nice to see old Slobberchops again! Isn't he a beauty? Seven hundred and fifty pounds if he's an ounce. We've been able to identify him on photos taken as far back as eighty years ago, and he wasn't much smaller then. It's a wonder he escaped the spear fishers before this area was made a reservation."

"I should think," said Franklin, "that it was a wonder the spear fishers escaped him."

"Oh, he's not really dangerous. Groupers only swallow

things they can get down whole—those silly little teeth aren't much good for biting. And a full-sized man would be a trifle too much for him. Give him another century for that."

They left the giant grouper still patrolling the entrance to its cave, and continued on along the edge of the reef. For the next ten minutes they saw nothing of interest except a large ray, which was lying on the bottom and took off with an agitated flapping of its wings as soon as they approached. As it flew away into the distance, it seemed an uncannily accurate replica of the big delta-winged aircraft which had ruled the air for a short while, sixty or seventy years ago. It was strange, thought Franklin, how Nature had anticipated so many of man's inventions—for example, the precise shape of the vehicle on which he was riding, and even the jet principle by which it was propelled.

"I'm going to circle right around the reef," said Don. "It will take us about forty minutes to get home. Are you feeling O.K.?"

"I'm fine."

"No ear trouble?"

"My left ear bothered me a bit at first, but it seems to have popped now."

"Right—let's go. Follow just above and behind me, so I can see you in my rearview mirror. I was always afraid of running into you when you were on my right."

In the new formation, they sped on toward the east at a steady ten knots, following the irregular line of the reef. Don was well satisfied with the trip; Franklin had seemed perfectly at home under water—though one could never be sure of this until one had seen how he faced an emergency. That would be part of the next lesson; Franklin did not know it yet, but an emergency had been arranged.

CHAPTER

It was hard to distinguish one day from another on the island. The weather had settled in for a period of prolonged calm, and the Sun rose and set in a cloudless sky. But there was no danger of monotony, for there was far too much to learn and do.

Slowly, as his mind absorbed new knowledge and skills, Franklin was escaping from whatever nightmare must have engulfed him in the past. He was, Don sometimes thought, like an overtightened spring that was now unwinding. It was true that he still showed occasional signs of nervousness and impatience when there was no obvious cause for them, and once or twice there had been flare-ups that had caused brief interruptions in the training program. One of these had been partly Don's fault, and the memory of it still left him annoyed with himself.

He had not been too bright that morning, owing to a late night with the boys who had just completed their course and were now full-fledged third wardens (probationary), very proud of the silver dolphins on their tunics. It would not be true to say that he had a hangover, but all his mental processes were extremely sluggish, and as bad luck would have it they were dealing with a subtle point in underwater acoustics. Even at the best of times, Don would have passed it by somewhat hastily, with a lame: "I've never been into the math, but it seems that if you take the compressibility and temperature curves this is what happens. . . ."

This worked on most pupils, but it failed to work on Franklin, who had an annoying fondness for going into unnecessary details. He began to draw curves and to differentiate equations while Don, anxious to conceal his ignorance, fumed in the background. It was soon obvious that Franklin had bitten off more than he could chew, and he appealed to his tutor for assistance. Don, both stupid and stubborn that morning, would not admit frankly that he didn't know, with the result that he gave the impression of refusing to cooperate. In no time at all, Franklin lost his temper and walked out in a huff, leaving Don to wander to the dispensary. He was not pleased to find that the entire stock of "morning-after" pills had already been consumed by the departing class.

Fortunately, such incidents were rare, for the two men had grown to respect each other's abilities and to make those allowances that are essential in every partnership. With the rest of the staff, and with the trainees, however, Franklin was not popular. This was partly because he avoided close contacts, which in the little world of the island gave him a reputation for being standoffish. The trainees also resented his special privileges—particularly the fact that he had a room of his own. And the staff, while grumbling mildly at the extra work he involved, were also annoyed because they could discover so little about him. Don had several times found himself, rather to his surprise, defending Franklin against the criticisms of his colleagues.

"He's not a bad chap when you get to know him," he had said. "If he doesn't want to talk about his past, that's his affair. The fact that a lot of people way up in the administration must be backing him is good enough for me. Besides, when I've fin-

ished with him he'll be a better warden than half the people in
this room."

There were snorts of disbelief at this statement, and someone asked:

"Have you tried any tricks on him yet?"

"No, but I'm going to soon. I've thought up a nice one.
Will let you know how he makes out."

"Five to one he panics."

"I'll take that. Start saving up your money."

Franklin knew nothing of his financial responsibilities
when he and Don left the garage on their second torpedo ride,
nor had he reason to suspect the entertainment that had been
planned for him. This time they headed south as soon as they
had cleared the jetty, cruising about thirty feet below the surface. In a few minutes they had passed the narrow channel
blasted through the reef so that small ships could get in to the
Research Station, and they circled once round the observation
chamber from which the scientists could watch the inhabitants
of the seabed in comfort. There was no one inside at the moment to look out at them through the thick plate-glass windows; quite unexpectedly, Franklin found himself wondering
what the little shark fancier was doing today.

"We'll head over to the Wistari Reef," said Don. "I want to
give you some practice in navigation."

Don's torpedo swung round to the west as he set a new
course, out into the deeper water. Visibility was not good
today—less than thirty feet—and it was difficult to keep him
in sight. Presently he halted and began to orbit slowly as he
gave Franklin his instructions.

"I want you to hold course 250 for one minute at twenty
knots, then 010 for the same time and speed. I'll meet you
there. Got it?"

Franklin repeated the instructions and they checked the
synchronization of their watches. It was rather obvious what
Don was doing; he had given his pupil two sides of an equi-

lateral triangle to follow, and would doubtless proceed slowly along the third to make the appointment.

Carefully setting his course, Franklin pressed down the throttle and felt the surge of power as the torpedo leaped forward into the blue haze. The steady rush of water against his partly exposed legs was almost the only sensation of speed; without the shield, he would have been swept away in a moment. From time to time he caught a glimpse of the seabed—drab and featureless here in the channel between the great reefs—and once he overtook a school of surprised batfish which scattered in dismay at his approach.

For the first time, Franklin suddenly realized, he was alone beneath the sea, totally surrounded by the element which would be his new domain. It supported and protected him—yet it would kill him in two or three minutes at the most if he made a mistake or if his equipment failed. That knowledge did not disturb him; it had little weight against the increasing confidence and sense of mastery he was acquiring day by day. He now knew and understood the challenge of the sea, and it was a challenge he wished to meet. With a lifting of the heart, he realized that he once more had a goal in life.

The first minute was up, and he reduced speed to four knots with the reverse jet. He had now covered a third of a mile and it was time to start on the second leg of the triangle, to make his rendezvous with Don.

The moment he swung the little joy stick to starboard, he knew that something was wrong. The torpedo was wallowing like a pig, completely out of control. He cut speed to zero, and with all dynamic forces gone the vessel began to sink very slowly to the bottom.

Franklin lay motionless along the back of his recalcitrant steed, trying to analyze the situation. He was not so much alarmed as annoyed that his navigational exercise had been spoiled. It was no good calling Don, who would now be out of range—these little radio sets could not establish contact through more than a couple of hundred yards of water. What was the best thing to do?

Swiftly, his mind outlined alternative plans of action, and dismissed most of them at once. There was nothing he could do to repair the torp, for all the controls were sealed and, in any event, he had no tools. Since both rudder and elevator were out of action, the trouble was quite fundamental, and Franklin was unable to see how such a simultaneous breakdown could have happened.

He was now about fifty feet down, and gaining speed as he dropped to the bottom. The flat, sandy seabed was just coming into sight, and for a moment Franklin had to fight the automatic impulse to press the button which would blow the torpedo's tanks and take him up to the surface. That would be the worst thing to do, natural though it was to seek air and Sun when anything went wrong underwater. Once on the bottom, he could take his time to think matters out, whereas if he surfaced the current might sweep him miles away. It was true that the station would soon pick up his radio calls once he was above water—but he wanted to extricate himself from this predicament without any outside help.

The torp grounded, throwing up a cloud of sand which soon drifted away in the slight current. A small grouper appeared from nowhere, staring at the intruder with its characteristic popeyed expression. Franklin had no time to bother with spectators, but climbed carefully off his vehicle and pulled himself to the stern. Without flippers, he had little mobility under water, but fortunately there were sufficient handholds for him to move along the torpedo without difficulty.

As Franklin had feared—but was still unable to explain— the rudder and elevator were flopping around uselessly. There was no resistance when he moved the little vanes by hand, and he wondered if there was any way in which he could fix external control lines and steer the torpedo manually. He had some nylon line, and a knife, in the pouch on his harness, but there

seemed no practical way in which he could fasten the line to
the smooth, streamlined vanes.

It looked as if he would have to walk home. That should
not be too difficult—he could set the motor running at low
speed and let the torp pull him along the bottom while he
aimed it in the right direction by brute force. It would be
clumsy, but seemed possible in theory, and he could think of
nothing better.

He glanced at his watch; it had been only a couple of minutes since he had tried to turn at the leg of the triangle, so he
was no more than a minute late at his destination. Don would
not be anxious yet, but before long he would start searching for
his lost pupil. Perhaps the best thing to do would be to stay
right here until Don turned up, as he would be bound to do
sooner or later. . . .

It was at this moment that suspicion dawned in Franklin's
mind, and almost instantly became a full-fledged conviction.
He recalled certain rumors he had heard, and remembered that
Don's behavior before they set out had been—well, slightly
skittish was the only expression for it, as if he had been cher-
ishing some secret joke.

So that was it. The torpedo had been sabotaged. Probably
at this very moment Don was hovering out there at the limits
of visibility, waiting to see what he would do and ready to step
in if he ran into real trouble. Franklin glanced quickly around
his hemisphere of vision, to see if the other torp was lurking in
the mist, but was not surprised that there was no sign of it.
Burley would be too clever to be caught so easily. This, thought
Franklin, changed the situation completely. He not only had
to extricate himself from his dilemma, but, if possible, he had
to get his own back on Don as well.

He walked back to the control position, and switched on
the motor. A slight pressure on the throttle, and the torp began
to stir restlessly while a flurry of sand was gouged out of the sea
bed by the jet. A little experimenting showed that it was pos-

sible to "walk" the machine, though it required continual adjustments of trim to stop it from climbing up to the surface or burying itself in the sand. It was, thought Franklin, going to take him a long time to get home this way, but he could do it if there was no alternative.

He had walked no more than a dozen paces, and had acquired quite a retinue of astonished fish, when another idea struck him. It seemed too good to be true, but it would do no harm to try. Climbing onto the torpedo and lying in the normal prone position, he adjusted the trim as carefully as he could by moving his weight back and forth. Then he tilted the nose toward the surface, pushed his hands out into the slip stream on either side, and started the motor at quarter speed.

It was hard on his wrists, and his responses had to be almost instantaneous to check the weaving and bucking of the torpedo. But with a little experimenting, he found he could use his hands for steering, though it was as difficult as riding a bicycle with one's arms crossed. At five knots, the area of his flattened palms was just sufficient to give control over the vehicle.

He wondered if anyone had ever ridden a torp this way before, and felt rather pleased with himself. Experimentally, he pushed the speed up to eight knots, but the pressure on his wrists and forearms was too great and he had to throttle back before he lost control.

There was no reason, Franklin told himself, why he should not now make his original rendezvous, just in case Don was waiting there for him. He would be about five minutes late, but at least it would prove that he could carry out his assignment in the face of obstacles which he was not quite sure were entirely man-made.

Don was nowhere in sight when he arrived, and Franklin guessed what had happened. His unexpected mobility had taken Burley by surprise, and the warden had lost him in the submarine haze. Well, he could keep on looking. Franklin made one radio call as a matter of principle, but there was no reply from his tutor. "I'm going home!" he shouted to the watery world around him; still there was silence. Don was probably a good quarter of a mile away, conducting an increasingly more anxious search for his lost pupil.

There was no point in remaining below the surface and adding to the difficulties of navigation and control. Franklin took his vehicle up to the top and found that he was less than a thousand yards from the Maintenance Section jetty. By keeping the torp tail heavy and nose up he was able to scorch along on the surface like a speedboat without the slightest trouble, and he was home in five minutes.

As soon as the torpedo had come out of the anticorrosion sprays which were used on all equipment after salt-water dives, Franklin got to work on it. When he pulled off the panel of the control compartment, he discovered that his was a very special model indeed. Without a circuit diagram, it was not possible to tell exactly what the radio-operated relay unit he had located could do, but he did not doubt that it had an interesting repertory. It could certainly cut off the motor, blow or flood the buoyancy tanks, and reverse the rudder and elevator controls. Franklin suspected that compass and depth gauge could also be sabotaged if required. Someone had obviously spent a great deal of loving care making this torpedo a suitable steed for overconfident pupils. . . .

He replaced the panel and reported his safe return to the officer on duty. "Visibility's very poor," he said, truthfully enough. "Don and I lost each other out there, so I thought I'd better come in. I guess he'll be along later."

There was considerable surprise in the mess when Franklin turned up without his instructor and settled quietly down in a corner to read a magazine. Forty minutes later, a great slamming of doors announced Don's arrival. The warden's face was a study in relief and perplexity as he looked around the room and located his missing pupil, who stared back at him with his most innocent expression and said: "What kept you?"

Burley turned to his colleagues and held out his hand. "Pay up, boys," he ordered.

It had taken him long enough to make up his mind, but he realized that he was beginning to like Franklin.

CHAPTER

The two men leaning on the rails around the main pool of the aquarium did not, thought Indra as she walked up the road to the lab, look like the usual run of visiting scientists. It was not until she had come closer and was able to get a good look at them that she realized who they were. The big fellow was First Warden Burley, so the other must be the famous mystery man he was taking through a high-pressure course. She had heard his name but couldn't remember it, not being particularly interested in the activities of the training school. As a pure scientist, she tended to look down on the highly practical work of the Bureau of Whales—though had anyone accused her outright of such intellectual snobbery she would have denied it with indignation.

She had almost reached them before she realized that she had already met the smaller man. For his part, Franklin was looking at her with a slightly baffled, "Haven't we seen each other before?" expression.

"Hello," she said, coming to a standstill beside them. "Remember me? I'm the girl who collects sharks."

Franklin smiled and answered: "Of course I remember: It

still turns my stomach sometimes. I hope you found plenty of vitamins."

Yet strangely enough, the puzzled expression—so typical of a man straining after memories that will not come—still lingered in his eyes. It made him look lost and more than a little worried, and Indra found herself reacting with sympathy, which was disconcerting. She had already had several narrow escapes from emotional entanglements on the island, and she reminded herself firmly of her resolution: "Not until *after* I've got my master's degree . . ."

"So you know each other," said Don plaintively. "You might introduce me." Don, Indra decided, was perfectly safe. He would start to flirt with her at once, like any warden worthy of his calling. She did not mind that in the least; though big leonine blonds were not precisely her type, it was always flattering to feel that one was causing a stir, and she knew that there was no risk of any serious attachment here. With Franklin, however, she felt much less sure of herself.

They chattered pleasantly enough, with a few bantering undertones, while they stood watching the big fish and porpoises circling slowly in the oval pool. The lab's main tank was really an artificial lagoon, filled and emptied twice a day by the tides, with a little assistance from a pumping plant. Wire-mesh barriers divided it into various sections through which mutually incompatible exhibits stared hungrily at each other; a small tiger shark, with the inevitable sucker fish glued to its back, kept patrolling its underwater cage, unable to take its eyes off the succulent pompano parading just outside. In some enclosures, however, surprising partnerships had developed. Brilliantly colored crayfish, looking like overgrown shrimps that had been sprayed with paint guns, crawled a few inches away from the incessantly gaping jaws of a huge and hideous moray eel. A school of fingerlings, like sardines that had escaped from their tin, cruised past the nose of a quarter-ton grouper that could have swallowed them all at one gulp.

It was a peaceful little world, so different from the battle-field of the reef. But if the lab staff ever failed to make the normal feeding arrangements, this harmony would quickly vanish and in a few hours the population of the pool would start a catastrophic decline.

Don did most of the talking; he appeared to have quite forgotten that he had brought Franklin here to see some of the whale-recognition films in the lab's extensive library. He was clearly trying to impress Indra, and quite unaware of the fact that she saw through him completely. Franklin, on the other hand, obviously saw both sides of the game and was mildly entertained by it. Once, Indra caught his eye, when Don was holding forth about the life and hard times of the average warden, and they exchanged the smiles of two people who share the same amusing secret. And at that moment Indra decided that, after all, her degree might not be the most important thing in the world. She was still determined not to get herself involved—but she had to learn more about Franklin. What was his first name? Walter. It was not one of her favorites, but it would do.

In his calm confidence that he was laying waste another susceptible female heart, Don was completely unaware of the undercurrents of emotion that were sweeping around him yet leaving him utterly untouched. When he suddenly realized that they were twenty minutes late for their appointment in the projection room, he pretended to blame Franklin, who accepted the reproof in a good-natured but slightly absent-minded manner. For the rest of the morning, indeed, Franklin was rather far away from his studies; but Don noticed nothing at all.

The first part of the course was now virtually completed; Franklin had learned the basic mechanics of the warden's profession and now needed the experience that only time would give. In almost every respect, he had exceeded Burley's hopes, partly because of his original scientific training, partly because of his innate intelligence. Yet there was more to it even than this; Franklin had a drive and determination that was sometimes frightening. It was as if success in this course was a matter of life and death to him. True, he had been slow in starting; for the first few days he had been listless and seemingly almost uninterested in his new career. Then he had come to life, as he awoke to the wonder and challenge—the endless opportunity—of the element he was attempting to master. Though Don was not much given to such fancies, it seemed to him that Franklin was like a man awakening from a long and troubled sleep.

The real test had been when they had first gone underwater with the torpedoes. Franklin might never use a torp again—except for amusement—during his entire career; they were purely shallow-water units designed for very short-range work, and as a warden, Franklin would spend all his operational time snug and dry behind the protective walls of a sub. But unless a man was at ease and confident—though not overconfident—when he was actually immersed in water, the service had no use for him, however qualified he might be in other respects.

Franklin had also passed, with a satisfactory safety margin, the decompression, CO_2, and nitrogen narcosis tests. Burley had put him in the station's "torture chamber," where the doctors slowly increased the air pressure and took him down on a simulated dive. He had been perfectly normal down to 150 feet; thereafter his mental reactions became sluggish and failed to do simple sums correctly when they were given to him over the intercom. At 300 feet he appeared to be mildly drunk and started cracking jokes which reduced him to tears of helpless laughter but which were quite unfunny to those outside—and embarrassingly so to Franklin himself when they played them back to him later. Three hundred and fifty feet down he still appeared to be conscious but refused to react to Don's voice, even when it started shouting outrageous insults. And at 400 feet he passed out completely, and they brought him slowly back to normal.

Though he would never have occasion to use them, he was also tested with the special breathing mixtures which enable a man to remain conscious and active at far greater depths. When he did any deep dives, he would not be wearing underwater breathing gear but would be sitting comfortably inside a sub breathing normal air at normal pressure. But a warden had to be a Jack of all underwater trades, and never knew what equipment he might have to use in an emergency.

Burley was no longer scared—as he had once been—at the thought of sharing a two-man training sub with Franklin. Despite the other's underlying reticence and the mystery which still surrounded him, they were partners now and knew how to work together. They had not yet become friends, but had reached a state which might be defined as one of tolerant respect.

On their first sub run, they kept to the shallow waters between the Great Barrier Reef and the mainland, while Franklin familiarized himself with the control, and above all with the navigational instruments. If you could run a sub here, said Don, in this labyrinth of reefs and islands, you could run it anywhere. Apart from trying to charge Masthead Island at sixty knots, Franklin performed quite creditably. His fingers began to move over the complex control board with a careful precision which, Don knew, would soon develop into automatic skill. His scanning of the many meters and display screens would soon be unconscious, so that he would not even be aware that he saw them—until something called for his attention.

Don gave Franklin increasingly more complicated tasks to perform, such as tracing out improbable courses by dead reckoning and then checking his position on the sonar grid to see where he had actually arrived. It was not until he was quite sure that Franklin was proficient in handling a sub that they finally went out into deep water over the edge of the continental shelf.

Navigating a Scoutsub was merely the beginning; one had to learn to see and feel with its senses, to interpret all the patterns of information displayed on the control board by the many instruments which were continually probing the underwater world. The sonic senses were, perhaps, the most important. In utter darkness, or in completely turbid water, they could detect all obstacles out to a range of ten miles, with great accuracy and in considerable detail. They could show the contours of the ocean bed, or with equal ease could detect any fish more than two or three feet long that came within half a mile. Whales and the larger marine animals they could spot right out to the extreme limit of range, fixing them with pinpoint accuracy.

Visible light had a more limited role. Sometimes, in deep ocean waters far from the eternal rain of silt which sloughs down from the edges of the continents, it was possible to see as much as two hundred feet—but that was rare. In shallow coastal waters, the television eye could seldom peer more than fifty feet, but within its range it gave a definition unmatched by the sub's other senses.

Yet the subs had not only to see and feel; they also had to act. Franklin must learn to use a whole armory of tools and weapons: borers to collect specimens of the seabed, meters to check the efficiency of the fences, sampling devices, branders for painlessly marking uncooperative whales, electric probes to discourage marine beasts that became too inquisitive—and, most seldom used of all, the tiny torpedoes and poisoned darts that could slay in seconds the mightiest creatures of the seas.

In daily cruises far out into the Pacific, Franklin learned to use these tools of his new trade. Sometimes they went through the fence, and it seemed to Franklin that he could feel its eternal high-pitched shrieking in his very bones. Halfway around the world it now extended, its narrow fans of radiation reaching up to the surface from the deeply submerged generators.

What, wondered Franklin, would earlier ages have thought of this? In some ways it seemed the greatest and most daring of all man's presumptions. The sea, which had worked its will with man since the beginning of time, had been humbled at last. Not even the conquest of space had been a greater victory than this.

And yet—it was a victory that could never be final. The sea would always be waiting, and every year it would claim its victims. There was a roll of honor that Franklin had glimpsed briefly during his visit to the head office. Already it bore many names, and there was room for many more.

Slowly, Franklin was coming to terms with the sea, as must all men who have dealings with it. Though he had had little time for nonessential reading, he had dipped into *Moby Dick*, which had been half-jokingly, half-seriously called the bible of the Bureau of Whales. Much of it had seemed to him tedious, and so far removed from the world in which he was living that it had no relevance. Yet occasionally Melville's archaic, sonorous prose touched some chord in his own mind, and gave him a closer understanding of the ocean which he, too, must learn to hate and love.

Don Burley, however, had no use at all for *Moby Dick* and frequently made fun of those who were always quoting from it.

"We could show Melville a thing or two!" he had once remarked to Franklin, in a very condescending tone.

"Of course we could," Franklin had answered. "But would you have the guts to stick a spear into a sperm whale from an open boat?"

Don did not reply. He was honest enough to admit that he did not know the answer.

Yet there was one question he was now close to answering. As he watched Franklin learn his new skills, with a swiftness which could undoubtedly make him a first warden in no more than four or five years, he knew with complete certainty what his pupil's last profession had been. If he chose to keep it a secret, that was his own affair. Don felt a little aggrieved by such lack of trust; but sooner or later, he told himself, Franklin would confide in him.

Yet it was not Don who was the first to learn the truth. By the sheerest of accidents, it was Indra.

CHAPTER

They now met at least once a day in the mess, though Franklin had not yet made the irrevocable, almost unprecedented, step of moving from his table to the one at which the research staff dined. That would be a flamboyant declaration which would set every tongue on the island wagging happily, and in any case it would not be justified by the circumstances. As far as Indra and Franklin were concerned, the much-abused phrase "we're just friends" was still perfectly true.

Yet it was also true that they had grown very fond of each other, and that almost everyone except Don was aware of it. Several of Indra's colleagues had said to her approvingly, "You're thawing out the iceberg," and the compliment had flattered her. The few people who knew Franklin well enough to banter with him had made warning references to Don, pointing out that first wardens had reputations to maintain. Franklin's reaction had been a somewhat forced grin, concealing feelings which he could not fully analyze himself.

Loneliness, the need to escape from memories, a safety valve to guard him against the pressure under which he was working—these factors were at least as important as the normal feelings of any man for a girl as attractive as Indra.

Whether this companionship would develop into anything more serious, he did not know. He was not even sure if he wished it to do so.

Nor, for her part, was Indra, though her old resolve was weakening. Sometimes she indulged in reveries wherein her career took very much of a second place. One day, of course, she was going to marry, and the man she would choose would be very much like Franklin. But that it might *be* Franklin was a thought from which she still shied away.

One of the problems of romance on Heron Island was that there were far too many people in too small a space. Even the fragment that was left of the original forest did not provide enough seclusion. At night, if one wandered through its paths and byways, carrying a flashlight to avoid the low-hanging branches, one had to be very tactful with the beam. One was liable to find that favorite spots had already been requisitioned, which would be extremely frustrating if there was nowhere else to go.

The fortunate scientists at the Research Station, however, had an invaluable escape route. All the large surface craft and all the underwater vessels belonged to Administration, though they were made available to the lab for official business. But by some historical accident, the lab had a tiny private fleet consisting of one launch and two catamarans. No one was quite sure who owned the latter, and it was noticeable that they were always at sea when the auditors arrived for the annual inventory.

The little cats did a great deal of work for the lab, since they drew only six inches of water and could operate safely over the reef except at low tide. With a stiff wind behind them, they could do twenty knots with ease, and races between the two craft were frequently arranged. When they were not being used for other business, the scientists would sail them to the neighboring reefs and islands to impress their friends—usually of the opposite sex—with their prowess as seamen.

It was a little surprising that ships and occupants had always come back safely from these expeditions. The only casualties had been to morale; one first warden of many years seniority had had to be carried off the boat after a pleasure trip, and had sworn that nothing would ever induce him to travel on the *surface* of the sea again.

When Indra suggested to Franklin that he might like to sail to Masthead Island, he accepted at once. Then he said cautiously: "Who'll run the boat?"

Indra looked hurt.

"I will, of course," she answered. "I've done it dozens of times." She seemed to be half-expecting him to doubt her competence, but Franklin knew better than to do so. Indra, he had already discovered, was a very levelheaded girl—perhaps too levelheaded. If she said she could do a job, that was that.

There was still, however, one other point to be settled. The cats could take four people; who would the other two be?

Neither Indra nor Franklin actually voiced the final decision. It hovered in the air while they discussed various possible companions, starting with Don and working down the list of Indra's friends at the lab. Presently the conversation died out into one of those portentous pauses which can sometimes occur even in a roomful of chattering people.

In the sudden silence, each realized that the other was thinking the same thought, and that a new phase had begun in their relationship. They would take no one with them to Masthead; for the first time, they would have the solitude that had never been possible here. That this could lead only to one logical conclusion they refused to admit, even to themselves, the human mind having a remarkable capacity for self-deceit.

It was well into the afternoon before they were able to make all their arrangements and escape. Franklin felt very guilty about Don, and wondered what his reactions would be when he found out what had happened. He would probably be mortified, but he was not the sort to hold a grudge and he would take it like a man.

Indra had thought of everything. Food, drinks, sunburn lotion, towels—she had overlooked nothing that such an expedition might need. Franklin was impressed by her thoroughness, and was amused to find himself thinking that so competent a woman would be very useful to have around the house. Then he reminded himself hastily that women who were too efficient were seldom happy unless they ran their husbands' lives as well as their own.

There was a steady wind blowing from the mainland, and the cat bounded across the waves like a living creature. Franklin had never before been in a sailing boat, and he found the experience an exhilarating one. He lay back on the worn but comfortable padding of the open cockpit, while Heron Island receded into the distance at an astonishing speed. It was restful to watch the twin, creamy wakes trace their passage across the sea, and to caress with the eye the straining, power-filled curves of the sails. With a mild and fleeting regret, Franklin wished that all man's machines could be as simple and efficient as this one. What a contrast there was between this vessel and the crowded complexities of the subs he was now learning to handle! The thought passed swiftly; there were some tasks which could not be achieved by simple means, and one must accept the fact without complaint.

On their left, they were now skirting the long line of rounded coral boulders which centuries of storms had cast up upon the edge of the Wistari Reef. The waves were breaking against the submerged ramparts with a relentless and persistent fury which had never impressed Franklin so much as now. He had seen them often enough before—but never from so close at hand, in so frail a craft.

The boiling margin of the reef fell astern; now they had merely to wait while the winds brought them to their goal. Even if the wind failed—which was most unlikely—they could still make the trip on the little auxiliary hydro-jet engine, though that would only be used as a last resort. It was a matter of principle to return with a full fuel tank.

Although they were now together and alone for almost the first time since they had met, neither Franklin nor Indra felt any need to talk. There seemed a silent communion between them which they did not wish to break with words, being content to share the peace and wonder of the open sea and the open sky. They were enclosed between two hemispheres of flawless blue, clamped together at the misty rim of the horizon, and nothing else of the world remained. Even time seemed to have faltered to a stop; Franklin felt he could lie here forever, relaxing in the gentle motion of the boat as it skimmed effortlessly over the waves.

Presently a low, dark cloud began to solidify, then to reveal itself as a tree-clad island with its narrow sandy shore and inevitable fringing reef. Indra bestirred herself and began to take an active interest in navigation once more, while Franklin looked rather anxiously at the breakers which seemed to surround the island in one continuous band.

"How are we going to get in?" he asked.

"Round the lee side; it won't be rough there, and the tide should be high enough for us to go in across the reef. If it isn't, we can always anchor and wade ashore."

Franklin was not altogether happy about so casual an approach to what seemed a serious problem, and he could only hope that Indra really did know what she was doing. If she made a mistake, they might have an uncomfortable though not particularly dangerous swim ahead, followed after a long wait by an ignominious rescue when someone came from the lab to look for them.

Either it was easier than it appeared to an anxious novice, or else Indra's seamanship was of a high order. They circled halfway around the island, until they came to a spot where the breakers subsided into a few choppy waves. Then Indra turned the prow of the cat toward the land, and headed straight for shore.

There were no sounds of grinding coral or splintering plastic. Like a bird, the catamaran flew in across the narrow edge of the reef, now clearly visible just below the broken and unsettled water. It skimmed past this danger zone, and then was over the peaceful surface of the lagoon, seeming to gain speed as it approached the beach. Seconds before impact, Indra furled the mainsail. With a soft thud, the vessel hit the sand and coasted up the gentle slope, coming to rest with more than half its length above the water line.

"Here we are," said Indra. "One uninhabited coral island, in full working order." She seemed more relaxed and lighthearted than Franklin had ever before seen her; he realized that she, too, had been working under pressure and was glad to escape from the daily routine for a few hours. Or was it the stimulating effect of his company that was turning her from a serious student into a vivacious girl? Whatever the explanation, he liked the change.

They climbed out of the boat and carried their gear up the beach into the shade of the coconut palms, which had been imported into these islands only during the last century to challenge the predominance of the Pisonia and the stilt-rooted pandanus. It seemed that someone else had also been here recently, for curious tracks apparently made by narrow-gauge caterpillar treads marched up out of the water and vanished inland. They would have been quite baffling to anyone who did not know that the big turtles had been coming ashore to lay their eggs.

As soon as the cat had been made secure, Franklin and Indra began a tour of exploration. It was true that one coral island was almost exactly the same as another; the same pattern was repeated endlessly over and over again, with few variations. Yet even when one was aware of that, and had landed on dozens of islands, every new one presented a fresh challenge which had to be accepted.

They began the circumnavigation of their little world, walking along the narrow belt of sand between the forest and the sea. Sometimes, when they came to a clearing, they made short forays inland, deliberately trying to lose themselves in the tangle of trees so that they could pretend that they were in the heart of Africa and not, at the very most, a hundred yards from the sea.

Once they stopped to dig with their hands at the spot where one of the turtle tracks terminated on a flat-ended sand dune. They gave up when they were two feet down and there was still no sign of the leathery, flexible eggs. The mother turtle, they solemnly decided, must have been making false trails to deceive her enemies. For the next ten minutes, they elaborated this fantasy into a startling thesis on reptile intelligence, which, far from gaining Indra new qualifications, would undoubtedly have cost her the degree she already possessed.

Inevitably the time came when, having helped each other over a patch of rough coral, their hands failed to separate even though the path was smooth once more. Neither speaking, yet each more conscious of the other's presence than they had ever been before, they walked on in the silence of shared contentment.

At a leisurely stroll, pausing whenever they felt like it to examine some curiosity of the plant or animal world, it took them almost two hours to circumnavigate the little island. By the time they had reached the cat they were very hungry, and Franklin began to unpack the food hamper with unconcealed eagerness while Indra started working on the stove.

"Now I'm going to brew you a billy of genuine Australian tea," she said.

Franklin gave her that twisted, whimsical smile which she found so attractive.

"It will hardly be a novelty to me," he said. "After all, I was born here."

She stared at him in astonishment which gradually turned to exasperation. "Well, you might have told me!" she said. "In fact, I really think—" Then she stopped, as if by a deliberate effort of will, leaving the uncompleted sentence hanging in mid-air. Franklin had no difficulty in finishing it. She had intended to say, "It's high time you told me something about yourself, and abandoned all this silly reticence."

The truth of the unspoken accusation made him flush, and for a moment some of his carefree happiness—the first he had known for so many months—drained away. Then a thought struck him which he had never faced before, since to do so might have jeopardized his friendship with Indra. She was a scientist and a woman, and therefore doubly inquisitive. Why was it that she had never asked him any questions about his past life? There could be only one explanation. Dr. Myers, who was unobtrusively watching over him despite the jovial pretense that he was doing nothing of the sort, must have spoken to her.

A little more of his contentment ebbed as he realized that Indra must feel sorry for him and must wonder, like everyone else, exactly what had happened to him. He would not, he told himself bitterly, accept a love that was founded on pity.

Indra seemed unaware of his sudden brooding silence and the conflict that now disturbed his mind. She was busy filling the little stove by a somewhat primitive method that involved siphoning fuel out of the hydrojet's tank, and Franklin was so amused by her repeated failures that he forgot his momentary annoyance. When at last she had managed to light the stove, they lay back under the palms, munching sandwiches and waiting for the water to boil. The Sun was already far down the sky, and Franklin realized that they would probably not get back to Heron Island until well after nightfall. However, it would not be dark, for the Moon was nearing full, so even without the aid of the local beacons the homeward journey would present no difficulties.

The billy-brewed tea was excellent, though doubtless far too anemic for any old-time swagman. It washed down the remainder of their food very efficiently, and as they relaxed with sighs of satisfaction their hands once again found each other. Now, thought Franklin, I should be perfectly content. But he knew that he was not; something that he could not define was worrying him.

His unease had grown steadily stronger during the last few minutes, but he had tried to ignore it and force it down into his mind. He knew that it was utterly ridiculous and irrational to expect any danger here, on this empty and peaceful island. Yet little warning bells were ringing far down in the labyrinths of his brain, and he could not understand their signals.

Indra's casual question came as a welcome distraction. She was staring intently up into the western sky, obviously searching for something.

"Is it really true, Walter," she asked, "that if you know where to look for her you can see Venus in the daytime? She was so bright after sunset last night that I could almost believe it."

"It's perfectly true," Franklin answered. "In fact, it isn't even difficult. The big problem is to locate her in the first place; once you've done that, she's quite easy to see."

He propped himself up against a palm trunk, shaded his eyes from the glare of the descending Sun, and began to search the western sky with little hope of discovering the elusive silver speck he knew to be shining there. He had noticed Venus dominating the evening sky during the last few weeks, but it was hard to judge how far she was from the Sun when both were above the horizon at the same time.

Suddenly—unexpectedly—his eyes caught and held a solitary silver star hanging against the milky blue of the sky. "I've found her!" he exclaimed, raising his arm as a pointer. Indra squinted along it, but at first could see nothing.

"You've got spots before the eyes," she taunted.

"No—I'm not imagining things. Just keep on looking," Franklin answered, his eyes still focused on the dimensionless star which he knew he would lose if he turned away from it even for a second.

"But Venus *can't* be there," protested Indra. "That's much too far north."

In a single, sickening instant Franklin knew that she was right. If he had any doubt, he could see now that the star he was watching was moving swiftly across the sky, rising out of the west and so defying the laws which controlled all other heavenly bodies.

He was staring at the Space Station, the largest of all the satellites now circling Earth, as it raced along its thousand-mile-high orbit. He tried to turn his eyes away, to break the hypnotic spell of that man-made, unscintillating star. It was as if he was teetering on the edge of an abyss; the terror of those endless, trackless wastes between the worlds began to invade and dominate his mind, to threaten the very foundations of his sanity.

He would have won the struggle, no more than a little shaken, had it not been for a second accident of fate. With the explosive suddenness with which memory sometimes yields to persistent questioning, he knew what it was that had been worrying him for the last few minutes. It was the smell of the fuel that Indra had siphoned from the hydrojet—the unmistakable, slightly aromatic tang of synthene. And crowding hard upon that recognition was the memory of where he had last met that all-too-familiar odor.

Synthene—first developed as a rocket propellant—now obsolete like all other chemical fuels, except for low-powered applications like the propulsion of space suits.

Space suits.

It was too much; the double assault defeated him. Both sight and smell had turned traitor in the same instant. Within seconds, the patiently built dikes which now protected his mind went down before the rising tide of terror.

He could feel the Earth beneath him spinning dizzily through space. It seemed to be whirling faster and faster on its axis, trying to hurl him off like a stone from a sling by the sheer speed of its rotation. With a choking cry, he rolled over on his stomach, buried his face in the sand, and clung desperately to the rough trunk of the palm. It gave him no security; the endless fall began again. . . . Chief Engineer Franklin, second in command of the *Arcturus,* was in space once more, at the beginning of the nightmare he had hoped and prayed he need never retrace.

CHAPTER

In the first shock of stunned surprise, Indra sat staring foolishly at Franklin as he groveled in the sand and wept like a heartbroken child. Then compassion and common sense told her what to do; she moved swiftly to his side and threw her arms around his heaving shoulders.

"Walter!" she cried. "You're all right—there's nothing to be afraid of!"

The words seemed flat and foolish even as she uttered them, but they were the best she had to offer. Franklin did not seem to hear; he was still trembling uncontrollably, still clinging to the tree with desperate determination. It was pitiful to see a man reduced to such a state of abject fear, so robbed of all dignity and pride. As Indra crouched over him, she realized that between his sobs he was calling a name—and even at such a moment as this she could not repress a stab of jealousy. For it was the name of a woman; over and over again, in a voice so low as to be barely audible, Franklin would whisper "Irene!" and then be convulsed by a fresh paroxysm of weeping.

There was something here beyond Indra's slight knowledge of medicine. She hesitated for a moment, then hurried to the catamaran and broke open its little first-aid kit. It con-

tained a vial of potent painkilling capsules, prominently la-
beled ONLY ONE TO BE TAKEN AT ANY TIME, and with some
difficulty she managed to force one of these into Franklin's
mouth. Then she held him in her arms while his tremors
slowly subsided and the violence of the attack ebbed away.

It is hard to draw any line between compassion and love. If
such a division exists, Indra crossed it during this silent vigil.
Franklin's loss of manhood had not disgusted her; she knew
that something terrible indeed must have happened in his past
to bring him to this state. Whatever it was, her own future
would not be complete unless she could help him fight it.

Presently Franklin was quiet, though apparently still conscious. He did not resist when she rolled him over so that his face
was no longer half-buried in the sand, and he relaxed his frenzied
grip upon the tree. But his eyes were empty, and his mouth still
moved silently though no words came from it.

"We're going home," whispered Indra, as if soothing a
frightened child. "Come along—it's all right now."

She helped him to his feet, and he rose unresistingly. He
even assisted her, in a mechanical way, to pack their equipment
and to push the catamaran off the beach. He seemed nearly
normal again, except that he would not speak and there was a
sadness in his eyes that tore at Indra's heart.

They left the island under both sail and power, for Indra
was determined to waste no time. Even now it had not occurred to her that she might be in any personal danger, so
many miles from any help, with a man who might be mad.
Her only concern was to get Franklin back to medical care as
quickly as she could.

The light was failing fast; the Sun had already touched the
horizon and darkness was massing in the east. Beacons on the
mainland and the surrounding islands began, one by one, to
spring to life. And, more brilliant than any of them, there
in the west was Venus, which had somehow caused all this
trouble. . . .

Presently Franklin spoke, his words forced but perfectly rational.

"I'm very sorry about this, Indra," he said. "I'm afraid I spoiled your trip."

"Don't be silly," she answered. "It wasn't your fault. Just take it easy—don't talk unless you want to." He relapsed into silence, and spoke no more for the rest of the voyage. When Indra reached out to hold his hand again, he stiffened defensively in a way which said, without actually rejecting her, that he would prefer no such contact. She felt hurt, but obeyed his unspoken request. In any event, she was busy enough picking out the beacons as she made the tricky passage between the reefs.

She had not intended to be out as late as this, even though the rising Moon was now flooding the sea with light. The wind had freshened, and all too close at hand the breakers along the Wistari Reef were appearing and vanishing in deadly lines of luminous, ghostly white. She kept one eye on them, and the other on the winking beacon that marked the end of the Heron jetty. Not until she could see the jetty itself and make out the details of the island was she able to relax and give her attention once more to Franklin.

He appeared almost normal again when they had berthed the catamaran and walked back to the lab. Indra could not see his expression, for there were no lights here on this part of the beach, and the palms shaded them from the Moon. As far as she could tell, his voice was under full control when he bade her good night.

"Thank you for everything, Indra. No one could have done more."

"Let me take you to Dr. Myers right away. You've got to see him."

"No—there's nothing he can do. I'm quite all right now—it won't happen again."

"I still think you should see him. I'll take you to your room and then go and call him."

Franklin shook his head violently.

"That's one thing I don't want you to do. Promise me you won't call him."

Sorely troubled, Indra debated with her conscience. The wisest thing to do, she was sure, was to make the promise— and then to break it. Yet if she did so, Franklin might never forgive her. In the end, she compromised.

"Will you go and see him yourself, if you won't let me take you?"

Franklin hesitated before answering. It seemed a shame that his parting words with this girl, whom he might have loved, should be a lie. But in the drugged calm that had come upon him now he knew what he must do.

"I'll call him in the morning—and thanks again." Then he broke away, with a fierce finality, before Indra could question him further.

She watched him disappear into the darkness, along the path that led to the training and administration section. Happiness and anxiety were contending for her soul—happiness because she had found love, anxiety because it was threatened by forces she did not understand. The anxiety resolved itself into a single nagging fear: Should she have insisted, even against his will, that Franklin see Dr. Myers at once?

She would have had no doubt of the answer could she have watched Franklin double back through the moonlit forest and make his way, like a man in a waking dream, to the dock from which had begun all his journeys down into the sea.

The rational part of his mind was now merely the passive tool of his emotions, and they were set upon a single goal. He had been hurt too badly for reason to control him now; like an injured animal, he could think of nothing but the abating of his pain. He was seeking the only place where for a little while he had found peace and contentment.

The jetty was deserted as he made the long, lonely walk out to the edge of the reef. Down in the submarine hangar, twenty feet below the water line, he made his final preparations with as much care as he had ever done on his many earlier trips. He felt a fleeting sense of guilt at robbing the bureau of some fairly valuable equipment and still more valuable training time; but it was not his fault that he had no other choice.

Very quietly, the torp slipped out beneath the submerged archway and set course for the open sea. It was the first time that Franklin had ever been out at night; only the fully enclosed subs operated after darkness, for night navigation involved dangers which it was foolhardy for unprotected men to face. That was the least of Franklin's worries as he set the course he remembered so well and headed out into the channel that would lead him to the sea.

Part of the pain, but none of the determination, lifted from his mind. This was where he belonged; this was where he had found happiness. This was where he would find oblivion.

He was in a world of midnight blue which the pale rays of the Moon could do little to illumine. Around him strange shapes moved like phosphorescent ghosts, as the creatures of the reef were attracted or scattered by the sound of his passing. Below him, no more than shadows in a deeper darkness, he could see the coral hills and valleys he had grown to know so well. With a resignation beyond sadness, he bade them all adieu.

There was no point in lingering, now that his destiny was clear before him. He pushed the throttle full down, and the torpedo leaped forward like a horse that had been given the spur. The islands of the Great Barrier Reef were falling swiftly behind him, and he was heading out into the Pacific at a speed which no other creature of the sea could match.

Only once did he glance up at the world he had abandoned. The water was fantastically clear, and a hundred feet above his head he could see the silver track of the Moon upon the sea, as few men could ever have witnessed it before. He could even see the hazy, dancing patch of light that was the Moon itself, refracted through the water surface yet occasionally freezing, when the moving waves brought a moment of stability, into a perfect, flawless image.

And once a very large shark—the largest he had ever seen—tried to pursue him. The great streamlined shadow, leaving its phosphorescent wake, appeared suddenly almost dead ahead of him, and he made no effort to avoid it. As it swept past he caught a glimpse of the inhuman, staring eye, the slatted gills, and the inevitable retinue of pilot fish and remora. When he glanced back the shark was following him—whether motivated by curiosity, sex, or hunger he neither knew nor cared. It remained in sight for almost a minute before his superior speed left it behind. He had never met a shark that had reacted in this way before; usually they were terrified of the turbine's warning scream. But the laws that ruled the reef during the day were not those that prevailed in the hours of darkness.

He raced on through the luminous night that covered half the world, crouching behind his curved shield for protection against the turbulent waters he was sundering in his haste to reach the open sea. Even now he was navigating with all his old skill and precision; he knew exactly where he was, exactly when he would reach his objective—and exactly how deep were the waters he was now entering. In a few minutes, the seabed would start slanting sharply down and he must say his last farewell to the reef.

He tilted the nose of the torp imperceptibly toward the depths and at the same time cut his speed to a quarter. The mad, roaring rush of waters ceased; he was sliding gently down a long, invisible slope whose end he would never see.

Slowly the pale and filtered moonlight began to fade as the water thickened above him. Deliberately, he avoided looking at the illuminated depth gauge, avoided all thought of the fathoms that now lay overhead. He could feel the pressure on his body increasing minute by minute, but it was not in the least unpleasant. Indeed, he welcomed it; he gave himself, a willing sacrifice, gladly into the grasp of the great mother of life.

The darkness was now complete. He was alone, driving through a night stranger and more palpable than any to be found upon the land. From time to time he could see, at an unguessable distance below him, tiny explosions of light as the unknown creatures of the open sea went about their mysterious business. Sometimes an entire, ephemeral galaxy would thrust forth and within seconds die; perhaps that other galaxy, he told himself, was of no longer duration, of no greater importance, when seen against the background of eternity.

The dreamy sleep of nitrogen narcosis was now almost upon him; no other human being, using a compressed-air lung alone, could ever have been so deep and returned to tell the tale. He was breathing air at more than ten times normal pressure, and still the torpedo was boring down into the lightless depths. All responsibility, all regrets, all fears had been washed away from his mind by the blissful euphoria that had invaded every level of consciousness.

And yet, at the very end, there was one regret. He felt a mild and wistful sadness that Indra must now begin again her search for the happiness he might have given her.

Thereafter there was only the sea, and a mindless machine creeping ever more slowly down to the hundred-fathom line and the far Pacific wastes.

CHAPTER

T here were four people in the room, and not one of them was talking now. The chief instructor was biting his lip nervously, Don Burley sat looking stunned, and Indra was trying not to cry. Only Dr. Myers seemed fairly well under control, and was silently cursing the fantastic, the still inexplicable bad luck that had brought this situation upon them. He would have sworn that Franklin was well on the road to recovery, well past any serious crisis. And now this!

"There's only one thing to do," said the chief instructor suddenly. "And that's to send out all our underwater craft on a general search."

Don Burley stirred himself, slowly and as if carrying a great weight upon his shoulders.

"It's twelve hours now. In that time he could have covered five hundred miles. And there are only six qualified pilots on the station."

"I know—it would be like looking for a needle in a haystack. But it's the only thing we can do."

"Sometimes a few minutes of thought can save a good many hours of random searching," said Myers. "After half a day, a little extra time will make no difference. With your permission, I'd like to have a private talk with Miss Langenburg."

"Of course—if she agrees."

Indra nodded dumbly. She was still blaming herself bitterly for what had happened—for not going to the doctor immediately when they had returned to the island. Her intuition had failed her then; now it told her that there was no possibility of any hope, and she could only pray that it was wrong again.

"Now, Indra," said Myers kindly when the others had left the room, "if we want to help Franklin we've got to keep our heads, and try to guess what he's done. So stop blaming yourself—this isn't your fault. I'm not sure if it's anyone's fault."

It might be mine, he added grimly to himself. But who could have guessed? We understand so little about astrophobia, even now . . . and heaven knows it's not in my line.

Indra managed a brave smile. Until yesterday, she had thought she was very grown-up and able to take care of herself in any situation. But yesterday was a very, very long time ago.

"Please tell me," she said, "what is the matter with Walter. I think it would help me to understand."

It was a sensible and reasonable request; even before Indra had made it, Myers had come to the same conclusion.

"Very well—but remember, this is confidential, for Walter's own sake. I'm only telling it to you because this is an emergency and you may be able to help him if you know the facts.

"Until a year ago, Walter was a highly qualified spaceman. In fact, he was chief engineer of a liner on the Martian run, which as you know is a very responsible position indeed, and that was certainly merely the beginning of his career.

"Well, there was some kind of emergency in mid-orbit, and the ion drive had to be shut off. Walter went outside in a space suit to fix it—nothing unusual about that, of course. Before he had finished the job, however, his suit failed. No—I don't mean it leaked. What happened was that the propulsion system jammed *on,* and he couldn't shut off the rockets that allowed him to move around in space.

"So there he was, millions of miles from anywhere, building up speed away from his ship. To make matters worse, he'd crashed against some part of the liner when he started, and that had snapped off his radio antenna. So he couldn't talk or receive messages—couldn't call for help or find out what his friends were doing for him. He was completely alone, and in a few minutes he couldn't even see the liner.

"Now, no one who has not been in a situation like that can possibly imagine what it's like. We can try, but we can't really picture being absolutely isolated, with stars all around us, not knowing if we'll ever be rescued. No vertigo that can ever be experienced on Earth can match it—not even seasickness at its worst, and that's bad enough.

"It was four hours before Walter was rescued. He was actually quite safe, and probably knew it—but that didn't make any difference. The ship's radar had tracked him, but until the drive was repaired it couldn't go after him. When they did get him aboard he was—well, let's say he was in a pretty bad way.

"It took the best psychologists on Earth almost a year to straighten him out, and as we've seen, the job wasn't finished properly. And there was one factor that the psychologists could do nothing about."

Myers paused, wondering how Indra was taking all this, how it would affect her feelings toward Franklin. She seemed to have got over her initial shock; she was not, thank God, the hysterical type it was so difficult to do anything with.

"You see, Walter was married. He had a wife and family on Mars, and was very fond of them. His wife was a second-generation colonist, the children, of course, third-generation ones. They had spent all their lives under Martian gravity—had been conceived and born in it. And so they could never come to Earth, where they would be crushed under three times their normal weight.

"At the same time, Walter could never go back into space. We could patch up his mind so that he could function efficiently here on Earth, but that was the best we could do. He could never again face free fall, the knowledge that there was space all around him, all the way out to the stars. And so he was an exile on his own world, unable ever to see his family again.

"We did our best for him, and I still think it was a good best. This work here could use his skills, but there were also profound psychological reasons why we thought it might suit him, and would enable him to rebuild his life. I think you probably know those reasons as well as I do, Indra—if not better. You are a marine biologist and know the links we have with the sea. We have no such links with space, and so we shall never feel at home there—at least as long as we are men.

"I studied Franklin while he was here; he knew I was doing it, and didn't mind. All the while he was improving, getting to love the work. Don was very pleased with his progress—he was the best pupil he'd ever met. And when I heard—don't ask me how!—that he was going around with you, I was delighted. For he has to rebuild his life all along the line, you know. I hope you don't mind me putting it this way, but when I found he was spending his spare time with you, and even making time to do it, I knew he had stopped looking back.

"And now—this breakdown. I don't mind admitting that I'm completely in the dark. You say that you were looking up at the Space Station, but that doesn't seem enough cause. Walter had a rather bad fear of heights when he came here, but he'd largely got over that. Besides, he must have seen the station dozens of times in the morning or evening. There must have been some other factor we don't know."

Dr. Myers stopped his rapid delivery, then said gently, as if the thought had only just struck him: "Tell me, Indra—had you been making love?"

"No," she said without hesitation or embarrassment. "There was nothing like that."

It was a little hard to believe, but he knew it was the truth. He could detect—so clear and unmistakable!—the note of regret in her voice.

"I was wondering if he had any guilty feelings about his wife. Whether he knows it or not, you probably remind him of her, which is why he was attracted to you in the first place. Anyway, *that* line of reasoning isn't enough to explain what happened, so let's forget it.

"All we know is that there was an attack, and a very bad one. Giving him the sedative was the best thing you could have done in the circumstances. You're *quite* sure that he never gave any indication of what he intended to do when you got him back to Heron?"

"Quite sure. All he said was, 'Don't tell Dr. Myers.' He said there was nothing you could do."

That, thought Myers grimly, might well be true, and he did not like the sound of it. There was only one reason why a man might hide from the only person who could help him. That was because he had decided he was now beyond help.

"But he promised," Indra continued, "to see you in the morning."

Myers did not reply. By this time they both knew that that promise had been nothing more than a ruse.

Indra still clung desperately to one last hope.

"Surely," she said, her voice quavering as if she did not really believe her own words, "if he'd intended to do—something drastic—he'd have left a message for somebody."

Myers looked at her sadly, his mind now completely made up.

"His parents are dead," he replied. "He said good-bye to his wife long ago. What message was there for him to leave?"

Indra knew, with a sickening certainty, that he spoke the truth. She might well be the only person on Earth for whom

Franklin felt any affection. And he had made his farewell with her. . . .

Reluctantly, Myers rose to his feet.

"There's nothing we can do," he said, "except to start a general search. There may be a chance that he's just blowing off steam at full throttle, and will creep in shamefaced some time this morning. It's happened before."

He patted Indra's bowed shoulders, then helped her out of the chair. "Don't be too upset, my dear. Everyone will do his best." But in his heart, he knew it was too late. It had been too late hours before, and they were going through the motions of search and rescue because there were times when no one expected logic to be obeyed.

They walked together to the assistant chief instructor's office, where the C.I. and Burley were waiting for them. Dr. Myers threw open the door—and stood paralyzed on the threshold. For a moment he thought that he had two more patients—or that he had gone insane himself. Don and the chief instructor, all distinctions of rank forgotten, had their arms around each other's shoulders and were shaking with hysterical laughter. There was no doubt of the hysteria; it was that of relief. And there was equally no doubt about the laughter.

Dr. Myers stared at this improbable scene for perhaps five seconds, then glanced swiftly around the room. At once he saw the message form lying on the floor where one of his temporarily disordered colleagues had dropped it. Without asking their permission, he rushed forward and picked it up.

He had to read it several times before it made any sense; then he, too, began to laugh as he had not done for years.

CHAPTER

Captain Bert Darryl was looking forward to a quiet trip; if there was any justice in this world, he was certainly due for one. Last time there had been that awkward affair with the cops at Mackay; the time before there had been that uncharted rock off Lizard Island; and before *that,* by crikey, there'd been that trigger-happy young fool who had used a nondetachable harpoon on a fifteen-foot tiger and had been towed all over the seabed.

As far as one could tell by appearances, his customers seemed a reasonable lot this time. Of course, the Sports Agency always guaranteed their reliability as well as their credit—but all the same it was surprising what he sometimes got saddled with. Still, a man had to earn a living, and it cost a lot to keep this old bucket waterproof.

By an odd coincidence, his customers always had the same names—Mr. Jones, Mr. Robinson, Mr. Brown, Mr. Smith. Captain Bert thought it was a crazy idea, but that was just another of the agency's little ways. It certainly made life interesting, trying to figure out who they really were. Some of them were so cautious that they wore rubber face masks the whole trip—yes, even under their diving masks. They would be the important boys who were scared of being recognized. Think of the scandal, for instance, if a supreme court judge or chief secretary of the Space Department was found poaching on a World Food reservation! Captain Bert thought of it, and chuckled.

The little five-berth sports cruiser was still forty miles off the outer edge of the reef, feeling her way in from the Pacific. Of course, it was risky operating so near the Capricorns, right in enemy territory as it were. But the biggest fish were here, just because they were the best protected. You had to take a chance if you wanted to keep your clients satisfied. . . .

Captain Bert had worked out his tactics carefully, as he always did. There were never any patrols out at night, and even if there were, his long-range sonar would spot them and he could run for it. So it would be perfectly safe creeping up during darkness, getting into position just before dawn, and pushing his eager beavers out of the air lock as soon as the Sun came up. He would lie doggo on the bottom, keeping in touch through the radios. If they got out of range, they'd still have his low-powered sonar beacon to home on. And if they got too far away to pick up *that,* serve 'em jolly well right. He patted his jacket where the four blood chits reposed safely, absolving him of all responsibility if anything happened to Messrs. Smith, Jones, Robinson, or Brown. There were times when he wondered if it was really any use, considering these weren't their real names, but the agency told him not to worry. Captain Bert was not the worrying type, or he would have given up this job long ago.

At the moment, Messrs. S., J., R., and B. were lying on their respective couches, putting the final touches to the equipment they would not need until morning. Smith and Jones had brand-new guns that had obviously never been fired before, and their webbing was fitted with every conceivable underwater gadget. Captain Bert looked at them sardonically; they represented a type he knew very well. They were the boys who were so keen on their equipment that they never did any shooting, either with the guns or their cameras. They would wander happily around the reef, making such a noise that every fish within miles would know exactly what they were up to. Their beautiful guns, which could drill a thousand-pound shark at fifty feet, would probably never be fired. But they wouldn't really mind; they would enjoy themselves.

Now Robinson was a very different matter. His gun was slightly dented, and about five years old. It had seen service, and he obviously knew how to handle it. He was not one of those catalogue-obsessed sportsmen who had to buy the current year's model as soon as it came out, like a woman who couldn't bear to be behind the fashion. Mr. Robinson, Captain Bert decided, would be the one who would bring back the biggest catch.

As for Brown—Robinson's partner—he was the only one that Captain Bert hadn't been able to classify. A well-built, strong-featured man in the forties, he was the oldest of the hunters and his face was vaguely familiar. He was probably some official in the upper echelons of the state, who had felt the need to sow a few wild oats. Captain Bert, who was constitutionally unable to work for the World State or any other employer, could understand just how he felt.

There were more than a thousand feet of water below them, and the reef was still miles ahead. But one never took anything for granted in this business, and Captain Bert's eyes were seldom far from the dials and screens of the control board, even while he watched his little crew preparing for their morning's fun. The clear and tiny echo had barely appeared on the sonar scanner before he had fastened on to it.

"Big shark coming, boys," he announced jovially. There was a general rush to the screen.

"How do you know it's a shark?" someone asked.

"Pretty sure to be. Couldn't be a whale—they can't leave the channel inside the reef."

"Sure it's not a sub?" said one anxious voice.

"Naow. Look at the size of it. A sub would be ten times as bright on the screen. Don't be a nervous Nelly."

The questioner subsided, duly abashed. No one said anything for the next five minutes, as the distant echo closed in toward the center of the screen.

"It'll pass within a quarter of a mile of us," said Mr. Smith. "What about changing course and seeing if we can make contact?"

"Not a hope. He'll run for it as soon as he picks up our motors. If we stopped still he might come and sniff us over. Anyway, what would be the use? You couldn't get at him. It's night and he's well below the depth where you could operate."

Their attention was momentarily distracted by a large school of fish—probably tuna, the captain said—which appeared on the southern sector of the screen. When that had gone past, the distinguished-looking Mr. Brown said thoughtfully: "Surely a shark would have changed course by now."

Captain Bert thought so too, and was beginning to be puzzled. "Think we'll have a look at it," he said. "Won't do any harm."

He altered course imperceptibly; the strange echo continued on its unvarying way. It was moving quite slowly, and there would be no difficulty in getting within visual distance without risk of collision. At the point of nearest approach, Captain Bert switched on the camera and the U.V. searchlight—and gulped.

"We're rumbled, boys. It's a cop."

There were four simultaneous gasps of dismay, then a chorus of "But you told us . . ." which the captain silenced with a few well-chosen words while he continued to study the screen.

"Something funny here," he said. "I was right first time. That's no sub—it's only a torp. So it can't detect us, anyway—they don't carry that kind of gear. But what the hell's it doing out here at night?"

"Let's run for it!" pleaded several anxious voices.

"Shurrup!" shouted Captain Bert. "Let me think." He glanced at the depth indicator. "Crikey," he muttered, this time in a much more subdued voice. "We're a hundred fathoms down. Unless that lad's breathing some fancy mixture, he's had it."

He peered closely at the image on the TV screen; it was hard to be certain, but the figure strapped to the slowly moving torp seemed abnormally still. Yes—there was no doubt of it; he could tell from the attitude of the head. The pilot was certainly unconscious, probably dead.

"This is a bloody nuisance," announced the skipper, "but there's nothing else to do. We've got to fetch that guy in."

Someone started to protest, then thought better of it. Captain Bert was right, of course. The later consequences would have to be dealt with as they arose.

"But how are you going to do it?" asked Smith. "We can't go outside at this depth."

"It won't be easy," admitted the captain. "It's lucky he's moving so slowly. I think I can flip him over."

He nosed in toward the torp, making infinitely delicate adjustments with the controls. Suddenly there was a clang that made everybody jump except the skipper, who knew when it was coming and exactly how loud it would be.

He backed away, and breathed a sigh of relief.

"Made it first time!" he said smugly. The torp had rolled over on its back, with the helpless figure of its rider now dangling beneath it in his harness. But instead of heading down into the depths, it was now climbing toward the distant surface.

They followed it up to the two-hundred-foot mark while Captain Bert gave his detailed instructions. There was still a chance, he told his passengers, that the pilot might be alive. But if he reached the surface, he'd certainly be dead—compression sickness would get him as he dropped from ten atmospheres to one.

"So we've got to haul him in around the hundred-and-fifty-foot level—no higher—and then start staging him in the air lock. Well, who's going to do it? *I* can't leave the controls."

No one doubted that the captain was giving the single and sufficient reason, and that he would have gone outside without hesitation had there been anyone else aboard who could operate the sub. After a short pause, Smith said: "I've been three hundred feet down on normal air."

"So have I," interjected Jones. "Not at night, of course," he added thoughtfully.

They weren't exactly volunteering, but it would do. They listened to the skipper's instructions like men about to go over the top, then put on their equipment and went reluctantly into the air lock.

Fortunately, they were in good training and he was able to bring them up to the full pressure in a couple of minutes. "O.K., boys," he said. "I'm opening the door—here you go!"

It would have helped them could they have seen his searchlight, but it had been carefully filtered to remove all visible light. Their hand torches were feeble glow-worms by comparison, as he watched them moving across to the still-ascending torp. Jones went first, while Smith played out the line from the air lock. Both vessels were moving faster than a man could swim, and it was necessary to play Jones like a fish on a line so that as he trailed behind the sub he could work his way across to the torpedo. He was probably not enjoying it, thought the skipper, but he managed to reach the torp on the second try.

After that, the rest was straightforward. Jones cut out the torp's motor, and when the two vessels had come to a halt Smith went to help him. They unstrapped the pilot and carried him back to the sub; his face mask was unflooded, so there was still hope for him. It was not easy to manhandle his helpless body into the tiny air lock, and Smith had to stay outside, feeling horribly lonely, while his partner went ahead.

And thus it was that, thirty minutes later, Walter Franklin woke in a surprising but not totally unfamiliar environment. He was lying in a bunk aboard a small cruiser-class sub, and five men were standing around him. Oddest of all, four of the men had handkerchiefs tied over their faces so that he could only see their eyes. . . .

He looked at the fifth man—at his scarred and grizzled countenance and his rakish goatee. The dirty nautical cap was really quite superfluous; no one would have doubted that this was the skipper.

A raging headache made it hard for Franklin to think straight. He had to make several attempts before he could get out the words: "Where am I?"

"Never you mind, mate," replied the bearded character. "What *we* want to know is what the hell were you doing at a hundred fathoms with a standard compressed-air set. Crikey, he's fainted again!"

The second time Franklin revived, he felt a good deal better, and sufficiently interested in life to want to know what was going on around him. He supposed he should be grateful to these people, whoever they were, but at the moment he felt neither relief nor disappointment at having been rescued.

"What's all this for?" he said, pointing to the conspiratorial handkerchiefs. The skipper, who was now sitting at the controls, turned his head and answered laconically: "Haven't you worked out where you are yet?"

"No."

"Mean ter say you don't know who *I* am?"

"Sorry—I don't."

There was a grunt that might have signified disbelief or disappointment.

"Guess you must be one of the new boys. I'm Bert Darryl,

and you're on board the *Sea Lion.* Those two gentlemen behind you risked their necks getting you in."

Franklin turned in the direction indicated, and looked at
the blank triangles of linen.

"Thanks," he said, and then stopped, unable to think of
any further comment. Now he knew where he was, and could
guess what had happened.

So this was the famous—or notorious, depending on the
point of view—Captain Darryl, whose advertisements you saw
in all the sporting and marine journals. Captain Darryl, the or-
ganizer of thrilling underwater safaris; the intrepid and skillful
hunter—and the equally intrepid and skillful poacher, whose
immunity from prosecution had long been a source of cynical
comment among the wardens. Captain Darryl—one of the
few genuine adventurers of this regimented age, according to
some. Captain Darryl, the big phony, according to others. . . .

Franklin now understood why the rest of the crew was
masked. This was one of the captain's less legitimate enterprises, and Franklin had heard that on these occasions his customers were often from the very highest ranks of society. No
one else could afford to pay his fees; it must cost a lot to run
the *Sea Lion,* even though Captain Darryl was reputed never to
pay cash for anything and to owe money at every port between
Sydney and Darwin.

Franklin glanced at the anonymous figures around him,
wondering who they might be and whether he knew any of
them. Only a halfhearted effort had been made to hide the
powerful big-game guns piled on the other bunk. Just where
was the captain taking his customers, and what were they after?
In the circumstances, he had better keep his eyes shut and
learn as little as possible.

Captain Darryl had already come to the same conclusion.

"You realize, mate," he said over his shoulder as he carefully
blocked Franklin's view of the course settings, "that your presence aboard is just a little bit embarrassing. Still, we couldn't

let you drown, even though you deserved it for a silly stunt like that. The point is—what are we going to do with you now?"

"You could put me ashore on Heron. We can't be very far away." Franklin smiled as he spoke, to show how seriously he intended the suggestion to be taken. It was strange how cheerful and lighthearted he now felt; perhaps it was a merely physical reaction—and perhaps he was really glad at having been given a second chance, a new lease on life.

"What a hope!" snorted the captain. "These gentlemen have paid for their day's sport, and they don't want you boy scouts spoiling it."

"They can take off those handkerchiefs, anyway. They don't look very comfortable—and if I recognize someone, I won't give him away."

Rather reluctantly, the disguises were removed. As he had expected—and hoped—there was no one here whom he knew, either from photographs or direct contact.

"Only one thing for it," said the captain. "We'll have to dump you somewhere before we go into action." He scratched his head as he reviewed his marvelously detailed mental image of the Capricorn Group, then came to a decision. "Anyway, we're stuck with you for tonight, and I guess we'll have to sleep in shifts. If you'd like to make yourself useful, you can get to work in the galley."

"Aye, aye, sir," said Franklin.

The dawn was just breaking when he hit the sandy beach, staggered to his feet, and removed his flippers. ("They're my second-best pair, so mind you post them back to me," Captain Bert had said as he pushed him through the air lock.) Out there beyond the reef, the *Sea Lion* was departing on her dubious business, and the hunters were getting ready for their sortie. Though it was against his principles and his duties, Franklin could not help wishing them luck.

Captain Bert had promised to radio Brisbane in four hours' time, and the message would be passed on to Heron Island immediately. Presumably that four hours would give the captain and his clients the time they needed to make their assault and to get clear of W.F.O. waters.

Franklin walked up the beach, stripped off his wet equipment and clothes, and lay down to watch the sunrise he had never dreamed he would see. He had four hours to wait, to wrestle with his thoughts and to face life once more. But he did not need the time, for he had made the decision hours ago.

His life was no longer his to throw away if he chose; not when it had been given back to him, at the risk of their own, by men he had never met before and would never see again.

CHAPTER

"Y ou realize, of course," said Myers, "that I'm only the station doctor, not a high-powered psychiatrist. So I'll have to send you back to Professor Stevens and his merry men."

"Is that really necessary?" asked Franklin.

"I don't think it is, but I can't accept the responsibility. If I was a gambler like Don, I'd take very long odds that you'll never play this trick again. But doctors can't afford to gamble, and anyway I think it would be a good idea to get you off Heron for a few days."

"I'll finish the course in a couple of weeks. Can't it wait until then?"

"Don't argue with doctors, Walt—you can't win. And if my arithmetic is correct, a month and a half is *not* a couple of weeks. The course can wait for a few days; I don't think Prof. Stevens will keep you very long. He'll probably give you a good dressing-down and will send you straight back. Meanwhile, if you're interested in my views, I'd like to get 'em off my chest."

"Go ahead."

"First of all, we know *why* you had that attack when you did. Smell is the most evocative of all the senses, and now that you've told me that a spaceship air lock always smells of syn-thene the whole business makes sense. It was hard luck that you got a whiff of the stuff just when you were looking at the Space Station: The damn thing's nearly hypnotized me some-times when I've watched it scuttling across the sky like some mad meteor.

"But that isn't the whole explanation, Walter. You had to be, let's say, emotionally sensitized to make you susceptible. Tell me—have you got a photograph of your wife here?"

Franklin seemed more puzzled than disturbed by the un-expected, indeed apparently incongruous, question.

"Yes," he said. "Why do you ask?"

"Never mind. May I have a look at it?"

After a good deal of searching, which Myers was quite sure was unnecessary, Franklin produced a leather wallet and handed it over. He did not look at Myers as the doctor stud-ied the woman who was now parted from her husband by laws more inviolable than any that man could make.

She was small and dark, with lustrous brown eyes. A single glance told Myers all that he wanted to know, yet he contin-ued to gaze at the photograph with an unanalyzable mixture of compassion and curiosity. How, he wondered, was Franklin's wife meeting her problem? Was she, too, rebuilding her life on that far world to which she was forever bound by genetics and gravity? No, forever was not quite accurate. She could safely journey to the Moon, which had only the gravity of her native world. But there would be no purpose in doing so, for Franklin could never face even the trifling voyage from Earth to Moon.

With a sigh, Dr. Myers closed the wallet. Even in the most perfect of social systems, the most peaceful and contented of worlds, there would still be heartbreak and tragedy. And as man extended his powers over the universe, he would in-evitably create new evils and new problems to plague him. Yet, apart from its details, there was nothing really novel

about this case. All down the ages, men had been separated—
often forever—from those they loved by the accident of geography or the malice of their fellows.

"Listen, Walt," said Myers as he handed back the wallet. "I
know a few things about you that even Prof. Stevens doesn't,
so here's my contribution.

"Whether you realize it consciously or not, Indra is like your
wife. That, of course, is why you were attracted to her in the
first place. At the same time, that attraction has set up a conflict in your mind. You don't want to be unfaithful even to
someone—please excuse me for speaking so bluntly—who
might as well be dead as far as you are concerned. Well—do you
agree with my analysis?"

Franklin took a long time to answer. Then he said at last:
"I think there may be something in that. But what am I to
do?"

"This may sound cynical, but there is an old saying which
applies in this case. 'Cooperate with the inevitable.' Once you
admit that certain aspects of your life are fixed and have to be
accepted, you will stop fighting against them. It won't be a sur-
render; it will give you the energy you need for the battles that
still have to be won."

"What does Indra really think about me?"

"The silly girl's in love with you, if that's what you want to
know. So the least you can do is make it up to her for all the
trouble you've caused."

"Then do you think I should marry again?"

"The fact that you can ask that question is a good sign, but
I can't answer it with a simple 'yes' or 'no.' We've done our best
to rebuild your professional life; we can't give you so much
help with your emotional one. Obviously, it's highly desirable
for you to establish a firm and stable relationship to replace
the one you have lost. As for Indra—well, she's a charming
and intelligent girl, but no one can say how much of her pres-

ent feelings are due to sympathy. So don't rush matters; let them take their time. You can't afford to make any mistakes.

"Well, that finishes the sermon—except for one item. Part of the trouble with you, Walter Franklin, is that you've always been too independent and self-reliant. You refused to admit that you had limitations, that you needed help from anyone else. So when you came up against something that was too big for you, you really went to pieces, and you've been hating yourself for it ever since.

"Now that's all over and done with; even if the old Walt Franklin was a bit of a stinker, we can make a better job of the Mark II. Don't you agree?"

Franklin gave a wry smile; he felt emotionally exhausted, yet at the same time most of the remaining shadows had lifted from his mind. Hard though it had been for him to accept help, he had surrendered at last and he felt better for it.

"Thanks for the treatment, Doc," he said. "I don't believe the specialists could do any better, and I'm quite sure now that this trip back to Prof. Stevens isn't necessary."

"So am I—but you're going just the same. Now clear out and let me get on with my proper work of putting sticking plaster on coral cuts."

Franklin was halfway through the door when he paused with a sudden, anxious query.

"I almost forgot—Don particularly wants to take me out tomorrow in the sub. Will that be O.K.?"

"Oh, sure—Don's big enough to look after you. Just get back in time for the noon plane, that's all I ask."

As Franklin walked away from the office and two rooms grandly called "Medical Center" he felt no resentment at having been ordered off the island. He had received far more tolerance and consideration than he had expected—perhaps more than he deserved. All the mild hostility that had been focused upon him by the less-privileged trainees had vanished at a stroke, but it would be best for him to escape for a few days from an atmosphere that had become embarrassingly sympathetic. In particular, he found it hard to talk without a sense of strain with Don and Indra.

He thought again of Dr. Myers' advice, and remembered the jolting leap his heart had given at the words "the silly girl's in love with you." Yet it would be unfair, he knew, to take advantage of the present emotional situation; they could only know what they meant to each other when they had both had time for careful and mature thought. Put that way, it seemed a little cold-blooded and calculating. If one was really in love, did one stop to weigh the pros and cons?

He knew the answer to that. As Myers had said, he could not afford any more mistakes. It was far better to take his time and be certain than to risk the happiness of two lives.

The Sun had barely lifted above the miles of reef extending to the east when Don Burley hauled Franklin out of bed. Don's attitude toward him had undergone a change which it was not easy to define. He had been shocked and distressed by what had occurred and had tried, in his somewhat boisterous manner, to express sympathy and understanding. At the same time, his *amour propre* had been hurt; he could not quite believe, even now, that Indra had never been seriously interested in him but only in Franklin, whom he had never thought of as a rival. It was not that he was jealous of Franklin; jealousy was an emotion beyond him. He was worried—as most men are occasionally throughout their lives—by his discovery that he did not understand women as well as he had believed.

Franklin had already packed, and his room looked bleak and bare. Even though he might be gone for only a few days, the accommodation was needed too badly for it to be left vacant just to suit his convenience. It served him right, he told himself philosophically.

Don was in a hurry, which was not unusual, but there was also a conspiratorial air about him, as if he had planned some big surprise for Franklin and was almost childishly anxious that everything should come off as intended. In any other circumstances, Franklin would have suspected some practical joke, but that could hardly be the explanation now.

By this time, the little training sub had become practically an extension of his own body, and he followed the courses Don gave him until he knew, by mental dead reckoning, that they were somewhere out in the thirty-mile-wide channel between Wistari Reef and the mainland. For some reason of his own, which he refused to explain, Don had switched off the pilot's main sonar screen, so that Franklin was navigating blind. Don himself could see everything that was in the vicinity by looking at the repeater set at the rear of the cabin, and though Franklin was occasionally tempted to glance back at it he managed to resist the impulse. This was, after all, a legitimate part of his training; one day he might have to navigate a sub that had been blinded by a breakdown of its underwater senses.

"You can surface now," said Don at last. He was trying to be casual, but the undercurrent of excitement in his voice could not be concealed. Franklin blew the tanks, and even without looking at the depth gauge knew when he broke surface by the unmistakable rolling of the sub. It was not a comfortable sensation, and he hoped that they would not stay here for long.

Don gave one more glance at his private sonar screen, then gestured to the hatch overhead.

"Open up," he said. "Let's have a look at the scenery."

"We may ship some water," protested Franklin. "It feels pretty rough."

"With the two of us in that hatch, not much is going to leak past. Here—put on this cape. That'll keep the spray out of the works."

It seemed a crazy idea, but Don must have a good reason. Overhead, a tiny elliptical patch of sky appeared as the outer seal of the conning tower opened. Don scrambled up the ladder first; then Franklin followed, blinking his eyes against the windswept spray.

Yes, Don had known what he was doing. There was little wonder that he had been so anxious to make this trip before Franklin left the island. In his own way, Don was a good psychologist, and Franklin felt an inexpressible gratitude toward him. For this was one of the great moments of his life; he could think of only one other to match it: the moment when he had first seen Earth, in all its heart-stopping beauty, floating against the infinitely distant background of the stars. This scene, also, filled his soul with the same awe, the same sense of being in the presence of cosmic forces.

The whales were moving north, and he was among them. During the night, the leaders must have passed through the Queensland Gate, on the way to the warm seas in which their young could be safely born. A living armada was all around him, plowing steadfastly through the waves with effortless power. The great dark bodies emerged streaming from the water, then sank with scarcely a ripple back into the sea. As Franklin watched, too fascinated to feel any sense of danger, one of the enormous beasts surfaced less than forty feet away. There was a roaring whistle of air as it emptied its lungs, and he caught a mercifully weakened breath of the fetid air. A ridiculously tiny eye stared at him—an eye that seemed lost in the monstrous, misshapen head. For a moment the two mammals—the biped who had abandoned the sea, the quadruped who had returned to it—regarded each other across the evolutionary gulf that separated them. What did a man look like to a whale? Franklin asked himself, and wondered if there was any way of finding the answer. Then the titanic bulk tilted down into the sea, the great flukes lifted themselves into the air, and the waters flowed back to fill the sudden void.

A distant clap of thunder made him look toward the mainland. Half a mile away, the giants were playing. As he watched, a shape so strange that it was hard to relate it to any of the films and pictures he had seen emerged from the waves with breathtaking slowness, and hung poised for a moment completely out of the water. As a ballet dancer seems at the climax of his leap to defy gravity, so for an instant the whale appeared to hang upon the horizon. Then, with that same un-hurried grace, it tumbled back into the sea, and seconds later the crash of the impact came echoing over the waves.

The sheer slowness of that huge leap gave it a dreamlike quality, as if the sense of time had been distorted. Nothing else conveyed so clearly to Franklin the immense size of the beasts that now surrounded him like moving islands. Rather belatedly, he wondered what would happen if one of the whales surfaced beneath the sub, or decided to take too close an interest in it. . . .

"No need to worry," Don reassured him. "They know who we are. Sometimes they'll come and rub against us to remove parasites, and then it gets a bit uncomfortable. As for bump-ing into us accidentally—they can see where they're going a good deal better than we can."

As if to refute this statement, a streamlined mountain emerged dripping from the sea and showered water down upon them. The sub rocked crazily, and for a moment Franklin feared it was going to overturn; then it righted itself, and he realized that he could, quite literally, reach out and touch the barnacle-encrusted head now lying on the waves. The weirdly shaped mouth opened in a prodigious yawn, the hundreds of strips of whalebone fluttering like a Venetian blind in a breeze.

Had he been alone, Franklin would have been scared stiff, but Don seemed the complete master of the situation. He leaned out of the hatch and yelled in the direction of the whale's invisible ear: "Move over momma! We're not your baby!"

The great mouth with its hanging draperies of bone

snapped shut, the beady little eye—strangely like a cow's and seemingly not much larger—looked at them with what might have been a hurt expression. Then the sub rocked once more, and the whale was gone.

"It's quite safe, you see," Don explained. "They're peaceful, good-natured beasts, except when they have their calves with them. Just like any other cattle."

"But would you get this close to any of the toothed whales—the sperm whale, for instance?"

"That depends. If it was an old rogue male—a real Moby Dick—I wouldn't care to try it. Same with killer whales; they might think I was good eating, though I could scare them off easily enough by turning on the hooter. I once got into a harem of about a dozen sperm whales, and the ladies didn't seem to mind, even though some of them had calves with them. Nor did the old man, oddly enough. I suppose he knew I wasn't a rival." He paused thoughtfully, then continued. "That was the only time I've actually seen whales mating. It was pretty awe-inspiring—gave me such an inferiority complex it put me off my stroke for a week."

"How many would you say there are in this school?" asked Franklin.

"Oh, about a hundred. The recorders at the gate will give the exact figure. So you can say there are at least five thousand tons of the best meal and oil swimming around us—a couple of million dollars, if it's worth a penny. Doesn't all that cash make you feel good?"

"No," said Franklin. "And I'm damn sure it doesn't make any difference to you. Now I know why you like this job, and there's no need to put on an act about it."

Don made no attempt to answer. They stood together in the cramped hatchway, not feeling the spray upon their faces, sharing the same thoughts and emotions, as the mightiest animals the world had ever seen drove purposefully past them to the north. It was then that Franklin knew, with a final certainty, that his life was firmly set upon its new course. Though much had been taken from him which he would never cease to regret, he had passed the stage of futile grief and solitary brooding. He had lost the freedom of space, but he had won the freedom of the seas.

That was enough for any man.

CHAPTER

CONFIDENTIAL
To Be Kept in Sealed Envelope

Attached is the medical report on Walter Franklin, who has now successfully completed his training and has qualified as third warden with the highest rating ever recorded. In view of certain complaints from senior members of Establishment and Personnel Branch that earlier reports were too technical for comprehension, I am giving this summary in language understandable even to administrative officers.

Despite a number of personality defects, W.F.'s capability rating places him in that small group from which future heads of technical departments must be drawn—a group so desperately small that, as I have frequently pointed out, the very existence of the state is threatened unless we can enlarge it. The accident which eliminated W.F. from the Space Service, in which he would have undoubtedly had a distinguished career, left him in full possession of all his talents and presented us with an opportunity which it would have been criminal to waste. Not only did it give us a chance of studying what has since become the classic textbook case of astrophobia, but it offered us a striking challenge in rehabilitation. The analogies between sea and space have often been pointed out, and a man used to one can readily adapt to the other. In this case, however, the differences between the two media were equally important; at the simplest level, the fact that the sea is a continuous and sustaining fluid, in which vision is always limited to no more than a few yards, gave W.F. the sense of security he had lost in space.

.The fact that, toward the end of his training, he attempted suicide may at first appear to argue against the correctness of our treatment. This is not the case; the attempt was due to a combination of quite unforeseeable factors (Paragraphs 57–86 of attached report), and its outcome, as often happens, was an improvement in the stability of the subject. The method chosen for the attempt is also highly significant in itself and proves that we had made a correct choice of W.F.'s new vocation. The seriousness of the attempt may also be questioned; had W.F. been really determined to kill himself, he would have chosen a simpler and less fallible method of doing so.

Now that the subject has reestablished—apparently successfully—his emotional life and has shown only trivial symptoms of disturbance, I am confident that we need expect no more trouble. Above all, it is important that we interfere with him as little as possible. His independence and originality of mind, though no longer as exaggerated as they were, are a fundamental part of his personality and will largely determine his future progress.

Only time will show whether all the skill and effort lavished on this case will be repaid in cents and dollars. Even if it is not, those engaged upon it have already received their reward in the rebuilding of a life, which will certainly be useful and may be invaluable.

IAN K. STEVENS
Director, Division of Applied Psychiatry,
World Health Organization

II

THE WARDEN

CHAPTER

Second Warden Walter Franklin was having his monthly shave when the emergency call came through. It had always seemed a little surprising to him that, after so many years of research, the biochemists had not yet found an inhibitor that would put one's bristles permanently out of action. Still, one should not be ungrateful; only a couple of generations ago, incredible though it seemed, men had been forced to shave themselves every day, using a variety of complicated, expensive, and sometimes lethal instruments.

Franklin did not stop to wipe the layer of cream from his face when he heard the shrill whining of the communicator alarm. He was out of the bathroom, through the kitchen, and into the hall before the sound had died away and the instrument had been able to get its second breath. As he punched the Receive button, the screen lighted up and he was looking into the familiar but now harassed face of the Headquarters operator.

"You're to report for duty at once, Mr. Franklin," she said breathlessly.

"What's the trouble?"

"It's Farms, sir. The fence is down somewhere and one of

the herds has broken through. It's eating the spring crop, and we've got to get it out as quickly as we can."

"Oh, is that all?" said Franklin. "I'll be over at the dock in ten minutes."

It was an emergency all right, but not one about which he could feel very excited. Of course, Farms would be yelling its head off as its production quota was being whittled down by thousands of half-ton nibbles. But he was secretly on the side of the whales; if they'd managed to break into the great plankton prairies, then good luck to them.

"What's all the fuss about?" said Indra as she came out of the bedroom, her long, dark hair looking attractive even at this time of the morning as it hung in lustrous tresses over her shoulders. When Franklin told her, she appeared worried.

"It's a bigger emergency than you seem to think," she said. "Unless you act quickly, you may have some very sick whales on your hands. The spring overturn was only two weeks ago, and it's the biggest one we've ever had. So your greedy pets will be gorging themselves silly."

Franklin realized that she was perfectly right. The plankton farms were no affair of his, and formed a completely independent section of the Marine Division. But he knew a great deal about them, since they were an alternative and to some extent rival method of getting food from the sea. The plankton enthusiasts claimed, with a good deal of justice, that crop growing was more efficient than herding, since the whales themselves fed on the plankton and were therefore farther down the food chain. Why waste ten pounds of plankton, they argued, to produce one pound of whale, when you could harvest it directly?

The debate had been in progress for at least twenty years, and so far neither side could claim to have won. Sometimes the argument had been quite acrimonious and had echoed, on an infinitely larger and more sophisticated scale, the rivalry between homesteaders and cattle barons in the days when the

American Midwest was being settled. But unfortunately for latter-day mythmakers, competing departments of the Marine Division of the World Food Organization fought each other purely with official minutes and the efficient but unspectacular weapons of bureaucracy. There were no gunfighters prowling the range, and if the fence had gone down it would be due to purely technical troubles, not midnight sabotage. . . .

In the sea as on the land, all life depends upon vegetation. And the amount of vegetation in turn depends upon the mineral content of the medium in which it grows—the nitrates, phosphates, and scores of other basic chemicals. In the ocean, there is always a tendency for these vital substances to accumulate in the depths, far below the regions where light penetrates and therefore plants can exist and grow. The upper few hundred feet of the sea is the primary source of its life; everything below that level preys, at second or third hand, on the food formed above.

Every spring, as the warmth of the new year seeps down into the ocean, the waters far below respond to the invisible Sun. They expand and rise, lifting to the surface, in untold billions of tons, the salts and minerals they bear. Thus fertilized by food from below and Sun from above, the floating plants multiply with explosive violence, and the creatures which browse upon them flourish accordingly. And so spring comes to the meadows of the sea.

This was the cycle that had repeated itself at least a billion times before man appeared on the scene. And now he had changed it. Not content with the upwelling of minerals produced by Nature, he had sunk his atomic generators at strategic spots far down into the sea, where the raw heat they produced would start immense, submerged fountains lifting their chemical treasure toward the fruitful Sun. This artificial enhancement of the natural overturn had been one of the most unexpected, as well as the most rewarding, of all the many applications of nuclear energy. By this means alone, the output of food from the sea had been increased by almost ten per cent.

And now the whales were busily doing their best to restore the balance.

The roundup would have to be a combined sea and air operation. There were too few of the subs, and they were far too slow, to do the job unassisted. Three of them—including Franklin's one-man scout—were being flown to the scene of the breakthrough by a cargo plane which would drop them and then cooperate by spotting the movements of the whales from the air, if they had scattered over too large an area for the subs' sonar to pick them up. Two other planes would also try to scare the whales by dropping noise generators near them, but this technique had never worked well in the past and no one really expected much success from it now.

Within twenty minutes of the alarm, Franklin was watching the enormous food-processing plants of Pearl Harbor falling below as the jets of the freighter hauled him up into the sky. Even now, he was still not fond of flying and tried to avoid it when he could. But it no longer worried him, and he could look down on the world beneath without qualms.

A hundred miles east of Hawaii, the sea turned suddenly from blue to gold. The moving fields, rich with the year's first crop, covered the Pacific clear out to the horizon, and showed no sign of ending as the plane raced on toward the rising sun. Here and there the mile-long skimmers of the floating harvesters lay upon the surface like the enigmatic toys of some giant children, while beside them, smaller and more compact, were the pontoons and rafts of the concentration equipment. It was an impressive sight, even in these days of mammoth engineering achievements, but it did not move Franklin. He could not become excited over a billion tons of assorted diatoms and shrimps—not even though he knew that they fed a quarter of the human race.

"Just passing over the Hawaiian Corridor," said the pilot's voice from the speaker. "We should see the break in a minute."

"I can see it now," said one of the other wardens, leaning past Franklin and pointing out to sea. "There they are—having the time of their lives."

It was a spectacle which must be making the poor farmers tear their hair. Franklin suddenly remembered an old nursery rhyme he had not thought of for at least thirty years:

Little Boy Blue, come blow your horn,
The sheep's in the meadow, the cow's in the corn.

There was no doubt that the cows were in the corn, and Little Boy Blue was going to have a busy time getting them out. Far below, myriads of narrow swathes were being carved in the endless yellow sea, as the ravenous, slowly moving mountains ate their way into the rich plankton meadows. A blue line of exposed water marked the track of each whale as it meandered through what must be a cetacean heaven—a heaven from which it was Franklin's job to expel it as promptly as possible.

The three wardens, after a final radio briefing, left the cabin and went down to the hold, where the little subs were already hanging from the davits which would lower them into the sea. There would be no difficulty about this operation; what might not be so easy would be getting them back again, and if the sea became rough they might have to go home under their own power.

It seemed strange to be inside a submarine inside an airplane, but Franklin had little time for such thoughts as he went through the routine cockpit drill. Then the speaker on his control panel remarked: "Hovering at thirty feet; now opening cargo hatches. Stand by, Number One Sub." Franklin was Number Two; the great cargo craft was poised so steadily, and the hoists moved down so smoothly, that he never felt any impact as the sub dropped into its natural element. Then the three scouts were fanning out along the tracks that had been assigned to them, like mechanized sheep dogs rounding up a flock.

Almost at once, Franklin realized that this operation was not going to be as simple as it looked. The sub was driving through a thick soup that completely eliminated vision and even interfered seriously with sonar. What was still more serious, the hydrojet motors were laboring unhappily as their impellers chewed through the mush. He could not afford to get his propulsion system clogged; the best thing to do would be to dive below the plankton layer and not to surface until it was absolutely necessary.

Three hundred feet down, the water was merely murky and though vision was still impossible he could make good speed. He wondered if the greedily feasting whales above his head knew of his approach and realized that their idyll was coming to an end. On the sonar screen he could see their luminous echoes moving slowly across the ghostly mirror of the air-water surface which his sound beams could not penetrate. It was odd how similar the surface of the sea looked from below both to the naked eye and to the acoustical senses of the sonar.

The characteristically compact little echoes of the two other subs were moving out to the flanks of the scattered herd. Franklin glanced at the chronometer; in less than a minute, the drive was due to begin. He switched on the external microphones and listened to the voices of the sea.

How could anyone have ever thought that the sea was silent! Even man's limited hearing could detect many of its sounds—the clashing of chitinous claws, the moan of great boulders made restive by the ocean swell, the highpitched squeak of porpoises, the unmistakable "flick" of a shark's tail as it suddenly accelerated on a new course. But these were merely the sounds in the audible spectrum; to listen to the full music of the sea one must go both below and above the range of human hearing. This was a simple enough task for the sub's frequency converters; if he wished, Franklin could tune in to any sounds from almost a million cycles a second down to vibrations as sluggish as the slow opening of an ancient, rusty door.

He set the receiver to the broadest band, and at once his mind began to interpret the multitudinous messages that came pouring into the little cabin from the watery world outside. The man-made noises he dismissed at once; the sounds of his own sub and the more distant whines of his companion vessels were largely eliminated by the special filters designed for that purpose. But he could just detect the distinctive whistles of the three sonar sets—his own almost blanketing the others—and beyond those the faint and far-off BEEP-BEEP-BEEP of the Hawaiian Corridor. The double fence which was supposed to channel the whales safely through the rich sea farm sent out its pulses at five-second intervals, and though the nearest portion of the fence was out of action the more distant parts of the sonic barrier could be clearly heard. The pulses were curiously distorted and drawn-out into a faint continuous echo as each new burst of sound was followed at once by the delayed waves from more and more remote regions of the fence. Franklin could hear each pulse running away into the distance, as sometimes a clap of thunder may be heard racing across the sky.

Against this background, the sounds of the natural world stood out sharp and clear. From all directions, with never a moment's silence, came the shrill shrieks and squealings of the whales as they talked to one another or merely gave vent to their high spirits and enjoyment. Franklin could distinguish between the voices of the males and the females, but he was not one of those experts who could identify individuals and even interpret what they were trying to express.

There is no more eerie sound in all the world than the screaming of a herd of whales, when one moves among it in the depths of the sea. Franklin had only to close his eyes and he could imagine that he was lost in some demon-haunted forest, while ghosts and goblins closed in upon him. Could Hector Berlioz have heard this banshee chorus, he would have known that Nature had already anticipated his "Dream of the Witches' Sabbath."

But weirdness lies only in unfamiliarity, and this sound was now part of Franklin's life. It no longer gave him nightmares, as it had sometimes done in his early days. Indeed, the main emotion that it now inspired in him was an affectionate amusement, together with a slight surprise that such enormous animals produced such falsetto screams.

Yet there was a memory that the sound of the sea sometimes evoked. It no longer had power to hurt him, though it could still fill his heart with a wistful sadness. He remembered all the times he had spent in the signals rooms of space ships or space stations, listening to the radio waves coming in as the monitors combed the spectrum in their automatic search. Sometimes there had been, like these same ghostly voices calling in the night, the sound of distant ships or beacons, or the torrents of high-speed code as the colonies talked with Mother Earth. And always one could hear a perpetual murmuring background to man's feeble transmitters, the endless susurration of the stars and galaxies themselves as they drenched the whole universe with radiation.

The chronometer hand came around to zero. It had not scythed away the first second before the sea erupted in a hellish cacophony of sound—a rising and falling ululation that made Franklin reach swiftly for the volume control. The sonic mines had been dropped, and he felt sorry for any whales who were unlucky enough to be near them. Almost at once the pattern of echoes on the screen began to change, as the terrified beasts started to flee in panic toward the west. Franklin watched closely, preparing to head off any part of the herd that looked like it would miss the gap in the fence and turn back into the farms.

The noise generators must have been improved, he decided,

since the last time this trick had been tried—or else these whales were more amenable. Only a few strugglers tried to break away, and it was no more than ten minutes' work to round them up on the right path and scare them back with the subs' own sirens. Half an hour after the mines had been dropped, the entire herd had been funneled back through the invisible gap in the fence, and was milling around inside the narrow corridor. There was nothing for the subs to do but to stand by until the engineers had carried out their repairs and the curtain of sound was once more complete.

No one could claim that it was a famous victory. It was just another day's work, a minor battle in an endless campaign. Already the excitement of the chase had died away, and Franklin was wondering how long it would be before the freighter could hoist them out of the ocean and fly them back to Hawaii. This was, after all, supposed to be his day off, and he had promised to take Peter down to Waikiki and start teaching him how to swim.

Even when he is merely standing by, a good warden never lets his attention stray for long from his sonar screen. Every three minutes, without any conscious thought, Franklin switched to the long-range scan and tilted the transmitter down toward the seabed, just to keep track of what was going on around him. He did not doubt that his colleagues were doing exactly the same, between wondering how long it would be before they were relieved. . . .

At the very limit of his range, ten miles away and almost two miles down, a faint echo had crawled onto the edge of the screen. Franklin looked at it with mild interest; then his brows knit in perplexity. It must be an unusually large object to be visible at such a distance—something quite as large as a whale. But no whale could be swimming at such a depth; though sperm whales had been encountered almost a mile down, this was beyond the limits at which they could operate, fabulous divers though they were. A deep-sea shark? Possibly, thought Franklin; it would do no harm to have a closer look at it.

He locked the scanner onto the distant echo and expanded the image as far as the screen magnification would allow. It was too far away to make out any detail, but he could see now that he was looking at a long, thin object—and that it was moving quite rapidly. He stared at it for a moment, then called his colleagues. Unnecessary chatter was discouraged on operations, but here was a minor mystery that intrigued him.

"Sub Two calling," he said. "I've a large echo bearing 185 degrees, range 9.7 miles, depth 1.8 miles. Looks like another sub. You know if anyone else is operating around here?"

"Sub One calling Sub Two," came the first reply. "That's outside my range. Could be a Research Department sub down there. How big would you say your echo is?"

"About a hundred feet long. Maybe more. It's doing over ten knots."

"Sub Three calling. There's no research vessel around here. The *Nautilus IV* is laid up for repairs, and the *Cousteau*'s in the Atlantic. Must be a fish you've got hold of."

"There aren't any fish this size. Have I permission to go after it? I think we ought to check up."

"Permission granted," answered Sub One. "We'll hold the gap here. Keep in touch."

Franklin swung the sub around to the south, and brought the little vessel up to maximum speed with a smooth rush of power. The echo he was chasing was already too deep for him to reach, but there was always the chance that it might come back to the surface. Even if it did not, he would be able to get a much clearer image when he had shortened his range.

He had traveled only two miles when he saw that the chase was hopeless. There could be no doubt; his quarry had detected either the vibrations of his motor or his sonar and was plunging at full speed straight down to the bottom. He managed to get within four miles, and then the signal was lost in the confused maze of echoes from the ocean bed. His last glimpse of it confirmed his earlier impression of great length and relative thinness, but he was still unable to make out any details of its structure.

"So it got away from you," said Sub One. "I thought it would."

"Then you know what it was?"

"No—nor does anyone else. And if you'll take my advice, you won't talk to any reporters about it. If you do, you'll never live it down."

Momentarily frozen with astonishment, Franklin stared at the little loudspeaker from which the words had just come. So they had not been pulling his leg, as he had always assumed. He remembered some of the tales he had heard in the bar at Heron Island and wherever wardens gathered together after duty. He had laughed at them then, but now he knew that the tales were true.

That nervous echo skittering hastily out of range had been nothing less than the Great Sea Serpent.

Indra, who was still doing part-time work at the Hawaii Aquarium when her household duties permitted, was not as impressed as her husband had expected. In fact, her first comment was somewhat deflating.

"Yes, but *which* sea serpent? You know there are at least three totally different types."

"I certainly didn't."

"Well, first of all there's a giant eel which has been seen on three or four occasions but never properly identified, though its larvae were caught back in the 1940s. It's known to grow up to sixty feet long, and that's enough of a sea serpent for most people. But the really spectacular one is the oarfish—*Regalecus glesne.* That's got a face like a horse, a crest of brilliant red quills like an Indian brave's headdress—and a snakelike body which may be seventy feet long. Since we know that these things exist, how do you expect us to be surprised at anything the sea can produce?"

"What about the third type you mentioned?"

"That's the one we haven't identified or even described. We just call it 'X' because people still laugh when you talk about sea serpents. The only thing that we know about it is that it undoubtedly exists, that it's extremely sly, and that it lives in deep water. One day we'll catch it, but when we do it will probably be through pure luck."

Franklin was very thoughtful for the rest of the evening. He did not like to admit that, despite all the instruments that man now used to probe the sea, despite his own continual patrolling of the depths, the ocean still held many secrets and would retain them for ages yet to come. And he knew that, though he might never see it again, he would be haunted all his life by the memory of that distant, tantalizing echo as it descended swiftly into the abyss that was its home.

CHAPTER

There are many misconceptions about the glamour of a warden's life. Franklin had never shared them, so he was neither surprised nor disappointed that so much of his time was spent on long, uneventful patrols far out at sea. Indeed, he welcomed them. They gave him time to think, yet not time to brood—and it was on these lonely missions in the living heart of the sea that his last fears were shed and his mental scars finally healed.

The warden's year was dominated by the pattern of whale migration, but that pattern was itself continually changing as new areas of the sea were fenced and fertilized. He might spend summer moving cautiously through the polar ice, and winter beating back and forth across the equator. Sometimes he would operate from shore stations, sometimes from mobile bases like the *Rorqual,* the *Pequod,* or the *Cachelot.* One season he might be wholly concerned with the great whalebone or baleen whales, who literally strained their food from the sea as they swam, mouth open, through the rich plankton soup. And another season he would have to deal with their very different cousins, the fierce, toothed cetaceans of whom the sperm whales were the most important representatives. These were no gentle herbivores, but pursued and fought their monstrous prey in the lightless deep half a mile from the last rays of the Sun.

There would be weeks or even months when a warden would never see a whale. The bureau had many calls on its equipment and personnel, and whales were not its only business. Everyone who had dealings with the sea appeared to come, sooner or later, to the Bureau of Whales with an appeal for help. Sometimes the requests were tragic; several times a year subs were sent on usually fruitless searches for drowned sportsmen or explorers.

At the other extreme, there was a standing joke that a senator had once asked the Sydney office to locate his false teeth, lost when the Bondi surf worked its will upon him. It was said that he had received, with great promptness, the foot-wide jaws of a tiger shark, with an apologetic note saying that these were the only unwanted teeth that an extensive search had been able to find off Bondi Beach.

Some tasks that came the warden's way had a certain glamour, and were eagerly sought after when they arose. A very small and understaffed section of the Bureau of Fisheries was concerned with pearls, and during the slack season wardens were sometimes detached from their normal work and allowed to assist on the pearl beds.

Franklin had one such tour of duty in the Persian Gulf. It was straightforward work, not unlike gardening, and since it involved diving to depths never greater than two hundred feet simple compressed-air equipment was used and the diver employed a torpedo for moving around. The best areas for pearl cultivation had been carefully populated with selected stock, and the main problem was protecting the oysters from their natural enemies—particularly starfish and rays. When they had time to mature, they were collected and carried back to the surface for inspection—one of the few jobs that no one had ever been able to mechanize.

Any pearls discovered belonged, of course, to the Bureau of Fisheries. But it was noticeable that the wives of all the wardens posted to this duty very soon afterward sported pearl necklaces or earrings—and Indra was no exception to this rule.

She had received her necklace the day she gave birth to Peter, and with the arrival of his son it seemed to Franklin that the old chapter of his life had finally closed. It was not true, of course; he could never forget—nor did he wish to—that Irene had given him Roy and Rupert, on a world which was now as remote to him as a planet of the farthest star. But the ache of that irrevocable parting had subsided at last, for no grief can endure forever.

He was glad—though he had once bitterly resented it—that it was impossible to talk to anyone on Mars, or indeed anywhere in space beyond the orbit of the Moon. The six-minute time lag for the round trip, even when the planet was at its nearest, made conversation out of the question, so he could never torture himself by feeling in the presence of Irene and the boys by calling them up on the visiphone. Every Christmas they exchanged recordings and talked over the events of the year; apart from occasional letters, that was the only personal contact they now had, and the only one that Franklin needed.

There was no way of telling how well Irene had adjusted to her virtual widowhood. The boys must have helped, but there were times when Franklin wished that she had married again, for their sakes as well as hers. Yet somehow he had never been able to suggest it, and she had never raised the subject, even when he had made this step himself.

Did she resent Indra? That again was hard to tell. Perhaps some jealousy was inevitable; Indra herself, during the occasional quarrels that punctuated their marriage, made it clear that she sometimes disliked the thought of being only the second woman in Franklin's life.

Such quarrels were rare, and after the birth of Peter they

were rarer. A married couple forms a dynamically unstable system until the arrival of the first child converts it from a double
to a triple group.

Franklin was as happy now as he had ever hoped to be. His
family gave him the emotional security he needed; his work
provided the interest and adventure which he had sought in
space, only to lose again. There was more life and wonder in
the sea than in all the endless empty leagues between the planets, and it was seldom now that his heart ached for the blue
beauty of the crescent Earth, the swirling silver mist of the
Milky Way, or the tense excitement of landfall on the moons
of Mars at the end of a long voyage.

The sea had begun to shape his life and thought, as it must
that of all men who try to master it and learn its secrets. He
felt a kinship with all the creatures that moved throughout its
length and depth, even when they were enemies which it was
his duty to destroy. But above all, he felt a sympathy and an almost mystical reverence, of which he was half ashamed, toward
the great beasts whose destinies he ruled.

He believed that most wardens knew that feeling, though
they were careful to avoid admitting it in their shoptalk. The
nearest they came to it was when they accused each other of
being "whale happy," a somewhat indefinable term which
might be summed up as acting more like a whale than a man
in a given situation. It was a form of identification without
which no warden could be really good at his job, but there
were times when it could become too extreme. The classic
case—which everyone swore was perfectly true—was that of
the senior warden who felt he was suffocating unless he
brought his sub up to blow every ten minutes.

Being regarded—and regarding themselves—as the elite of
the world's army of underwater experts, the wardens were always called upon when there was some unusual job that no
one else cared to perform. Sometimes these jobs were so suici-

dal that it was necessary to explain to the would-be client that he must find another way out of his difficulties.

But occasionally there was no other way, and risks had to be taken. The bureau still remembered how Chief Warden Kircher, back in '22, had gone up the giant intake pipes through which the cooling water flowed into the fusion power plant supplying half the South American continent. One of the filter grilles had started to come loose, and could be fixed only by a man on the spot. With strong ropes tied around his body to prevent him from being sucked through the wire meshing, Kircher had descended into the roaring darkness. He had done the job and returned safely; but that was the last time he ever went underwater.

So far, all Franklin's missions had been fairly conventional ones; he had had to face nothing as hair-raising as Kircher's exploit, and was not sure how he would react if such an occasion arose. Of course, he could always turn down any assignment that involved abnormal risks; his contract was quite specific on that point. But the "suicide clause," as it was sardonically called, was very much a dead letter. Any warden who invoked it, except under the most extreme circumstances, would incur no displeasure from his superiors, but he would thereafter find it very hard to live with his colleagues.

Franklin's first operation beyond the call of duty did not come his way for almost five years—five busy, crowded, yet in retrospect curiously uneventful, years. But when it came, it more than made up for the delay.

CHAPTER

The chief accountant dropped his tables and charts on the desk, and peered triumphantly at his little audience over the rims of his antiquated spectacles.

"So you see, gentlemen," he said, "there's no doubt about it. In this area here"—he stabbed at the map again—"sperm whale casualties have been abnormally high. It's no longer a question of the usual random variations in the census numbers. During the migrations of the last five years, no less than nine plus or minus two whales have disappeared in this rather small area.

"Now, as you are all aware, the sperm whale has no natural enemies, except for the orcas that occasionally attack small females with calves. But we are quite sure that no killer packs have broken into this area for several years, and at least three adult males have disappeared. In our opinion, that left only one possibility.

"The seabed here is slightly less than four thousand feet down, which means that a sperm whale can just reach it with a few minutes' time for hunting on the bottom before it has to return for air. Now, ever since it was discovered that Physeter feeds almost exclusively on squids, naturalists have wondered whether a squid can ever win when a whale attacks it. The general opinion was that it couldn't, because the whale is much larger and more powerful.

"But we must remember that even today no one knows how big the giant squid does grow; the Biology Section tells me that tentacles of *Bathyteutis Maximus* have been found up to eighty feet long. Moreover, a squid would only have to keep a whale held down for a matter of a few minutes at this depth, and the animal would drown before it could get back to the surface. So a couple of years ago we formulated the theory that in this area there lives at least one abnormally large squid. We—ahem—christened him Percy.

"Until last week, Percy was only a theory. Then, as you know, Whale S.87693 was found dead on the surface, badly mauled and with its body covered with the typical scars caused by squid claws and suckers. I would like you to look at this photograph."

He pulled a set of large glossy prints out of his briefcase and passed them around. Each showed a small portion of a whale's body which was mottled with white streaks and perfectly circular rings. A foot ruler lay incongruously in the middle of the picture to give an idea of the scale.

"Those, gentlemen, are sucker marks. They go up to six inches in diameter. I think we can say that Percy is no longer a theory. The question is: What do we do about him? He is costing us at least twenty thousand dollars a year. I should welcome any suggestions."

There was a brief silence while the little group of officials looked thoughtfully at the photographs. Then the director said: "I've asked Mr. Franklin to come along and give his opinion. What do you say, Walter? Can you deal with Percy?"

"If I can find him, yes. But the bottom's pretty rugged down there, and it might be a long search. I couldn't use a normal sub, of course—there'd be no safety margin at that depth, especially if Percy started putting on the squeeze. Incidentally, what size do you think he is?"

The chief accountant, usually so glib with figures, hesitated for an appreciable instant before replying.

"This isn't *my* estimate," he said apologetically, "but the biologists say he may be a hundred and fifty feet long."

There were some subdued whistles, but the director seemed unimpressed. Long ago he had learned the truth of the old cliché that there were bigger fish in the sea than ever came out of it. He knew also that, in a medium where gravity set no limit to size, a creature could continue to grow almost indefinitely as long as it could avoid death. And of all the inhabitants of the sea, the giant squid was perhaps the safest from attack. Even its one enemy, the sperm whale, could not reach it if it remained below the four-thousand-foot level.

"There are dozens of ways we can kill Percy if we can locate him," put in the chief biologist. "Explosives, poison, electrocution—any of them would do. But unless there's no alternative, I think we should avoid killing. He must be one of the biggest animals alive on this planet, and it would be a crime to murder him."

"*Please,* Dr. Roberts!" protested the director. "May I remind you that this bureau is only concerned with food production—not with research or the conservation of any animals except whales. And I do think that murder is rather a strong term to apply to an overgrown mollusk."

Dr. Roberts seemed quite unabashed by the mild reprimand.

"I agree, sir," he said cheerfully, "that production is our main job, and that we must always keep economic factors in mind. At the same time, we're continually cooperating with the Department of Scientific Research and this seems another case where we can work together to our mutual advantage. In fact, we might even make a profit in the long run."

"Go on," said the director, a slight twinkle in his eye. He

wondered what ingenious plan the scientists who were supposed to be working for him had cooked up with their opposite numbers in Research.

"No giant squid has ever been captured alive, simply because we've never had the tools for the job. It would be an expensive operation, but if we are going to chase Percy anyway, the additional cost should not be very great. So I suggest that we try to bring him back alive."

No one bothered to ask how. If Dr. Roberts said it could be done, that meant he had already worked out a plan of campaign. The director, as usual, bypassed the minor technical details involved in hauling up several tons of fighting squid from a depth of a mile, and went straight to the important point.

"Will Research pay for any of this? And what will you do with Percy when you've caught him?"

"Unofficially, Research will provide the additional equipment if we make the subs and pilots available. We'll also need that floating dock we borrowed from Maintenance last year; it's big enough to hold two whales, so it can certainly hold one squid. There'll be some additional expenditure here—extra aeration plant for the water, electrified mesh to stop Percy climbing out, and so on. In fact, I suggest that we use the dock as a lab while we're studying him."

"And after that?"

"Why, we sell him."

"The demand for hundred-and-fifty-foot squids as household pets would seem to be rather small."

Like an actor throwing away his best line, Dr. Roberts casually produced his trump card.

"If we can deliver Percy alive and in good condition, Marineland will pay fifty thousand dollars for him. That was Professor Milton's first informal offer when I spoke to him this morning. I've no doubt that we can get more than that; I've even been wondering if we could arrange things on a royalty basis. After all, a giant squid would be the biggest attraction Marineland ever had."

"Research was bad enough," grumbled the director. "Now it looks as if you're trying to get us involved in the entertainment business. Still, as far as I'm concerned it sounds fairly plausible. If Accounts can convince me that the project is not too expensive, and if no other snags turn up, we'll go ahead with it. That is, of course, if Mr. Franklin and his colleagues think it can be done. They're the people who'll have to do the work."

"If Dr. Roberts has any practical plan, I'll be glad to discuss it with him. It's certainly a very interesting project."

That, thought Franklin, was the understatement of the year. But he was not the sort of man who ever waxed too enthusiastic over any enterprise, having long ago decided that this always resulted in eventual disappointment. If "Operation Percy" came off, it would be the most exciting job he had ever had in his five years as a warden. But it was too good to be true; something would turn up to cancel the whole project.

It did not. Less than a month later, he was dropping down to the seabed in a specially modified deep-water scout. Two hundred feet behind him, Don Burley was following in a second machine. It was the first time they had worked together since those far-off days on Heron Island, but when Franklin had been asked to choose his partner he had automatically thought of Don. This was the chance of a lifetime, and Don would never forgive him if he selected anyone else.

Franklin sometimes wondered if Don resented his own rapid rise in the service. Five years ago, Don had been a first warden; Franklin, a completely inexperienced trainee. Now they were both first wardens, and before long Franklin would probably be promoted again. He did not altogether welcome this, for, though he was ambitious enough, he knew that the higher he rose in the bureau the less time he would spend at sea. Perhaps Don knew what he was doing; it was very hard to picture him settling down in an office. . . .

"Better try your lights," said Don's voice from the speaker. "Doc Roberts wants me to get a photograph of you."

"Right," Franklin replied. "Here goes."

"My—you *do* look pretty! If I was another squid, I'm sure I'd find you irresistible. Swing broadside a minute. Thanks. Talk about a Christmas tree! It's the first time I've ever seen one making ten knots at six hundred fathoms."

Franklin grinned and switched off the illuminations. This idea of Dr. Roberts' was simple enough, but it remained to be seen if it would work. In the lightless abyss, many creatures carry constellations of luminous organs which they can switch on or off at will, and the giant squid, with its enormous eyes, is particularly sensitive to such lights. It uses them not only to lure its prey into its clutches, but also to attract its mates. If squids were as intelligent as they were supposed to be, thought Franklin, Percy would soon see through his disguise. It would be ironic, however, if a deep-diving sperm whale was deceived and he had an unwanted fight on his hands.

The rocky bottom was now only five hundred feet below, every detail of it clearly traced on the short-range sonar scanner. It looked like an unpromising place for a search; there might be countless caves here in which Percy could hide beyond all hope of detection. On the other hand, the whales had detected him—to their cost. And anything that Physeter can do, Franklin told himself, my sub can do just as well.

"We're in luck," said Don. "The water's as clear as I've ever seen it down here. As long as we don't stir up any mud, we'll be able to see a couple of hundred feet."

That was important; Franklin's luminous lures would be useless if the water was too turbid for them to be visible. He switched on the external TV camera, and quickly located the faint glow of Don's starboard light, two hundred feet away. Yes, this was extremely good luck; it should simplify their task enormously.

Franklin tuned in to the nearest beacon and fixed his position with the utmost accuracy. To make doubly sure, he got Don to do the same, and they split the difference between them. Then, cruising slowly on parallel courses, they began their careful search of the seabed.

It was unusual to find bare rock at such a depth, for the ocean bed is normally covered with a layer of mud and sediment hundreds or even thousands of feet thick. There must, Franklin decided, be powerful currents scouring this area clear—but there was certainly no current now, as his drift meter assured him. It was probably seasonal, and associated with the ten-thousand-foot-deeper cleft of the Miller Canyon, only five miles away.

Every few seconds, Franklin switched on his pattern of colored lights, then watched the screen eagerly to see if there was any response. Before long he had half a dozen fantastic deep-sea fish following him—nightmare creatures, two or three feet long, with enormous jaws and ridiculously attenuated feelers and tendrils trailing from their bodies. The lure of his lights apparently overcame their fear of his engine vibration, which was an encouraging sign. Though his speed quickly left them behind, they were continually replaced by new monsters, no two of which appeared to be exactly the same.

Franklin paid relatively little attention to the TV screen; the longer-range senses of the sonar, warning him of what lay in the thousand feet ahead of him, were more important. Not only had he to keep a lookout for his quarry, but he had to avoid rocks and hillocks which might suddenly rear up in the track of the sub. He was doing only ten knots, which was slow enough, but it required all his concentration. Sometimes he felt as if he was flying at treetop height over hilly country in a thick fog.

They traveled five uneventful miles, then made a hairpin

turn and came back on a parallel course. If they were doing nothing else, thought Franklin, at least they were producing a survey of this area in more detail than it had ever been mapped before. Both he and Don were operating with their recorders on, so that the profile of the seabed beneath them was being automatically mapped.

"Whoever said this was an exciting life?" said Don when they made their fourth turn. "I've not even seen a baby octopus. Maybe we're scaring the squids away."

"Roberts said they're not very sensitive to vibrations, so I don't think that's likely. And somehow I feel that Percy isn't the sort who's easily scared."

"*If* he exists," said Don skeptically.

"Don't forget those six-inch sucker marks. What do you think made them—mice?"

"Hey!" said Don. "Have a look at that echo on bearing 250, range 750 feet. Looks like a rock, but I thought it moved then."

Another false alarm, Franklin told himself. No—the echo did seem a bit fuzzy. By God, it *was* moving!

"Cut speed to half a knot," he ordered. "Drop back behind me—I'll creep up slowly and switch on my lights."

"It's a weird-looking echo. Keeps changing size all the time."

"That sounds like our boy. Here we go."

The sub was now moving across an endless, slightly tilted plain, still accompanied by its inquisitive retinue of finned dragons. On the TV screen all objects were lost in the haze at a distance of about a hundred and fifty feet; the full power of the ultraviolet projectors could probe the water no farther than this. Franklin switched off his headlights and all external illumination, and continued his cautious approach using the sonar screen alone.

At five hundred feet the echo began to show its unmistakable structure; at four hundred feet there was no longer any doubt; at three hundred feet Franklin's escort of fish suddenly fled at high speed as if aware that this was no healthy spot. At two hundred feet he turned on his visual lures, but he waited a few seconds before switching on the searchlights and TV.

A forest was walking across the seabed—a forest of writhing, serpentine trunks. The great squid froze for a moment as if impaled by the searchlights; probably it could see them, though they were invisible to human eyes. Then it gathered up its tentacles with incredible swiftness, folding itself into a compact, streamlined mass—and shot straight toward the sub under the full power of its own jet propulsion.

It swerved at the last minute, and Franklin caught a glimpse of a huge and lidless eye that must have been at least a foot in diameter. A second later there was a violent blow on the hull, followed by a scraping sound as of great claws being dragged across metal. Franklin remembered the scars he had so often seen on the blubbery hides of sperm whales, and was glad of the thickness of steel that protected him. He could hear the wiring of his external illumination being ripped away; no matter—it had served its purpose.

It was impossible to tell what the squid was doing; from time to time the sub rocked violently, but Franklin made no effort to escape. Unless things got a little too rough, he proposed to stay here and take it.

"Can you see what he's doing?" he asked Don, rather plaintively.

"Yes—he's got his eight arms wrapped around you, and the two big tentacles are waving hopefully at me. And he's going through the most beautiful color changes you can imagine—I can't begin to describe them. I wish I knew whether he's really trying to eat you—or whether he's just being affectionate."

"Whichever it is, it's not very comfortable. Hurry up and take your photos so that I can get out of here."

"Right—give me another couple of minutes so I can get a movie sequence as well. Then I'll try to plant my harpoon."

It seemed a long two minutes, but at last Don had finished. Percy still showed none of the shyness which Dr. Roberts had rather confidently predicted, though by this time he could hardly have imagined that Franklin's sub was another squid.

Don planted his dart with neatness and precision in the thickest part of Percy's mantle, where it would lodge securely but would do no damage. At the sudden sting, the great mollusk abruptly released its grip, and Franklin took the opportunity for going full speed ahead. He felt the horny palps grating over the stern of the sub; then he was free and rising swiftly up toward the distant sky. He felt rather pleased that he had managed to escape without using any of the battery of weapons that had been provided for this very purpose.

Don followed him at once, and they circled five hundred feet above the seabed—far beyond visual range. On the sonar screen the rocky bottom was a sharply defined plane, but now at its center pulsed a tiny, brilliant star. The little beacon—less than six inches long and barely an inch wide—that had been anchored in Percy was already doing its job. It would continue to operate for more than a week before its batteries failed.

"We've tagged him!" cried Don gleefully. "Now he can't hide."

"As long as he doesn't get rid of that dart," said Franklin cautiously. "If he works it out, we'll have to start looking for him all over again."

"*I* aimed it," pointed out Don severely. "Bet you ten to one it stays put."

"If I've learned one thing in this game," said Franklin, "it's not to accept your bets." He brought the drive up to maximum cruising power, and pointed the sub's nose to the surface, still more than half a mile away. "Let's not keep Doc Roberts waiting—the poor man will be crazy with impatience. Besides, I want to see those pictures myself. It's the first time I've ever played a starring role with a giant squid."

And this, he reminded himself, was only the curtain raiser. The main feature had still to begin.

CHAPTER

"How nice it is," said Franklin, as he relaxed lazily in the contour-form chair on the porch, "to have a wife who's not scared stiff of the job I'm doing."

"There are times when I am," admitted Indra. "I don't like these deep-water operations. If anything goes wrong down there, you don't have a chance."

"You can drown just as easily in ten feet of water as ten thousand."

"That's silly, and you know it. Besides, no warden has ever been killed by drowning, as far as I've ever heard. The things that happen to them are never as nice and simple as that."

"I'm sorry I started this conversation," said Franklin ruefully, glancing around to see if Peter was safely out of earshot. "Anyway, you're not worried about Operation Percy, are you?"

"No, I don't think so. I'm as anxious as everybody else to see you catch him—and I'm still more interested to see if Dr. Roberts can keep him alive." She rose to her feet and walked over to the bookshelf recessed into the wall. Plowing through the usual pile of papers and magazines that had accumulated there, she finally unearthed the volume for which she was looking.

"Listen to this," she continued, "and remember that it was written almost two hundred years ago." She began to read in her best lecture-room voice, while Franklin listened at first with mild reluctance, and then with complete absorption.

"In the distance, a great white mass lazily rose, and rising higher and higher, and disentangling itself from the azure, at last gleamed before our prow like a snow-slide, new slid from the hills. Thus glistening for a moment, as slowly it subsided, and sank. Then once more arose, and slightly gleamed. It seemed not a whale; and yet is this Moby Dick? thought Daggoo. Again the phantom went down, but on reappearing once more, like a stiletto-like cry that startled every man from his nod, the negro yelled out—'There! there again! there she breaches! Right ahead! The White Whale! The White Whale!'

"The four boats were soon on the water; Ahab's in advance, and all swiftly pulling towards their prey. Soon it went down, and while, with oars suspended, we were awaiting its appearance, lo! in the same spot where it sank, once more it slowly rose. Almost forgetting for the moment all thoughts of Moby Dick, we now gazed at the most wondrous phenomenon which the secret seas have hitherto revealed to mankind. A vast pulpy mass, furlongs in length and breadth, of a glancing cream-colour, lay floating on the water, innumerable long arms radiating from its centre, and curling and twisting like a nest of anacondas, as if blindly to catch at any hapless object within reach. No perceptible face or front did it have; no conceivable token of either sensation or instinct; but undulated there on the billows, an unearthly, formless, chance-like apparition of life.

"As with a low sucking sound it slowly disappeared again, Starbuck still gazing at the agitated waters where it had sunk, with a wild voice exclaimed—'Almost rather had I seen Moby Dick and fought him, than to have seen thee, thou white ghost!'

"'What was it, Sir?' said Flask.

" 'The great live squid, which, they say, few whaleships ever beheld, and returned to their ports to tell of it.'

"But Ahab said nothing; turning his boat, he sailed back to the vessel; the rest as silently following."

Indra paused, closed the book, and waited for her husband's response. Franklin stirred himself in the too-comfortable couch and said thoughtfully: "I'd forgotten that bit—if I ever read as far. It rings true to life, but what was a squid doing on the surface?"

"It was probably dying. They sometimes surface at night, but never in the daytime, and Melville says this was on 'one transparent blue morning.' "

"Anyway, what's a furlong? I'd like to know if Melville's squid was as big as Percy. The photos make him a hundred and thirty feet from his flukes to the tips of his feelers."

"So he beats the largest blue whale ever recorded."

"Yes, by a couple of feet. But of course he doesn't weigh a tenth as much."

Franklin heaved himself from his couch and went in search of a dictionary. Presently Indra heard indignant noises coming from the living room, and called out: "What's the matter?"

"It says here that a furlong is an obsolete measure of length equal to an eighth of a mile. Melville was talking through his hat."

"He's usually very accurate, at least as far as whales are concerned. But 'furlong' is obviously ridiculous—I'm surprised no one's spotted it before. He must have meant fathoms, or else the printer got it wrong."

Slightly mollified, Franklin put down the dictionary and came back to the porch. He was just in time to see Don Burley arrive, sweep Indra off her feet, plant a large but brotherly kiss on her forehead, and dump her back in her chair.

"Come along, Walt!" he said. "Got your things packed? I'll give you a lift to the airport."

"Where's Peter hiding?" said Franklin. "Peter! Come and say good-bye—Daddy's off to work."

A four-year-old bundle of uncontrollable energy came flying into the room, almost capsizing his father as he jumped into his arms.

"Daddy's going to bring me back a 'quid?" he asked.

"Hey—how did you know about all this?"

"It was on the news this morning, while you were still asleep," explained Indra. "They showed a few seconds of Don's film, too."

"I was afraid of that. Now we'll have to work with a crowd of cameramen and reporters looking over our shoulders. That means that something's sure to go wrong."

"They can't follow us down to the bottom, anyway," said Burley.

"I hope you're right—but don't forget we're not the only people with deep-sea subs."

"I don't know how you put up with him," Don protested to Indra. "Does he *always* look on the black side of things?"

"Not always," smiled Indra, as she unraveled Peter from his father. "He's cheerful at least twice a week."

Her smile faded as she watched the sleek sportster go whispering down the hill. She was very fond of Don, who was practically a member of the family, and there were times when she worried about him. It seemed a pity that he had never married and settled down; the nomadic, promiscuous life he led could hardly be very satisfying. Since they had known him, he had spent almost all his time on or under the sea, apart from hectic leaves when he had used their home as a base—at their invitation but often to their embarrassment when there were unexpected lady guests to entertain at breakfast.

Their own life, by many standards, had been nomadic enough, but at least they had always had a place they could call home. That apartment in Brisbane, where her brief but happy

career as a lecturer at the University of Queensland had ended
with the birth of Peter; that bungalow in Fiji, with the roof
that had a mobile leak which the builders could never find; the
married quarters at the South Georgia whaling station (she
could still smell the mountains of offal, and see the gulls
wheeling over the flensing yards); and finally, this house looking out across the sea to the other islands of Hawaii. Four
homes in five years might seem excessive to many people, but
for a warden's wife Indra knew she had done well.

She had few regrets for the career that had been temporarily
interrupted. When Peter was old enough, she told herself, she
would go back to her research; even now she read all the literature and kept in touch with current work. Only a few months
ago the *Journal of Selachians* had published her letter "On the
possible evolution of the Goblin Shark (*Scapanorhynchus ow-
stoni*)," and she had since been involved in an enjoyable controversy with all five of the scientists qualified to discuss the
subject.

Even if nothing came of these dreams, it was pleasant to
have them and to know you might make the best of both
worlds. So Indra Franklin, housewife and ichthyologist, told
herself as she went back into the kitchen to prepare lunch for
her ever-hungry son.

The floating dock had been modified in many ways that
would have baffled its original designers. A thick steel mesh,
supported on sturdy insulators, extended its entire length, and
above this mesh was a canvas awning to cut out the sunlight
which would injure Percy's sensitive eyes and skin. The only illumination inside the dock came from a battery of amber-
tinted bulbs; at the moment, however, the great doors at either
end of the huge concrete box were open, letting in both sunlight and water.

The two subs, barely awash, lay tied up beside the crowded
catwalk as Dr. Roberts gave his final instructions.

"I'll try not to bother you too much when you're down there," he said, "but for heaven's sake tell me what's going on."

"We'll be too busy to give a running commentary," answered Don with a grin, "but we'll do our best. And if anything goes wrong, trust us to yell right away. All set, Walt?"

"O.K.," said Franklin, climbing down into the hatch. "See you in five hours, with Percy—I hope."

They wasted no time in diving to the seabed; less than ten minutes later there was four thousand feet of water overhead, and the familiar rocky terrain was imaged on TV and sonar screen. But there was no sign of the pulsing star that should have indicated the presence of Percy.

"Hope the beacon hasn't packed up," said Franklin as he reported this news to the hopefully waiting scientists. "If it has, it may take us days to locate him again."

"Do you suppose he's left the area? I wouldn't blame him," added Don.

Dr. Roberts' voice, still confident and assured, came down to them from the distant world of Sun and light almost a mile above.

"He's probably hiding in a cleft, or shielded by rock. I suggest you rise five hundred feet so that you're well clear of all the seabed irregularities, and start a high-speed search. That beacon has a range of more than a mile, so you'll pick him up pretty quickly."

An hour later even the doctor sounded less confident, and from the comments that leaked down to them over the sonar communicator it appeared that the reporters and TV networks were getting impatient.

"There's only one place he can be," said Roberts at last. "If he's there at all, and the beacon's still working, he must have gone down into the Miller Canyon."

"That's fifteen thousand feet deep," protested Don. "These subs are only cleared for twelve."

"I know—I know. But he won't have gone to the bottom.

He's probably hunting somewhere down the slope. You'll see him easily if he's there."

"Right," replied Franklin, not very optimistically. "We'll go and have a look. But if he's more than twelve thousand feet down, he'll have to stay there."

On the sonar screen, the canyon was clearly visible as a sudden gap in the luminous image of the seabed. It came rapidly closer as the two subs raced toward it at forty knots—the fastest creatures, Franklin mused, anywhere beneath the surface of the sea. He had once flown low toward the Grand Canyon, and seen the land below suddenly whipped away as the enormous cavity gaped beneath him. And now, though he must rely for vision solely on the pattern of echoes brought back by his probing sound waves, he felt exactly that same sensation as he swept across the edge of this still mightier chasm in the ocean floor.

He had scarcely finished the thought when Don's voice, high-pitched with excitement, came yelling from the speaker.

"There he is! A thousand feet down!"

"No need to break my eardrums," grumbled Franklin. "I can see him."

The precipitous slope of the canyon wall was etched like an almost vertical line down the center of the sonar screen. Creeping along the face of that wall was the tiny, twinkling star for which they had been searching. The patient beacon had betrayed Percy to his hunters.

They reported the situation to Dr. Roberts; Franklin could picture the jubilation and excitement up above, some hints of which trickled down through the open microphone. Presently Dr. Roberts, a little breathless, asked: "Do you think you can still carry out our plan?"

"I'll try," he answered. "It won't be easy with this cliff face right beside us, and I hope there aren't any caves Percy can crawl into. You ready, Don?"

"All set to follow you down."

"I think I can reach him without using the motors. Here we go."

Franklin flooded the nose tanks, and went down in a long, steep glide—a silent glide, he hoped. By this time, Percy would have learned caution and would probably run for it as soon as he knew that they were around.

The squid was cruising along the face of the canyon, and Franklin marveled that it could find any food in such a forbidding and apparently lifeless spot. Every time it expelled a jet of water from the tube of its siphon it moved forward in a distinct jerk; it seemed unaware that it was no longer alone, since it had not changed course since Franklin had first observed it.

"Two hundred feet—I'm going to switch on my lights again," he told Don.

"He won't see you—visibility's only about eighty today."

"Yes, but I'm still closing in—he's spotted me! Here he comes!"

Franklin had not really expected that the trick would work a second time on an animal as intelligent as Percy. But almost at once he felt the sudden thud, followed by the rasping of horny claws as the great tentacles closed around the sub. Though he knew that he was perfectly safe, and that no animal could harm walls that had been built to withstand pressures of a thousand tons on every square foot, that grating, slithering sound was one calculated to give him nightmares.

Then, quite suddenly, there was silence. He heard Don exclaim, "Christ, that stuff acts quickly! He's out cold." Almost at once Dr. Roberts interjected anxiously: "Don't give him too much! And keep him moving so that he'll still breathe!"

Don was too busy to answer. Having carried out his role as decoy, Franklin could do nothing but watch as his partner maneuvered dexterously around the great mollusk. The anesthetic bomb had paralyzed it completely; it was slowly sinking, its tentacles stretched limply upward. Pieces of fish, some of them over a foot across, were floating away from the cruel beak as the monster disgorged its last meal.

"Can you get underneath?" Don asked hurriedly. "He's sinking too fast for me."

Franklin threw on the drive and went around in a tight curve. There was a soft thump, as of a snowdrift falling from a roof, and he knew that five or ten tons of gelatinous body were now draped over the sub.

"Fine—hold him there—I'm getting into position."

Franklin was now blind, but the occasional clanks and whirs coming from the water outside told him what was happening. Presently Don said triumphantly: "All set! We're ready to go."

The weight lifted from the sub, and Franklin could see again. Percy had been neatly gaffed. A band of thick, elastic webbing had been fastened around his body at the narrowest part, just behind the flukes. From this harness a cable extended to Don's sub, invisible in the haze a hundred feet away. Percy was being towed through the water in his normal direction of motion—backward. Had he been conscious and actively resisting, he could have escaped easily enough, but in his present state the collar he was wearing enabled Don to handle him without difficulty. The fun would begin when he started to revive. . . .

Franklin gave a brief eyewitness description of the scene for the benefit of his patiently waiting colleagues a mile above. It was probably being broadcast, and he hoped that Indra and Peter were listening. Then he settled down to keep an eye on Percy as the long haul back to the surface began.

They could not move at more than two knots, lest the collar lose its none-too-secure grip on the great mass of jelly it was towing. In any event, the trip back to the surface had to take at least three hours, to give Percy a fair chance of adjusting to the pressure difference. Since an air-breathing—and therefore more vulnerable—animal like a sperm whale could endure almost the same pressure change in ten or twenty minutes, this caution was probably excessive. But Dr. Roberts was taking no chances with his unprecedented catch.

They had been climbing for nearly an hour, and had reached the three-thousand-foot level, when Percy showed signs of life. The two long arms, terminating in their great sucker-covered palps, began to writhe purposefully; the monstrous eyes, into which Franklin had been staring half hypnotized from a distance of no more than five feet, began to light once more with intelligence. Quite unaware that he was speaking in a breathless whisper, he swiftly reported these symptoms to Dr. Roberts.

The doctor's first reaction was a hearty sigh of relief: "Good!" he said. "I was afraid we might have killed him. Can you see if he's breathing properly? Is the siphon contracting?"

Franklin dropped a few feet so that he could get a better view of the fleshy tube projecting from the squid's mantle. It was opening and closing in an unsteady rhythm which seemed to be getting stronger and more regular at every beat.

"Splendid!" said Dr. Roberts. "He's in fine shape. As soon as he starts to wriggle too hard, give him one of the small bombs. But leave it until the last possible moment."

Franklin wondered how that moment was to be decided. Percy was now beginning to glow a beautiful blue; even with the searchlights switched off he was clearly visible. Blue, he remembered Dr. Roberts saying, was a sign of excitement in squids. In that case, it was high time he did something.

"Better let go that bomb. I think he's getting lively," he told Don.

"Right—here it is."

A glass bubble floated across Franklin's screen and swiftly vanished from sight.

"The damn thing never broke!" he cried. "Let go another one!"

"O.K.—here's number two. I hope this works; I've only got five left."

But once again the narcotic bomb failed. This time Franklin never saw the sphere; he only knew that instead of relaxing into slumber once more Percy was becoming more active second by second. The eight short tentacles—short, that is, compared with the almost hundred-foot reach of the pair carrying the grasping palps—were now beginning to twine briskly together. He recalled Melville's phrase: "Like a nest of anacondas." No; somehow that did not seem to fit. It was more like a miser—a submarine Shylock—twisting his fingers together as he gloated over his wealth. In any event, it was a disconcerting sight when those fingers were a foot in diameter and were operating only two yards away. . . .

"You'll just have to keep on trying," he told Don. "Unless we stop him soon, he'll get away."

An instant later he breathed a sigh of relief as he saw broken shards of glass drifting by. They would have been quite invisible, surrounded as they were by water, had they not been fluorescing brilliantly under the light of his ultraviolet searchlight. But for the moment he was too relieved to wonder why he had been able to see something as proverbially elusive as a piece of broken glass in water; he only knew that Percy had suddenly relaxed again and no longer appeared to be working himself into a rage.

"What happened?" said Dr. Roberts plaintively from above.

"These confounded knockout drops of yours. Two of them didn't work. That leaves me with just four—and at the present rate of failure I'll be lucky if even one goes off."

"I don't understand it. The mechanism worked perfectly every time we tested it in the lab."

"Did you test it at a hundred atmospheres pressure?"

"Er—no. It didn't seem necessary."

Don's "Huh!" seemed to say all that was needful about biologists who tried to dabble with engineering, and there was silence on all channels for the next few minutes of slow ascent. Then Dr. Roberts, sounding a little diffident, came back to the subject.

"Since we can't rely on the bombs," he said, "you'd better come up more quickly. He'll revive again in about thirty minutes."

"Right—I'll double speed. I only hope this collar doesn't slip off."

The next twenty minutes were perfectly uneventful; then everything started to happen at once.

"He's coming around again," said Franklin. "I think the higher speed has waked him up."

"I was afraid of that," Dr. Roberts answered. "Hold on as long as you can, and then let go a bomb. We can only pray that *one* of them will work."

A new voice suddenly cut into the circuit.

"Captain here. Lookout has just spotted some sperm whales about two miles away. They seem to be heading toward us; I suggest you have a look at them—we've got no horizontal search sonar on this ship."

Franklin switched quickly over to the long-range scanner and picked up the echoes at once.

"Nothing to worry about," he said. "If they come too close, we can scare them away." He glanced back at the TV screen and saw that Percy was now getting very restive.

"Let go your bomb," he told Don, "and keep your fingers crossed."

"I'm not betting on *this*," Don answered. "Anything happen?"

"No; another dud. Try again."

"That leaves three. Here goes."

"Sorry—I can see that one. It isn't cracked."

"Two left. Now there's only one."

"That's a dud too. What had we better do, Doc? Risk the last one? I'm afraid Percy will slip off in a minute."

"There's nothing else we can do," replied Dr. Roberts, his voice now clearly showing the strain. "Go ahead, Don."

Almost at once Franklin gave a cry of satisfaction.

"We've made it!" he shouted. "He's knocked cold again! How long do you think it will keep him under this time?"

"We can't rely on more than twenty minutes, so plan your ascent accordingly. We're right above you—and remember what I said about taking at least ten minutes over that last two hundred feet. I don't want any pressure damage after all the trouble we've been to."

"Just a minute," put in Don. "I've been looking at those whales. They've put on speed and they're coming straight toward us. I think they've detected Percy—or the beacon we put in him."

"So what?" said Franklin. "We can frighten them with—oh."

"Yes—I thought you'd forgotten that. These aren't patrol subs, Walt. No sirens on them. And you can't scare sperm whales just by revving your engines."

That was true enough, though it would not have been fifty years ago, when the great beasts had been hunted almost to extinction. But a dozen generations had lived and died since then; now they recognized the subs as harmless, and certainly no obstacle to the meal they were anticipating. There was a real danger that the helpless Percy might be eaten before he could be safely caged.

"I think we'll make it," said Franklin, as he anxiously calculated the speed of the approaching whales. This was a hazard that no one could have anticipated; it was typical of the way in which underwater operations developed unexpected snags and complications.

"I'm going straight up to the two-hundred-foot level," Don told him. "We'll wait there just as long as it's safe, and then run for the ship. What do you think of that, Doc?"

"It's the only thing to do. But remember that those whales can make fifteen knots if they have to."

"Yes, but they can't keep it up for long, even if they see their dinner slipping away. Here we go."

The subs increased their rate of ascent, while the water brightened around them and the enormous pressure slowly relaxed. At last they were back in the narrow zone where an unprotected man could safely dive. The mother ship was less than a hundred yards away, but this final stage in the climb back to the surface was the most critical of all. In this last two hundred feet, the pressure would drop swiftly from eight atmospheres to only one—as great a change in ratio as had occurred in the previous quarter of a mile. There were no enclosed air spaces in Percy which might cause him to explode if the ascent was too swift, but no one could be certain what other internal damage might occur.

"Whales only half a mile away," reported Franklin. "Who said they couldn't keep up that speed? They'll be here in two minutes."

"You'll have to hold them off somehow," said Dr. Roberts, a note of desperation in his voice.

"Any suggestions?" asked Franklin, a little sarcastically.

"Suppose you pretend to attack; that might make them break off."

This, Franklin told himself, was not his idea of fun. But there seemed no alternative; with a last glance at Percy, who was now beginning to stir again, he started off at half-speed to meet the advancing whales.

There were three echoes dead ahead of him—not very large ones, but he did not let that encourage him. Even if those were the relatively diminutive females, each one was as big as ten elephants and they were coming toward him at a combined speed of forty miles an hour. He was making all the noise he could, but so far it seemed to be having no effect.

Then he heard Don shouting: "Percy's waking up fast! I can feel him starting to move."

"Come straight in," ordered Dr. Roberts. "We've got the doors open."

"And get ready to close the back door as soon as I've slipped the cable. I'm going straight through—I don't want to share your swimming pool with Percy when he finds what's happened to him."

Franklin heard all this chattering with only half an ear. Those three approaching echoes were ominously close. Were they going to call his bluff? Sperm whales were among the most pugnacious animals in the sea, as different from their vegetarian cousins as wild buffaloes from a herd of prize Guernseys. It was a sperm whale that had rammed and sunk the *Essex* and thus inspired the closing chapter of *Moby Dick*; he had no desire to figure in a submarine sequel.

Yet he held stubbornly to his course, though now the racing echoes were less than fifteen seconds away. Then he saw that they were beginning to separate; even if they were not scared, the whales had become confused. Probably the noise of his motors had made them lose contact with their target. He cut his speed to zero, and the three whales began to circle him inquisitively, at a range of about a hundred feet. Sometimes he caught a shadowy glimpse of them on the TV screen. As he had thought, they were young females, and he felt a little sorry to have robbed them of what should have been their rightful food.

He had broken the momentum of their charge; now it was up to Don to finish his side of the mission. From the brief and occasionally lurid comments from the loudspeaker, it was obvious that this was no easy task. Percy was not yet fully conscious, but he knew that something was wrong and he was beginning to object.

The men on the floating dock had the best view of the final stages. Don surfaced about fifty yards away—and the sea behind him became covered with an undulating mass of jelly, twisting and rolling on the waves. At the greatest speed he dared to risk, Don headed for the open end of the dock. One of Percy's tentacles made a halfhearted grab at the entrance, as if in a somnambulistic effort to avoid captivity, but the speed at which he was being hurried through the water broke his grip. As soon as he was safely inside, the massive steel gates began to close like horizontally operating jaws, and Don jettisoned the towrope fastened around the squid's flukes. He wasted no time in leaving from the other exit, and the second set of lock gates started to close even before he was through. The caging of Percy had taken less than a quarter of a minute.

When Franklin surfaced, in company with three disappointed but not hostile sperm whales, it was some time before he could attract any attention. The entire personnel of the dock were busy staring, with awe, triumph, scientific curiosity, and even downright disbelief, at the monstrous captive now swiftly reviving in his great concrete tank. The water was being thoroughly aerated by the streams of bubbles from a score of pipes, and the last traces of the drugs that had paralyzed him were being flushed out of Percy's system. Beneath the dim amber light that was now the sole illumination inside the dock, the giant squid began to investigate its prison.

First it swam slowly from end to end of the rectangular concrete box, exploring the sides with its tentacles. Then the two immense palps started to climb into the air, waving toward the breathless watchers gathered round the edge of the dock. They touched the electrified netting—and flicked away with a speed that almost eluded the eye. Twice again Percy repeated the experiment before he had convinced himself that there was no way out in this direction, all the while staring up at the puny spectators with a gaze that seemed to betoken an intelligence every wit as great as theirs.

By the time Don and Franklin came aboard, the squid appeared to have settled down in captivity, and was showing a mild interest in a number of fish that had been dropped into its tank. As the two wardens joined Dr. Roberts behind the wire meshing, they had their first clear and complete view of the monster they had hauled up from the ocean depths.

Their eyes ran along the hundred and more feet of flexible, sinewy strength, the countless claw-ringed suckers, the slowly pulsing jet, and the huge staring eyes of the most superbly equipped beast of prey the world had ever seen. Then Don summed up the thoughts that they were both feeling.

"He's all yours, Doc. I hope you know how to handle him."

Dr. Roberts smiled confidently enough. He was a very happy man, though a small worry was beginning to invade his mind. He had no doubt at all that he could handle Percy, and he was perfectly right. But he was not so sure that he could handle the director when the bills came in for the research equipment he was going to order—and for the mountains of fish that Percy was going to eat.

CHAPTER

The secretary of the Department of Scientific Research had listened to him attentively enough—and not merely with attention, Franklin told himself, but with a flattering interest. When he had finished the sales talk which had taken such long and careful preparation, he felt a sudden and unexpected emotional letdown. He knew that he had done his best; what happened now was largely out of his hands.

"There are a few points I would like to clear up," said the secretary. "The first is a rather obvious one. Why didn't you go to the Marine Division's own research department instead of coming all the way up to World Secretariat level and contacting D.S.R.?"

It was, Franklin admitted, a rather obvious point—and a somewhat delicate one. But he knew that it would be raised, and he had come prepared.

"Naturally, Mr. Farlan," he answered, "I did my best to get support in the division. There was a good deal of interest, especially after we'd captured that squid. But Operation Percy turned out to be much more expensive than anyone had calculated, and there were a lot of awkward questions about it.

The whole affair ended with several of our scientists transferring to other divisions."

"I know," interjected the secretary with a smile. "We've got some of them." .

"So any research that isn't of direct practical importance is now frowned on in the division, which is one reason why I came to you. And, frankly, it hasn't the authority to do the sort of thing I propose. The cost of running even two deep-sea subs is considerable, and would have to be approved at higher than divisional level."

"But if it was approved, you are confident that the staff could be made available?"

"Yes, at the right time of the year. Now that the fence is practically one hundred per cent reliable—there's been no major breakdown for three years—we wardens have a fairly slack time except at the annual roundups and slaughterings. That's why it seemed a good idea—"

"To utilize the wasted talents of the wardens?"

"Well, that's putting it a little bluntly. I don't want to give the idea that there is any inefficiency in the bureau."

"I wouldn't dream of suggesting such a thing," smiled the secretary. "The other point is a more personal one. Why are you so keen on this project? You have obviously spent a lot of time and trouble on it—and, if I may say so, risked the disapproval of your superiors by coming directly to me."

That question was not so easy to answer, even to someone you knew well, still less to a stranger. Would this man, who had risen so high in the service of the state, understand the fascination of a mysterious echo on a sonar screen, glimpsed only once, and that years ago? Yes, he would, for he was at least partly a scientist.

"As a chief warden," explained Franklin, "I probably won't be on sea duty much longer. I'm thirty-eight, and getting old for this kind of work. And I've an inquisitive type of mind; perhaps I should have been a scientist myself. This is a problem I'd like to see settled, though I know the odds against it are pretty high."

"I can appreciate that. This chart of confirmed sightings covers about half the world's oceans."

"Yes, I know it looks hopeless, but with the new sonar sets we can scan a volume three times as great as we used to, and an echo that size is easy to pick up. It's only a matter of time before somebody detects it."

"And you want to be that somebody. Well, that's reasonable enough. When I got your original letter I had a talk with my marine biology people, and got about three different opinions—none of them very encouraging. Some of those who admit that these echoes have been seen say that they are probably ghosts due to faults in the sonar sets or returns from discontinuities of some kind in the water."

Franklin snorted. "Anyone who's seen them would know better than that. After all, we're familiar with all the ordinary sonar ghosts and false returns. We have to be."

"Yes, that's what I feel. Some more of my people think that the—let us say—conventional sea serpents have already been accounted for by squids, oarfish, and eels, and that what your patrols have been seeing is either one of these or else a large deep-sea shark."

Franklin shook his head. "I know what all those echoes look like. This is quite different."

"The third objection is a theoretical one. There simply isn't enough food in the extreme ocean depths to support any very large and active forms of life."

"No one can be sure of that. Only in the last century scientists were saying that there could be no life at all on the ocean bed. We know what nonsense *that* turned out to be."

"Well, you've made a good case. I'll see what can be done."

"Thank you very much, Mr. Farlan. Perhaps it would be best if no one in the bureau knew that I'd come to see you."

"We won't tell them, but they'll guess." The secretary rose

to his feet, and Franklin assumed that the interview was over. He was wrong.

"Before you go, Mr. Franklin," said the secretary, "you might be able to clear up one little matter that's been worrying me for a good many years."

"What's that, sir?"

"I've never understood what a presumably well-trained warden would be doing in the middle of the night off the Great Barrier Reef, breathing compressed air five hundred feet down."

There was a long silence while the two men, their relationship suddenly altered, stared at each other across the room. Franklin searched his memory, but the other's face evoked no echoes; that was so long ago, and he had met so many people during the intervening years.

"Were you one of the men who pulled me in?" he asked. "If so, I've a lot to thank you for." He paused for a moment, then added, "You see, that wasn't an accident."

"I rather thought so; that explains everything. But before we change the subject, just what happened to Bert Darryl? I've never been able to find the true story."

"Oh, eventually he ran out of credit; he could never make the *Sea Lion* pay its way. The last time I ever saw him was in Melbourne; he was heartbroken because customs duties had been abolished and there was no way an honest smuggler could make a living. Finally he tried to collect the insurance on the *Sea Lion*; he had a convincing fire and had to abandon ship off Cairns. She went to the bottom, but the appraisers went after her, and started asking some very awkward questions when they found that all the valuable fittings had been removed before the fire. I don't know how the captain got out of that mess.

"That was about the end of the old rascal. He took to the bottle in earnest, and one night up in Darwin he decided to go for a swim off the jetty. But he'd forgotten that it was low tide—and in Darwin the tide drops thirty feet. So he broke his neck, and a lot of people besides his creditors were genuinely sorry."

"Poor old Bert. The world will be a dull place when there aren't any more people like him."

That was rather a heretical remark, thought Franklin, coming from the lips of so senior a member of the World Secretariat. But it pleased him greatly, and not merely because he agreed with it. He knew now that he had unexpectedly acquired an influential friend, and that the chances of his project going forward had been immeasurably improved.

He did not expect anything to happen in a hurry, so was not disappointed as the weeks passed in silence. In any event, he was kept busy; the slack season was still three months away, and meanwhile a whole series of minor but annoying crises crowded upon him.

And there was one that was neither minor nor annoying, if indeed it could be called a crisis at all. Anne Franklin arrived wide-eyed and wide-mouthed into the world, and Indra began to have her first serious doubts of continuing her academic career.

Franklin, to his great disappointment, was not home when his daughter was born. He had been in charge of a small task force of six subs, carrying out an offensive sweep off the Pribilof Islands in an attempt to cut down the number of killer whales. It was not the first mission of its kind, but it was the most successful, thanks to the use of improved techniques. The characteristic calls of seals and the smaller whales had been recorded and played back into the sea, while the subs had waited silently for the killers to appear.

They had done so in hundreds, and the slaughter had been immense. By the time the little fleet returned to Base, more than a thousand orcas had been killed. It had been hard and sometimes dangerous work, and despite its importance Franklin had found this scientific butchery extremely depressing. He could not help admiring the beauty, speed, and ferocity of the hunters he was himself hunting, and toward the end of the mission he was almost glad when the rate of kill began to fall off. It seemed that the orcas were learning by bitter experience, and the bureau's statisticians would have to decide whether or not it would be economically worthwhile repeating the operation next season.

Franklin had barely had time to thaw out from this mission and to fondle Anne gingerly, without extracting any signs of recognition from her, when he was shot off to South Georgia. His problem there was to discover why the whales, who had previously swum into the slaughtering pens without any qualms, had suddenly become suspicious and shown a great reluctance to enter the electrified sluices. As it turned out, he did nothing at all to solve the mystery; while he was still looking for psychological factors, a bright young plant inspector discovered that some of the bloody waste from the processing plants was accidentally leaking back into the sea. It was not surprising that the whales, though their sense of smell was not as strongly developed as in other marine animals, had become alarmed as the moving barriers tried to guide them to the place where so many of their relatives had met their doom.

As a chief warden, already being groomed for higher things, Franklin was now a kind of mobile trouble shooter who might be sent anywhere in the world on the bureau's business. Apart from the effect on his home life, he welcomed this state of affairs. Once a man had learned the mechanics of a warden's trade, straightforward patrolling and herding had little future in it. People like Don Burley got all the excitement and pleasure they needed from it, but then Don was neither ambitious nor much of an intellectual heavyweight. Franklin told himself this without any sense of superiority; it was a simple statement of fact which Don would be the first to admit.

He was in England, giving evidence as an expert witness before the Whaling Commission—the bureau's state-appointed watchdog—when he received a plaintive call from Dr. Lundquist, who had taken over when Dr. Roberts had left the Bureau of Whales to accept a much more lucrative appointment at the Marineland aquarium.

"I've just had three crates of gear delivered from the Department of Scientific Research. It's nothing we ever ordered, but your name is on it. What's it all about?"

Franklin thought quickly. It *would* arrive when he was away, and if the director came across it before he could prepare the ground there would be fireworks.

"It's too long a story to give now," Franklin answered. "I've got to go before the committee in ten minutes. Just push it out of the way somewhere until I get back—I'll explain everything then."

"I hope it's all right—it's most unusual."

"Nothing to worry about—see you the day after tomorrow. If Don Burley comes to Base, let him have a look at the stuff. But I'll fix all the paperwork when I get back."

That, he told himself, would be the worst part of the whole job. Getting equipment that had never been officially requisitioned onto the bureau's inventory without too many questions was going to be at least as difficult as locating the Great Sea Serpent. . . .

He need not have worried. His new and influential ally, the secretary of the Department of Scientific Research, had already anticipated most of his problems. The equipment was to be on loan to the bureau, and was to be returned as soon as it had done its job. What was more, the director had been given the impression that the whole thing was a D.S.R. project; he might have his doubts, but Franklin was officially covered.

"Since you seem to know all about it, Walter," he said in the lab when the gear was finally unpacked, "you'd better explain what it's supposed to do."

"It's an automatic recorder, much more sophisticated than the ones we have at the gates for counting the whales as they go through. Essentially, it's a long-range sonar scanner that explores a volume of space fifteen miles in radius, clear down to the bottom of the sea. It rejects all fixed echoes, and will only record moving objects. And it can also be set to ignore all objects of less than any desired size. In other words, we can use it to count the number of whales more than, say, fifty feet long, and take no notice of the others. It does this once every six minutes—two hundred and forty times a day—so it will give a virtually continuous census of any desired region."

"Quite ingenious. I suppose D.S.R. wants us to moor the thing somewhere and service it?"

"Yes—and to collect the recordings every week. They should be very useful to us as well. Er—there are three of the things, by the way."

"Trust D.S.R. to do it in style! I wish we had as much money to throw around. Let me know how the things work—if they do."

It was as simple as that, and there had been no mention at all of sea serpents.

Nor was there any sign of them for more than two months. Every week, whatever patrol sub happened to be in the neighborhood would bring back the records from the three instruments, moored half a mile below sea level at the spots Franklin had chosen after a careful study of all the known sightings. With an eagerness which slowly subsided to a stubborn determination, he examined the hundreds of feet of old-fashioned sixteen-millimeter film—still unsurpassed in its own field as a recording medium. He looked at thousands of echoes as he projected the film, condensing into minutes the comings and goings of giant sea creatures through many days and nights.

Usually the pictures were blank, for he had set the discriminator to reject all echoes from objects less than seventy feet in length. That, he calculated, should eliminate all but the very largest whales—and the quarry he was seeking. When the herds were on the move, however, the film would be dotted with echoes which would jump across the screen at fantastically exaggerated speeds as he projected the images. He was watching the life of the sea accelerated almost ten thousand times.

After two months of fruitless watching, he began to wonder if he had chosen the wrong places for all three recorders, and was making plans to move them. When the next rolls of film came back, he told himself, he would do just that, and he had already decided on the new locations.

But this time he found what he had been looking for. It was on the edge of the screen, and had been caught by only four sweeps of the scanner. Two days ago that unforgotten, curiously linear echo had appeared on the recorder; now he had evidence, but he still lacked proof.

He moved the other two recorders into the area, arranging the three instruments in a great triangle fifteen miles on a side, so that their fields overlapped. Then it was a question of waiting with what patience he could until another week had passed.

The wait was worth it; at the end of that time he had all the ammunition he needed for his campaign. The proof was there, clear and undeniable.

A very large animal, too long and thin to be any of the known creatures of the sea, lived at the astonishing depth of twenty thousand feet and came halfway to the surface twice a day, presumably to feed. From its intermittent appearance on the screens of the recorders, Franklin was able to get a fairly good idea of its habits and movements. Unless it suddenly left the area and he lost track of it, there should be no great difficulty in repeating the success of Operation Percy.

He should have remembered that in the sea nothing is ever twice the same.

CHAPTER

"Y ou know, dear," said Indra, "I'm rather glad this is going to be one of your last missions."

"If you think I'm getting too old—"

"Oh, it's not only that. When you're on headquarters duty we'll be able to start leading a normal social life. I'll be able to invite people to dinner without having to apologize because you've suddenly been called out to round up a sick whale. And it will be better for the children; I won't have to keep explaining to them who the strange man is they sometimes meet around the house."

"Well, it's not *that* bad, is it, Pete?" laughed Franklin, tousling his son's dark, unruly hair.

"When are you going to take me down in a sub, Daddy?" asked Peter, for approximately the hundredth time.

"One of these days, when you're big enough not to get in the way."

"But if you wait until I am big, I *will* get in the way."

"There's logic for you!" said Indra. "I told you my child was a genius."

"He may have got his hair from you," said Franklin, "but it doesn't follow that you're responsible for what lies beneath it." He turned to Don, who was making ridiculous noises for Anne's benefit. She seemed unable to decide whether to laugh or to burst into tears, but was obviously giving the problem her urgent attention. "When are you going to settle down to the joys of domesticity? You can't be an honorary uncle all your life."

For once, Don looked a little embarrassed.

"As a matter of fact," he said slowly, "I am thinking about it. I've met someone at last who looks as if she might be willing."

"Congratulations! I thought you and Marie were seeing a lot of each other."

Don looked still more embarrassed.

"Well—ah—it isn't Marie. I was just trying to say goodbye to *her*."

"Oh," said Franklin, considerably deflated. "Who is it?"

"I don't think you know her. She's named June—June Curtis. She isn't in the bureau at all, which is an advantage in some ways. I've not quite made up my mind yet, but I'll probably ask her next week."

"There's only one thing to do," said Indra firmly. "As soon as you come back from this hunt, bring her around to dinner and I'll tell you what we think of her."

"And I'll tell her what we think of *you*," put in Franklin. "We can't be fairer than that, can we?"

He remembered Indra's words—"this is going to be one of your last missions"—as the little depth ship slanted swiftly down into the eternal night. It was not strictly true, of course; even though he had now been promoted to a permanent shore position, he would still occasionally go to sea. But the opportunities would become fewer and fewer; this was his swan song as a warden, and he did not know whether to be sorry or glad.

For seven years he had roamed the oceans—one year of his

life to each of the seas—and in that time he had grown to know the creatures of the deep as no man could ever have done in any earlier age. He had watched the sea in all its moods; he had coasted over mirror-flat waters, and had felt the surge of mighty waves lifting his vessel when it was a hundred feet below the storm-tossed surface. He had looked upon beauty and horror and birth and death in all their multitudinous forms, as he moved through a liquid world so teeming with life that by comparison the land was an empty desert.

No man could ever exhaust the wonder of the sea, but Franklin knew that the time had come for him to take up new tasks. He looked at the sonar screen for the accompanying cigar of light which was Don's ship, and thought affectionately of their common characteristics and of the differences which now must take them further and further apart. Who would have imagined, he told himself, that they would become such good friends, that far-off day when they had met warily as instructor and pupil?

That had been only seven years ago, but already it was hard for him to remember the sort of person he had been in those days. He felt an abiding gratitude for the psychologists who had not only rebuilt his mind but had found him the work that could rebuild his life.

His thoughts completed the next, inevitable step. Memory tried to recreate Irene and the boys—good heavens, Rupert would be twelve years old now!—around whom his whole existence had once revolved, but who now were strangers drifting further and further apart year by year. The last photograph he had of them was already more than a year old; the last letter from Irene had been posted on Mars six months ago, and he reminded himself guiltily that he had not yet answered it.

All the grief had gone long ago; he felt no pain at being an exile in his own world, no ache to see once more the faces of friends he had known in the days when he counted all space his empire. There was only a wistful sadness, not even wholly unpleasant, and a mild regret for the inconstancy of sorrow.

Don's voice broke into his reverie, which had never taken his attention away from his crowded instrument panel.

"We're just passing my record, Walt. Ten thousand's the deepest I've ever been."

"And we're only halfway there. Still, what difference does it make if you've got the right ship? It just takes a bit longer to go down, and a bit longer to come up. These subs would still have a safety factor of five at the bottom of the Philippine Trench."

"That's true enough, but you can't convince me there's no psychological difference. Don't *you* feel two miles of water on your shoulders?"

It was most unlike Don to be so imaginative; usually it was Franklin who made such remarks and was promptly laughed at. If Don was getting moody, it would be best to give him some of his own medicine.

"Tell me when you've got to start bailing," said Franklin. "If the water gets up to your chin, we'll turn back."

He had to admit that the feeble joke helped his own morale. The knowledge that the pressure around him was rising steadily to five tons per square inch did have a definite effect on his mind—an effect he had never experienced in shallow-water operations where disaster could be just as instantaneous, just as total. He had complete confidence in his equipment and knew that the sub would do all that he asked it to; but he still felt that curious feeling of depression which seemed to have taken most of the zest out of the project into which he had put so much effort.

Five thousand feet lower down, that zest returned with all its old vigor. They both saw the echo simultaneously, and for a moment were shouting at cross purposes until they remembered their signals discipline. When silence had been restored, Franklin gave his orders.

"Cut your motor to quarter speed," he said. "We know the beast's very sensitive and we don't want to scare it until the last minute."

"Can't we flood the bow tanks and glide down?"

"Take too long—he's still three thousand feet below. And cut your sonar to minimum power; I don't want him picking up our pulses."

The animal was moving in a curiously erratic path at a constant depth, sometimes making little darts to right or left as if in search of food. It was following the slopes of an unusually steep submarine mountain, which rose abruptly some four thousand feet from the seabed. Not for the first time, Franklin thought what a pity it was that the world's most stupendous scenery was all sunk beyond sight in the ocean depths. Nothing on the land could compare with the hundred-mile-wide canyons of the North Atlantic, or the monstrous potholes that gave the Pacific the deepest soundings on Earth.

They sank slowly below the summit of the submerged mountain—a mountain whose topmost peak was three miles below sea level. Only a little way beneath them now that mysteriously elongated echo seemed to be undulating through the water with a sinuous motion which reminded Franklin irresistibly of a snake. It would, he thought, be ironic if the Great Sea Serpent turned out to be exactly that. But that was impossible, for there were no water-breathing snakes.

Neither man spoke during the slow and cautious approach to their goal. They both realized that this was one of the great moments of their lives, and wished to savor it to the full. Until now, Don had been mildly skeptical, believing that whatever they found would be no more than some already-known species of animal. But as the echo on the screen expanded, so its strangeness grew. This was something wholly new.

The mountain was now looming above them; they were skirting the foot of a cliff more than two thousand feet high, and their quarry was less than half a mile ahead. Franklin felt his hand itching to throw on the ultraviolet searchlights which in an instant might solve the oldest mystery of the sea, and bring him enduring fame. How important to him was that? he asked himself, as the seconds ticked slowly by. That it was important, he did not attempt to hide from himself. In all his career, he might never have another opportunity like this. . . .

Suddenly, without the slightest warning, the sub trembled as if struck by a hammer. At the same moment Don cried out: "My God—what was that?"

"Some damn fool is letting off explosives," Franklin replied, rage and frustration completely banishing fear. "Wasn't everyone notified of our dive?"

"That's no explosion. I've felt it before—it's an earthquake."

No other word could so swiftly have conjured up once more all that terror of the ultimate depths which Franklin had felt brushing briefly against his mind during their descent. At once the immeasurable weight of the waters crushed down upon him like a physical burden; his sturdy craft seemed the frailest of cockleshells, already doomed by forces which all man's science could no longer hold at bay.

He knew that earthquakes were common in the deep Pacific, where the weights of rock and water were forever poised in precarious equilibrium. Once or twice on patrols he had felt distant shocks—but this time, he felt certain, he was near the epicenter.

"Make full speed for the surface," he ordered. "That may be just the beginning."

"But we only need another five minutes," Don protested. "Let's chance it, Walt."

Franklin was sorely tempted. That single shock might be the only one; the strain on the tortured strata miles below might have been relieved. He glanced at the echo they had been chasing; it was moving much faster now, as if it, too, had been frightened by this display of Nature's slumbering power.

"We'll risk it," Franklin decided. "But if there's another one we'll go straight up."

"Fair enough," answered Don. "I'll bet you ten to one—"

He never completed the sentence. This time the hammer blow was no more violent, but it was sustained. The entire ocean seemed to be in travail as the shock waves, traveling at almost a mile a second, were reflected back and forth between surface and seabed. Franklin shouted the one word "Up!" and tilted the sub as steeply as he dared toward the distant sky.

But the sky was gone. The sharply defined plane which marked the water-air interface on the sonar screen had vanished, replaced by a meaningless jumble of hazy echoes. For a moment Franklin assumed that the set had been put out of action by the shocks; then his mind interpreted the incredible, the terrifying picture that was taking shape upon the screen.

"Don," he yelled, "run for the open sea—the mountain's falling!"

The billions of tons of rock that had been towering above them were sliding down into the deep. The whole face of the mountain had split away and was descending in a waterfall of stone, moving with a deceptive slowness and an utterly irresistible power. It was an avalanche in slow motion, but Franklin knew that within seconds the waters through which his sub was driving would be torn with falling debris.

He was moving at full speed, yet he seemed motionless. Even without the amplifiers, he could hear through the hull the rumble and roar of grinding rock. More than half the sonar image was now obliterated, either by solid fragments or by the immense clouds of mud and silt that were now beginning to fill the sea. He was becoming blind; there was nothing he could do but hold his course and pray.

With a muffled thud, something crashed against the hull and the sub groaned from end to end. For a moment Franklin thought he had lost control; then he managed to fight the vessel back to an even keel. No sooner had he done this than he realized he was in the grip of a powerful current, presumably due to water displaced by the collapsing mountain. He welcomed it, for it was sweeping him to the safety of the open sea, and for the first time he dared to hope.

Where was Don? It was impossible to see his echo in the shifting chaos of the sonar screen. Franklin switched his communication set to high power and started calling through the moving darkness. There was no reply; probably Don was too busy to answer, even if he had received the signal.

The pounding shock waves had ceased; with them had gone the worst of Franklin's fears. There was no danger now of the hull being cracked by pressure, and by this time, surely, he was clear of the slowly toppling mountain. The current that had been aiding his engines had now lost its strength, proving that he was far away from its source. On the sonar screen, the luminous haze that had blocked all vision was fading minute by minute as the silt and debris subsided.

Slowly the wrecked face of the mountain emerged from the mist of conflicting echoes. The pattern on the screen began to stabilize itself, and presently Franklin could see the great scar left by the avalanche. The seabed itself was still hidden in a vast fog of mud; it might be hours before it would be visible again and the damage wrought by Nature's paroxysm could be ascertained.

Franklin watched and waited as the screen cleared. With each sweep of the scanner, the sparkle of interference faded; the water was still turbid, but no longer full of suspended matter. He could see for a mile—then two—then three.

And in all that space there was no sign of the sharp and brilliant echo that would mark Don's ship. Hope faded as his radius of vision grew and the screen remained empty. Again and again he called into the lonely silence, while grief and helplessness strove for the mastery of his soul.

He exploded the signal grenades that would alert all the hydrophones in the Pacific and send help racing to him by sea and air. But even as be began his slowly descending spiral search, he knew that it was in vain.

Don Burley had lost his last bet.

III

THE BUREAUCRAT

CHAPTER

18

T he great Mercator chart that covered the whole of one wall
was a most unusual one. All the land areas were completely
blank; as far as this mapmaker was concerned, the continents had never been explored. But the sea was crammed with
detail, and scattered over its face were countless spots of colored light, projected by some mechanism inside the wall.
Those spots moved slowly from hour to hour, recording as
they did so, for skilled eyes to read, the migration of all the
main schools of whales that roamed the seas.

Franklin had seen the master chart scores of times during
the last fourteen years—but never from this vantage point. For
he was looking at it now from the director's chair.

"There's no need for me to warn you, Walter," said his ex-
chief, "that you are taking over the bureau at a very tricky time.
Sometime in the next five years we're going to have a show-
down with the farms. Unless we can improve our efficiency,
plankton-derived proteins will soon be substantially cheaper
than any we can deliver.

"And that's only one of our problems. The staff position is
getting more difficult every year—and this sort of thing isn't
going to help."

He pushed a folder across to Franklin, who smiled wryly when he saw what it contained. The advertisement was familiar enough; it had appeared in all the major magazines during the past week, and must have cost the Space Department a small fortune.

An underwater scene of improbable clarity and color was spread across two pages. Vast scaly monsters, more huge and hideous than any that had lived on Earth since the Jurassic period, were battling each other in the crystalline depths. Franklin knew, from the photographs he had seen, that they were very accurately painted, and he did not grudge the illustrator his artistic license in the matter of underwater clarity.

The text was dignified and avoided sensationalism; the painting was sensational enough and needed no embellishment. The Space Department, he read, urgently needed young men as wardens and food production experts for the exploitation of the seas of Venus. The work, it was added, was probably the most exciting and rewarding to be found anywhere in the Solar System; pay was good and the qualifications were not as high as those needed for space pilot or astrogator. After the short list of physical and educational requirements, the advertisement ended with the words which the Venus Commission had been plugging for the last six months, and which Franklin had grown heartily tired of seeing: HELP TO BUILD A SECOND EARTH.

"Meanwhile," said the ex-director, "our problem is to keep the first one going, when the bright youngsters who might be joining us are running away to Venus. And between you and me, I shouldn't be surprised if the Space Department has been after some of our men."

"They wouldn't do a thing like that!"

"Wouldn't they now? Anyway, there's a transfer application in from First Warden McRae; if you can't talk him out of it, try to find what made him want to leave."

Life was certainly going to be difficult, Franklin thought.

Joe McRae was an old friend; could he impose on that friendship now that he was Joe's boss?

"Another of your little problems is going to be keeping the scientists under control. Lundquist is worse than Roberts ever was; he's got about six crazy schemes going, and at least Roberts only had one brainstorm at a time. He spends half his time over on Heron Island. It might be a good idea to fly over and have a look at him. That was something I never had a chance to get around to."

Franklin was still listening politely as his predecessor continued, with obvious relish, to point out the many disadvantages of his new post. Most of them he already knew, and his mind was now far away. He was thinking how pleasant it would be to begin his directorate with an official visit to Heron Island, which he had not seen for nearly five years, and which had so many memories of his first days in the bureau.

Dr. Lundquist was flattered by the new director's visit, being innocent enough to hope that it might lead to increased support for his activities. He would not have been so enthusiastic had he guessed that the opposite was more likely to be the case. No one could have been more sympathetic than Franklin to scientific research, but now that he had to approve the bills himself he found that his point of view was subtly altered. Whatever Lundquist was doing would have to be of direct value to the bureau. Otherwise it was out—unless the Department of Scientific Research could be talked into taking it over.

Lundquist was a small, intense little man whose rapid and somewhat jerky movements reminded Franklin of a sparrow. He was an enthusiast of a type seldom met these days, and he combined a sound scientific background with an unfettered imagination. How unfettered, Franklin was soon to discover.

Yet at first sight it seemed that most of the work going on at the lab was of a fairly routine nature. Franklin spent a dull half-hour while two young scientists explained the methods they were developing to keep whales free of the many parasites that plagued them, and then escaped by the skin of his teeth from a lecture on cetacean obstetrics. He listened with rare interest to the latest work on artificial insemination, having in the past helped with some of the early—and often hilariously unsuccessful—experiments along this line. He sniffed cautiously at some synthetic ambergris, and agreed that it seemed just like the real thing. And he listened to the recorded heartbeat of a whale before and after the cardiac operation that had saved its life, and pretended that he could hear the difference.

Everything here was perfectly in order, and just as he had expected. Then Lundquist steered him out of the lab and down to the big pool, saying as he did so: "I think you'll find this more interesting. It's only in the experimental stage, of course, but it has possibilities."

The scientist looked at his watch and muttered to himself, "Two minutes to go; she's usually in sight by now." He glanced out beyond the reef, then said with satisfaction, "Ah—there she is!"

A long black mound was moving in toward the island and a moment later Franklin saw the typical stubby spout of vapor which identified the humpback whale. Almost at once he saw a second, much smaller spout, and realized that he was watching a female and her calf. Without hesitation, both animals came in through the narrow channel that had been blasted through the coral years ago so that small boats could come up to the lab. They turned left into a large tidal pool that had not been here on Franklin's last visit, and remained there waiting patiently like well-trained dogs.

Two lab technicians, wearing oilskins, were trundling something that looked like a fire extinguisher to the edge of the pool. Lundquist and Franklin hurried to join them, and it was soon obvious why the oilskins were necessary on this bright and cloudless day. Every time the whales spouted there was a miniature rainstorm, and Franklin was glad to borrow protection from the descending and nauseous spray.

Even a warden seldom saw a live whale at such close quarters, and under such ideal conditions. The mother was about fifty feet long, and, like all humpbacks, very massively built. She was no beauty, Franklin decided, and the large, irregular warts along the leading edges of her flippers did nothing to add to her appearance. The little calf was about twenty feet in length, and did not appear to be too happy in its confined quarters, for it was anxiously circling its stolid mother.

One of the scientists gave a curious, high-pitched shout, and at once the whale rolled over on her side, bringing half of her pleated belly out of the water. She did not seem to mind when a large rubber cup was placed over the now-exposed teat; indeed, she was obviously cooperating, for the meter on the collecting tank was recording an astonishing rate of flow.

"You know, of course," explained Lundquist, "that the cows eject their milk under pressure, so that the calves can feed when the teats are submerged without getting water in their mouths. But when the calves are *very* young, the mother rolls over like this so that the baby can feed above water. It makes things a lot simpler for us."

The obedient whale, without any instructions that Franklin could detect, had now circled round in her pen and was rolling over on the other side, so that her second teat could be milked. He looked at the meter; it now registered just under fifty gallons, and was still rising. The calf was obviously getting worried, or perhaps it had become excited by the milk that had accidentally spilled into the water. It made several attempts to bunt its mechanical rival out of the way, and had to be discouraged by a few sharp smacks.

Franklin was impressed, but not surprised. He knew that this was not the first time that whales had been milked, though he did not know that it could now be done with such neatness and dispatch. But where was it leading? Knowing Dr. Lundquist, he could guess.

"Now," said the scientist, obviously hoping that the demonstration had made its desired impact, "we can get at least five hundred pounds of milk a day from a cow without interfering with the calf's growth. And if we start breeding for milk as the farmers have done on land, we should be able to get a ton a day without any trouble. You think that's a lot? I regard it as quite a modest target. After all, prize cattle have given over a hundred pounds of milk a day—and a whale weighs a good deal more than twenty times as much as a cow!"

Franklin did his best to interrupt the statistics.

"That's all very well," he said. "I don't doubt your figures. And equally I don't doubt that you can process the milk to remove that oily taste—yes, I've tried it, thanks. But how the devil are you going to round up all the cows in a herd—especially a herd that migrates ten thousand miles a year?"

"Oh, we've worked all that out. It's partly a matter of training, and we've learned a lot getting Susan here to obey our underwater recordings. Have you ever been to a dairy farm and watched how the cows walk into the autolactor at milking time and walk out again—without a human being coming within miles of the place? And believe me, whales are a lot smarter and more easily trained than cows! I've sketched out the rough designs for a milk tanker that can deal with four whales at once, and could follow the herd as it migrates. In any case, now that we can control the plankton yield we can stop migration if we want to, and keep the whales in the tropics without them getting hungry. The whole thing's quite practical, I assure you."

Despite himself, Franklin was fascinated by the idea. It had been suggested, in some form or other, for many years, but Dr. Lundquist seemed to have been the first to do anything about it.

The mother whale and her still somewhat indignant calf had now set out to sea, and were soon spouting and diving noisily beyond the edge of the reef. As Franklin watched them go, he wondered if in a few years' time he would see hundreds of the great beasts lined up obediently as they swam to the mobile milking plants, each delivering a ton of what was known to be one of the richest foods on earth. But it might remain only a dream; there would be countless practical problems to be faced, and what had been achieved on the laboratory scale with a single animal might prove out of the question in the sea.

"What I'd like you to do," he said to Lundquist, "is to let me have a report showing what an—er—whale dairy would require in terms of equipment and personnel. Try to give costs wherever you can. And then estimate how much milk it could deliver, and what the processing plants would pay for that. Then we'll have something definite to work on. At the moment it's an interesting experiment, but no one can say if it has any practical application."

Lundquist seemed slightly disappointed at Franklin's lack of enthusiasm, but rapidly warmed up again as they walked away from the pool. If Franklin had thought that a little project like setting up a whale dairy had exhausted Lundquist's powers of extrapolation, he was going to learn better.

"The next proposal I want to talk about," began the scientist, "is still entirely in the planning stage. I know that one of our most serious problems is staff shortage, and I've been trying to think of ways in which we can improve efficiency by releasing men from routine jobs."

"Surely that process has gone about as far as it can, short of making everything completely automatic? Anyway it's less than a year since the last team of efficiency experts went over us." (And, added Franklin to himself, the bureau isn't quite back to normal yet.)

"My approach to the problem," explained Lundquist, "is a little unconventional, and as an ex-warden yourself I think you'll be particularly interested in it. As you know, it normally takes two or even three subs to round up a large school of whales; if a single sub tries it, they'll scatter in all directions. Now this has often seemed to me a shocking waste of man-power and equipment, since all the thinking could be done by a single warden. He only needs his partners to make the right noises in the right places—something a machine could do just as well."

"If you're thinking of automatic slave subs," said Franklin, "it's been tried—and it didn't work. A warden can't handle two ships at once, let alone three."

"I know all about *that* experiment," answered Lundquist. "It could have been a success if they'd tackled it properly. But my idea is much more revolutionary. Tell me—does the name 'sheep dog' mean anything to you?"

Franklin wrinkled his brow. "I think so," he replied. "Weren't they dogs that the old-time shepherds used to protect their flocks, a few hundred years ago?"

"It happened until less than a hundred years ago. And 'pro-tect' is an understatement with a vengeance. I've been looking at film records of sheep dogs in action, and no one who hadn't seen them would believe some of the things they could do. Those dogs were so intelligent and so well-trained that they could make a flock of sheep do anything the shepherd wanted, merely at a word of command from him. They could split a flock into sections, single out one solitary sheep from its fel-lows, or keep a flock motionless in one spot as long as their master ordered.

"Do you see what I am driving at? We've been training dogs for centuries, so such a performance doesn't seem miraculous to us. What I am suggesting is that we repeat the pattern in the sea. We know that a good many marine mammals—seals and porpoises, for instance—are at least as intelligent as dogs, but except in circuses and places like Marineland there's been no attempt to train them. You've seen the tricks our porpoises here can do, and you know how affectionate and friendly they are. When you've watched these old films of sheep-dog trials, you'll agree that anything a dog could do a hundred years ago we can teach a porpoise to do today."

"Just a minute," said Franklin, a little overwhelmed. "Let me get this straight. Are you proposing that every warden should have a couple of—er—hounds working with him when he rounds up a school of whales?"

"For certain operations, yes. Of course, the technique would have limitations; no marine animal has the speed and range of a sub, and the hounds, as you've called them, couldn't always get to the places where they were needed. But I've done some studies and I think it would be possible to double the effectiveness of our wardens in this way, by eliminating the times when they had to work in pairs or trios."

"But," protested Franklin, "what notice would whales take of porpoises? They'd ignore them completely."

"Oh, I wasn't suggesting that we should use porpoises, that was merely an example. You're quite right—the whales wouldn't even notice them. We'll have to use an animal that's fairly large, at least as intelligent as the porpoise, and which whales will pay a great deal of attention to indeed. There's only one animal that fills the bill, and I'd like your authority to catch one and train it."

"Go on," said Franklin, with such a note of resignation in his voice that even Lundquist, who had little sense of humor, was forced to smile.

"What I want to do," he continued, "is to catch a couple of killer whales and train them to work with one of our wardens."

Franklin thought of the thirty-foot torpedoes of ravening power he had so often chased and slaughtered in the frozen polar seas. It was hard to picture one of these ferocious beasts tamed to man's bidding; then he remembered the chasm between the sheep dog and the wolf, and how that had long ago been bridged. Yes, it could be done again—if it was worthwhile.

When in doubt, ask for a report, one of his superiors had

once told him. Well, he was going to bring back at least two from Heron Island, and they would both make very thought-provoking reading. But Lundquist's schemes, exciting though they were, belonged to the future; Franklin had to run the bureau as it was here and now. He would prefer to avoid drastic changes for a few years, until he had learned his way about. Besides, even if Lundquist's ideas could be proved practical, it would be a long, stiff battle selling them to the people who approved the funds. "I want to buy fifty milking machines for whales, please." Yes, Franklin could picture the reaction in certain conservative quarters. And as for training killer whales—why, they would think he had gone completely crazy.

He watched the island fall away as the plane lifted him toward home (strange, after all his travels, that he should be living again in the country of his birth). It was almost fifteen years since he had first made this journey with poor old Don; how glad Don would have been, could he had seen this final fruit of his careful training! And Professor Stevens, too—Franklin had always been a little scared of him, but now he could have looked him in the face, had he still been alive. With a twinge of remorse, he realized that he had never properly thanked the psychologist for all that he had done.

Fifteen years from a neurotic trainee to director of the bureau; that wasn't bad going. And what now, Walter? Franklin asked himself. He felt no need of any further achievement; perhaps his ambition was now satisfied. He would be quite content to guide the bureau into a placid and uneventful future.

It was lucky for his peace of mind that he had no idea how futile that hope was going to be.

CHAPTER

19

The photographer had finished, but the young man who had been Franklin's shadow for the last two days still seemed to have an unlimited supply of notebooks and questions. Was it worth all this trouble to have your undistinguished features—probably superimposed on a montage of whales—displayed upon every bookstand in the world? Franklin doubted it, but he had no choice in the matter. He remembered the saying: "Public servants have no private lives." Like all aphorisms, it was only half true. No one had ever heard of the last director of the bureau, and he might have led an equally inconspicuous existence if the Marine Division's Public Relations Department had not decreed otherwise.

"Quite a number of your people, Mr. Franklin," said the young man from *Earth Magazine*, "have told me about your interest in the so-called Great Sea Serpent, and the mission in which First Warden Burley was killed. Have there been any further developments in this field?"

Franklin sighed; he had been afraid that this would come up sooner or later, and he hoped that it wouldn't be overplayed in the resulting article. He walked over to his private file cabinet, and pulled out a thick folder of notes and photographs.

"Here are all the sightings, Bob," he said. "You might like to have a glance through them—I've kept the record up to date. One day I hope we'll have the answer; you can say it's still a hobby of mine, but it's one I've had no chance of doing anything about for the last eight years. It's up to the Department of Scientific Research now—not the Bureau of Whales. We've other jobs to do."

He could have added a good deal more, but decided against it. If Secretary Farlan had not been transferred from D.S.R. soon after the tragic failure of their mission, they might have had a second chance. But in the inquiries and recriminations that had followed the disaster, the opportunity had been lost, possibly for years. Perhaps in every man's life there must be some cherished failure, some unfinished business which outweighed many successes.

"Then there's only one other question I want to ask," continued the reporter. "What about the future of the bureau? Have you any interesting long-term plans you'd care to talk about?"

This was another tricky one. Franklin had learned long ago that men in his position must cooperate with the press, and in the last two days his busy interrogator had practically become one of the family. But there were some things that sounded a little too farfetched, and he had contrived to keep Dr. Lundquist out of the way when Bob had flown over to Heron Island. True, he had seen the prototype milking machine and been duly impressed by it, but he had been told nothing about the two young killer whales being maintained, at great trouble and expense, in the enclosure off the eastern edge of the reef.

"Well, Bob," he began slowly, "by this time you probably know the statistics better than I do. We hope to increase the size of our herds by ten per cent over the next five years. If this milking scheme comes off—and it's still purely experimental—we'll start cutting back on the sperm whales and will build up the humpbacks. At the moment we are providing twelve and a half per cent of the total food requirements of the human race, and that's quite a responsibility. I hope to see it fifteen per cent while I'm still in office."

"So that everyone in the world will have whale steak at least once a week, eh?"

"Put it that way if you like. But people are eating whale all day without knowing it—every time they use cooking fat or spread margarine on a piece of bread. We could double our output and we'd get no credit for it, since our products are almost always disguised in something else."

"The Art Department is going to put that right; when the story appears, we'll have a picture of the average household's groceries for a week, with a clock face on each item showing what percentage of it comes from whales."

"That'll be fine. Er—by the way—have you decided what you're going to call me?"

The reporter grinned.

"That's up to my editor," he answered. "But I'll tell him to avoid the word 'whaleboy' like the plague. It's too hackneyed, anyway."

"Well, I'll believe you when we see the article. Every journalist promises he won't call us that, but it seems they can never resist the temptation. Incidentally, when do you expect the story to appear?"

"Unless some news story crowds it off, in about four weeks. You'll get the proofs, of course, before that—probably by the end of next week."

Franklin saw him off through the outer office, half sorry to lose an entertaining companion who, even if he asked awkward questions, more than made up for it by the stories he could tell about most of the famous men on the planet. Now, he supposed, he belonged to that group himself, for at least a hundred million people would read the current "Men of *Earth*" series.

*   *   *

The story appeared, as promised, four weeks later. It was accurate, well-written, and contained one mistake so trivial that Franklin himself had failed to notice it when he checked the proofs. The photographic coverage was excellent and contained an astonishing study of a baby whale suckling its mother—a shot obviously obtained at enormous risk and after months of patient stalking. The fact that it was actually taken in the pool at Heron Island without the photographer even getting his feet wet was an irrelevance not allowed to distract the reader.

Apart from the shocking pun beneath the cover picture ("Prince of Whales," indeed!), Franklin was delighted with it; so was everyone else in the bureau, the Marine Division, and even the World Food Organization itself. No one could have guessed that within a few weeks it was to involve the Bureau of Whales in the greatest crisis of its entire history.

It was not lack of foresight; sometimes the future can be charted in advance, and plans made to meet it. But there are also times in human affairs when events that seem to have no possible connection—to be as remote as if they occurred on different planets—may react upon each other with shattering violence.

The Bureau of Whales was an organization which had taken half a century to build up, and which now employed twenty thousand men and possessed equipment valued at over two billion dollars. It was a typical unit of the scientific world state, with all the power and prestige which that implied.

And now it was to be shaken to its foundations by the gentle words of a man who had lived half a thousand years before the birth of Christ.

Franklin was in London when the first hint of trouble came. It was not unusual for officers of the World Food Organization to bypass his immediate superiors in the Marine Division and to contact him directly. What was unusual, however, was for the secretary of the W.F.O. himself to interfere with the everyday working of the bureau, causing Franklin to cancel all his engagements and to find himself, still a little dazed, flying halfway around the world to a small town in Ceylon of which he had never heard before and whose name he could not even pronounce.

Fortunately, it had been a hot summer in London and the extra ten degrees at Colombo was not unduly oppressive. Franklin was met at the airport by the local W.F.O. representative, looking very cool and comfortable in the sarong which had now been adopted by even the most conservative of westerners. He shook hands with the usual array of minor officials, was relieved to see that there were no reporters around who might tell him more about this mission than he knew himself, and swiftly transferred to the cross-country plane which would take him on the last hundred miles of his journey.

"Now," he said, when he had recovered his breath and the miles of neatly laid-out automatic tea plantations were flashing past beneath him, "you'd better start briefing me. Why is it so important to rush me to Anna—whatever you call the place?"

"Anuradhapura. Hasn't the secretary told you?"

"We had just five minutes at London Airport. So you might as well start from scratch."

"Well, this is something that has been building up for several years. We've warned Headquarters, but they've never taken us seriously. Now your interview in *Earth* has brought matters to a head; the Mahanayake Thero of Anuradhapura—he's the most influential man in the East, and you're going to hear a lot more about him—read it and promptly asked us to grant him facilities for a tour of the bureau. We can't refuse, of course, but we know perfectly well what he intends to do. He'll take a team of cameramen with him and will collect enough material to launch an all-out propaganda campaign against the bureau. Then, when it's had time to sink in, he'll demand a referendum. And if that goes against us, we *will* be in trouble."

The pieces of the jigsaw fell into place; the pattern was at last clear. For a moment Franklin felt annoyed that he had been diverted across the world to deal with so absurd a challenge. Then he realized that the men who had sent him here did not consider it absurd; they must know, better than he did, the strength of the forces that were being marshaled. It was never wise to underestimate the power of religion, even a religion as pacific and tolerant as Buddhism.

The position was one which, even a hundred years ago, would have seemed unthinkable, but the catastrophic political and social changes of the last century had all combined to give it a certain inevitability. With the failure or weakening of its three great rivals, Buddhism was now the only religion that still possessed any real power over the minds of men.

Christianity, which had never fully recovered from the shattering blow given it by Darwin and Freud, had finally and unexpectedly succumbed before the archaeological discoveries of the late twentieth century. The Hindu religion, with its fantastic pantheon of gods and goddesses, had failed to survive in an age of scientific rationalism. And the Mohammedan faith, weakened by the same forces, had suffered additional loss of prestige when the rising Star of David had outshone the pale crescent of the Prophet.

These beliefs still survived, and would linger on for generations yet, but all their power was gone. Only the teachings of the Buddha had maintained and even increased their influence, as they filled the vacuum left by the other faiths. Being a philosophy and not a religion, and relying on no revelations vulnerable to the archaeologist's hammer, Buddhism had been largely unaffected by the shocks that had destroyed the other giants. It had been purged and purified by internal reformations, but its basic structure was unchanged.

One of the fundamentals of Buddhism, as Franklin knew well enough, was respect for all other living creatures. It was a law that few Buddhists had ever obeyed to the letter, excusing themselves with the sophistry that it was quite in order to eat the flesh of an animal that someone else had killed. In recent years, however, attempts had been made to enforce this rule more rigorously, and there had been endless debates between vegetarians and meat eaters covering the whole spectrum of crankiness. That these arguments could have any practical effect on the work of the World Food Organization was something that Franklin had never seriously considered.

"Tell me," he asked, as the fertile hills rolled swiftly past beneath him, "what sort of man is this Thero you're taking me to see?"

"Thero is his title; you can translate it by archbishop if you like. His real name is Alexander Boyce, and he was born in Scotland sixty years ago."

"Scotland?"

"Yes—he was the first westerner ever to reach the top of the Buddhist hierarchy, and he had to overcome a lot of opposition to do it. A bhikku—er, monk—friend of mine once complained that the Maha Thero was a typical elder of the kirk, born a few hundred years too late—so he'd reformed Buddhism instead of the church of Scotland."

"How did he get to Ceylon in the first place?"

"Believe it or not, he came out as a junior technician in a film company. He was about twenty then. The story is that he went to film the statue of the Dying Buddha at the cave temple of Dambulla, and became converted. After that it took him twenty years to rise to the top, and he's been responsible for most of the reforms that have taken place since then. Religions get corrupt after a couple of thousand years and need a spring-cleaning. The Maha Thero did that job for Buddhism in Ceylon by getting rid of the Hindu gods that had crept into the temples."

"And now he's looking around for fresh worlds to conquer?"

"It rather seems like it. He pretends to have nothing to do with politics, but he's thrown out a couple of governments just by raising his finger, and he's got a huge following in the East. His 'Voice of Buddha' programs are listened to by several hundred million people, and it's estimated that at least a billion are sympathetic toward him even if they won't go all the way with his views. So you'll understand why we are taking this seriously."

Now that he had penetrated the disguise of an unfamiliar name, Franklin remembered that the Venerable Alexander Boyce had been the subject of a cover story in *Earth Magazine* two or three years ago. So they had something in common; he wished now that he had read that article, but at the time it had been of no interest to him and he could not even recall the Thero's appearance.

"He's a deceptively quiet little man, very easy to get on with," was the reply to his question. "You'll find him reasonable and friendly, but once he's made up his mind he grinds through all opposition like a glacier. He's not a fanatic, if that's what you are thinking. If you can prove to him that any course of action is essential, he won't stand in the way even though he may not like what you're doing. He's not happy about our local drive for increased meat production, but he realizes that everybody can't be a vegetarian. We compromised with him by not building our new slaughterhouse in either of the sacred cities, as we'd intended to do originally."

"Then why should he suddenly have taken an interest in the Bureau of Whales?"

"He's probably decided to make a stand somewhere. And besides—don't you think whales are in a different class from other animals?" The remark was made half apologetically, as if in the expectation of denial or even ridicule.

Franklin did not answer; it was a question he had been trying to decide for twenty years, and the scene now passing below absolved him from the necessity.

He was flying over what had once been the greatest city in the world—a city against which Rome and Athens in their prime had been no more than villages—a city unchallenged in size or population until the heydays of London and New York, two thousand years later. A ring of huge artificial lakes, some of them miles across, surrounded the ancient home of the Singhalese kings. Even from the air, the modern town of Anuradhapura showed startling contrasts of old and new. Dotted here and there among the colorful, gossamer buildings of the twenty-first century were the immense, bell-shaped domes of the great dagobas. The mightiest of all—the Abhayagiri Dagoba—was pointed out to Franklin as the plane flew low over it. The brickwork of the dome had long ago been overgrown with grass and even small trees, so that the great temple now appeared no more than a curiously symmetrical hill surmounted by a broken spire. It was a hill exceeded in size by one only of the pyramids that the Pharaohs had built beside the Nile.

By the time that Franklin had reached the local Food Production office, conferred with the superintendent, donated a few platitudes to a reporter who had somehow discovered his presence, and eaten a leisurely meal, he felt that he knew how to handle the situation. It was, after all, merely another public-relations problem; there had been a very similar one about three weeks ago, when a sensational and quite inaccurate newspaper story about methods of whale slaughtering had brought a dozen Societies for the Prevention of Cruelty down upon his head. A fact-finding commission had disposed of the charges very quickly, and no permanent damage had been done to anybody except the reporter concerned.

He did not feel quite so confident, a few hours later, as he stood looking up at the soaring, gilded spire of the Ruanveliseya Dagoba. The immense white dome had been so skillfully restored that it seemed inconceivable that almost twenty-two centuries had passed since its foundations were laid. Completely surrounding the paved courtyard of the temple was a line of life-sized elephants, forming a wall more than a quarter of a mile long. Art and faith had united here to produce one of the world's masterpieces of architecture, and the sense of antiquity was overwhelming. How many of the creations of modern man, wondered Franklin, would be so perfectly preserved in the year 4000?

The great flagstones in the courtyard were burning hot, and he was glad that he had retained his stockings when he left his shoes at the gate. At the base of the dome, which rose like a shining mountain toward the cloudless blue sky, was a single-storied modern building whose clean lines and white plastic walls harmonized well with the work of architects who had died a hundred years before the beginning of the Christian era.

A saffron-robed bhikku led Franklin into the Thero's neat and comfortably air-conditioned office. It might have been that of any busy administrator, anywhere in the world, and the sense of strangeness, which had made him ill at ease ever since he had entered the courtyard of the temple, began to fade.

The Maha Thero rose to greet him; he was a small man, his head barely reaching the level of Franklin's shoulders. His gleaming, shaven scalp somehow depersonalized him, making it hard to judge what he was thinking and harder still to fit him into any familiar categories. At first sight, Franklin was not impressed; then he remembered how many small men had been movers and shakers of the world.

Even after forty years, the Mahanayake Thero had not lost the accent of his birth. At first it seemed incongruous, if not slightly comic, in these surroundings, but within a few minutes Franklin was completely unaware of it.

"It's very good of you to come all this way to see me, Mr. Franklin," said the Thero affably as he shook hands. "I must admit that I hardly expected my request to be dealt with quite so promptly. It hasn't inconvenienced you, I trust?"

"No," replied Franklin manfully. "In fact," he added with rather more truth, "this visit is a novel experience, and I'm grateful for the opportunity of making it."

"Excellent!" said the Thero, apparently with genuine pleasure. "I feel just the same way about my trip down to your South Georgia base, though I don't suppose I'll enjoy the weather there."

Franklin remembered his instructions—"Head him off if you possibly can, but don't try to put any fast ones across on him." Well, he had been given an opening here.

"That's one point I wanted to raise with you, Your Reverence," he answered, hoping he had chosen the correct honorific. "It's midwinter in South Georgia, and the base is virtually closed down until the late spring. It won't be operating again for about five months."

"How foolish of me—I should have remembered. But I've never been to the Antarctic and I've always wanted to; I suppose I was trying to give myself an excuse. Well—it will have to be one of the northern bases. Which do you suggest—Greenland or Iceland? Just tell me which is more convenient. We don't want to cause any trouble."

It was that last phrase which defeated Franklin before the battle had fairly begun. He knew now that he was dealing with an adversary who could be neither fooled nor deflected from his course. He would simply have to go along with the Thero, dragging his heels as hard as he could, and hoping for the best.

CHAPTER

The wide bay was dotted with feathery plumes of mist as the great herd milled around in uncertain circles, not alarmed by the voices that had called it to this spot between the mountains, but merely undecided as to their meaning. All their lives the whales had obeyed the orders that came, sometimes in the form of water-borne vibrations, sometimes in electric shocks, from the small creatures whom they recognized as masters. Those orders, they had come to learn, had never harmed them; often, indeed, they had led them to fertile pastures which they would never have found unaided, for they were in regions of the sea which all their experience and the memories of a million years told them should be barren. And sometimes the small masters had protected them from the killers, turning aside the ravening packs before they could tear their living victims into fragments.

They had no enemies and no fears. For generations now they had roamed the peaceful oceans of the world, growing fatter and sleeker and more contented than all their ancestors back to the beginning of time. In fifty years they had grown, on an average, ten per cent longer and thirty per cent heavier, thanks to the careful stewardship of the masters. Even now the lord of all their race, the hundred-and-fifty-one-foot blue whale B.69322, universally known as Leviathan, was sporting in the Gulf Stream with his mate and newborn calf. Leviathan could never have reached his present size in any earlier age; though such matters were beyond proof, he was probably the largest animal that had ever existed in the entire history of Earth. Order was emerging out of chaos as the directing fields started to guide the herd along invisible channels. Presently the electric barrier gave way to concrete ones; the whales were swimming along four parallel canals, too narrow for more than one to pass at a time. Automatic senses weighed and measured them, rejecting all those below a certain size and diverting them back into the sea—doubtless a little puzzled, and quite unaware how seriously their numbers had been depleted.

The whales that had passed the test swam on trustfully along the two remaining channels until presently they came to a large lagoon. Some tasks could not be left entirely to machines; there were human inspectors here to see that no mistakes had been made, to check the condition of the animals, and to log the numbers of the doomed beasts as they left the lagoon on their last, short swim into the killing pens.

"B.52111 coming up," said Franklin to the Thero as they stood together in the observation chamber. "Seventy-foot female, known to have had five calves—past the best age for breeding." Behind him, he knew the cameras were silently recording the scene as their ivory-skulled, saffron-robed operators handled them with a professional skill which had surprised him until he learned that they had all been trained in Hollywood.

The whale never had any warning; it probably never even felt the gentle touch of the flexible copper fingers as they brushed its body. One moment it was swimming quietly along the pen; a second later it was a lifeless hulk, continuing to move forward under its own momentum. The fifty-thousand-ampere current, passing through the heart like a stroke of lightning, had not even allowed time for a final convulsion.

At the end of the killing pen, the wide conveyor belt took the weight of the immense body and carried it up a short slope until it was completely clear of the water. Then it began to move slowly forward along an endless series of spinning rollers which seemed to stretch halfway to the horizon.

"This is the longest conveyor of its kind in the world," Franklin explained with justifiable pride. "It may have as many as ten whales—say a thousand tons—on it at one time. Although it involves us in considerable expense, and greatly restricts our choice of site, we always have the processing plant at least half a mile from the pens, so there is no danger of the whales being frightened by the smell of blood. I think you'll agree that not only is the slaughtering instantaneous but the animals show no alarm whatsoever right up to the end."

"Perfectly true," said the Thero. "It all seems very humane. Still, if the whales did get frightened it would be very difficult to handle them, wouldn't it? I wonder if you would go to all this trouble merely to spare their feelings?"

It was a shrewd question, and like a good many he had been asked in the last few days Franklin was not quite sure how to answer it.

"I suppose," he said slowly, "that would depend on whether we could get the money. It would be up to the World Assembly, in the final analysis. The finance committees would have to decide how kind we could afford to be. It's a theoretical question, anyway."

"Of course—but other questions aren't so theoretical," answered the Venerable Boyce, looking thoughtfully at the eighty tons of flesh and bone moving away into the distance. "Shall we get back to the car? I want to see what happens at the other end."

And I, thought Franklin grimly, will be very interested to

see how you and your colleagues take it. Most visitors who
went through the processing yards emerged rather pale and
shaken, and quite a few had been known to faint. It was a
standard joke in the bureau that this lesson in food production removed the appetites of all who watched it for several
hours after the experience.

The stench hit them while they were still a hundred yards
away. Out of the corner of his eye, Franklin could see that the
young bhikku carrying the sound recorder was already showing signs of distress, but the Maha Thero seemed completely
unaffected. He was still calm and dispassionate five minutes
later as he stared down into the reeking inferno where the
great carcasses were torn asunder into mountains of meat and
bone and guts.

"Just think of it," said Franklin, "for almost two hundred
years this job was done by men, often working on board a
pitching deck in filthy weather. It's not pretty to watch even
now, but can you imagine being down there hacking away
with a knife nearly as big as yourself?"

"I think I could," answered the Thero, "but I'd prefer not
to." He turned to his cameramen and gave some brief instructions, then watched intently as the next whale arrived on
the conveyor belt.

The great body had already been scanned by photoelectric
eyes and its dimensions fed into the computer controlling the
operations. Even when one knew how it was done, it was uncanny to watch the precision with which the knives and saws
moved out on their extensible arms, made their carefully
planned pattern of cuts, and then retreated again. Huge grabs
seized the foot-thick blanket of blubber and stripped it off as
a man peels a banana, leaving the naked, bleeding carcass to
move on along the conveyor to the final stage of its dismem-
berment.

The whale traveled as fast as a man could comfortably
walk, and disintegrated before the eyes of the watchers as they

kept pace with it. Slabs of meat as large as elephants were torn away and went sliding down side chutes; circular saws whirred through the scaffolding of ribs in a cloud of bone dust; the interlinked plastic bags of the intestines, stuffed with perhaps a ton of shrimps and plankton from the whale's last meal, were dragged away in noisome heaps.

It had taken less than two minutes to reduce a lord of the sea to a bloody shambles which no one but an expert could have recognized. Not even the bones were wasted; at the end of the conveyor belt, the disarticulated skeleton fell into a pit where it would be ground into fertilizer.

"This is the end of the line," said Franklin, "but as far as the processing side is concerned it's only the beginning. The oil has to be extracted from the blubber you saw peeled off in stage one; the meat has to be cut down into more manageable portions and sterilized—we use a high-intensity neutron source for that—and about ten other basic products have to be sorted out and packed for shipment. I'll be glad to show you around any part of the factory you'd like to see. It won't be quite so gruesome as the operations we've just been watching."

The Thero stood for a moment in thoughtful silence, studying the notes he had been making in his incredibly tiny handwriting. Then he looked back along the bloodstained quarter-mile of moving belt, toward the next whale arriving from the killing pen.

"There's one sequence I'm not sure we managed to film properly," he said, coming to a sudden decision. "If you don't mind, I'd like to go back to the beginning and start again."

Franklin caught the recorder as the young monk dropped it. "Never mind, son," he said reassuringly, "the first time is always the worst. When you've been here a few days, you'll be quite puzzled when newcomers complain of the stink."

That was hard to believe, but the permanent staff had assured him that it was perfectly true. He only hoped that the

Venerable Boyce was not so thoroughgoing that he would have a chance of putting it to the proof.

"And now, Your Reverence," said Franklin, as the plane lifted above the snow-covered mountains and began the homeward flight to London and Ceylon, "do you mind if I ask how you intend to use all the material you've gathered?"

During the two days they had been together, priest and administrator had established a degree of friendship and mutual respect that Franklin, for his part, still found as surprising as it was pleasant. He considered—as who does not?—that he was good at summing men up, but there were depths in the Mahanayake Thero beyond his powers of analysis. It did not matter; he now knew instinctively that he was in the presence not only of power but also of—there was no escaping from that trite and jejune word—goodness. He had even begun to wonder, with a mounting awe that at any moment might deepen into certainty, if the man who was now his companion would go down into history as a saint.

"I have nothing to hide," said the Thero gently, "and, as you know, deceit is contrary to the teachings of the Buddha. Our position is quite simple. We believe that all creatures have a right to life, and it therefore follows that what you are doing is wrong. Accordingly, we would like to see it stopped."

That was what Franklin had expected, but it was the first time he had obtained a definite statement. He felt a slight sense of disappointment; surely someone as intelligent as the Thero must realize that such a move was totally impracticable, since it would involve cutting off one eighth of the total food supply of the world. And for that matter, why stop at whales? What about cows, sheep, pigs—all the animals that man kept in luxury and then slaughtered at his convenience?

"I know what you are thinking," said the Thero, before he could voice his objections. "We are fully aware of the problems involved, and realize that it will be necessary to move slowly. But a start must be made somewhere, and the Bureau of Whales gives us the most dramatic presentation of our case."

"Thank you," answered Franklin dryly. "But is that altogether fair? What you've seen here happens in every slaughterhouse on the planet. The fact that the scale of operation is different hardly alters the case."

"I quite agree. But we are practical men, not fanatics. We know perfectly well that alternative food sources will have to be found before the world's meat supplies can be cut off."

Franklin shook his head in vigorous disagreement.

"I'm sorry," he said, "but even if you could solve the supply problem, you're not going to turn the entire population of the planet into vegetarians—unless you are anxious to encourage emigration to Mars and Venus. I'd shoot myself if I thought I could never eat a lamb chop or a well-done steak again. So your plans are bound to fail on two counts: human psychology and the sheer facts of food production."

The Maha Thero looked a little hurt.

"My dear Director," he said, "surely you don't think we would overlook something as obvious as that? But let me finish putting our point of view before I explain how we propose to implement it. I'll be interested in studying your reactions, because you represent the maximum—ah—consumer resistance we are likely to meet."

"Very well," smiled Franklin. "See if you can convert me out of my job."

"Since the beginning of history," said the Thero, "man has assumed that the other animals exist only for his benefit. He has wiped out whole species, sometimes through sheer greed, sometimes because they destroyed his crops or interfered with his other activities. I won't deny that he often had justification, and frequently no alternative. But down the ages man has blackened his soul with his crimes against the animal kingdom—some of the very worst, incidentally, being in your particular profession, only sixty or seventy years ago. I've read of cases where harpooned whales died after hours of such frightful torment that not a scrap of their meat could be used—it was poisoned with the toxins produced by the animal's death agonies."

"Very exceptional," interjected Franklin. "And anyway we've put a stop to that."

"True, but it's all part of the debt we have to discharge."

"Svend Foyn wouldn't have agreed with you. When he invented the explosive harpoon, back in the 1870's, he made an entry in his diary thanking God for having done all the work."

"An interesting point of view," answered the Thero dryly. "I wish I'd had a chance of arguing it with him. You know, there is a simple test which divides the human race into two classes. If a man is walking along the street and sees a beetle crawling just where he is going to place his foot—well, he can break his stride and miss it or he can crush it into pulp. Which would *you* do, Mr. Franklin?"

"It would depend on the beetle. If I knew it was poisonous, or a pest, I'd kill it. Otherwise I'd let it go. That, surely, is what any reasonable man would do."

"Then we are not reasonable. We believe that killing is only justified to save the life of a higher creature—and it is surprising how seldom that situation arises. But let me get back to my argument; we seem to have lost our way.

"About a hundred years ago an Irish poet named Lord Dunsany wrote a play called *The Use of Man*, which you'll be seeing on one of our TV programs before long. In it a man dreams that he's magically transported out of the Solar System to appear before a tribunal of animals—and if he cannot find two to speak on his behalf, the human race is doomed. Only the dog will come forward to fawn over its master; all the others remember their old grievances and maintain that they would have been better off if man had never existed. The sentence of annihilation is about to be pronounced when another sponsor arrives in the nick of time, and humanity is saved. The only other creature who has any use for man is—the mosquito.

"Now you may think that this is merely an amusing jest; so, I am sure, did Dunsany—who happened to be a keen hunter. But poets often speak hidden truths of which they themselves are unaware, and I believe that this almost forgotten play contains an allegory of profound importance to the human race.

"Within a century or so, Franklin, we will literally be going outside the Solar System. Sooner or later we will meet types of intelligent life much higher than our own, yet in forms completely alien. And when that time comes, the treatment man receives from his superiors may well depend upon the way he has behaved toward the other creatures of his own world."

The words were spoken so quietly, yet with such conviction, that they struck a sudden chill into Franklin's soul. For the first time he felt that there might be something in the other's point of view—something, that is, besides mere humanitarianism. (But could humanitarianism ever be "mere"?) He had never liked the final climax of his work, for he had long ago developed a great affection for the monstrous charges, but he had always regarded it as a regrettable necessity.

"I grant that your points are well made," he admitted, "but whether we like them or not, we have to accept the realities of life. I don't know who coined the phrase 'Nature red in tooth and claw,' but that's the way she is. And if the world has to choose between food and ethics, I know which will win."

The Thero gave that secret, gentle smile which, consciously or otherwise, seemed to echo the benign gaze that so many generations of artists had made the hallmark of the Buddha.

"But that is just the point, my dear Franklin," he answered.

"There is no longer any need for a choice. Ours is the first generation in the world's history that can break the ancient cycle, and eat what it pleases without spilling the blood of innocent creatures. I am sincerely grateful to you for helping to show me how."

"Me!" exploded Franklin.

"Exactly," said the Thero, the extent of his smile now far exceeding the canons of Buddhist art. "And now, if you will excuse me, I think I'll go to sleep."

CHAPTER

S o this," grumbled Franklin, "is my reward for twenty years
of devoted public service—to be regarded even by my own
family as a bloodstained butcher."

"But all that was true, wasn't it?" said Anne, pointing to the
TV screen, which a few seconds ago had been dripping with
gore.

"Of course it was. But it was also very cleverly edited propaganda. I could make out just as good a case for our side."

"Are you sure of that?" asked Indra. "The division will certainly want you to, but it may not be easy."

Franklin snorted indignantly.

"Why, those statistics are all nonsense! The very idea of
switching our entire herds to milking instead of slaughtering is
just crazy. If we converted all our resources to whalemilk production we couldn't make up a quarter of the loss of fats and
protein involved in closing down the processing plants."

"Now, Walter," said Indra placidly, "there's no need to break
a blood vessel trying to keep calm. What's really upset you is
the suggestion that the plankton farms should be extended to
make up the deficit."

"Well, you're the biologist. Is it practical to turn that pea soup into prime ribs of beef or T-bone steaks?"

"It's obviously *possible*. It was a very clever move, having the chef of the Waldorf tasting both the genuine and the synthetic product, and being unable to tell the difference. There's no doubt you're going to have a lovely fight on your hands—the farm people will jump right in on the Thero's side of the fence, and the whole Marine Division will be split wide open."

"He probably planned that," said Franklin with reluctant admiration. "He's diabolically well-informed. I wish now I hadn't said so much about the possibilities of milk production during that interview—and they did overplay it a bit in the final article. I'm sure that's what started the whole business."

"That's another thing I was going to mention. Where did he get the figures on which he based his statistics? As far as I know, they have never been published anywhere outside the bureau."

"You're right," conceded Franklin. "I should have thought of that before. First thing tomorrow morning I'm going out to Heron Island to have a little talk with Dr. Lundquist."

"Will you take me, Daddy?" pleaded Anne.

"Not this time, young lady. I wouldn't like an innocent daughter of mine to hear some of the things I may have to say."

"Dr. Lundquist is out in the lagoon, sir," said the chief lab assistant. "There's no way of contacting him until he decides to come up."

"Oh, isn't there? I could go down and tap him on the shoulder."

"I don't think that would be at all wise, sir. Attila and Genghis Khan aren't very fond of strangers."

"Good God—is he swimming with *them*!"

"Oh yes—they're quite fond of him, and they've got very friendly with the wardens who work with them. But anyone else might be eaten rather quickly."

Quite a lot seemed to be going on, thought Franklin, that he knew very little about. He decided to walk to the lagoon; unless it was extremely hot, or one had something to carry, it was never worthwhile to take a car for such short distances.

He had changed his mind by the time he reached the new eastern jetty. Either Heron Island was getting bigger or he was beginning to feel his years. He sat down on the keel of an upturned dinghy, and looked out to sea. The tide was in, but the sharp dividing line marking the edge of the reef was clearly visible, and in the fenced-off enclosure the spouts of the two killer whales appeared as intermittent plumes of mist. There was a small boat out there, with somebody in it, but it was too far away for him to tell whether it was Dr. Lundquist or one of his assistants.

He waited for a few minutes, then telephoned for a boat to carry him out to the reef. In slightly more time than it would have taken him to swim there, he arrived at the enclosure and had his first good look at Attila and Genghis Khan.

The two killer whales were a little under thirty feet long, and as his boat approached them they simultaneously reared out of the water and stared at him with their huge, intelligent eyes. The unusual attitude, and the pure white of the bodies now presented to him, gave Franklin the uncanny impression that he was face to face not with animals but with beings who might be higher in the order of creation than himself. He knew that the truth was far otherwise, and reminded himself that he was looking at the most ruthless killer in the sea.

No, that was not quite correct. The *second* most ruthless killer in the sea. . . .

The whales dropped back into the water, apparently satisfied with their scrutiny. It was then that Franklin made out Lundquist, working about thirty feet down with a small torpedo loaded with instruments. Probably the commotion had disturbed him, because he came quickly to the surface and lay treading water, with his face mask pushed back, as he recognized his visitor.

"Good morning, Mr. Franklin. I wasn't expecting you today. What do you think of my pupils?"

"Very impressive. How well are they learning their lessons?"

"There's no doubt about it—they're brilliant. Even cleverer than porpoises, and surprisingly affectionate when they get to know you. I can teach them to do anything now. If I wanted to commit the perfect murder, I could tell them that you were a seal on an ice floe, and they'd have the boat over in two seconds."

"In that case, I'd prefer to continue our conversation back on land. Have you finished whatever you're doing?"

"It's never finished, but that doesn't matter. I'll ride the torp back—no need to lift all this gear into the boat."

The scientist swung his tiny metal fish around toward the island, and promptly set off at a speed which the dinghy could not hope to match. At once the two killers streaked after him, their huge dorsal fins leaving a creamy wake in the water. It seemed a dangerous game of tag to play, but before Franklin could discover what would happen when the killers caught the torpedo, Lundquist had crossed the shallow but clearly marked mesh around the enclosure, and the two whales broke their rush in a flurry of spray.

Franklin was very thoughtful on the way back to land. He had known Lundquist for years, but now he felt that this was the first time he had ever really seen him. There had never been any doubt concerning his originality—indeed, his brilliance—but he also appeared to possess unsuspected courage and initiative. None of which, Franklin determined grimly, would help him unless he had a satisfactory answer to certain questions.

Dressed in his everyday clothes, and back in the familiar laboratory surroundings, Lundquist was the man Franklin had always known. "Now, John," he began, "I suppose you've seen this television propaganda against the bureau?"

"Of course. But is it *against* us?"

"It's certainly against our main activity, but we won't argue that point. What I want to know is this: Have you been in touch with the Maha Thero?"

"Oh yes. He contacted me immediately after that article appeared in *Earth Magazine*."

"And you passed on confidential information to him?"

Lundquist looked sincerely hurt.

"I resent that, Mr. Franklin. The only information I gave him was an advance proof of my paper on whalemilk production, which comes out in the *Cetological Review* next month. You approved it for publication yourself."

The accusations that Franklin was going to make collapsed around his ears, and he felt suddenly rather ashamed of himself.

"I'm sorry, John," he said. "I take that back. All this has made me a bit jumpy, and I just want to sort out the facts before HQ starts chasing me. But don't you think you should have told me about this inquiry?"

"Frankly, I don't see why. We get all sorts of queries every day, and I saw no reason to suppose that this was not just another routine one. Of course, I was pleased that somebody was taking a particular interest in my special project, and I gave them all the help I could."

"Very well," said Franklin resignedly. "Let's forget the postmortem. But answer for me this question: As a scientist, do you really believe that we can afford to stop whale slaughtering and switch over to milk and synthetics?"

"Given ten years, we can do it if we have to. There's no technical objection that I can see. Of course I can't guarantee the figures on the plankton-farming side, but you can bet your life that the Thero had accurate sources of information there as well."

"But you realize what this will mean! If it starts with whales, sooner or later it will go right down the line through all the domestic animals."

"And why not? The prospect rather appeals to me. If science and religion can combine to take some of the cruelty out of Nature, isn't that a good thing?"

"You sound like a crypto-Buddhist—and I'm tired of pointing out that there's no cruelty in what we are doing. Meanwhile, if the Thero asks any more questions, kindly refer him to me."

"Very good, Mr. Franklin," Lundquist replied rather stiffly. There was an awkward pause, providentially broken by the arrival of a messenger.

"Headquarters wants to speak to you, Mr. Franklin. It's urgent."

"I bet it is," muttered Franklin. Then he caught sight of Lundquists's still somewhat hostile expression, and could not suppress a smile.

"If you can train orcas to be wardens, John," he said, "you'd better start looking around for a suitable mammal—preferably amphibious—to be the next director."

On a planet of instantaneous and universal communications, ideas spread from pole to pole more rapidly than they could once have done by word of mouth in a single village. The skillfully edited and presented program which had spoiled the appetites of a mere twenty million people on its first appearance had a far larger audience on its second. Soon there were few other topics of conversation; one of the disadvantages of life in a peaceful and well-organized world state was that with the disappearance of wars and crises very little was left of what was once called "news." Indeed, the complaint had often been made that since the ending of national sovereignty, history had also been abolished. So the argument raged in club and kitchen, in World Assembly and lonely space freighter, with no competition from any other quarter.

The World Food Organization maintained a dignified silence, but behind the scenes there was furious activity. Matters were not helped by the brisk lobbying of the farm group, which it had taken no great foresight on Indra's part to predict. Franklin was particularly annoyed by the efforts of the rival department to profit from his difficulties, and made several protests to the Director of Plankton Farms when the infighting became a little too rough. "Damn it all, Ted," he had snarled over the viewphone on one occasion, "you're just as big a butcher as I am. Every ton of raw plankton you process contains half a billion shrimps with as much right to life, liberty, and the pursuit of happiness as my whales. So don't try to stand in a white sheet. Sooner or later the Thero will work down to you—this is only the thin edge of the wedge."

"Maybe you're right, Walter," the culprit had admitted cheerfully enough, "but I think the farms will last out my time. It's not easy to make people sentimental over shrimps—they don't have cute little ten-ton babies to nurse."

That was perfectly true; it was very hard to draw the line between maudlin sentimentality and rational humanitarianism. Franklin remembered a recent cartoon showing the Thero raising his arms in protest while a shrieking cabbage was brutally dragged from the ground. The artist had taken no sides; he had merely summed up the viewpoint of those who considered that a great deal of fuss was being made about nothing. Perhaps this whole affair would blow over in a few weeks when people became bored and started arguing about something else—but he doubted it. That first television program had shown that the Thero was an expert in molding public opinion; he could be relied upon not to let his campaign lose momentum.

It took less than a month for the Thero to obtain the ten per cent vote needed under the constitution to set up a commission of inquiry. The fact that one tenth of the human race was sufficiently interested in the matter to request that all the facts be laid before it did not mean that they agreed with the Thero; mere curiosity and the pleasure of seeing a department of the state fighting a defensive rearguard action was quite enough to account for the vote. In itself, a commission of inquiry meant very little. What would matter would be the final referendum on the commission's report, and it would be months before that could be arranged.

One of the unexpected results of the twentieth century's electronic revolution was that for the first time in history it was possible to have a truly democratic government—in the sense that every citizen could express his views on matters of policy. What the Athenians, with indifferent success, had tried to do with a few thousand score of free men could now be achieved in a global society of five billion. Automatic sampling devices originally devised for the rating of television programs had turned out to have a far wider significance, by making it a relatively simple and inexpensive matter to discover exactly what the public really thought on any subject.

Naturally, there had to be safeguards, and such a system would have been disastrous before the days of universal education—before, in fact, the beginning of the twenty-first century. Even now, it was possible for some emotionally laden issue to force a vote that was really against the best interests of the community, and no government could function unless it held the final right to decide matters of policy during its term of office. Even if the world demanded some course of action by a ninety-nine per cent vote, the state could ignore the expressed will of the people—but it would have to account for its behavior at the next election.

Franklin did not relish the privilege of being a key witness at the commission's hearings, but he knew that there was no way in which he could escape this ordeal. Much of his time was now spent in collecting data to refute the arguments of those who wished to put an end to whale slaughtering, and it proved to be a more difficult task than he had imagined. One could not present a neat, clear-cut case by saying that processed whale meat cost so much per pound by the time it reached the consumer's table whereas synthetic meats derived from plankton or algae would cost more. Nobody knew—there were far too many variables. The biggest unknown of all was the cost of running the proposed sea dairies, if it was decided to breed whales purely for milk and not for slaughter.

The data were insufficient. It would be honest to say so, but there was pressure on him to state outright that the suspension of whale slaughtering would never be a practical or economic possibility. His own loyalty to the bureau, not to mention the security of his present position, prompted him in the same direction.

But it was not merely a matter of economics; there were emotional factors which disturbed Franklin's judgment and made it impossible for him to make up his mind. The days he had spent with the Maha Thero, and his brief glimpse of a civilization and a way of thought far older than his own, had affected him more deeply than he had realized. Like most men of his highly materialistic era, he was intoxicated with the scientific and sociological triumphs which had irradiated the opening decades of the twenty-first century. He prided himself on his skeptical rationalism, and his total freedom from superstition. The fundamental questions of philosophy had never bothered him greatly; he knew that they existed, but they had seemed the concern of other people.

And now, whether he liked it or not, he had been challenged from a quarter so unexpected that he was almost defenseless. He had always considered himself a humane man, but now he had been reminded that humanity might not be enough. As he struggled with his thoughts, he became progressively more and more irritable with the world around him, and matters finally became so bad that Indra had to take action.

"Walter," she said firmly, when Anne had gone tearfully to

bed after a row in which there was a good deal of blame on both sides, "it will save a lot of trouble if you face the facts and stop trying to fool yourself."

"What the devil do you mean?"

"You've been angry with everybody this last week—with just one exception. You've lost your temper with Lundquist— though that was partly my fault—with the press, with just about every other bureau in the division, with the children, and any moment you're going to lose it with me. But there's one person you're not angry with—and that's the Maha Thero, who's the cause of all the trouble."

"Why should I be? He's crazy, of course, but he's a saint— or as near it as I ever care to meet."

"I'm not arguing about that. I'm merely saying that you really agree with him, but you won't admit it."

Franklin started to explode. "That's utterly ridiculous!" he began. Then his indignation petered out. It *was* ridiculous; but it was also perfectly true.

He felt a great calm come upon him; he was no longer angry with the world and with himself. His childish resentment of the fact that *he* should be the man involved in a dilemma not of his making suddenly evaporated. There was no reason why he should be ashamed of the fact that he had grown to love the great beasts he guarded; if their slaughter could be avoided, he should welcome it, whatever the consequences to the bureau.

The parting smile of the Thero suddenly floated up into his memory. Had that extraordinary man foreseen that he would win him around to his point of view? If his gentle persuasiveness—which he had not hesitated to combine with the shock tactics of that bloodstained television program—could work with Franklin himself, then the battle was already half over.

CHAPTER

22

L ife was a good deal simpler in the old days, thought Indra
with a sigh. It was true that Peter and Anne were both at
school or college most of the time, but somehow that had
given her none of the additional leisure she had expected.
There was so much entertaining and visiting to do now that
Walter had moved into the upper echelons of the state.
Though perhaps that was exaggerating a little; the director of
the Bureau of Whales was still a long way—at least six steps—
down from the rarefied heights in which the president and his
advisers dwelt.

But there were some things that cut right across official
rank. No one could deny that there was a glamour about Walt's
job and an interest in his activities that had made him known
to a far wider circle than the other directors of the Marine Division, even before the *Earth Magazine* article or the present
controversy over whale slaughtering. How many people could
name the director of Plankton Farms or of Fresh-Water Food
Production? Not one to every hundred that had heard of Walter. It was a fact that made her proud, even though at the same
time it exposed Walter to a good deal of interdepartmental
jealousy.

Now, however, it seemed likely to expose him to worse than that. So far, no one in the bureau, still less any of the higher officials of the Marine Division or the World Food Organization imagined for one moment that Walter had any private doubts or that he was not wholeheartedly in support of the *status quo*.

Her attempts to read the current *Nature* were interrupted by the private-line viewphone. It had been installed, despite her bitter protests, the day that Walter had become director. The public service, it seemed, was not good enough; now the office could get hold of Walter whenever it liked, unless he took precautions to frustrate it.

"Oh, good morning, Mrs. Franklin," said the operator, who was now practically a friend of the family. "Is the director in?"

"I'm afraid not," said Indra with satisfaction. "He hasn't had a day off for about a month, and he's out sailing in the bay with Peter. If you want to catch him, you'll have to send a plane out; J.94's radio has broken down again."

"*Both* sets? That's odd. Still, it's not urgent. When he comes in, will you give him this memo?"

There was a barely audible click, and a sheet of paper drifted down into the extra large-sized memorandum basket. Indra read it, gave the operator an absent-minded farewell, and at once called Franklin on his perfectly serviceable radio.

The creak of the rigging, the soft rush of water past the smooth hull—even the occasional cry of a sea bird—these sounds came clearly from the speaker and transported her at once out into Moreton Bay.

"I thought you'd like to know, Walter," she said, "the Policy Board is having its special meeting next Wednesday, here in Brisbane. That gives you three days to decide what you're going to tell them."

There was a slight pause during which she could hear her husband moving about the boat; then Franklin answered: "Thanks, dear. I know what I've got to say—I just don't know how to say it. But there's something I've thought of that you can do to help. You know all the warden's wives—suppose you call up as many as you can, and try to find what their husbands feel about this business. Can you do that without making it look too obvious? It's not so easy for me, nowadays, to find what the men in the field are thinking. They're too liable to tell me what they imagine I want to know."

There was a wistful note in Franklin's voice which Indra had been hearing more and more frequently these days, though she knew her husband well enough to be quite sure that he had no real regrets for having taken on his present responsibilities.

"That's a good idea," she said. "There are at least a dozen people I should have called up weeks ago, and this will give me an excuse. It probably means that we'll have to have another party though."

"I don't mind that, as long as I'm still director and can afford to pay for it. But if I revert to a warden's pay in a month or so, we'll have to cut out the entertaining."

"You don't really think—"

"Oh, it won't be as bad as that. But they may shift me to some nice safe job, though I can't imagine what use I am now outside the bureau. GET OUT OF THE WAY, YOU BLASTED FOOL—CAN'T YOU SEE WHERE YOU'RE GOING? Sorry, dear— too many week-end sailors around. We'll be back in ninety minutes, unless some idiot rams us. Pete says he wants honey for tea. Bye now."

Indra looked thoughtfully at the radio as the sounds of the distant boat ceased abruptly. She half wished that she had accompanied Walter and Pete on their cruise out into the bay, but she had faced the fact that her son now needed his father's company rather than hers. There were times when she grudged this, realizing that in a few months they would both lose the boy whose mind and body they had formed, but who was now slipping from their grasp.

It was inevitable, of course; the ties that bound father and son together must now drive them apart. She doubted if Peter realized why he was so determined to get into space; after all, it was a common enough ambition among boys of his age. But he was one of the youngest ever to obtain a triplanetary scholarship, and it was easy to understand why. He was determined to conquer the element that had defeated his father.

But enough of this daydreaming, she told herself. She got out her file of visiphone numbers, and began to tick off the names of all the wardens' wives who would be at home.

The Policy Board normally met twice a year, and very seldom had much policy to discuss, since most of the bureau's work was satisfactorily taken care of by the committees dealing with finance, production, staff, and technical development. Franklin served on all of these, though only as an ordinary member, since the chairman was always someone from the Marine Division or the World Secretariat. He sometimes came back from the meetings depressed and discouraged; what was very unusual was for him to come back in a bad temper as well.

Indra knew that something had gone wrong the moment he entered the house. "Let me know the worst," she said resignedly as her exhausted husband flopped into the most comfortable chair in sight. "Do you have to find a new job?"

She was only half joking, and Franklin managed a wan smile. "It's not as bad as that," he answered, "but there's more in this business than I thought. Old Burrows had got it all worked out before he took the chair; someone in the Secretariat had briefed him pretty thoroughly. What it comes to is this: Unless it can be proved that food production from whale milk and synthetics will be *drastically* cheaper than the present method, whale slaughtering will continue. Even a ten percent saving isn't regarded as good enough to justify a switch-over. As Burrows put it, we're concerned with cost accounting, not abstruse philosophical principles like justice to animals.

"That's reasonable enough, I suppose, and certainly I

wouldn't try to fight it. The trouble started during the break for coffee, when Burrows got me into a corner and asked me what the wardens thought about the whole business. So I told him that eighty per cent of them would like to see slaughtering stopped, even if it meant a rise in food costs. I don't know why he asked me this particular question, unless news of our little survey has leaked out.

"Anyway, it upset him a bit and I could see him trying to get around to something. Then he put it bluntly that I'd be a key witness when the inquiry started, and that the Marine Division wouldn't like me to plead the Thero's case in open court with a few million people watching. 'Suppose I'm asked for my personal opinion?' I said. 'No one's worked harder than me to increase whale-meat and oil production, but as soon as it's possible I'd like to see the bureau become a purely conservation service.' He asked if this was my considered viewpoint and I told him that it was.

"Then things got a bit personal, though still in a friendly sort of way, and we agreed that there was a distinct cleavage of opinion between the people who handled whales as whales and those who saw them only as statistics on food-production charts. After that Burrows went off and made some phone calls, and kept us all waiting around for half an hour while he talked to a few people up in the Secretariat. He finally came back with what were virtually my orders, though he was careful not to put it that way. It comes to this: I've got to be an obedient little ventriloquist's dummy at the inquiry."

"But suppose the other side asks you outright for your personal views?"

"Our counsel will try to head them off, and if he fails I'm not supposed to have any personal views."

"And what's the point of all this?"

"That's what I asked Burrows, and I finally managed to get it out of him. There are political issues involved. The Secretariat is afraid that the Maha Thero will get too powerful if he wins this case, so it's going to be fought whatever its merits."

"Now I understand," said Indra slowly. "Do you think that the Thero is after political power?"

"For its own sake—no. But he may be trying to gain influence to put across his religious ideas, and that's what the Secretariat's afraid of."

"And what are you going to do about it?"

"I don't know," Franklin answered. "I really don't know."

He was still undecided when the hearings began and the Maha Thero made his first personal appearance before a worldwide audience. He was not, Franklin could not help thinking as he looked at the small, yellow-robed figure with his gleaming skull, very impressive at first sight. Indeed, there was something almost comic about him—until he began to speak, and one knew without any doubt that one was in the presence both of power and conviction.

"I would like to make one thing perfectly clear," said the Maha Thero, addressing not only the chairman of the commission but also the unseen millions who were watching this first hearing. "It is not true that we are trying to enforce vegetarianism on the world, as some of our opponents have tried to maintain. The Buddha himself did not abstain from eating meat, when it was given to him; nor do we, for a guest should accept gratefully whatever his host offers.

"Our attitude is based on something deeper and more fundamental than food prejudices, which are usually only a matter of conditioning. What is more, we believe that most reasonable men, whether their religious beliefs are the same as ours or not, will eventually accept our point of view.

"It can be summed up very simply, though it is the result of twenty-six centuries of thought. We consider that it is wrong to inflict injury or death on any living creature, but we are not so foolish as to imagine that it can be avoided altogether. Thus we recognize, for example, the need to kill microbes and insect pests, much though we may regret the necessity.

"But as soon as such killing is no longer essential, it should cease. We believe that this point has now arrived as far as many of the higher animals are concerned. The production of all types of synthetic protein from purely vegetable sources is now an economic possibility—or it will be if the effort is made to achieve it. Within a generation, we can shed the burden of guilt which, however lightly or heavily it has weighed on individual consciences, must at some time or other have haunted all thinking men as they look at the world of life which shares their planet.

"Yet this is not an attitude which we seek to enforce on anyone against his will. Good actions lose any merit if they are imposed by force. We will be content to let the facts we will present speak for themselves, so that the world may make its own choice."

It was, thought Franklin, a simple, straightforward speech, quite devoid of any of the fanaticism which would have fatally prejudiced the case in this rational age. And yet the whole matter was one that went beyond reason; in a purely logical world, this controversy could never have arisen, for no one would have doubted man's right to use the animal kingdom as he felt fit. Logic, however, could be easily discredited here; it could be used too readily to make out a convincing case for cannibalism.

The Thero had not mentioned, anywhere in his argument, one point which had made a considerable impact on Franklin. He had not raised the possibility that man might someday come into contact with alien life forms that might judge him by his conduct toward the rest of the animal kingdom. Did he think that this was so far-fetched an idea that the general public would be unable to take it seriously, and would thus grow to regard his whole campaign as a joke? Or had he realized that it was an argument that might particularly appeal to an ex-astronaut? There was no way of guessing; in either event it proved that the Thero was a shrewd judge both of private and public reactions.

Franklin switched off the receiver; the scenes it was showing now were quite familiar to him, since he had helped the Thero to film them. The Marine Division, he thought wryly, would now be regretting the facilities it had offered His Reverence, but there was nothing else it could have done in the circumstances.

In two days he would be appearing to give his evidence; already he felt more like a criminal on trial than a witness. And in truth he was on trial—or, to be more accurate, his conscience was. It was strange to think that having once tried to kill himself, he now objected to killing other creatures. There was some connection here, but it was too complicated for him to unravel—and even if he did, it would not help him to solve his dilemma.

Yet the solution was on the way, and from a totally unexpected direction.

CHAPTER

23

Franklin was boarding the plane that would take him to the hearings when the "Sub-Smash" signal came through. He stood in the doorway, reading the scarlet-tabbed message that had been rushed out to him, and at that moment all his other problems ceased to exist.

The SOS was from the Bureau of Mines, the largest of all the sections of the Marine Division. Its title was a slightly misleading one, for it did not run a single mine in the strict sense of the word. Twenty or thirty years ago there had indeed been mines on the ocean beds, but now the sea itself was an inexhaustible treasure chest. Almost every one of the natural elements could be extracted directly and economically from the millions of tons of dissolved matter in each cubic mile of sea water. With the perfection of selective ion-exchanged filters, the nightmare of metal shortages had been banished forever.

The Bureau of Mines was also responsible for the hundreds of oil wells that now dotted the seabeds, pumping up the precious fluid that was the basic material for half the chemical plants on earth—and which earlier generations, with criminal shortsightedness, had actually burned for fuel.

There were plenty of accidents that could befall the bureau's worldwide empire; only last year Franklin had lent it a whaling sub in an unsuccessful attempt to salvage a tank of gold concentrate. But this was far more serious, as he discovered after he had put through a few priority calls.

Thirty minutes later he was airborne, though not in the direction he had expected to be going. And it was almost an hour after he had taken off before all the orders had been given and he at last had a chance of calling Indra.

She was surprised at the unexpected call, but her surprise quickly turned to alarm. "Listen, dear," Franklin began. "I'm not going to Berne after all. Mines has had a serious accident and has appealed for our help. One of their big subs is trapped on the bottom—it was drilling a well and hit a high-pressure gas pocket. The derrick was blown over and toppled on the sub so that it can't get away. There's a load of VIP's aboard, including a senator and the director of Mines. I don't know how we're going to pull them out, but we'll do our best. I'll call you again when I've got time."

"Will you have to go down yourself?" asked Indra anxiously.

"Probably. Now don't look so upset! I've been doing it for years!"

"I'm *not* upset," retorted Indra, and Franklin knew better than to contradict her. "Good-bye, darling," he continued, "give my love to Anne, and don't worry."

Indra watched the image fade. It had already vanished when she realized that Walter had not looked so happy for weeks. Perhaps that was not the right word to use when men's lives were at stake; it would be truer to say that he looked full of life and enthusiasm. She smiled, knowing full well the reason why.

Now Walter could get away from the problems of his office, and could lose himself again, if only for a while, in the clear-cut and elemental simplicities of the sea.

*   *   *

"There she is," said the pilot of the sub, pointing to the image forming at the edge of the sonar screen. "On hard rock eleven hundred feet down. In a couple of minutes we'll be able to make out the details."

"How's the water clarity—can we use TV?"

"I doubt it. That gas geyser is still spouting—there it is— that fuzzy echo. It's stirred up all the mud for miles around."

Franklin stared at the screen, comparing the image forming there with the plans and sketches on the desk. The smooth ovoid of the big shallow-water sub was partly obscured by the wreckage of the drills and derrick—a thousand or more tons of steel pinning it to the ocean bed. It was not surprising that, though it had blown its buoyancy tanks and turned its jets on to full power, the vessel had been unable to move more than a foot or two.

"It's a nice mess," said Franklin thoughtfully. "How long will it take for the big tugs to get here?"

"At least four days. *Hercules* can lift five thousand tons, but she's down at Singapore. And she's too big to be flown here; she'll have to come under her own steam. You're the only people with subs small enough to be airlifted."

That was true enough, thought Franklin, but it also meant that they were not big enough to do any heavy work. The only hope was that they could operate cutting torches and carve up the derrick until the trapped sub was able to escape.

Another of the bureau's scouts was already at work; someone, Franklin told himself, had earned a citation for the speed with which the torches had been fitted to a vessel not designed to carry them. He doubted if even the Space Department, for all its fabled efficiency, could have acted any more swiftly than this.

"Captain Jacobsen calling," said the loudspeaker. "Glad to have you with us, Mr. Franklin. Your boys are doing a good job, but it looks as if it will take time."

"How are things inside?"

"Not so bad. The only thing that worries me is the hull between bulkheads three and four. It took the impact there, and there's some distortion."

"Can you close off the section if a leak develops?"

"Not very well," said Jacobsen dryly. "It happens to be the middle of the control room. If we have to evacuate that, we'll be completely helpless."

"What about your passengers?"

"Er—they're fine," replied the captain, in a tone suggesting that he was giving some of them the benefit of a good deal of doubt. "Senator Chamberlain would like a word with you."

"Hello, Franklin," began the senator. "Didn't expect to meet you again under these circumstances. How long do you think it will take to get us out?"

The senator had a good memory, or else he had been well briefed. Franklin had met him on not more than three occasions—the last time in Canberra, at a session of the Committee for the Conservation of Natural Resources. As a witness, Franklin had been before the C.C.N.R. for about ten minutes, and he would not have expected its busy chairman to remember the fact.

"I can't make any promises, Senator," he answered cautiously. "It may take some time to clear away all this rubbish. But we'll manage all right—no need to worry about that."

As the sub drew closer, he was not so sure. The derrick was over two hundred feet long, and it would be a slow business nibbling it away in sections that the little scout-subs could handle.

For the next ten minutes there was a three-cornered conference between Franklin, Captain Jacobsen, and Chief Warden Barlow, skipper of the second scoutsub. At the end of that time they had agreed that the best plan was to continue to cut away the derrick; even taking the most pessimistic view, they should be able to finish the job at least two days before the *Hercules* could arrive. Unless, of course, there were any unexpected snags; the only possible danger seemed to be the one that Captain Jacobsen had mentioned. Like all large undersea vessels, his ship carried an air-purifying plant which would keep the atmosphere breathable for weeks, but if the hull failed in the region of the control room all the sub's essential services would be disrupted. The occupants might retreat behind the pressure bulkheads, but that would give them only a temporary reprieve, because the air would start to become foul immediately. Moreover, with part of the sub flooded, it would be extremely difficult even for the *Hercules* to lift her.

Before he joined Barlow in the attack on the derrick, Franklin called Base on the long-range transmitter and ordered all the additional equipment that might conceivably be needed. He asked for two more subs to be flown out at once, and started the workshops mass producing buoyancy tanks by the simple process of screwing air couplings onto old oil drums. If enough of these could be hitched to the derrick, it might be lifted without any help from the submarine salvage vessel.

There was one other piece of equipment which he hesitated for some time before ordering. Then he muttered to himself: "Better get too much than too little," and sent off the requisition, even though he knew that the Stores Department would probably think him crazy.

The work of cutting through the girders of the smashed derrick was tedious, but not difficult. The two subs worked together, one burning through the steel while the other pulled away the detached section as soon as it came loose. Soon Franklin became completely unconscious of time; all that existed was the short length of metal which he was dealing with at that particular moment. Messages and instructions continually came and went, but another part of his mind dealt with them. Hands and brain were functioning as two separate entities.

The water, which had been completely turbid when they arrived, was now clearing rapidly. The roaring geyser of gas that was bursting from the seabed barely a hundred yards away must have sucked in fresh water to sweep away the mud it had originally disturbed. Whatever the explanation, it made the task of salvage very much simpler, since the subs' external eyes could function again.

Franklin was almost taken aback when the reinforcements arrived. It seemed impossible that he had been here for more than six hours; he felt neither tired nor hungry. The two subs brought with them, like a long procession of tin cans, the first batch of the buoyancy tanks he had ordered.

Now the plan of campaign was altered. One by one the oil drums were clipped to the derrick, air hoses were coupled to them, and the water inside them was blown out until they strained upward like captive balloons. Each had a lifting power of two or three tons; by the time a hundred had been attached, Franklin calculated, the trapped sub might be able to escape without any further help.

The remote handling equipment on the outside of the scoutsub, so seldom used in normal operations, now seemed an extension of his own arms. It had been at least four years since he had manipulated the ingenious metal fingers that enabled a man to work in places where his unprotected body could never go—and he remembered, from ten years earlier still, the first time he had attempted to tie a knot and the hopeless tangle he had made of it. That was one of the skills he had hardly ever used; who would have imagined that it would be vital now that he had left the sea and was no longer a warden?

They were starting to pump out the second batch of oil drums when Captain Jacobsen called.

"I'm afraid I've got bad news, Franklin," he said, his voice heavy with apprehension. "There's water coming in, and the leak's increasing. At the present rate, we'll have to abandon the control room in a couple of hours."

This was the news that Franklin had feared. It transformed a straightforward salvage job into a race against time—a race hopelessly handicapped, since it would take at least a day to cut away the rest of the derrick.

"What's your internal air pressure?" he asked Captain Jacobsen.

"I've already pushed it up to five atmospheres. It's not safe to put it up any farther."

"Take it up to eight if you can. Even if half of you pass out, that won't matter as long as someone remains in control. And it may help to keep the leak from spreading, which is the important thing."

"I'll do that—but if most of us are unconscious, it won't be easy to evacuate the control room."

There were too many people listening for Franklin to make the obvious reply—that if the control room had to be abandoned it wouldn't matter anyway. Captain Jacobsen knew that as well as he did, but some of his passengers might not realize that such a move would end any chance of rescue.

The decision he had hoped he would not have to make was now upon him. This slow whittling away of the wreckage was not good enough; they would have to use explosives, cutting the fallen derrick at the center, so that the lower, unsupported portion would drop back to the seabed and its weight would no longer pin down the sub.

It had been the obvious thing to do, even from the beginning, but there were two objections: one was the risk of using explosives so near the sub's already weakened hull; the other was the problem of placing the charges in the correct spot. Of the derrick's four main girders, the two upper ones were easily accessible, but the lower pair could not be reached by the remote handling mechanisms of the scoutsubs. It was the sort of job that only an unencumbered diver could do, and in shallow water it would not have taken more than a few minutes.

Unfortunately, this was not shallow water; they were eleven hundred feet down—and at a pressure of over thirty atmospheres.

CHAPTER

24

t's too great a risk, Franklin. I won't allow it." It was not often, thought Franklin, that one had a chance of arguing with a senator. And if necessary he would not merely argue; he would defy.

"I know there's a danger, sir," he admitted, "but there's no alternative. It's a calculated risk—one life against twenty-three."

"But I thought it was suicide for an unprotected man to dive below a few hundred feet."

"It is if he's breathing compressed air. The nitrogen knocks him out first, and then oxygen poisoning gets him. But with the right mixture it's quite possible. With the gear I'm using, men have been down fifteen hundred feet."

"I don't want to contradict you, Mr. Franklin," said Captain Jacobsen quietly, "but I believe that only one man has reached fifteen hundred—and then under carefully controlled conditions. *And* he wasn't attempting to do any work."

"Nor am I; I just have to place those two charges."

"But the pressure!"

"Pressure never makes any difference, Senator, as long as it's balanced. There may be a hundred tons squeezing on my lungs—but I'll have a hundred tons inside and won't feel it."

"Forgive me mentioning this—but wouldn't it be better to send a younger man?"

"I won't delegate this job, and age makes no difference to diving ability. I'm in good health, and that's all that matters." Franklin turned to his pilot and cut the microphone switch.

"Take her up," he said. "They'll argue all day if we stay here. I want to get into that rig before I change my mind."

He was wrestling with his thoughts all the way to the surface. Was he being a fool, taking risks which a man in his position, with a wife and family, ought never to face? Or was he still, after all these years, trying to prove that he was no coward, by deliberately meeting a danger from which he had once been rescued by a miracle?

Presently he was aware of other and perhaps less flattering motives. In a sense, he was trying to escape from responsibility. Whether his mission failed or succeeded, he would be a hero—and as such it would not be quite so easy for the Secretariat to push him around. It was an interesting problem; could one make up for lack of moral courage by proving physical bravery?

When the sub broke surface, he had not so much resolved these questions as dismissed them. There might be truth in every one of the charges he was making against himself; it did not matter. He knew in his heart that what he was doing was the right thing, the only thing. There was no other way in which the men almost a quarter of a mile below him could be saved, and against that fact all other considerations were meaningless.

The escaping oil from the well had made the sea so flat that the pilot of the cargo plane had made a landing, though his machine was not intended for amphibious operations. One of the scoutsubs was floating on the surface while her crew wrestled with the next batch of buoyancy tanks to be sunk. Men from the plane were helping them, working in collapsible boats that had been tossed into the water and automatically inflated.

Commander Henson, the Marine Division's master diver, was waiting in the plane with the equipment. There was another brief argument before the commander capitulated with good grace and, Franklin thought, a certain amount of relief. If anyone else was to attempt this mission, there was no doubt that Henson, with his unparalleled experience, was the obvious choice. Franklin even hesitated for a moment, wondering if by stubbornly insisting on going himself, he might not be reducing the chances of success. But he had been on the bottom and knew exactly what conditions were down there; it would waste precious time if Henson went down in the sub to make a reconnaissance.

Franklin swallowed his pH pills, took his injections, and climbed into the flexible rubber suit which would protect him from the near-zero temperature on the seabed. He hated suits—they interfered with movement and upset one's buoyancy—but this was a case where he had no choice. The complex breathing unit, with its three cylinders—one the ominous red of compressed hydrogen—was strapped to his back, and he was lowered into the sea.

Commander Henson swam around him for five minutes while all the fittings were checked, the weight belt was adjusted, and the sonar transmitter tested. He was breathing easily enough on normal air, and would not switch over to the oxyhydrogen mixture until he had reached a depth of three hundred feet. The change-over was automatic, and the demand regulator also adjusted the oxygen flow so that the mixture ratio was correct at any depth. As correct as it could be, that is, for a region in which man was never intended to live. . . .

At last everything was ready. The explosive charges were securely attached to his belt, and he gripped the handrail around the tiny conning tower of the sub. "Take her down," he said to the pilot. "Fifty feet a minute, and keep your forward speed below two knots."

"Fifty feet a minute it is. If we pick up speed, I'll kill it with the reverse jets."

Almost at once, daylight faded to a gloomy and depressing green. The water here on the surface was almost opaque, owing to the debris thrown up by the oil well. Franklin could not even see the width of the conning tower; less than two feet from his eyes the metal rail blurred and faded into nothingness. He was not worried; if necessary, he could work by touch alone, but he knew that the water was much clearer on the bottom.

Only thirty feet down, he had to stop the descent for almost a minute while he cleared his ears. He blew and swallowed frantically before the comforting "click" inside his head told him that all was well; how humiliating it would have been, he thought, had he been forced back to the surface because of a blocked Eustachian tube! No one would have blamed him, of course; even a mild cold could completely incapacitate the best diver—but the anticlimax would have been hard to live down.

The light was fading swiftly as the Sun's rays lost their battle with the turbid water. A hundred feet down, he seemed to be in a world of misty moonlight, a world completely lacking color or warmth. His ears were giving him no trouble now, and he was breathing without effort, but he felt a subtle depression creeping over him. It was, he was sure, only an effect of the failing light—not a premonition of the thousand feet of descent that still lay ahead of him.

To occupy his mind, he called the pilot and asked for a progress report. Fifty drums had now been attached to the derrick, giving a total lift of well over a hundred tons. Six of the passengers in the trapped sub had become unconscious but appeared to be in no danger; the remaining seventeen were uncomfortable, but had adapted themselves to the increased pressure. The leak was getting no worse, but there were now three inches of water in the control room, and before long there would be danger of short circuits.

"Three hundred feet down," said Commander Henson's voice. "Check your hydrogen-flow meter—you should be starting the switch-over now."

Franklin glanced down at the compact little instrument panel. Yes, the automatic change-over was taking place. He could detect no difference in the air he was breathing, but in the next few hundred feet of descent most of the dangerous nitrogen would be flushed out. It seemed strange to replace it with hydrogen, a far more reactive—and even explosive—gas, but hydrogen produced no narcotic effects and was not trapped in the body tissues as readily as nitrogen.

It seemed to have grown no darker in the last hundred feet; his eyes had accustomed themselves to the low level of illumination, and the water was slightly clearer. He could now see for two or three yards along the smooth hull he was riding down into the depths where only a handful of unprotected men had ever ventured—and fewer still returned to tell the story.

Commander Henson called him again. "You should be on fifty per cent hydrogen now. Can you taste it?"

"Yes—a metallic sort of flavor. Not unpleasant, though."

"Talk as slowly as you can," said the commander. "It's hard to understand you—your voice sounds so high-pitched now. Are you feeling quite O.K.?"

"Yes," replied Franklin, glancing at his depth gauge. "Will you increase my rate of descent to a hundred feet a minute? We've no time to waste."

At once he felt the vessel sinking more swiftly beneath him as the ballast tanks were flooded, and for the first time he began to feel the pressure around him as something palpable. He was going down so quickly that there was a slight lag as the insulating layer of air in his suit adjusted to the pressure change; his arms and legs seemed to be gripped as if by a huge and gentle vise, which slowed his movements without actually restricting them.

The light had now nearly gone, and as if in anticipation of his order the pilot of the sub switched on his twin searchlights. There was nothing for them to illumine, here in this empty void midway between seabed and sky, but it was reassuring to see the double nimbus of scattered radiance floating in the water ahead of him. The violet filters had been removed, for his benefit, and now that his eyes had something distant to focus upon he no longer felt so oppressively shut in and confined.

Eight hundred feet down—more than three quarters of the way to the bottom. "Better level off here for three minutes," advised Commander Henson. "I'd like to keep you here for half an hour, but we'll have to make it up on the way back."

Franklin submitted to the delay with what grace he could. It seemed incredibly long; perhaps his time sense had been distorted, so that what was really a minute appeared like ten. He was going to ask Commander Henson if his watch had stopped when he suddenly remembered that he had a perfectly good one of his own. The fact that he had forgotten something so obvious was, he realized, rather a bad sign; it suggested that he was becoming stupid. However, if he was intelligent enough to know that he was becoming stupid things could not be too bad. . . . Luckily the descent started again before he could get too involved in this line of argument.

And now he could hear, growing louder and louder each minute, the incessant roar of the great geyser of gas belching from the shaft which inquisitive and interfering man had drilled in the ocean bed. It shook the sea around him, already making it hard to hear the advice and comments of his helpers. There was a danger here as great as that of pressure itself; if the gas jet caught him, he might be tossed hundreds of feet upward in a matter of seconds and would explode like a deep-sea fish dragged suddenly to the surface.

"We're nearly there," said the pilot, after they had been sinking for what seemed an age. "You should be able to see the derrick in a minute; I'll switch on the lower lights."

Franklin swung himself over the edge of the now slowly moving sub and peered down the misty columns of light. At first he could see nothing; then, at an indeterminate distance, he made out mysterious rectangles and circles. They baffled him for a moment before he realized that he was seeing the air-filled drums which were now straining to lift the shattered derrick.

Almost at once he was able to make out the framework of twisted girders below them, and presently a brilliant star—fantastically out of place in this dreary underworld—burst into life just outside the cone of his searchlights. He was watching one of the cutting torches at work, manipulated by the mechanical hands of a sub just beyond visual range.

With great care, his own vessel positioned him beside the derrick, and for the first time he realized how hopeless his task would have been had he been compelled to rely on touch to find his way around. He could see the two girders to which he had to attach his charge; they were hemmed in by a maze of smaller rods, beams, and cables through which he must somehow make his way.

Franklin released his hold of the sub which had towed him so effortlessly into the depths, and with slow, easy strokes swam toward the derrick. As he approached, he saw for the first time the looming mass of the trapped sub, and his heart sank as he thought of all the problems that must still be solved before it could be extricated. On a sudden impulse, he swam toward the helpless vessel and banged sharply on the hull with the pair of wire cutters from his little tool kit. The men inside knew that he was here, of course, but the signal would have an altogether disproportionate effect on their morale.

Then he started work. Trying to ignore the throbbing vibration which filled all the water around him and made it difficult to think, he began a careful survey of the metal maze into which he must swim.

It would not be difficult to reach the nearest girder and place the charge. There was an open space between three I beams, blocked only by a loop of cable which could be easily pushed out of the way (but he'd have to watch that it didn't tangle in his equipment when he swam past it). Then the girder would be dead ahead of him; what was more, there was room to turn around, so that he could avoid the unpleasant necessity of creeping out backward.

He checked again, and could see no snags. To make doubly sure, he talked it over with Commander Henson, who could see the situation almost as well on the TV screen of the sub. Then he swam slowly into the derrick, working his way along the metal framework with his gloved hands. He was quite surprised to find that, even at this depth, there was no shortage of the barnacles and other marine growths which always make it dangerous to touch any object which had been under water for more than a few months.

The steel structure was vibrating like a giant tuning fork; he could feel the roaring power of the uncapped well both through the sea surrounding him and through the metal beneath his hands. He seemed to be imprisoned in an enormous, throbbing cage; the sheer noise, as well as the awful pressure, was beginning to make him dull and lethargic. It now needed a positive effort of will to take any action; he had to keep reminding himself that many lives besides his own depended upon what he was doing.

He reached the girder and slowly taped the flat package against the metal. It took a long time to do it to his satisfaction, but at last the explosive was in place and he felt sure that the vibration would not dislodge it. Then he looked around for his second objective—the girder forming the other edge of the derrick.

He had stirred up a good deal of dirt and could no longer

see so clearly, but it seemed to Franklin that there was nothing to stop him crossing the interior of the derrick and completing the job. The alternative was to go back the way he had come, and then swim right around to the other side of the wreckage. In normal circumstances that would have been easy enough— but now every movement had to be considered with care, every expenditure of effort made grudgingly only after its need had been established beyond all doubt.

With infinite caution, he began to move through the throbbing mist. The glare of the searchlights, pouring down upon him, was so dazzling that it pained his eyes. It never occurred to him that he had only to speak into his microphone and the illumination would be reduced instantly to whatever level he wished. Instead, he tried to keep in whatever shadow he could find among the confused pile of wreckage through which he was moving.

He reached the girder, and crouched over it for a long time while he tried to remember what he was supposed to be doing here. It took Commander Henson's voice, shouting in his ears like some far-off echo, to call him back to reality. Very carefully and slowly he taped the precious slab into position; then he floated beside it, admiring his meaningless handiwork, while the annoying voice in his ear grew ever more insistent. He could stop it, he realized, by throwing away his face mask and the irritating little speaker it contained. For a moment he toyed with this idea, but discovered that he was not strong enough to undo the straps holding the mask in place. It was too bad; perhaps the voice would shut up if he did what it told him to.

Unfortunately, he had no idea which was the right way out of the maze in which he was now comfortably ensconced. The light and noise were very confusing; when he moved in any direction, he sooner or later banged into something and had to turn back. This annoyed but did not alarm him, for he was quite happy where he was.

But the voice would not give him any peace. It was no longer at all friendly and helpful; he dimly realized that it was being downright rude, and was ordering him about in a manner in which—though he could not remember why—people did not usually speak to him. He was being given careful and detailed instructions which were repeated over and over again, with increasing emphasis, until he sluggishly obeyed them. He was too tired to answer back, but he wept a little at the indignity to which he was being subjected. He had never been called such things in his life, and it was very seldom indeed that he had heard such shocking language as was now coming through his speaker. Who on Earth would yell at him this way? "Not that way, you goddammed fool, sir! To the left—LEFT! That's fine—now forward a bit more—don't stop there! Christ, he's gone to sleep again. WAKE UP—SNAP OUT OF IT OR I'LL KNOCK YOUR BLOODY BLOCK OFF!! That's a good boy—you're nearly there—just another couple of feet . . ." and so on endlessly, and some of it with very much worse language than that.

Then, quite to his surprise, there was no longer twisted metal around him. He was swimming slowly in the open, but he was not swimming for long. Metal fingers closed upon him, none too gently, and he was lifted into the roaring night.

From far away he heard four short, muffled explosions, and something deep down in his mind told him that for two of these he was responsible. But he saw nothing of the swift drama a hundred feet below as the radio fuses detonated and the great derrick snapped in two. The section lying across the trapped submarine was still too heavy to be lifted clear by the buoyancy tanks, but now that it was free to move it teetered for a moment like a giant seesaw, then slipped aside and crashed onto the seabed.

The big sub, all restraint removed, began to move upward with increasing speed; Franklin felt the wash of its close passage, but was too bemused to realize what it meant. He was still struggling back into hazy consciousness; around eight hundred feet, quite abruptly, he started to react to Henson's bullying ministrations, and, to the commander's vast relief, began to answer him back in kind. He cursed wildly for about a hundred feet, then became fully aware of his surroundings and ground to an embarrassed halt. Only then did he realize that his mission had been successful and that the men he had set out to rescue were already far above him on their way back to the surface.

Franklin could make no such speed. A decompression chamber was waiting for him at the three-hundred-foot level, and in its cramped confines he was to fly back to Brisbane and spend eighteen tedious hours before all the absorbed gas had escaped from his body. And by the time the doctors let him out of their clutches, it was far too late to suppress the tape recording that had circulated throughout the entire bureau. He was a hero to the whole world, but if he ever grew conceited he need only remind himself that all his staff had listened gleefully to every word of Commander Henson's fluently profane cajoling of their director.

CHAPTER

P eter never looked back as he walked up the gangplank into
the projectile from which, in little more than half an hour,
he would have his first view of the receding Earth.
Franklin could understand why his son kept his head averted;
young men of eighteen do not cry in public. Nor, for that matter, he told himself fiercely, do middle-aged directors of important bureaus.

Anne had no such inhibitions; she was weeping steadily despite all that Indra could do to comfort her. Not until the doors
of the spaceship had finally sealed and the thirty-minute warning siren had drowned all other noises did she subside into an
intermittent sniffling.

The tide of spectators, of friends and relatives, of cameramen and Space Department officials, began to retreat before
the moving barriers. Clasping hands with his wife and daughter, Franklin let himself be swept along with the flood of humanity. What hopes and fears, sorrows and joys surrounded
him now! He tried to remember his emotions at his first take-
off; it must have been one of the great moments of his life—
yet all recollection of it had gone, obliterated by thirty years of
later experience.

And now Peter was setting out on the road his father had traveled half a lifetime before. May you have better luck among the stars than I did, Franklin prayed. He wished he could be there at Port Lowell when Irene greeted the boy who might have been her son, and wondered how Roy and Rupert would receive their half-brother. He was sure that they would be glad to meet him; Peter would not be as lonely on Mars as Ensign Walter Franklin had once been.

They waited in silence while the long minutes wore away. By this time, Peter would be so interested in the strange and exciting world that was to be his home for the next week that he would already have forgotten the pain of parting. He could not be blamed if his eyes were fixed on the new life which lay before him in all its unknown promise.

And what of his own life? Franklin asked himself. Now that he had launched his son into the future, could he say that he had been a success? It was a question he found very hard to answer honestly. So many things that he had attempted had ended in failure or even in disaster. He knew now that he was unlikely to rise any farther in the service of the state; he might be a hero, but he had upset too many people when he became the surprised and somewhat reluctant ally of the Maha Thero. Certainly he had no hope of promotion—nor did he desire it—during the five or ten years which would be needed to complete the reorganization of the Bureau of Whales. He had been told in as many words that since he was partly responsible for the situation—the mess, it was generally called—he could sort it out himself.

One thing he would never know. If fate had not brought him public admiration and the even more valuable—because less fickle—friendship of Senator Chamberlain, would he have had the courage of his newfound convictions? It had been easy, as the latest hero that the world had taken to its heart but would forget tomorrow, to stand up in the witness box and state his beliefs. His superiors could fume and fret, but there was nothing they could do but accept his defection with the best grace they could muster. There were times when he almost wished that the accident of fame had not come to his rescue. And had his evidence, after all, been decisive? He suspected that it had. The result of the referendum had been close, and the Maha Thero might not have carried the day without his help.

The three sharp blasts of the siren broke into his reverie. In that awe-inspiring silence which still seemed so uncanny to those who remembered the age of rockets, the great ship sloughed away its hundred thousand tons of weight and began the climb back to its natural element. Half a mile above the plain, its own gravity field took over completely, so that it was no longer concerned with terrestrial ideas of "up" or "down." It lifted its prow toward the zenith, and hung poised for a moment like a metal obelisk miraculously supported among the clouds. Then, in that same awful silence, it blurred itself into a line—and the sky was empty.

The tension broke. There were a few stifled sobs, but many more laughs and jokes, perhaps a little too high-pitched to be altogether convincing. Franklin put his arms around Anne and Indra, and began to shepherd them toward the exit.

To his son, he willingly bequeathed the shoreless seas of space. For himself, the oceans of this world were sufficient. Therein dwelt all his subjects, from the moving mountain of Leviathan to the newborn dolphin that had not yet learned to suckle under water.

He would guard them to the best of his knowledge and ability. Already he could see clearly the future role of the bureau, when its wardens would be in truth the protectors of all the creatures moving in the sea. All? No—that, of course, was absurd; nothing could change or even greatly alleviate the incessant cruelty and slaughter that raged through all the oceans of the world. But with the great mammals who were his kindred, man could make a start, imposing his truce upon the battlefield of Nature.

What might come of that in the ages ahead, no one could guess. Even Lundquist's daring and still unproved plan for taming the killer whales might no more than hint of what the next few decades would bring. They might even bring the answer to the mystery which haunted him still, and which he had so nearly solved when that submarine earthquake robbed him of his best friend.

A chapter—perhaps the best chapter—of his life was closing. The future would have many problems, but he did not believe that ever again would he have to face such challenges as he had met in the past. In a sense, his work was done, even though the details were merely beginning.

He looked once more at the empty sky, and the words that the Mahanayake Thero had spoken to him as they flew back from the Greenland station rose up out of memory like a ground swell on the sea. He would never forget that chilling thought: *"When that time comes, the treatment man receives from his superiors may well depend upon the way he has behaved toward the other creatures of his own world."*

Perhaps he was a fool to let such phantasms of a remote and unknowable future have any influence upon his thoughts and acts, but he had no regrets for what he had done. As he stared into the blue infinity that had swallowed his son, the stars seemed suddenly very close. "Give us another hundred years," he whispered, "and we'll face you with clean hands and hearts—whatever shape you be."

"Come along, dear," said Indra, her voice still a little unsteady. "You haven't much time. The office asked me to remind you—the Committee on Interdepartmental Standardization meets in half an hour."

"I know," said Franklin, blowing his nose firmly and finally. "I wouldn't dream of keeping it waiting."

About the Author

Sir Arthur Charles Clarke was born in Minehead, England, in 1917 and now lives in Colombo, Sri Lanka. He is a graduate, and Fellow, of King's College, London, and Chancellor of the International Space University and the University of Moratuwa, near the Arthur C. Clarke Centre for Modern Technologies.

Sir Arthur has twice been Chairman of the British Interplanetary Society. While serving as an RAF radar officer in 1945, he published the theory of communications satellites, most of which operate in what is now called the Clarke Orbit. The impact of this invention upon global politics resulted in his nomination for the 1994 Nobel Peace Prize.

He has written over seventy books and shared an Oscar nomination with Stanley Kubrick for the movie based on his novel *2001: A Space Odyssey.* The recipient of three Hugo Awards and three Nebula Awards as well as an International Fantasy Award and a John W. Campbell Award, he was named a Grand Master by the Science Fiction Writers of America. His *Mysterious World*, *Strange Powers*, and *Mysterious Universe* TV series have been shown worldwide. His many honors include several doctorates in science and literature and a host of prizes and awards, including the Vidya Jyothi ("Light of Science") Award by the President of Sri Lanka in 1986 and the CBE (Commander of the British Empire) from H.M. Queen Elizabeth in 1989. In a global satellite ceremony in 1995 he received NASA's highest civilian honor, its Distinguished Public Service Medal. And in 1998 he was awarded a Knighthood "for services to literature" in the New Year's Honours List.

His recreations include scuba diving on Indian Ocean wrecks with his company, Underwater Safaris, table tennis (despite post-polio syndrome), observing the Moon through his fourteen-inch telescope, and playing with his Chihuahua Pepsi and his six computers.